THE LINGERING

DANI MATHEWSON

THE LINGERING

Smashwords edition

ISBN: 978-0-6452286-1-8 - Paperback

ISBN: 978-0-6452286-0-1 - Ebook

Cover design & formatting by Damonza www.damonza.com

For Rafferty and Ruari with love

"Aye, the mental telescope is now discovered which may pierce the depths of the past and bring us in full view of the grand and tragic passages of ancient history."

Joseph Rodes Buchanan,

1842

PRELUDE

ALEXANDRIA, EGYPT – 48 BC

CHILL MIDNIGHT WIND blew off the harbour. It raked its cold fingers through the man's silver hair and billowed his robes as he hurried through Alexandria's moonless streets toward the library.

The papyrus scroll in his hand seemed to drag its own darkness behind it, lending his old legs haste for fear that its blackness might catch up and swallow him. Still, he clutched it tighter. The terrible knowledge it preserved weighed down every step as he slugged up the hill, near breathless. Rumours of its curse felt real enough.

He paused at the library's stone steps to catch his breath. The columns towered over him, ghostly against the cloudy night. Imposing and frightful to some, the library was home to him; it was life to him. He loved it as Alexander the Great had loved the very *idea* of it three hundred years earlier; the grand idea of a universal library to house the greatest works ever written from across the globe.

His footsteps made no sound as he crossed the vast tiled space of The Great Hall. He breathed the familiar peppery smell of dry papyrus scrolls and felt their protective spells settle on his skin. He swept down the stone passageway to his private chamber. Not until the heavy timber door was locked behind him did he feel a tiny measure of calm return with each laboured breath.

He lit a candle and sat at his desk to unfurl the papyrus, weighting the top with his official Chief Administrator's bronze seal. The rest of the document trailed over the edge of the desk to curl near the floor. He leaned back and regarded the roll of papyrus in front of him with a strange mix of curiosity and repulsion. He wiped his hands on his robes for fear he'd been tainted somehow. It was a relief not to have to touch it.

Ink-stained fingertips absently worked the ruby ring on his left hand while he agonised over what to do with the mysterious find. It wasn't a written document but a charcoal rubbing of ancient carvings – primeval tellings so old that some of the glyphs had been lost to time. Parts of it were indecipherable, with arcane formulas and complex diagrams. The rest of it was made up of confounding riddles that teased the mind into hunting for meaning.

He stroked his cropped beard and stared into the candle's flame until it backlit his thoughts.

His sources assured him the host carvings were genuine and ancient. He hadn't doubted it. His problem was not their authenticity; his problem was how to keep the dangerous knowledge they contained a secret. In the wrong hands, the document might spell the end of life on earth. Its secrecy was paramount. How could he ensure its accurate transcription and archiving in total secrecy? How could he *protect* the people? Sweet Isis, he was just the library's keeper, a nobody in his seventy-ninth year, a boyhood scribe whom the gods had blessed with opportunity.

He exhaled with a rush. The candle blew out. The sudden darkness was suffocating.

He didn't want to admit that he already had the solution. It had gnawed at the edge of his mind since the moment he'd made the exchange with his source in the deep shadows of the lighthouse. He had rejected the idea before it had even properly surfaced. He simply would not put his granddaughter in danger like that.

But... The old man pinched the bridge of his nose.

But Aisha was the best scribe he had. Even on the cusp of her seventeenth year, she far outstripped the older, more experienced scribes. Hers was surely a gift from the gods. She was already commissioned to work on the most sensitive documents in the Isolation Room, and not just because she was the best. Aisha could be trusted.

He let his head fall back to stare at the blackness above.

It was the only solution. He would commission his granddaughter to begin work on its transcription as soon as he'd had time to make the preparations, prepare the spells. That would take a few days.

He closed his eyes and prayed he was strong enough to protect her. He prayed that there were spells powerful enough to shield her body, to offer her safe passage to the Afterlife, at least.

And he prayed for forgiveness.

Yet he knew that come the time of his death – come the time of the weighing of his heart against the feather of Ma'at on the Scales of Justice – the great Anubis would find him wanting. Everlasting life would not be his. It was a trade he was willing to make – the world's future for his own. But could he risk his beloved granddaughter, his only family?

He shivered.

His tragic destiny had been written in the night skies long before he was adept enough to read it there. But was his violent fate the same as that shared by the world? Or was it his alone? It remained obscure, unlike the message in last night's stars. There had been no mistaking that.

Death.

But for whom? His own name was a whispered chant in the back of his mind. Even so, the sense of dread he felt seeped beyond his existence.

His eyes flew open to repel it.

He was surprised by the welcome wedge of blue moonlight that streamed through the window, momentarily victorious over the cloudy night.

The light had won. This time.

It lent him hope. Perhaps even *his* dark fate could be salvaged, changed at least. There was something else in the stars last night. He hoped his interpretation was accurate. It seemed they foretold of a Deliverer from afar.

"Deliverer." His own voice made a harsh intrusion on the silence.

He was unsure what it meant but he felt it was somehow connected to the mysterious text. A Deliverer could only mean protection from something dark, protection for his granddaughter, for the citizens of Alexandria.

"Isis Almighty, let it be true," he whispered.

He stared at the papyrus, its strange text highlighted in moon-washed relief against the charcoal rub. The glyphs seemed to squirm and writhe against the black background like a pit of vipers until a sudden shadow obliterated the moon, pitching him into a darkness so thick, so suffocating, it robbed him of his next breath.

His chair crashed to the floor as he lunged for the window, tearing at his robes, desperate for air.

The shadow passed.

Moonlight returned.

Shaking hands relit the candle.

The papyrus lay in a roll on the floor. He made no move to pick it up.

It was evil.

It was dangerous.

And it was very real.

CHAPTER ONE

ALEXANDRIA, EGYPT – PRESENT DAY

MAC SANDERSON CLOSED his eyes and inhaled deeply. The desert's hot breath became his own. He lay still and let his body absorb the warmth from the ancient stone tiles beneath him. The Egyptian breeze ruffled his hair. All reason, all judgement, all reality was suspended.

Peace.

Connectedness.

His accelerated heartbeat became erratic, his breathing quick and shallow. He felt his chest tighten as he surrendered to the increasingly familiar sensation. The quickening swept over him. The Now was lost.

Snaps and flashes of light streaked across his mind. A distant whisper of sound became a roar in his head, a hurricane. He was overtaken by the sickening sensation of falling through space. Instinctively, he clawed at the sandy floor. Goosebumps swept over his trembling body. His inner vision narrowed to a pinprick of bright light, which he accelerated toward at lightning speed. Just as he felt he would disintegrate, he burst into another world.

CHAPTER TWO

FIRE!

This world was on fire! Flames surrounded him. The air was choked with smoke. Mac coughed violently. He threw his arms up to shield his stinging eyes.

Where the hell had he ended up this time?

A burning beam fell from the ceiling with a deafening crash. It splintered, sending a flurry of sparks skyward.

On the brink of panic, he tried to focus his energy for the return trip back through the void to his own time – to the Now – when his focus was pulled to a figure huddled in the corner of the burning room.

Mac adjusted his glasses, straining to see as he squinted against the murderous heat.

A girl in a blue hooded robe hugged her knees to her chest and buried her head in the crook of her arm. The fallen beam had her trapped.

Mac reeled at the sick imagining of her charred and blackened body. He was torn. Every instinct of survival told him to get out of there, to flash back to the Present, but he couldn't just leave her to die in the fire.

Look but don't touch. His mother's deathbed advice

echoed in his head. Mac rubbed his left wrist. Even after all these years, he could still feel her desperate fingers gripping it, begging him. *Promise me, Mac.* So he had. But he couldn't do that, not this time. He wasn't a kid anymore.

In silent apology, he clutched her wedding ring necklace at his throat.

His eyes swept the space for something he could use to lever the beam out of the way. He spotted a tall brass candelabrum. He whipped the bandana off his head and wrapped it around the hot shaft. It was heavy and awkward but many hours on the end of a shovel digging up the Past had made him strong. Melted candles dribbled to the floor as Mac tipped the stand. He wedged the shaft under the burning hunk of timber that blocked the girl's escape. With his free hand, he grabbed a footstool and shoved it under the pole for leverage.

The *heat*... Mac felt as though his flesh was about to shrivel and peel right off his bones.

With every bit of strength he could muster, he pushed down on the end of the pole to lever the beam off the ground. Just as it started to lift, it suddenly split in two amid a violent eruption of sparks. The flames leapt higher but a narrow gap had opened up. He dropped the brass pole and darted through.

Mac grabbed the hooded girl by the arm and hauled her to her feet.

"Come on!" he yelled over the roar of the flames.

She coughed uncontrollably. Mac tightened his grip on her arm and dragged her through the inferno, stopping only to retrieve his bandana off the floor. He clamped it over the girl's mouth. He thought maybe it was supposed to be wet like he'd seen in the movies but who the hell knew?

"Breathe through this," he yelled.

He knew she probably couldn't understand a word he said yet she held the bandana to her mouth with her free hand and tried to catch her breath.

Mac gasped in the choking smoke, straining to see a way out.

There! A door.

Sweeping the girl off her feet and into his arms, he bolted toward it.

It swung open into a much larger room. Flames roared high overhead. Sparks and tiny pieces of burning paper rained down on them. Through the ash that coated his glasses, Mac caught glimpses of the tiled floor as he ran. With a jolt, he recognized the design of blue lapis lazuli and black obsidian that twinned the one his 'other' body was lying on, back in present-day Egypt. The thought of the Present spurred him on. He ran faster. The stranger in his arms weighed next to nothing yet his rubbery legs argued. He heard shouts nearby and could just make out the shadowy forms of people running through the smoke in different directions. Timber beams crashed to the floor somewhere behind them.

Total chaos.

Suddenly, his boot jammed up against something solid and they were airborne. For a split second he thought he'd tripped up a step until they splash-landed in some sort of shallow indoor pond. Mac struggled to his feet in the knee-deep water. He shook his dripping fringe out of his eyes and reached for the girl. She was coughing and splashing, trying to find her feet, tripping on her robes.

"Come on!"

He wrapped an arm around her waist and hauled her up.

They waded through the pool and stumbled out onto solid ground once more. The floor was slippery with ash and soot. Twice they fell but got up and ran on blindly, eventually bursting out of the thick smoke into the night air.

They collapsed on a wide set of stone steps that ran the length of the building.

Mac sucked in huge gulps of the cool air. He was shaking. His lungs burned and his stinging eyes streamed. As he rubbed them, he realised that he'd lost his glasses. He cursed under his breath. They must have fallen off when he fell in the pond.

The girl lay on her back next to him, coughing and gasping for breath.

Mac managed to sit up.

They were on the steps of a huge building.

A temple... he thought. *A real-life ancient Egyptian temple...* Though it looked decidedly Greek as he watched thick clouds of smoke billow out between the fluted columns.

Flames leapt high into the night sky. A crowd of hundreds had gathered to watch in horror as the building burned. Men were running back and forth frantically, shouting instructions.

He turned to look at the girl.

She had rolled onto her knees. Trembling hands pressed against her lips. Her shoulders heaved and great shuddering gasps racked her body as she watched the place burn.

Mac repositioned himself to curl an awkward arm around her shoulders. Even if he could have spoken her language, he couldn't think of a single thing to say. He rubbed the tops of her arms, wishing he could make her stop crying. He couldn't stand it.

He looked away from the flames to shake his wet hair

out of his eyes. Although he really had to squint to see without his glasses, he could still make out detail.

Nearby, an old man lay belly-down on the steps. His long, silver hair blew a wispy halo in the gusts of heat from the furnace. His arms were flung out in front of him in desperation. He was crying. His whole body shook with each painful sob. His rheumy eyes swam with tears that reflected the orange flames as he watched the fire devour everything.

Mac dropped his eyes to the man's wrinkled hands.

Something glinted in the firelight. Mac squinted even harder to make it out. There was a gold ring on the man's left hand. A large square-cut ruby flashed bright as his outstretched arms slowly retracted like shriveling vines toward his body until he lay in a fetal curl, whimpering.

Mac swallowed hard and looked away.

A short Asian man with a shaved head was standing at the front of the crowd. He wore flowing orange robes over a wiry frame. Mac thought he looked about a hundred years old. His wizened face was expressionless and he stood perfectly still. His palms were pressed together in front, fingertips pointing upward in prayer. He resembled the Shao Lin monks of Tibet that Mac had seen in pictures. It was hard to tear his attention away from the strange man.

"Ugh!" Someone slammed Mac in the shoulder, knocking him forward. He steadied himself amid a torrent of angry shouts from a soldier carrying a barrel of water. He watched the uniformed man disappear into the flames. The soldier could have been lifted straight off the tattered pages of the old illustrated children's Bible his Gran used to have. As a kid, Mac had loved the story of Moses, probably because it was set in Egypt.

He turned to the girl. "You okay?"

She had stopped crying at least.

"Come on. We can't stay here."

Mac helped her to her feet and was about to lead her down the steps into the crowd when she yanked back on his arm. She fished in her pocket then pressed something into his palm. She curled his fingers over it with her own and gave it a squeeze. He opened his hand. It was his red bandana. Something was wrapped in it. His glasses! They were filthy but undamaged.

Mac rolled his eyes in relief. "You're an angel."

He wiped his glasses with the wet bandana and put them on.

She *was* an angel.

In one strange frozen moment, the earth seemed to tilt under his feet. He couldn't breathe. Some unseen force tugged at his chest and a matrix of… of… possibilities, outcomes – he didn't have the right words, *enough* words – flashed through his mind like complex electric circuitry. Past, Present and Future fused into a single excruciating nanosecond.

He exhaled.

Beautiful…

She looked about sixteen; around his age, he figured. Her large almond eyes sparkled like emeralds atop high cheekbones. Under a layer of tear-streaked soot, her skin was mocha. There was a small crescent-shaped mole high on her left cheek. It looked like a tiny chocolate moon. Although unusual and distinctive, it certainly didn't detract from her beauty. Her lips were full and parted to reveal perfect white teeth. Wet hair was plastered slick and black to the side of her face and neck. A long thick plait draped over her shoulder, sending a trickle of water down her front. Mac couldn't help noticing that her wet robes were enticingly see-through as they clung to her slender frame.

Around her neck she wore a spectacular gold necklace set with colourful jewels that spilled onto her chest. It glittered in the light of the flames, throwing reflections up under her chin. She wore a cluster of gold bangles on each wrist. A spiralling gold band in the shape of a snake with red rubies for eyes was wrapped around her left upper arm. With jewels like that, Mac guessed the girl was of noble Egyptian blood, possibly even royal.

A shy smile forced a fresh tear down her cheek. Mac leaned over and wiped it away with his thumb to reveal glowing skin beneath. It was warm and soft.

His heart was beating hard but it wasn't like anything he'd experienced before. He held her gaze a moment longer before the spell broke.

Taking her by the hand, he led her through the crowd of onlookers to a small rocky hill at the rear. They sat and watched the blaze in silence.

From that vantage point, Mac was able to get a better idea of what was going on. Flames and smoke rose skyward. He was sure the building was some sort of temple. It was enormous. There looked to be further rooms built on at the end of the columned center, with adjoining wings to the sides. The roof had to have been more than ten metres high. Wide stone steps flanked the building on all sides.

Scores of soldiers were running in and out of the burning building. It seemed most of them were on water duty, bringing load after load of water to dowse the flames. Their muscled bodies gleamed with sweat. Teams of other soldiers, faces blackened and coughing in fits, were staggering out of the inferno carrying armloads of cylinders – *scrolls*, Mac realised. They passed them on to others waiting outside and disappeared back into the flames to emerge moments later with more scrolls.

It took Mac a few minutes to realise that not all of the soldiers were Egyptian. He recognised the uniform of the Roman navy. What were they doing there? After all, he was sure he was still in Egypt, even though he had landed somewhere in the distant Past. In fact, he was pretty sure he was still in the city of Alexandria, only its ancient version.

He nodded to himself. It *had* to be. The tiled floor in the temple – it was the same design. There was no other explanation.

Mac looked to his right. Below him in the distance, he could make out the reflection of the moon on a harbour filled with many ships, mostly Roman, he judged by the shape of them.

Just then, a beam of light flashed in the distance. A lighthouse.

Mac gasped. *The Lighthouse of Alexandria!*

It was one of the Seven Ancient Wonders of the World. He had goosebumps. It hadn't existed for over a thousand years and there he was, staring right at it.

Suddenly, he made the connection.

"The Library!" Mac was on his feet again. "Of course! The Library of Alexandria!"

He stared in disbelief as the flames engulfed the building. He ran his hands through his wet hair and continued to stare open-mouthed at the scene before him. "I am witnessing the destruction of the Library of Alexandria," he whispered, as if voicing the fact might convince him it wasn't just a bad dream.

The strength seeped from his knees. He sat. It wasn't a temple after all. It was a library. It was *the* library. Back in the Now, he'd just won a twenty-dollar bet with his friend, Ru. Yet the thought didn't gladden him any.

The girl slipped her hand into his. Mac held it but found he could not look away from the tragic spectacle below.

From what he could recall of his studies, the famous Library of Alexandria had, at one time, housed the greatest collection of written works in living memory. He remembered reading somewhere that the library was home to over half a million scrolls from around the world. It preserved knowledge from the dawn of civilization. He could only wonder at what ancient wisdom and secrets had been lost – *were being lost* right before his eyes!

According to the history books he'd read, no one knew for sure what had happened to the library, except that at some stage it had burned down and the hundreds of thousands of written works of history, science and literature were lost forever. Its destruction remained a lively source of controversy among historians.

He couldn't remember the details but one popular theory was that Julius Caesar somehow started the fire during his fight against Cleopatra's brother.

Mac looked back toward the harbour. He was pretty sure the ships he could see at anchor were Roman. Could they be Caesar's? He wondered what year it was. Had he paid more attention to his history lessons, he might have a clue what year – or *century* – he was in. Not that it probably mattered; remembering dates wasn't his thing.

The girl shivered in the cool night air. She was still soaking wet. Feeling a little awkward, Mac disengaged his hand to wrap an arm around her shoulders. She leaned closer.

He could feel her staring at him and turned to face her curious green gaze. There was a strange sensation of butterflies in his stomach when he looked at her.

She leaned forward and tapped the lens of his glasses.

"Glasses," said Mac and pointed to them.

All of a sudden, he felt very self-conscious. He adjusted his glasses on the bridge of his nose. He looked down and fidgeted with the red bandana in his hand. When he glanced up again, the girl was still staring at him.

"Here. You try." His voice was still croaky from the smoke. He uncurled his arm from around her to take off his glasses and offer them to her.

After a moment's hesitation, she took them. She studied them before putting them on upside down.

"No, like this," Mac corrected her and turned them up the right way.

Her eyes looked enormous through the lenses. She reminded him of an Anime cartoon, with fine elfin features and oversized sparkling eyes. She held the glasses to her face, squinting then widening her eyes as she tried to adjust to the wonky distortions of the lenses. She shrugged and handed them back.

Mac put them on, his mouth tweaking into a half-smile.

There was an awkward pause.

"Aisha," said the girl eventually. She pressed the palm of her hand against her chest.

Mac had studied just enough ancient Egyptian to know that her name meant 'peace'. It was a nice name. It suited her, he thought, though it seemed strangely out of context this night.

"Mac," he replied, tapping his chest.

She repeated his name and smiled.

His heart skipped a beat while he searched for his next breath.

A sudden shiver swept over the girl and her bottom lip quivered. He didn't have anything warm to offer her except his arms so he wrapped her up in them and held her.

His gaze was drawn to the flames once more.

Crazy night...

But he didn't want it to end.

He knew he should be getting back to the Present. He had no idea how much time had elapsed. Time seemed to be sort of elastic. Often he would return to the Present from one of his trips to find hardly any time had elapsed at all. On other occasions, it seemed more time had passed in the Present while he was out than expected. Either way, he couldn't be sure. He knew if Ru or the workers, came back from noon break to find him zoned out on the floor of the dig, he'd be in big trouble.

Mac stood up and pulled Aisha to her feet. He turned to face her. She was a good bit shorter than him. He looked down at her. The moonlight cast one side of her face blue and the flames painted the other side amber. She looked exotic. His heart was off and racing again. For an instant, he had the wild idea of kissing her. He had never kissed a girl before. Not properly, anyway.

Once, when he was twelve years old, he pecked the daughter of one of the volunteer workers on the lips then ran away as fast as he could. Right now, he didn't want to run away. He wanted to stay.

He squeezed his eyes shut and shook his head.

Madness!

The gold bangles on her wrists jingled as he took her tiny hands in his. He glanced away briefly. "Um," he started. "Ah, I have to… You know. Go home." It sounded absurd, like he was just hopping on a bus to the next suburb instead of traversing vast millennia through space-time.

The girl said nothing. She just stared up at him.

Mac took a deep breath. He released her hands. "Aisha," he said. He hesitated before going on. He pointed to her then he placed his crossed palms flat on his chest, over his heart. "I won't forget you." He bowed slightly. He felt kind of stupid and a little melodramatic but he wasn't sure what else to do. It was true. He would never forget how he saved the life of the most beautiful girl in the world from the burning Library of Alexandria. It sounded completely insane, even to him. Yet he was right there and it was very real.

He puffed out a breath and turned to go.

Without warning, she threw her arms around his neck and kissed him full on the lips. It was electric! It was also fleeting. Before Mac had time to register what was happening, it was over.

The girl pulled away and ran down the hill, her long plait flying behind her.

Slowly, he raised his fingertips to his lips. He stared after her as she disappeared into the crowd. He couldn't help grinning. He thought it kind of funny that he had done the very same thing when he was twelve – peck and run. Only, this was more than just a peck. He guessed it was what his cousin,

Corey, referred to as a 'pash and dash'. Whatever it was, it was incredible. It tasted like smoke but it was still incredible.

Mac collected himself. He took one last long look at the ancient city of Alexandria and its burning library.

Clouds scudded across the moon and lightning flashed over the harbour. The sea breeze, laden with the promise of rain, ruffled his hair.

SWOOSH!

A shadow.

Instinctively he ducked as something huge – a bird of some kind – swooped low overhead. Startled, he looked up but couldn't see anything. Whatever it was, it was fast. There was no sign of it. The beat of wings and the rush of air had been unmistakable though. It left him feeling jittery.

Time to go.

CHAPTER THREE

The disapproving face of Rupert Cheswick came into focus as Mac blinked heavily in the blinding daylight of the Now. The chubby Englishman stood over him, blocking out the sun.

"Ru," croaked Mac.

His heart sank. He knew he was in big trouble. Rupert grabbed him by the arm and hauled him up into a sitting position. His face looked like a ripe plum that was about to explode.

"I can explain –"

"Shut thy pie hole, MacKinley," hissed Rupert. "Not impressed."

"I know I said –"

"Enough! Let's get you cleaned up before your father sees you and has my head on a platter. What the devil happened to you?"

Mac peeled his palms off the tiled floor, breaking the energetic 'signal' that linked him with the Past. He examined his hands. They should have been black with soot but, strangely, they weren't. That made the burns and blisters all the more obvious. His injuries weren't serious but they were raw and painful.

Ru sucked in a sympathy breath when he saw Mac's burnt hands.

"It's nothing," said Mac, looking down. Remarkably, his white cotton shirt was still clean and intact but the hairs on his legs and arms had been singed. His knees were bruised where he'd fallen over on the tiles.

He pulled his bandana from his pocket, dragged it over his face and inspected the fabric. No soot, just sweat. Yet the smell of smoke clung to the inside of his nostrils. Or was it merely in his mind?

"Here, give me that," said Rupert, snatching the bandana out of the boy's hands. He soaked it in water from the canteen around his neck and dabbed at Mac's red face.

The boy had his mother's eyes, thought Ru. He had his mother's gift too, only stronger. Much stronger.

Softening, Rupert asked him again, "So, what happened?"

Mac wasn't sure where to begin. The first thing that came to mind was the kiss. Even now, the thought caused a strange stirring in his belly. He decided not to mention it.

"There was a fire," he began.

"Evidently. And?"

Mac paused, staring up at the fluted edges of towering ancient columns made of huge, stone blocks that lined the edge of the excavation on one side. Some of the columns had collapsed millennia ago and the blocks were strewn about on the floor of the dig. A wall of scaffolding and fine synthetic mesh had been erected to keep the desert from encroaching on the excavation. Behind the mesh, he could just make out the hieroglyphics and painted scenes beneath the dust. He was amazed any of it had survived the fire. Although far from being fully unearthed, there was no doubt in his mind that this was the building he'd just escaped from.

"The Library. Ru, this is – *was* – the Library of Alexandria."

Rupert froze, the wet bandana just inches from Mac's face. His eyes were wide and his mouth hung open.

"It's true," continued Mac. "I was there."

He spat into the palm of his hand then wiped it across the tiles to remove a layer of ever-shifting sand. The stone floor was inlaid with squares of black obsidian, which were in turn inlaid with bright blue triangular wedges of polished lapis lazuli that gleamed in the noon sun.

"The floor, Ru. The tiles – they're *exactly* the same!"

The man stared at him in disbelief.

His voice still hoarse from the smoke, Mac recounted everything. Almost everything. His cheeks flushed redder as he remembered Aisha's kiss.

Rupert exhaled. "Positively staggering. Staggering, indeed."

"Here, I'll show you." Mac knelt on the ancient, tiled floor and roughly sketched the layout of the building in the sand with his finger. "See here," he said pointing to his drawing. "There should be another wing off here. And here."

Ru stared at him. "Well, that certainly matches the read out from the thermal scanner."

Mac's father's archaeological dig team was well equipped with the latest imaging technology, plus they had a long-standing arrangement with the local authorities and airfield. For a generous 'donation', Alexandrian government officials were more than happy to oblige the Sanderson team by authorising the use of drones for aerial photography that used infrared radiation and thermal scanners to pick up the presence of subsurface stone structures. Months ago, when the surveys hinted at the strong possibility of a large man-made structure under the desert on the outskirts of Alexandria, his father had organised the thermal scanning to determine if the project was worth pursuing. No one in their wildest dreams expected to turn up the famed Library of Alexandria.

"Can you be certain this is the library then?" Ru asked.

"Absolutely. Everything fits. There's no other explanation. The tiles tell the story."

Ru's eyes narrowed. "The tiles. So, that's what you used as the trigger for your psycho-whatever."

"Psychometry," said Mac, rolling his eyes.

"MacKinley, you know you're not to dabble in that stuff unsupervised."

"Yeah, yeah," droned Mac.

After a recent incident, his father had forbidden him to practise psychometry when he was alone. It was one thing to hold an object and receive impulses or visions, but it was entirely another to actually teleport back in time, leaving a duplicate of his body behind. He had done it several times over the years but lately these episodes were getting stronger and more frequent.

"And that pond," Mac said, pointing. "I fell in it."

They both looked at the shallow rectangle that had already been excavated in the centre of the dig.

Ru knitted his dark, bushy brows and rubbed his silver goatee. "The Roman navy was at anchor, you said?"

Mac nodded.

"That puts it at around 48 BC," said Ru. "It fits with the

theory that Julius Caesar started the fire in the war against Ptolemy XIII. One account says that Caesar was forced to burn his own ships as a diversion when his enemies tried to cut off his communication by sea. Other accounts have Caesar setting fire to the *Egyptian* navy, not his own Roman fleet. Some even accuse Caesar's soldiers of starting the fire. Whatever the case, allegedly, it then got out of control and spread to the docks and then on to the library."

"No," Mac cut in. "That doesn't make sense. I watched the Roman soldiers try to put the fire *out*. If they started it, then it must have been by accident."

"Hmm." Ru took a deep breath and arched his eyebrows. "Very well," he said, straightening up. "But for now, we keep this strictly to ourselves. Agreed?"

"Agreed," echoed Mac with relief.

He was off the hook, at least for the moment. Still, he decided it would not be the best time to mention the twenty bucks he was owed. Just last week he had made a bet with Ru that the partially excavated ruins weren't that of a temple but something else. He'd had a psychometric inkling the first time he'd climbed down the ladder into the pit to study the structure. At the time, he didn't get a clear 'hit' so he figured that he wasn't exactly cheating by making the bet.

They climbed out of the pit and trudged up the hill toward Ru's tent. The sun was higher in the sky and most of the volunteer workers had retreated to the shade of their tents for a midday siesta. Mac had timed his trip perfectly it seemed.

He took off his shirt and sniffed it. He couldn't tell if it smelt like smoke or not. It was like the fire had permeated every cell in his body and he reeked of it though he was pretty sure that wasn't possible. The past stayed in the Past after all. He glanced at his blistered hands. Well, mostly.

He balled his shirt and tossed it aside before having a hasty splash in the drum of water behind Ru's tent. He rinsed his bandana and tied it pirate-style over his wet hair. Ru applied a blend of essential oils to treat the burns on his hands and dressed them with light gauze. Mac inspected his bandages while he tried to come up with a plausible story to tell his father.

As if reading his mind, Rupert said, "You spilt boiling water over yourself whilst making Ru's tea, you clumsy oaf."

Mac grinned. "You're a good man, Ru."

"I'm a *dead* man if your father finds out," he muttered as he re-packed the first aid kit.

Ru was his father's oldest and dearest friend. They'd met at university. As a young man, Leon Sanderson had left his family in Australia and travelled across the world to study archaeology at Oxford. He and Ru had hit it off instantly. Ru's family had practically adopted Leon. Ru had also introduced him to Emily, a pretty linguistics student who happened to be Ru's sister's best friend. They married and moved to Australia after graduating. Mac came along a few years later.

Mac left Ru's tent and wandered up through the site toward his own.

"Eh, dig kid, what'd you do to your 'ands?" The Welsh accent of Rhys, one of the volunteers from Cardiff University, rang out from behind him.

Mac cringed on the inside as he turned and feigned an off-handed greeting.

Rhys was with the other Cardiff volunteer, Gavyn. They

were always together, practically joined at the hip like freakish Siamese twins – one tall, dark and handsome, the other a freckled and flaming redhead.

For some reason, Mac always found them intimidating. He wasn't even sure why. They were nice enough guys though a good bit older – somewhere in their twenties. But their lightning wit and 'in' jokes always left Mac feeling small and stupid. It wasn't so much that he minded being called the dig kid. Everyone called him that. That's what he was – the kid on the dig who did all the digging. But around them, he reverted to a fifth-grader with a twitchy grin and nothing clever to say.

Mac just shrugged. "It's nothing."

"I told yer those local girls are too hot to handle," teased Rhys.

Mac blushed.

Gavyn laughed and added something in his thick accent that Mac didn't catch. They both roared with laughter and walked on. Mac knew it was just good-natured teasing so he was annoyed at the heat in his cheeks. It had almost cooled by the time he neared his tent, only to flare again as he realised that it was going to be next to impossible that his father wouldn't spot his bandaged hands.

Though he would never have said they were close, Mac adored his father in a weird, hero-worship way. Professor Leon Sanderson was reserved, remote. Mac saw him as a sort of nerdy Clint Eastwood, someone to be respected if not feared, yet admired from a distance. Sometimes, he wasn't altogether sure if his dad even liked him. He was loved, sure, but… Leon didn't really understand him or his psychometry, didn't try to either. He sensed his father still had a lot of reservations surrounding things that were somewhat supernatural, despite having had a wife and son to whom such things came naturally.

Ru, a little more open-minded, had had a huge influence on Leon's attitude toward the world of psychic phenomena. He was Mac's greatest ally, and had championed his cause on many occasions when his father had become difficult to get along with. Most of the time though, Ru walked a thin tightrope between upholding the professor's wishes and lending support and encouragement to Mac to further develop his talents.

Lately though, Leon was becoming particularly rigid.

Ever since that chariot thing…

In one of his recent psychometric expeditions into an ancient Roman sports arena, Mac had narrowly missed being run down by a chariot. He'd dived out of the way just in the nick of time but had grazed his knees and hands badly. To his father's horror, as Mac lay in a trance in the Present, huge bleeding grazes suddenly appeared on his knees and hands. In a panic, his father had pulled off the ancient leather sandal that Mac had found and put on, breaking the link with the Past. Mac had come out of the experience as shocked by his present-day injuries as his father had been.

As Mac studied Ru's neat bandaging, he was reminded again that his physical safety in the Past was as important as it was in the Now.

It wasn't a long walk from Ru's tent but Mac was exhausted. He knew time travel drained his energy and left him feeling flat and disoriented. Still, it didn't deter him. It was thrilling. Already he found himself looking forward to the next trip, the next kiss… He wondered if he would ever see Aisha again. He knew it would be foolish to try and sheer madness to not. Besides, he had already stepped way outside the bounds of "Look but don't touch." The rulebook had gone out the window.

What rulebook?

There was no rulebook. Hell, he was writing it as he went along! An uncharacteristic surge of arrogance squared his shoulders for an instant until he realised his rulebook was practically empty. There was still so much he didn't know.

Mac wished he had control over the entry and exit points of time travel. From past experience, he had learned that, even using the same object for his psychometric visions, he couldn't teleport back into exactly the same place from which he had just returned. Often he could get relatively close in terms of geographic location but not always the same year, or decade even. It were as though the object had a lifetime of its own and its energetic pull streamed from various intervals of its existence. He had no control over what came through, or what the object wished to communicate. In some ways, he was just a sort of medium through which the Past made itself known.

As he neared the tent, he rehearsed Ru's story about the spilt boiling water and tried to inject as much heartfelt emotion into it as he could. Deep down, he knew his dad probably wouldn't buy it. That man was freakishly good at spotting a lie.

Mac stooped through the front flap of the tent.

"Hey Dad," he said, as he wiped the back of his bandaged hand across his sweaty top lip.

Professor Leon Sanderson glanced up from his laptop computer. "Son." He nodded in greeting. "It's well past time for your lessons."

The middle-aged man offered his son a cold drink from the portable gas refrigerator and they settled into a couple of camping chairs in the shade of the lean-to.

In silence, they looked out on the view of the archaeological dig site that stretched across the plain below them. About a square kilometre of the surrounding desert had been excavated according to a grid formation staked out by small metal pegs and string. Little orange scraps of material tied at intervals along the perimeter fluttered wildly, and the loose cotton shirts of the volunteer workers billowed in the hot Egyptian breeze as they toiled in the trenches with brushes and trowels. A short distance away, they could make out the modern-day city of Alexandria, shrouded in haze, and beyond it, the occasional green twinkle of the Mediterranean Sea.

"What happened to your hands?"

The coolness in Mac's voice couldn't offset the hotness in his ears and cheeks as he delivered the carefully constructed lie.

The professor eyed the boy. He could hardly be called a boy anymore. He had grown so much. The sixteen years since he'd held his son for the first time had slipped by quickly. Leon shook his head. The boy's mother would have been proud, he thought to himself. A pang of grief squeezed his heart. She would have been pleased her son had turned out to be such a terrible liar. Leon smiled on the inside.

Mac kept his gaze on the horizon. He knew his dad didn't buy it.

Leon watched his son take another sip of his drink. MacKinley Sanderson was a tall boy with sun-bleached mousy hair that sprouted over the top of his faded red bandana. Leon noticed that the boy had inherited his dimples. He wore thin-rimmed glasses in front of eyes that belonged to his mother. Intelligent and alert, they were hazel with gold flecks radiating from the pupil and ringed by long dark lashes. His brows were habitually drawn together, creating a pair of neat creases in the middle. It gave him a certain intensity, as if he were concentrating very hard all the time. His naturally fair skin had been turned deep brown by many hours in the sun and the fine hairs on his arms glistened gold in the sunshine.

Leon was well aware of his son's unconscious charm with the ladies. It seemed MacKinley was quite a head-turner. He wondered how long it would take before he began to notice the admiring looks and flirtatious advances of the opposite sex.

"What?" demanded Mac.

"Nothing."

"You were looking at me all weird."

"Just thinking. That's all," said Leon.

Mac finished his drink and walked back inside the tent.

Leon rubbed a hand across his grey-stubbled chin and gazed out at the distant horizon that quivered and wavered in a haze of rising heat. Understandably, his son was a little defensive. Admiring looks weren't the only ones Mac got. He got a lot of weird looks too, especially once people found out about his unusual ability. As it turned out, his eyes weren't the only things he'd inherited from his mother.

The professor sighed and stared up at the cloudless sky. He often wondered if he was doing the right thing as a parent, carting Mac around from dig to dig across the globe with no formal schooling, no friends his own age. Still, the boy seemed happy and content. He was smart too. Certainly, he had proven an invaluable asset to the team. He mixed well with everyone and, although accustomed to the company of adults, he was still a typical teenager in a lot of ways.

Inside the tent, Mac sat in front of the laptop with an open book on the table beside him. He scrolled through a list of songs in the online music store.

"Don't even think of downloading any more music. You still owe me money from last week," came the voice of his father from outside the tent.

Mac could have sworn that man had eyes in the back of his head.

"I wasn't," he lied as he minimised the music window on the screen. Reluctantly, he turned his attention to his lessons. The next two hours could not go quickly enough. He was busting to get back out on the dig before sunset.

He closed his eyes. It was pointless trying to study. Dimples punctured his sun-tanned cheeks while thoughts of Aisha filled his head. Technically, it had been two thousand years since his first and only kiss. Surely he was due for another.

CHAPTER FOUR

LATER THAT NIGHT, Mac lay on his cot, his belly full of beef stew and crusty bread. His father hadn't mentioned his bandaged hands again. His missing shirt had gone unmentioned also but then it wasn't unusual for him to ditch his shirt on a hot day, despite his father's constant warnings about being sun smart. He should have felt relieved as he lay there but instead he was restless.

Mac stared out at the stars. They seemed brighter than usual. He stared at a particularly sparkly one and marvelled at the fact that the light from that star was only just now reaching his eyes from several hundred million years in the distant Past. Its energy had travelled light years to reach him. It was very possible that the star no longer existed in its Now. Its light had spanned millennia to arrive at that very point in his awareness. His mind toyed with the idea. He couldn't help feeling that the concept was somehow an analogy to the phenomena of psychometry and time travel. He drifted into sleep, still trying to make the connection.

Mac tossed and turned. He dreamed of burning buildings and papyrus scrolls. Words in ancient languages flashed across his mind. He dreamed of Aisha. She was even lovelier in his dreams. He tasted sweet berries on her lips. Then he dreamed of a boy pharaoh, his dark, outlined eyes gleaming with hatred as he held a dagger to Mac's throat.

Black wings.

White tower.

Death.

Mac woke with a start. He sat bolt upright, coughing and clutching his throat. He was sweating.

Through the flyscreen window of the tent, the dawn inched its way across the desert toward him. He pulled a light blanket about his shoulders to ward against the early morning chill and made his way outside to watch the sunrise.

His father was already sitting in the camper chair, a cup of tea in hand.

"You're up early," said Leon in his usual tone, as flat as the equatorial ocean. "Tea?"

"Thanks," croaked Mac. He plonked in the chair beside his dad.

Leon Sanderson poured his son a cup of hot black tea from an old teapot, sugared it generously, and handed it to him. Mac blew on it and slurped from the lip of the tin mug. He'd practically been brought up on black tea so it wasn't an unusual start to the day.

The sun crept higher in the sky as it turned the land from pink, to orange, to gold. They watched and sipped their tea.

"Ru reckons the temple may actually be the Library of Alexandria," said Leon eventually.

"Really?" Mac suppressed a smile.

"He reckons it's plausible. It's certainly in keeping with the thermal report at least."

"Interesting."

"I wonder what changed his mind," Leon said, eyeing his son suspiciously. "Just yesterday morning, he was so convinced it was a temple."

Mac wriggled uncomfortably in his chair but said nothing. The smile he wore on the inside vanished. He knew Ru wouldn't have ratted on him but it seemed his father suspected something.

Leon glanced at his son's bandaged hands then back up to his face. "What do *you* think?" he asked.

Mac swallowed hard. He chuckled unconvincingly. "You know Ru, Dad. He changes his mind like he changes his undies."

"Not as often as he should, you mean?" Leon said with the barest suggestion of a smile.

The fact that his father was in a good mood that morning was indeed a plus, however, Mac was under no illusions that he wasn't being watched very closely. He was fairly sure his dad had at least some idea that he was in it up to his neck and had influenced Ru's opinion via psychometric exploration. He was grateful when conversation turned to other things.

After an early breakfast of scrambled eggs on toast, Mac hoisted his tool bag and headed toward the dig. He felt strange – heavy somehow. He hadn't been able to get his mind off Aisha. When he thought of her, he felt elated but there was something – some other feeling – that tainted it.

As he reached his sector, Gabriella, a brilliant anthropologist and volunteer from Peru, greeted him. "Buenos días, MacKeenlee," she said in her charming Latin American accent.

Mac loved the way she said his name.

"Buenos días," replied Mac, returning her greeting.

Gabriella had been teaching him Spanish over the past few months. He thought she was amazing. She was a beautiful thirty-something-year-old, with dark hair that sparkled with premature greys and dark eyes to match. Her nose was a bit big but she wore it quite well above a large full mouth that was almost always smiling. She wore her cotton work shirts tied in a knot just above her navel and unbuttoned just far enough to sport a glimpse of her generous cleavage.

"Your hands. They are okay today?" she asked with concern.

"Yeah, they're fine," said Mac, shrugging and glancing at his bandaged hands.

He unpacked his brush and trowel and set to work nearby. Along with most of the crew, he'd had a slight crush on Gabriella ever since she joined the dig. Yet today, for some reason, he didn't seem to notice her belly button or her cleavage, or the flowery smell of her freshly shampooed hair. All he'd been able to think about since waking up that morning was Aisha, the lovely Aisha, with her emerald eyes and soft lips. He longed to see her again.

Using short brisk strokes, Mac brushed away the sand and grit from around a curved shard of pottery that protruded from the ground. Excavating the ancient odds and ends from the earth was time-consuming and painstaking work. It required much patience, which often went unrewarded when, after long hours of digging and brushing in the hot sun, only a broken fragment of an artefact was uncovered, the rest of it still buried or missing altogether. Still, as boring as it often was, it gave Mac time to think.

Today, he found himself wondering what it would be like to lead a normal life, where he went to a regular high school and had friends his own age, a girlfriend even. He wondered what it would be like to live in a house – the same house all the time – and not move around from place to place.

The Sandersons did, in fact, own a house right on the river in Brisbane, back in Australia, which they rarely visited. The last time Mac could remember being there for any length of time was almost a year ago when they'd gone home for the Christmas holidays. His father's sister and her family had flown up from Sydney to spend New Year with them. He'd spent two weeks hanging out with his cousins, Luke and Corey, who were around his own age, give or take a few years.

Granted, they'd had loads of fun together, as only boys on school holidays know how, but he was glad when he and his dad had finally left the house in the capable hands of the caretaker, Gladys, and returned to a dig in Nairobi.

He'd felt very inadequate in the company of his cousins. They made fun of his name, of his accent – it was a tad English – of his clothes, of his taste in music, and of pretty much everything about him.

They had teased him mercilessly about his glasses. Mac had spent much time in front of the mirror that summer and eventually came up with an idea. That was when the red bandana first made its appearance. He figured it somehow drew attention away from the fact that he wore glasses and so it became a permanent part of his attire. He didn't even care that his cousins would probably call him Karate Kid because of it.

Following his cousins' visit, Mac had spent the money he'd been given for Christmas on a pair of Nike Air Zoom sports shoes, like the ones Corey had worn. His cousin had gone on and on about how cool they were so Mac decided he just *had* to have a pair himself. They had cost him a small fortune and were sitting at the bottom of his trunk in the tent. They weren't exactly fit for work on site. Still, he felt better for at least owning a pair.

One good thing about that visit was Mac's introduction to the world of Manga comics and Anime cartoons. Luke and Corey were right into Japanese animation, which had Mac captivated from the outset. He especially loved one particular series that featured a character who was gifted in psychometry. He had watched it over and over. Mac's cousins knew nothing of his psychometric skills. They'd given him enough grief about everything else. He wasn't about to give them more ammunition.

He had to smile to himself though, as he remembered how his psychometry had come in handy on that particular visit. Corey had tried to convince Mac that the shark's tooth he wore on a piece of leather around his neck had been prised loose from his mauled surfboard when a shark had tried to attack him whilst surfing off Bondi. His cousin had constructed an elaborate story, complete with vivid details of how he'd narrowly escaped the shark attack. Corey's version finished with him clutching the tooth and looking off into the distance dramatically, muttering about how God had spared his life.

Mac had asked to hold the shark's tooth. Instantly, he got a clear vision of sideshow alley at the Royal Easter Show. He could see the toothless grin of the carnival attendant as he handed Corey the plastic-wrapped shark's tooth necklace over the row of gaping clown heads that turned from side to side in unison.

Mac had laughed as he handed the necklace back to his cousin and had told him he was full of crap. Corey had stalked off in a huff and they didn't see him for the rest of that afternoon.

Despite that small victory, Mac had felt somewhat self-conscious around people his own age ever since that holiday with the cousins. He was so aware that he just didn't fit in, no matter whether or not he owned a skateboard. He was – what was it his cousins had called him? A freak. That's right. And they didn't even know about his true freakishness. Hardly anyone did.

Mac stopped brushing at the piece of pottery and stretched his neck.

Maybe they were right. Maybe he *was* a freak. He should just concentrate on being more normal.

He started brushing again.

He had learned to limit the use of his extensive vocabulary and not to talk about any of the things he was actually interested in, like ancient history and conspiracy theories but rather to talk about sports and bands, and drop in a colourful swear word here and there, although he always managed to sound unconvincing.

Delicately, Mac extracted the ancient piece of pottery he'd been brushing away at from the surrounding earth and examined it.

It matched several pieces he'd found the previous morning. He was pretty sure he would unearth the rest of the pot, piece by piece, in the near vicinity. He placed the fragment in a yellow plastic crate with other bits and pieces and wiped the sweat from his brow. Already, it was hot.

Hours evaporated as Mac continued turning the rocky earth with his trowel in search of the Past. He glanced at his watch. It was almost time to down tools and return to the tent for lessons.

Just then, something in the crumbling baked earth at his feet caught his attention. He reached for his brush and leaned closer. There it was again. His eyes widened. The sun glinted off something red. Mac brushed away the sand and grit to reveal a large square-cut ruby. He brushed even more furiously around the stone to reveal the gold ring in which it was set.

Mac gasped. Goosebumps rose. He knew this ring. The old man on the steps of the burning library had been wearing it on the third finger of his bony left hand.

Mac picked up the ring, blew on it and held it up to inspect it more closely. It gleamed in the sunlight. The centre of the gem shone brightly with a fire of its own that turned to a deep crimson at the edges. Each facet of the stone caught the light perfectly. The ruby nestled in a setting of intricately engraved gold.

He squinted. No, it wasn't engraved.

The ruby was set into the top of a lion's head. Its mouth was open in a fierce roar. His flowing mane was etched into the gold around the stone. Mac tilted it up to get a better look. The lion's mane cushioned the ruby and trailed off into a twist, like rope, that narrowed as it completed the gold band and finished in the lion's mouth. It were as though the lion had swallowed its tail.

"Cool," he breathed.

The Sanderson team had unearthed many stunning pieces of jewellery in their travels but this piece was something else. It was mesmerising. He'd never seen anything like it.

"You found something?" called Gabriella from behind him.

Mac slipped it in the pocket of his cargos.

"Nah, it's nothing," he replied. "Just junk."

Gabriella turned back to her work.

After a furtive glance over his shoulder, he retrieved the ring from his pocket and stared at it again. Light burst from its core. Ancient whispers funneled through his head. He felt the sand shift beneath his feet and he had the sensation of vertigo.

Not here…

He crossed to the perimeter of the dig and stepped over the string.

"You study hard, no?" came the voice of Gabriella, assuming he was off to his lessons.

"Sí, señorita," replied Mac over his shoulder. "I study hard." Then, to himself, "But not today…" and he headed for a rocky outcrop nearby.

After checking for scorpions and other creepy things that love to hide in such places, he sank down with his back against the rocks and fumbled in his pocket for the ruby ring. He studied it. Again, came the strangeness in his head. There was a pull in his chest. Something powerful beckoned him. He knew he couldn't resist the pull. He *had* to go.

Mac glanced toward camp. He knew he was expected to return to the tent for lessons. There was no sign of his dad.

He looked back at the ring in his hand. "To hell with it!"

He was going on a trip. He knew he was doing the wrong thing by his father but he just had to explore this. The calling was too strong this time. He would just stay for a little while.

Look but don't touch… He silently repeated his mother's advice, which so far, he'd ignored. He took a deep breath and slipped the ring on the third finger of his left hand. It butted up against the bandage.

He had barely closed his eyes when a massive rush of energy swept through him. Every hair on his body stood on end. His heart banged furiously against his chest. Whispers became roars.

Lights.

Spinning, spinning, spinning… Faster now.

He thought he was going to be sick.

And then…

CHAPTER FIVE

THE BRIGHTNESS!

He scrunched his eyes up and peered through blinking slits. The white-hot glare of the mid-morning sun bounced off the sails of the Roman warships in the harbour. Dazzling reflections from the water's surface sparkled in all directions. A light breeze carried the strong smell of salt and seaweed, mixed with fish. A flock of seagulls glided over his head and landed on the wharf nearby, squawking and squabbling.

Mac studied the ships, with their curved sweeping prows that rose high in the air. Known as galleys or long ships, they had three rows of oars and it took three hundred oarsmen to propel them. His grandfather, whom he'd only met once, a few years ago, had models of them in his study. The old man was really into ships and had bored Mac almost to death. To witness the real thing, however, was a different story. It was amazing to see.

There were many other ships in the harbour besides the Roman navy. He spotted a particularly enormous craft with bright red triangular sails. It resembled a Chinese junk. There were also lots of small fishing boats dotted among the ships. All of them were dwarfed, however, by the magnificent structure that rose up from the ocean behind them – the Lighthouse of Alexandria.

Mac shivered. *White tower…*

He gazed at it open-mouthed. The lighthouse was built on a small island in the harbour that was linked to the mainland by a causeway known as the Heptastadion. This effectively divided the harbour into the Eastern and Western sectors. By Mac's reckoning, the lighthouse rose about a hundred and twenty metres in the air. In the morning sun, the white marble structure stood out in brilliant relief against the dark clouds that gathered far out to sea. Even though he had seen it by the light of the moon on his last visit, it was entirely something else to behold by day. It was nothing short of spectacular, especially in comparison to modern-day lighthouses, with its square tiered levels and columned turret that stretched skyward. He had viewed it from the hill last time. From sea level, it was immense. No wonder it was one of the Seven Ancient Wonders of the World, he thought.

Mac set off in no particular direction.

Huge warehouses and granaries lined the waterfront. The docks were crowded and bustling with people going about their daily business, selling their wares and trading goods from around the world. Nearby, there was what looked to be a marketplace or bazaar of some sort. The amazingly colourful sight struck him. For some reason, when he pictured the Past, it was always in faded muted tones, as if all the colour had been sucked out of the scene over time. This was vibrant and alive. The market pavilions were multicoloured with bright flags fluttering in the onshore winds. The people wore colourful fabrics of all sorts, not just the white cotton shifts that were so popular in Egyptian paintings.

The other thing that struck him was the stunning diversity of the place. Merchants and traders from all around the world were attracted to the great commercial emporium that was Alexandria. There were olive-skinned people that looked perhaps Greek; there were peppercorn-haired Africans whose skin was shiny chocolate and others whose skin was so black it was almost blue; there were some who looked more Middle Eastern, with hooked noses and turbans; there were yellow-skinned Asians in exotic silks with flowing moustaches; and there was even a large bearded man with very fair skin and long red hair.

A skinny brown man, bare-chested and barefoot, wearing a twisted length of material around his waist, brushed past Mac carrying a woven reed basket on his head. He gave the boy a strange glance but said nothing.

Mac was suddenly aware that he must look very odd, in his khaki cargo shorts and white button-up shirt with the sleeves ripped off at the shoulders. He did that to all his shirts, despite his father's protests. Mac thought it made his muscles look bigger. On his feet he wore a pair of steel-cap work boots. His glasses and wristwatch made him all the more conspicuous.

He lowered his head and made his way toward a row of tents. A few people shot him strange looks but, so far, no one had approached him. That was a good thing. He slipped into the gap between two tents and waited in the shade for a moment to collect his thoughts.

It was obvious to Mac that he had landed back in Alexandria and, judging by the fact that the Roman navy was at anchor in the harbour, he guessed it must be close to the time of his last visit. He had to find the library. If it lay in smouldering ruins then he'd know whether he had landed before or after about 48 BC, which was his guess as to when the Library of Alexandria burnt down.

He dared to wonder if he would see Aisha again. Given the hundreds of people in the street, he figured the odds were against him. If he were really honest with himself, he would have realised that Aisha was the main reason he so desperately wanted to return to the ancient city. But, for now, he was just content to be led by the ring. He could kid himself and pretend it was all about the history.

Mac noticed flapping sheets of cream cotton fabric draped over nearby tent ropes. He glanced around. Most of the people – men and women – were dressed in long flowing toga-like wraps of one sort or another. He checked no one was watching, then quickly whipped the sheet off the line and slipped around the back of the tent. He held the length of material up in front of him. Surely, it couldn't be too hard.

Mac took off his shirt and tucked it into the waistband of his shorts so it hung down at the back. He folded the sheet of cotton in half and wrapped it around his waist. That left a length of fabric trailing at the back, which he flipped up and over his opposite shoulder, then tucked it into his shorts at the front. He put his hands on his hips, well pleased with himself until he looked down at his boots sticking out from under the sheet. It looked ridiculous but he was reluctant to take them off and wander around barefoot. Besides, his dad would kill him if he got back to the Now with no boots. They would have to stay. He shuffled the fabric around until it dropped lower to cover the tops of his boots at least.

Satisfied, he stepped out into the street. He hadn't gone more than a few paces when he stopped. He didn't have any idea where he was going or what he was doing there. Did he even *have* a plan? He wasn't entirely sure, but he wasn't ready to go home just yet.

He looked at the ring. It seemed to pulse slowly. Maybe it was just his imagination. He decided to wander around and see if he could find the library at least, Aisha at best.

The marketplace was fascinating. Mac weaved his way through the crowd, pausing here and there to have a closer look at things. As he made his way from the docks toward the city, he noticed the smell had changed. Past the stinky fish markets, the air was filled with the smell of cooking and spices, and was laced with pungent wafts of burning incense. A group of old men sat in the shade, puffing on a sheesha pipe. Mac got a whiff of apple-flavoured smoke. They stared at him as he passed.

The street was hot and dusty. It was noisy. Merchants yelled in different languages while customers haggled over prices. Chickens squawked and goats bleated. Somewhere up ahead, an unseen drummer banged away rhythmically beneath the sound of flutes and bells. A seemingly endless array of fresh bananas, limes, lemons, melons and some other fruits he didn't recognise stretched before him.

A hooded old woman with a milky, blind eye shoved a bushel of dried herbs in Mac's face. She was shaking it and yelling at him, eyebrows raised, in the hope that he might buy. He shook is head and waved her away with open palms.

"Ah, no… No thanks…"

He sneezed.

She yelled some more.

He sneezed again and pushed past her. He glanced back at the woman over his shoulder to catch her pulling a nasty face at him. He wiped his nose on the back of his bandaged hand, and kept walking.

Moments later, his head was swimming. His vision was a little blurry and he felt unsteady on his feet. He was suddenly desperate to get out of there.

He turned sharply to his right, dodging a bunch of young girls, their enormous black eyes leering out of distorted faces. Their warped, twisted laughter seemed to echo in his brain. He rubbed his eyes behind his glasses and staggered forward.

Somehow his clumsy steps picked their way between the maze of ropes and tent pegs until he came to rest against the wall of a building behind the marketplace. He was breathing heavily and had trouble focusing. Sweat ran down his temples. He waited for his eyes to adjust to the gloom after the blazing sun of the open street and tried to make sense of his surroundings.

He was in a dark laneway between stone buildings. A crude thatched roof had been constructed over it. The alley looked to be a shortcut through to the next street. There was daylight at the other end. Although the shade was cool and it was much quieter, he felt uneasy in this place. The air was thick and the pressing darkness made it harder to breathe. Mac struggled to see as he made his way up the alley. He heard scrabbling noises beside him and caught a glimpse of movement. Rats! He hurried on. He could hear murmuring on either side of him and was vaguely aware of small clusters of people crouched against the walls. The glowing ends of cigarettes hovered in the darkness, giving off clouds of foul smoke that stung his throat. He coughed and kept walking. He was anxious to get out of there.

Suddenly, two youths appeared out of the shadows. They

stood right in front of him. Both of them were well muscled and a good few inches taller than Mac. The taller of the two stood with his arms crossed. The other stood slightly to the side and wielded a blunt length of wood like a baseball bat.

This was bad. Mac wasn't exactly a skinny kid but he'd never been in a fight in his life. He didn't speak the language so it wasn't like he could talk his way out of it. He couldn't even relax enough to concentrate on teleporting out of there either.

The tall guy smiled viciously and said something. Mac just looked from one to the other and said nothing. Without warning, the tall guy grabbed the front of Mac's toga and yanked him forward so that their faces were just inches apart. The youth yelled at him, spit flying.

Mac knew he was in trouble. He flipped his palms up, 'don't shoot' style. "Wait… Just…" What the hell did they speak? He remembered from his studies that they actually spoke ancient Greek, not Egyptian. In fact, they hadn't spoken the Egyptian language in Alexandria for almost three hundred years. He knew a smattering of ancient Greek but, in his panic, couldn't think of a single word.

The tall one spotted Mac's wristwatch. He squinted. He turned to his accomplice and mumbled something. He grabbed Mac's bandaged hand and wrenched it closer to inspect the watch.

Mac winced. His burns were still tender.

The guy with the bat leaned closer. They spoke to each other rapidly, eyes wide with wonder. Of course, Mac realised, they would never have seen a watch or a clock. The small amount of light in the dim alley glinted off the watch face and illuminated the hands and numbers so they glowed green. To them, it must have looked like magic.

The bat guy leaned close and yelled at Mac.

He flinched.

Then they were both yelling at him. It was clear they wanted the watch.

He unclipped it and held it up for them.

Tall Guy snatched it out of his hand and stared at it. Bat Boy leaned in, gibbering.

Mac just stood there with his hands up, thankful that his bandages had loosened enough to inch forward and cover the ruby lion ring. He wondered what would happen if the object he'd used to travel there were stolen. How did that work? Would he be stuck there? The object was the link between Past and Present. He knew from the Roman chariot incident that his father had been able to break the link to the Past by removing the sandal he'd been wearing. But could it work the other way?

In light of this new possibility, he decided the ring was suddenly far more valuable to him.

Just as Mac was considering making a run for it, his two would-be assailants turned and walked off, still deep in discussion. Bat Boy looked back over his shoulder and drew an invisible ring around his eye with his finger. Obviously, they were commenting on Mac's glasses.

He held his breath. *Not the glasses, not the glasses…*

They turned and started back towards him.

Mac ran. They gave chase.

His legs were rubbery and felt strangely disconnected from his body but somehow they propelled him forward. He could hear the youths gaining on him. They'd be on him in a second.

A faint glow on the edge of his vision caught his attention. A doorway!

Mac lunged for it, his boots splashing through a stream of stinking effluent before tripping up a step and landing on his hands and knees inside the door. He spun.

His attackers were no more than shadows that lingered outside for a second before taking off.

Mac was breathless. His shoulders sagged with relief as he gave in to the nauseating feeling that follows an adrenalin rush.

He looked around. He was sprawled just inside the door of a small, dimly lit room. Candles burned on a low table in the middle of the room. Aside from the table, a tattered rug on the floor and a woven screen in the corner, the place was empty of furniture. Bushels of dried herbs and strange objects dangled from the low ceiling. It was still and eerie.

Mac wrinkled his nose. The smell was dreadful. A sickly scent of burning incense and herbs barely masked the stench of… what? It smelt like…

Death.

He didn't know what death smelt like but that was the only word that came to mind. He scrambled to his feet and turned to go.

"AARGH!"

Terror bolted through him.

A milky white eye barred his escape.

Mac recognised her at once.

The wizened walnut of a mouth stretched into a smile. She hadn't a single tooth. Her one good eye glinted in the candlelight. Apart from a wispy lock of white hair dangling from one side of her head, she was completely bald.

She said something in a raspy voice.

Mac was frozen.

The woman smiled wider. She was a hideous thing. Taking him by the arm, she led him to the table and gestured for him to sit. He sank to the floor like stone. The woman sat opposite. She pushed the candles aside and laid a thick brown stick on the table between them.

He recoiled in horror.

It wasn't a stick at all but a length of bone. It very much resembled a human thigh bone. The fetid stench of death was suffocating.

The woman crinkled up her good eye until it was just a slit. A hoarse gurgle broke out between her gums. Her breath was utterly putrid.

Mac gagged. He was desperate to escape but his body felt like lead. It simply wouldn't obey his mental commands to move.

The old crone was abruptly serious. She emptied a drawstring pouch of white spiky pellets on the table. They scattered. She picked up the thigh bone and waved it over them, rasping a chilling intonation. When she'd finished, she whipped it away and stared at the pellets.

Bones!

They were individual vertebrae, bleached and finely painted all over with pictures and symbols. Some of them Mac recognised as hieroglyphs.

The woman rubbed her hands together and made a sound like air escaping from a tyre tube. She muttered something and picked up one of the bones. The candlelight flickered across it as she held it in front of Mac's face.

Even amid the strangeness of it all, a tiny voice in his

memory told him it was a lumbar vertebra from the lower back. It was slightly larger than the rest. There was a drawing of a bird – a heron, he thought – with a weird crown on its head. It was flanked by a sun and a moon. Strange symbols were etched along the pointy bit of the bone and all around the outside of it. He scanned his conscious mind for some meaning but found none. Yet when he looked at it, he felt a strange stirring, a foreboding.

The woman snatched it away and plucked another bone from the scattering. She held it up for him to examine as she hissed an explanation.

This one was painted black all over with a white tower on it.

A vague déjà vu rippled across his mind.

She picked through the bone runes and selected three. Her fists uncurled to reveal them. They were lined up in a perfect row across her palms. The first depicted a crown. The middle bone was the distinctive first vertebra of the spine with nothing painted on it and the third showed a lotus flower. The hag slipped a bony index finger through the wide hollow of the middle bone and jabbed it at Mac.

He flinched.

She spoke rapidly at him in a low voice. Her good eye was wide with near hysteria. He wanted to look away but couldn't. The glint of something red reflected in her eye.

No…

He shook his head. It felt heavy and slow. The room started to tilt and spin.

She went on and on, louder and louder.

Move…

He made a desperate lurch for the exit but he was too slow.

The hag's lightning grab for the ruby lion ring raked the skin off his knuckles. He screamed as her fingernails ripped at his bandages. He tore his hand away and rolled onto his belly. The floor felt like quicksand. Skeleton hands clawed at his legs until one took firm hold of his ankle. He kicked. He couldn't shake it.

The bone! Mac's hand closed around the thigh bone lying on the floor. He swung it in a backhanded arc with as much force as he could muster.

THWACK!

She released his ankle. He clawed his way to the door and tumbled through it into the alleyway sludge. Behind him, the hag's laughter sounded like an eruption of bubbles in warm mud.

Mac ran.

He was still shaking when he stumbled out into the bright sunshine. He squinted against the glare. The alley opened onto a dusty street lined with square, stone buildings. Unlike the mad bazaar, it was almost deserted. A scrawny dog that had obviously just had pups trotted past, teats swinging. A couple of women with large pots on their heads chatted casually nearby. They didn't even glance at him.

He put his back to the wall and let his legs fold under him. With trembling hands, he untied his bandana and wiped the sweat from his forehead.

Mac stared at the ring on his finger. It nestled amongst fresh rubies of bright blood. He dabbed at his knuckles with his bandana and wondered again just what would happen if he lost the ring. Would he be able to get home? He wished he knew more about how the whole time thing worked.

All he knew for sure was that he wasn't able to bring anything back from the Past with him. He'd tried that.

About a year ago, he'd found himself in a burial chamber laden with priceless treasure. He'd filled his pockets with as many precious gems and as much gold as he could carry, with the plan in mind to return for the rest later, only to find upon his return to the Present that his pockets were empty. Following Mac's temper tantrum, his father had lectured him at length about greed and ill intentions.

Until he had some answers, he decided it might be safer for him to keep the ring in his pocket.

The bleeding had eased. He went to take the ring off but it wouldn't budge. It was jammed tight against the bunched up skin on his knuckle, which was quickly springing more blood. He spat on it and strained harder. It was no use. The ruby ring was there to stay. He sighed.

Deciding he would just have to be more careful, Mac stood up and adjusted his toga. As filthy and stinky as it was, he made some improvement by flipping it over to the cleaner side and refastening it. It wasn't exactly high fashion of the day, he was sure, but it would have to do.

Feeling a little steadier on his feet, he headed in the direction in which he thought the library must be. Already, he was formulating a lie to tell his father that explained the disappearance of the watch he'd been given two Christmases ago.

He hadn't gone far when he realised the street was getting steeper. He knew he must have been heading in the right direction. The library had been on high ground.

He reached a busy intersection at the crest of the hill. There were people everywhere. Most were on foot, some pulling carts loaded with fresh produce, others bent double under the weight of heavy baskets strapped to their backs. A few hauled donkeys behind them, laden with market wares. He stood to the side of the human traffic. The road to his left led back to the marketplace. He looked to his right.

His heart almost stopped.

There on the hill, stood the grand Library of Alexandria, Royal Library of the Ptolemies.

CHAPTER SIX

Mac stared at the massive stone building. It was certainly impressive. The library gleamed against the blue sky. Wide stone steps with miniature sphinxes mounted on each side led up to a large, columned entry that was flanked by statues of royalty or gods. Mac wasn't sure which. The statues were the traditional Egyptian type – simplistic with arms crossed over chest, and one foot slightly in front.

As he approached, he noticed the flow of people going in and out of the library. Groups of what looked like students chatted as they passed clusters of scholarly old men in white robes. There were a couple of women sitting side by side on the steps in deep discussion. A bunch of kids nearby chanted rhymes as they played some sort of skipping game up and down the steps. No one even glanced at Mac.

He lingered at the entrance for a moment. Elaborate scenes were intricately sculpted in relief and inscriptions decorated the stone lintel of an immense set of timber doors that were opened wide. Serious-faced guards stood at attention on either side. They glanced sideways at him as he passed but made no move to stop him.

Inside, he soaked up the coolness while the greenish eye

fuzz from the harsh glare subsided enough for him to see indoors. As his eyes adjusted, his jaw dropped in wonder. If he thought the library was impressive from the outside, it was nothing compared to the splendour before him now.

He was standing in a cavernous hall, rimmed by balustraded walkways that ran all the way around the edges on two upper levels high above him. They were accessible by staircases at either end. The ground level was semi open to the outside in some parts via wooden folding doors that allowed light to stream in between the fluted columns. A section of the ceiling was open to the sky, which was spectacularly mirrored by a large shallow pool set into the floor, right in the centre of the hall. Mac realised it must have been the pond he and Aisha had stumbled into during their escape from the fire. The now familiar lapis lazuli and obsidian floor, with its stunning artistry of patterns and colours, stretched away before him. His eyes followed it to the far wall.

There, a set of white marble steps led up onto a platform from which three beautifully decorated doorways led off to other areas. On either side of the platform, were two giant wall murals. To the left, was a colourful portrait of Alexander the Great, founder and namesake of the city, and to the right, a depiction of the Hellenist-Egyptian god, Serapis. Mac recognised the deity immediately, with his almost Zeus-like features, grain basket on his head, scepter in hand, and the three-headed dog, Cerberus at his feet. Mac recalled from his studies in ancient Egyptian religion that the animal-headed gods were not so popular in Lower Egypt due to the strong Greek influence, so a more acceptable notion of a god was invented to keep everyone happy.

The walls were lined with boxed segments that were

quartered diagonally into pigeonholes that housed bundles of papyrus scrolls in cylinders. There were literally thousands of these pigeonholes and *hundreds* of thousands of scrolls. It was mind-boggling. Each box had inscriptions painted above it, which Mac figured must have been labels of some sort.

Tables were posted at intervals around the edges of the room, with clusters of library-goers pouring over lengths of papyrus. In one corner, a group sat cross-legged on the tiled floor around a stately man who stood with arms outstretched and spoke in a deep voice. Mac guessed it was some kind of poetry reading. The man's voice was the only sound in the otherwise quiet library.

A lean black cat stalked across the room. A cat?

Mac followed it with his eyes. Then he noticed another cat, and another. There were several of them, some hiding in the shadows, others preening themselves and lazing about. Mac found them a little spooky. He wondered what all those cats were doing in a library. Perhaps they were there to keep the rodents out. A storehouse of scrolls would probably be a haven for rats and mice, he figured. He also recalled that cats were sacred in ancient Egypt.

A bizarre-looking creature eyed him suspiciously from under a table. He thought it was a cat but he'd never seen one like it. It was grotesque. Oversized bat ears dwarfed its head. It had huge alien eyes that were blue instead of the usual cat-green, and it was completely hairless. Patchy pigmentation tattooed its body, the skin pooling in loose wrinkles between its ears, and around its chest and hips as it sat there staring. Its blue-eyed gaze was penetrating. Mac could almost read its thoughts: *I know who you are and I know you don't belong here.* It was unnerving.

WHACK!

Mac was almost knocked off his feet from behind by a teenager who had come rushing through the front doors, a bunch of scrolls tucked under his arm. The youth offered a hasty apology over his shoulder, amid a flurry of robes, as he ran toward the doors at the far end of the hall. An important-looking gentleman with a plaited beard directed a firm command at the running figure from the other side of the room. Mac watched with amusement as the youth slowed immediately to a barely restrained walk and kept going. It seemed libraries of the Past weren't that different from the Present, he thought.

The important-looking man glanced back at Mac. His gaze hovered a little longer than Mac was comfortable with so he lowered his eyes and turned to his left. He walked purposefully toward the wall of scrolls, chin up and brow furrowed slightly as if he were on a very important mission. He stood before the bundles of neatly pigeonholed scrolls and stole a glance over his shoulder. The man was still looking at him but then turned away and strode off in the other direction.

Relieved, Mac turned his attention to the wall of scrolls that rose above him. Some of the cylinders were made of wood and some of brass. Some looked as though they were carved out of ivory. Toward the corner of the room, the scrolls seemed much older. The cylinders were aged and dusty.

Mac glanced around to be sure no one was watching. Very gently, he slid one of the scrolls out of its quadrant and held the cylinder in his hands. He took a second to savour the moment.

I'm in the Library of Alexandria… This is real… This is actually happening…

His heart beat faster as he stared at the cylinder in his hands. He eased the papyrus scroll out of its container by the little knob on the end.

A shiver swept over him.

He wedged the empty cylinder between his knees and, using both hands, unrolled the scroll a few centimeters to reveal small neat writing of some sort. Mac thought he recognised it as the style of writing used by the ancient Greeks. It consisted of different combinations of strange symbols. Some almost resembled letters from the English alphabet. He didn't have a clue what it said. He desperately wished his mother had been there.

An archaeologist and a linguist, Emily Sanderson had been blessed with a unique psychic gift of her own. Hers allowed her to decipher ancient texts in forgotten languages just by placing part of the text or stone carving, or even a photograph of it, against her forehead. She could then translate it into English. The only problem was that, given the scientific nature of archaeology, she would then have to work backwards to establish the key to deciphering the text before she could submit the find with any real proof of authenticity. Her gift remained a well-kept secret as her reputation as an ancient languages expert astounded the academic world for years until her untimely death.

He stared at the scroll. An idea was forming. He looked around. No one was looking in his direction.

Placing the scroll on a nearby table, he positioned himself to face the wall. He placed a gentle hand on the fragile papyrus. With his other hand, he touched his mother's wedding band on the string around his neck. He dropped his chin to his chest and slipped the wedding ring between his lips.

He took a deep breath and closed his eyes.

At first, there was only black. Tiny sparks appeared and dashed away into the dark. Then he became aware that the sparks were bright symbols appearing then disappearing. They streaked across his mind in an instant. He wished they would slow down. The symbols morphed from one shape to the next, to the next. Mac felt as though his mind were expanding. The blackness stretched out further at the edges but the symbol sparks kept filling the space and began to clump together in vibrating clusters. Then they began to string together in sequences that seemed to flick and shuffle at lightning speed, like a slot machine. Then came the whispers, layers of them. They grew louder and filled his head until he thought he could stand it no longer.

Then silence.

Understanding.

Mac opened his eyes. He was sweating and breathing hard. He looked around. He'd remained unnoticed. A tiny droplet of perspiration plopped onto the scroll. He gasped in horror and delicately tried to dab at it with his robe. He had smudged the word 'perfume' and began to – *What?*

He understood the word!

His eyes scanned the papyrus rapidly. In fact, he understood all of it. All of it! Every word!

"…and the perfume of the rose and larkspur did softly embrace Persephone…" he read.

He had no idea what that meant.

The mutterings of a group of girls walking past interrupted his train of thought.

"…of course, I told him no. I just don't have time for this but all he said was…" Their voices trailed off as they walked on. They may as well have been speaking English. Mac understood every word perfectly.

Nearby, he overheard two men commenting on a very large-breasted woman on the far side of the room. He stared open-mouthed in her direction – not at her, or her breasts for that matter, but at what had just happened. He'd had some kind of total language download in his brain. It was mind blowing. All he'd hoped for was some inkling of what the text meant. He never imagined becoming instantly fluent in ancient Greek.

One of the leering men caught his eye and winked knowingly. Mac blushed and looked away.

He read a little more of the text in front of him. It seemed like a poem of some sort. He'd never really been into poetry. Carefully, he rolled up the scroll and replaced it in its proper place. He studied the labels on the adjacent compartments: *The Heart of Homer, Poetry of Old Times, The Dream Beyond – A Collection of Poems.*

Mac decided to explore further.

He craned his neck to look up. The view from the top level would be spectacular, he decided, so he headed for the staircase and climbed the two levels to the top.

It was darker and there were fewer people up there. He leaned over the railing and looked down. The patterns in the floor could be much better appreciated from high up. For a moment, he watched the people below come and go, and tried to soak up his surrounds.

The ugly cat was still staring at him. He poked his tongue out at it. It just stared back. It flicked its tail and wore a sinister half-smile.

An involuntary shiver rippled down Mac's spine. He turned back to the shelves of scrolls.

The cylinders looked even older than the ones on the ground level. Even the air smelt ancient. He strained to read the labels in the dim light. *Mysteries of the Ancients, Origins of Man – A Voyage Back in Time, The Destruction of Maldek, Visitors From the Skies…*

He followed along with his finger as he read in a whisper, "*Secrets from the Hall of Records, Atlantis and The Ten-Year War, Cultural Traditions of Mu and Lemuria…*"

Mac's eyes widened.

He thought they were supposed to be mythical civilizations. And Atlantis? He'd always believed it actually had existed – so did his dad and Ru – but here was proof, so it seemed. He was lost in thought for a moment. Perhaps, if enough time passed, eventually the modern-day cities of New York and London would be relegated to the realm of myth and legend.

He continued. "*Giant Creatures of Ancient Earth.*"

It struck him as kind of funny that the scrolls referred to 'ancient times'. Just how far back was 'ancient times' to the people of Alexandria? He wondered how old the scrolls could be. They looked hundreds of years old. And there he was in what, for him, was *ancient* Egypt. Just how far back did the information go? Knowledge and stories handed down from one generation to the next for perhaps thousands of years until such time as they could be scribed and preserved were begging to be heard. He felt like a little kid in a candy store. He didn't know what to read first.

He pulled out another scroll entitled *Flying Chariots – Ezekiel's Account.*

"Ah yes, a fine choice for the open mind," came a voice from behind him.

Mac jumped and spun around, almost dropping the scroll. He found himself face to face with an old man sporting a neatly cropped grey beard. His white robes reached to his ankles and he wore leather sandals with coloured beads stitched into them.

Wait.

This wasn't just any old man. It was the old man he had seen on the steps the night of the fire.

Mac's eyes darted to the man's left hand, which was gently entwined with the right. There was the ruby ring – the very same ring Mac wore on *his* left hand! He could feel it pulsing on his third finger. It was getting hotter. He hid his hand behind his back.

"You don't speak the language then," said the man and began to speak in a different tongue.

Mac cut him off. "I do. I do speak the language."

The man raised one eyebrow. "And rather well for a foreigner, I must add."

The intensity of his gaze seemed to pierce Mac's soul, searching it, mining it for information.

Mac couldn't hold his stare an instant longer. He glanced over the balcony. He was a long way from any exit.

A bony hand gripped his wrist and drew him close. The man smelt like rain on hot concrete. "And a time traveller at that," he whispered.

Mac's heart almost stopped. *How could he know?*

He was speechless.

The old man winked and tapped his head. "Strong in the touch, you see. Much like yourself. Though I do suspect your powers are much greater. I've not yet managed to master the art of time travel." He gave a wheezy chuckle and pointed to

Mac's glasses. "It gives you away. The device for clear seeing – it is of the Future."

Mac still couldn't speak. He reached up and dumbly touched his glasses.

The man grew very serious. "The stars foretold of your arrival… 'The Deliverer cometh from afar' they said," continued the old man.

"Deliverer?" asked Mac. "The stars?"

"Astrology, boy. You're trained in the art?"

"No. No, I'm not."

The man frowned. Clearly, he thought it unusual that Mac wasn't a skilled astrologist. "Never mind," he said.

Just then, the freaky hairless cat appeared from behind the man, twisted its slender body around his legs and rubbed its head against the man's shins. It turned to look at Mac.

"Ah, come to say 'hello' have we?" the man asked the cat. "This is Nefertiti."

Mac had to smile. Strangely, with her huge almond eyes and elegant neck, the cat did sort of resemble the famous statue of the ancient Egyptian queen after which she was named.

The cat shot him a haughty glance as if to say, "We've met" then turned away, disinterested.

"And I," said the man looking from the cat back to Mac, "am Elcor, Chief Administrator of the Library."

He offered his hand.

"Mac. MacKinley, actually. Just Mac is fine."

They shook hands. A nauseating instant of vertigo tilted time and space as they exchanged something unnameable.

Elcor withdrew his hand and tried to mask his momentary

unease with further comment. “Mac,” he repeated, nodding. “I like it. Strong.”

But Mac sensed a shadow of uncertainty hover over them.

Elcor inhaled and straightened, dispelling the tension. “Come. I’ll show you around,” he said. “Then we’ll eat. I can feel your hunger.”

The man was right. Mac was starving. Breakfast was eons ago – *literally.*

He followed Elcor along the walkway. The man’s long silver hair hung almost to his waist. It was clasped into a loose ponytail at several points by small leather bands. His footsteps made almost no sound. Mac was suddenly very aware of his work boots clomping along on the tiles in the relative silence of the place. He switched to tiptoes.

They made their way down the staircase and crossed to the far end of the hall to the platform with the three decorated doorways. There were other doors at the sides of the room that Mac hadn’t noticed before. They climbed the steps to stand on the platform. Elcor turned back to face the Great Hall.

With arms outstretched, he announced, “Welcome to the Royal Library of Alexandria.” He indicated to the mural on his left. “It is dedicated to the god, Serapis.”

“Oh yes, I’ve read about him,” said Mac.

“His name lives on then?”

“Um… Sort of. In the history books, at least.” Mac wasn’t sure what else to say.

The man raised his eyebrows and turned back to the doorways. Elcor proceeded with a flourish of hands that resembled a flight attendant’s safety presentation. Yet all his showiness couldn’t hide the unsettling sense of foreboding that Mac knew lurked beneath the façade. He knew because he felt it too.

"Through to the left is the Writing Room. That's where the scribes work. They copy manuscripts – some from here, some from afar. By law, all foreign merchant ships entering the harbour are boarded, their written works confiscated and brought here to the library, where they're translated and copied by our scribes. The originals become the property of the library and the copies are returned to the ships. This way, the Library of Alexandria will remain the largest and most extensive in the world." His scripted introduction lapsed as he added, "My granddaughter is one of the scribes. One of the best, actually."

Mac noticed the pride in his tone but there was something else in his eyes.

Elcor blinked rapidly and glanced at the tiles. "She has an uncanny gift for ancient languages and she's quite an accomplished mathematician."

He forced a smile before continuing. "Past that, is the Left Wing, which consists of a series of lecture halls. All up, we can seat almost five thousand students, you know."

Mac pretended to be impressed. He sort of was, in a distracted way.

"The door to the right leads to the administrative chambers, meeting rooms and dining hall."

"Dining hall?"

"Oh yes, yes. Many a healthy argument has been had over a long meal."

Elcor went on to explain that the hundred or so scholars who lectured and carried out research at the library shared meals in the common dining hall.

Mac imagined some of the greatest minds in history crowded together in the same room, eating, debating and exchanging ideas well into the night. He remembered reading that Aristotle once taught there and that the library housed his own private collection. With a little thrill, Mac wondered if he might even get to meet him.

"And this," continued Elcor, stepping through the middle doorway, "is the Temple of the Muses – The Musaeum."

Mac decided his bet with Ru was off. It seemed they were both right. It was a temple *and* a library. He vaguely remembered reading somewhere that the English word 'museum' originated from The Musaeum at Alexandria.

His thoughts were suspended as the grandeur of the temple loomed before him.

The other section of the library paled in comparison to the sheer magnificence of The Musaeum. In the very centre of the immense space was a columned circle supporting a staircase that spiralled up to a mezzanine level that was open to the sky directly above it. Sunlight poured in and bathed the temple in light.

"That's the observatory," said Elcor.

A rich blend of classical Greek and traditional Egyptian scenes were painted on the ceiling. The design on the tiled floor was even more colourful and intricate than that of the main library. Two long narrow ponds graced the floor on each side of the room, fed by waterfalls that cascaded from statues recessed into the walls.

Elaborate shrines to each of the nine Muses were stationed around the perimeter. The Muses, if Mac recalled his lessons correctly, were a sisterhood of goddesses who supposedly embodied the arts. According to Greek mythology, they were the daughters of Zeus.

Every inch of the walls was covered in the most incredible artwork and mosaics. Mac could have spent hours admiring the spectacle but it seemed he was getting the express tour. He trailed his guide, trying to take it all in as they crossed the space to the far end.

They passed mounted statues of draped women, their bodies styled in the classic 'S' bend of Hellenist sculpture, and monuments depicting muscled heroes of folklore. Noting the strong Greek influence in the artworks, it would have been easy to forget he was in Egypt.

Fragrant oils burned somewhere nearby, filling the place with the most heavenly scent. Robed priests moved about amid an air of quiet reverence.

"Where are all the people?" Mac whispered.

"The Musaeum is not open to the public. Only priests and scholars are allowed in here."

Elcor turned and winked at Mac. "Consider yourself privileged, young man."

They reached a heavy cedar door at the end of the Musaeum. Elcor lifted the latch and leaned against it. He paused to look back at Mac, his expression lighter than before. "Prepare to enter another world."

The door swung open.

Mac gaped.

CHAPTER SEVEN

THEY STEPPED INTO a lush courtyard garden, bordered by pillared walkways on all sides.

"May I present the Royal Gardens," said Elcor with a sweep of his hand.

It was tranquil and cool. The air was so fresh that Mac felt supercharged with energy. He did indeed feel like he'd entered another world. It was enchanting. The unspoken shadow that clung to them just moments ago was gone.

The huge trees that towered above the manicured lawns filtered the sunlight, casting a magical green glow throughout the garden. Birds twittered and butterflies danced from one exotic flower to the next. A circular fountain formed the centrepiece of the garden, from which four pathways radiated in each direction.

Students lazed on the grass while teachers strolled along the covered walkways, deep in conversation. A peacock strutted across the path in front of them, its magnificent tail sweeping along behind it.

Movement at the edge of his vision caught Mac's attention. He looked to his right to see two majestic giraffes rising above the foliage. They were so graceful that they seemed to be moving in slow motion.

"Giraffes..." He was entranced.

Elcor whistled. A white baby elephant came trotting out of the bushes toward them. Mac couldn't believe his eyes. Elcor slipped his hand into the folds of his robes and produced a treat for the elephant, which it snuffled up and stuffed in its mouth with its trunk. The old man cooed and scratched its trunk.

"It's perfectly safe," said Elcor, sensing Mac's eagerness.

Mac reached up and gently stroked the elephant's trunk. It batted its long, white lashes and sniffed him. He grinned as its trunk tickled the palm of his hand.

"This is Suru," said Elcor. "He was a gift to Pharaoh from visiting dignitaries from Carthage but he's really *my* baby. Aren't you? Aren't you, boy?" Elcor indulged the elephant. "Albino elephants are very rare and are considered good luck," he said.

"He's amazing..." Mac breathed.

He wished his dad and Ru were there to share the moment. A sick twinge of guilt nipped at his gut. He wondered how much time had passed in the Now. He took a deep breath and shook off the feeling. There was no way he was going home yet.

They made their way across the courtyard toward a massive gated archway with guards on either side.

"What's through there?" asked Mac.

"That's the entry to the palace grounds."

"Where the Pharaoh lives?"

"Yes, indeed. One of them at least."

Mac thought for a moment. "Would that be Ptolemy XIII?"

Elcor snorted. "Have there been that many of them?" He stopped walking and turned to Mac. "If you mean Ptolemy Theos Philopator, then yes. I'm not certain about the 'thirteenth' part."

Then Mac remembered that the numbering of the Ptolemy rulers was a modern-day convention. In ancient times, they were simply known by their names.

"What do you mean by 'one of them'? How many pharaohs are there?"

"You really *are* from the future, aren't you?" said the old man, cocking his head to one side. "There are currently two pharaohs but for how much longer I'm not sure. Trouble is brewing, you see. Ptolemy Philopator is married to his older sister, Cleopatra, and therefore, are joint rulers of Egypt."

Mac shuddered.

"You see," explained Elcor, "under Egyptian law a female ruler must have either her husband or son as co-ruler. Cleopatra has no children, therefore the obvious choice to ensure the strength of the Ptolemy Dynasty was her younger brother."

"That's one nasty law," said Mac in disgust.

"Is it not so in the future then?"

"Not only is it 'not so', it's not even legal."

Mac found the idea of Queen Elizabeth being married to Prince Charles, or Charles marrying Princess Anne, absolutely revolting.

"Times change, I suppose," said Elcor, and went on to explain the current situation.

There was much tension between Cleopatra and her

brother. Cleopatra was power-hungry and ambitious. Her brother, on the other hand, was weak and naïve. It was clear to Mac that Elcor wasn't a fan of Ptolemy at all.

Apparently, Cleopatra had coins minted with her image on them and didn't include her brother. In fact, his name was purposely omitted from all official documents. According to Elcor, it had been their father's dying will that his son and daughter rule Egypt together, with the Roman Republic as their guardians. Ptolemy's regent, or advisor, was a man named Pothinus. He managed to turn Ptolemy against his sister, which sparked a civil war. Fearing for her life, Cleopatra fled to Syria and now the Roman general, Julius Caesar, was stepping in to sort things out, in an effort to restore her to the throne.

"So you see," concluded Elcor, "it's not the best time to be in Alexandria. Things are very complicated right now. Just days ago, Ptolemy had Caesar's rival, General Pompey, beheaded and presented the head to Caesar as a gift in a desperate attempt to win favour with him. Well, what can I say? It had the opposite effect. Caesar is furious. Trouble is in the air, I tell you."

Elcor felt the darkness descend again. He stroked his short beard and tried to fight it off.

Mac sensed it too. He wanted to warn him about the fire but wasn't quite sure how to bring it up. The hard part was that he didn't exactly know when it was going to happen. He had no idea whether it was tomorrow or the next week or month, or even year. Plus, he didn't know how the fire started or who was to blame. What kind of warning was that? But he had to at least try. If there was some way he could help prevent one of history's greatest tragedies, he was certainly going to give it his best shot.

He opened his mouth to speak just as footsteps clattered on the path behind them.

"Grandfather!" came a girl's voice.

"There you are, Petal."

Elcor turned to embrace the girl. It wasn't until they pulled apart that Mac got the shock of his life. His heart almost stopped beating.

Aisha!

She smiled at her grandfather. Her emerald eyes seemed even greener in the garden light. The little chocolate moon high on her left cheek caught Mac's attention. It was the strangest-looking beauty spot he had ever seen. It could indeed be called a beauty spot as it somehow further enhanced her already exotic features. Her hair was plaited the same as last he'd seen her and she wore a long, white robe, nipped in at the waist by a purple cord. She was even more beautiful than he remembered.

"Did you hear, Grandfather? The Easterners are hosting a light show in the harbour for the festival!"

"Marvellous," said Elcor but his voice lacked expression. He held her by the elbows and studied her face.

"Is everything alright, Grandfather? You look worried."

Effort erased the concern that knotted his brow. "Not at all, Petal. There's someone I'd like you to meet." He turned to Mac. "This is my granddaughter –"

Mac cut him off with a stunned whisper. "Aisha."

The girl's eyes flew wide.

"How did you know my name?" she asked warily.

"He's a seer," explained Elcor.

"Oh…"

Elcor knew it wouldn't bother her. Aisha had grown up around psychic phenomena and was perfectly comfortable with it. Although she wasn't gifted in that way herself, her mother had been. Elcor let his daughter's memory intrude just long enough to feel the stab of loss in his chest. He stared at Aisha, so like her mother. Serapis be damned, he would not lose her too! He would find someone else to handle the cursed text.

Aisha reached out a bejewelled hand to Mac. "Peace and blessings be upon you."

He hesitated. Was he expected to shake her hand or kiss it? He stared at her fingertips, black with ink. That's right; Elcor had mentioned his granddaughter was a scribe. Mac took her hand. His gaze switched to her eyes and never left them as he gently raised her hand to his lips. They barely brushed her skin. She smelt wonderful; like summer jasmine, like something he wanted to eat. He knew he should say something but he couldn't speak. He simply stared into those green, green eyes as he watched them narrow slightly.

"Have we met? You look familiar," said Aisha.

Mac shook his head.

How could he explain that, yes, they had met but in the Future? How could he explain that she had kissed him and it was totally amazing? And how could he ask for another just like it, thanks very much?

The girl tugged her hand free of his lingering grasp and glanced sideways at her grandfather. Mac dropped his eyes and shuffled his feet as the colour rose in his cheeks.

"Let's get some lunch then, shall we?" said Elcor, deflecting the awkward moment.

They headed back the way they had come and entered a large dining hall. It was decorated simply and was open to the Royal Gardens on one side. The room was noisy and full of people, mostly men. Mac and Aisha were the youngest in the room by far. Accompanied by the library's Chief Administrator, they were accorded certain privileges, which included good seats in a quiet corner and their own personal waiter. Elcor ordered for them and within minutes a platter of food arrived on their table.

Mac waited until Elcor and Aisha had made their selection then reached for a flatbread parcel stuffed with mince. It was delicious. He followed it with glazed chicken wings marinated in a spicy sauce that had a real bite to it. He sipped his drink. It tasted a bit like ginger beer without the bubbles, laced with mint.

They ate in silence for a while before Elcor excused himself to speak to a group of gentlemen across the room. Mac and Aisha sat opposite each other. Neither broke the awkwardness as the minutes stretched out. Finally, Mac summoned the courage to speak to her.

"So, your grandfather tells me you're a scribe. One of the best, he says."

Aisha shrugged. "I don't know about that," she said. "But, yes, I am one of the scribes."

Mac nodded.

Silence settled once more.

Then, feeling a little bold, Aisha asked, "What happened to your hands?" and pointed at his bandages.

He blushed. "It's nothing. I just spilt some hot water. Clumsy."

The real story was so much better and he wished he could tell her how he really burnt his hands.

The silence lingered.

"What are those clear covers over your eyes?" Aisha finally asked.

"Glasses," said Mac, taking them off.

He used the English word, as he didn't have the equivalent in ancient Greek. He passed them to her.

She studied them. "I think I had a dream about these once…" she said in a faraway voice. She put them on. Only this time she put them on the right way up, first go. That wasn't lost on Mac. He wondered if some part of her 'remembered' the Future. Was it possible to get a sense of something that had happened in another dimension of time? Of course. What was he thinking? He did it all the time. It made perfect sense that it should work the other way. With a grandfather like Elcor, Mac thought it entirely possible that Aisha could grasp a sense of future events psychometrically, however vague they may be.

"This is glass?" she asked.

"Yes, glass."

"How is it so thin?"

Mac noticed the blue pitcher on the table. It was made of glass, he was certain, but it was thick and mostly opaque. The art of glass making had come a long way over the centuries, it seemed.

"Um… I don't really know how they do it," he answered.

"What is it for?"

"My eyes are not too good. These help me see better."

"See *better*?" she asked, surprised. She scrunched up her eyes and peered around the room, trying to focus on something.

"Yes, they're made especially for my eyes. They're no good for anyone else's eyes," he explained.

"Oh," she said. She understood. "That's because you're a seer," she whispered. "You're special."

Mac shook his head and considered explaining that it was just because he was a nerd that read too many books in bad light, or that maybe it was just genetic but he simply shrugged and bit into a ripe fig.

Feeling more confident, he decided to find out more about her. All he knew so far was that she was Elcor's granddaughter and a gifted scribe.

"So do you live around here?" he asked. Before she'd had time to answer, he was already kicking himself. It was a dumb question, and he cursed his lack of imagination. He was certain she already thought he was boring.

"I live with Grandfather in the library quarters just over there." She indicated a building on the other side of the courtyard with a toss of her lovely head.

Mac watched her peel the skin off a pomegranate with long delicate fingers. It was strangely alluring.

She continued. "My mother died when I was eight. She got sick from a mosquito bite. It was a long time ago but I still really miss her. My father's an ambassador stationed in Rome. I haven't seen him for years."

She looked sad. Mac reached across the table and gently placed a hand on hers. He didn't mind that it was sticky with pomegranate juice. Aisha blinked away the start of tears and took a deep breath. She looked at Mac with glistening eyes and forced a smile.

"It's silly but–"

"I lost my mother when I was eight too," he said.

"Really?" said Aisha, leaning forward. "How?"

He shrugged. "I don't really know what happened. She just... started to forget things. Then she got sick. I still miss her too. I don't think that ever really goes away."

He pulled the corners of his mouth into a 'cheer up' sort of smile, and his eyes crinkled at the edges.

Aisha gazed into them. All thoughts of further conversation evaporated from her head. She'd lost her train of thought entirely.

Behind those strange glass eye-covers, he had the most startling compelling eyes; not green, not brown but with gold flecks exploding from their core. And those long lashes... The neat creases between his brows reminded her of the Roman numeral two. His gaze was intense yet not rude or leering. She was quite used to the admiring stares of the local boys but this was different. Under that mesmerising stare, she found it difficult to speak. This had never happened before. She knew her place as a female in Egyptian society but she had never been shy in front of boys. Yet, here was this stranger that took away her ability to speak, to *think*. She fought a strange compunction to reach across the table and touch his face. What was happening?

Abruptly her mood changed. She slid her hand out from underneath his, her eyes roaming the room nervously.

She had to be careful. Her boyfriend was insanely jealous of any male that she spoke to and posted spies to follow her around and report back. She didn't speak to other boys unless she had to, mainly for their own protection. This had earned her the reputation of being snobby and aloof. Mistakenly, they thought she felt she was a cut above the rest and too good for anyone. The really stupid part was that she had actually started to behave that way. It was just easier, even if it wasn't authentic. She shook her head. If only they knew the truth.

Mac shifted in his seat and fidgeted with his bandana. He sensed the new mood and wondered if he'd upset her somehow.

The girl dabbed at the corner of her mouth with the back of her wrist and hid her sticky hands under the table.

An uncomfortable silence descended.

Eventually, Aisha broke it. "So will you be joining us for the festival at Week's End?" she said, sitting further back in her seat, her tone almost businesslike.

"Ah…" Mac had no idea what day it was. How could he possibly guarantee he could be back in ancient Alexandria in the right time frame for some event? He had no control over his time travel. He wasn't even sure he could get back at all. "I'm not sure I'll still be in town then."

"It's only four days away. Surely you could extend your stay that long. I promise you, you won't regret it. It'll be better than last year's. The visitors from the East are hosting a show in the harbour. They have magic lights of many colours that burst in the night sky, high above the ships. It's incredible! I saw it once when I was a little girl. It's like nothing you've ever seen before. I'd encourage you not to miss it."

He realised she was talking about fireworks.

Like most boys his age, he was into anything that went 'bang'. His cousins had managed to get hold of a bunch of firecrackers one New Year's Eve and had let them off down at the river near Mac's house. It was fun until Luke burnt his hand and scorched off his eyebrows. But it had been too late; Mac had the firebug by then. He'd researched fireworks, hoping to make his own but didn't get very far. They were illegal to own privately in his state so he couldn't even buy them. He gave up. Along the way, however, he discovered that China had fireworks over two thousand years ago.

He remembered seeing an Oriental-looking ship in the harbour. They must have been going to launch the fireworks display from the ship. For a second, his imagination held him hostage, playing images of standing hand in hand with Aisha, watching the spectacle light up the night sky.

"Sure, why not?" Mac's dimples pressed into his cheeks.

Aisha grinned.

There was a commotion in the dining hall. "All hail, Pharaoh!" a voice boomed.

Murmurings of the same thing rippled across the room as plates and cutlery clinked while everyone got down on bended knee for the pharaoh's entrance. Mac was a little slow on the uptake and was one of the last to make it to the floor. He glanced around. Everyone else knelt with heads bowed low. Mac copied them. He was excited at the prospect of actually seeing Pharaoh Ptolemy XIII in the flesh. It was more than he could have hoped for – except a kiss from Aisha.

The pharaoh's footsteps came closer. As his sandaled feet came into view, Mac stole a glance at the approaching king. Even though he knew from history that Ptolemy XIII was just fifteen years old when civil war broke out, he was still shocked to see a lean kid about his own age, wearing a large ornately decorated headdress. Around his waist he wore a white linen shift with a pleated section down the front. An ivory-handled dagger hung off a belt at his hip. He was bare-chested except for a dazzling breastplate of gold and precious gemstones.

His arrogant strut matched the smirk on his face. The pharaoh's eyes were dramatically outlined in dark kohl. Even at that distance, Mac could tell he was wearing make-up to cover a bad case of acne.

A tall man with a big nose and evil eyes followed closely behind. Mac assumed he must be the pharaoh's regent, Pothinus. He didn't like the look of the man at all. At that moment, Pothinus looked right at him. Mac dropped his eyes back to the tiles. They were walking directly toward him. He started to panic. What could they want with him? How could they possibly know who he was?

The pharaoh stopped just inches from him. Mac held his breath and waited for Pharaoh Ptolemy to speak.

"My pretty lotus, you look radiant today."

Mac's head snapped up. For a second, he thought the pharaoh had been speaking to him. To his horror, he watched as Ptolemy leaned down to plant a kiss on Aisha's cheek.

No…

CHAPTER EIGHT

HEARTSICK, MAC STARED at the floor.

Aisha and Ptolemy? But... Wasn't he already married to his sister?

He groaned inwardly as he remembered that the pharaoh was permitted to have more than one wife. Ptolemy was free to have anyone he wanted.

Mac wondered why he even cared. It wasn't like he was in love with her. Was he? He shook his head. That would just be plain ridiculous, falling in love with a girl from two thousand years ago when there was absolutely no hope of being with her – ever.

Besides, he and Aisha had only shared one tiny kiss.

Even so, he wondered why his chest hurt and his cheeks burned. He tried to convince himself it hadn't meant anything; that she was just showing her appreciation at being rescued. She probably kissed everyone like that.

He didn't really believe that though. They *had* shared something special, even if it was fleeting. There had been some connection. He felt it.

He hung his head lower. Aisha had kissed him because he'd saved her from a burning building. She had seen him as some sort of hero. Now he was just a weirdo in a bad toga. He couldn't even hope for her affection, let alone another kiss. He could never win her over. What would be the point in trying? How do you compete with a king?

"Compete for what?" said a little voice in his head. *"A dream? Compete for a dream?"*

The little voice was right. Aisha was an unattainable dream. He knew that once he returned, he would never lay eyes on her lovely face again, except in his dreams. She was perfect in every way apart from the fact that she didn't exist in his Now. Even if she had, she probably wouldn't look twice at him.

"… and this is Mac. He's a traveller from afar," came Aisha's voice.

Her introduction intruded on his thoughts as if someone had suddenly turned up the volume in his head.

Mac looked up to find he was the only one in the room still kneeling. He got to his feet, standing on the tip of his makeshift toga. It unravelled in an instant and fell in a heap around his ankles. He hesitated, caught in a split second of hellish dilemma – kiss the back of the pharaoh's outstretched hand or stoop to retrieve his sheet? He bobbed up and down uncertainly. Somehow he managed to half kneel, kiss Ptolemy's hand and grab a handful of sheet all at the same time. He had no idea what to say. What was the greeting Aisha had used earlier?

"Peace and blessings be upon you," he mumbled. "Your Majesty."

Mac was scarlet. His ears were on fire. He could feel every eye on him.

Ptolemy withdrew his hand and stared at him, not bothering to disguise his distaste.

Mac flicked his attention across to Aisha, just in time to catch her stealing an admiring glance at his bare chest. He hugged the sheet closer. His upper body was tanned and, although not big, it was nicely toned from long hours on the end of a shovel. The dig kid usually got stuck with the heavy labour on site and so he'd quite literally earned his title.

Aisha locked eyes with Mac. Realising she'd been caught staring at his naked chest, she managed an awkward smile and continued. "So will you join us for the festival? We'd be honoured to have you as our guest," she said.

Ptolemy glared at her but recovered swiftly. "Er… Of course," he said.

Mac looked across at Pothinus. The man was staring at him in amazement – or was it horror? Mac couldn't be sure but it wasn't in a good way. The regent's dark, slitty eyes roamed every inch of him. He must have looked a sight in his khaki shorts and work boots, not to mention 'the device for clear seeing' on his face.

For a few seconds, Mac's mouth opened and shut but not a single sound escaped. He just stood there gulping like a goldfish and clutching his sheet.

"Certainly," he finally managed to get out. "That would be… to my liking." He winced at his clumsy choice of words.

He turned his attention from Aisha to Ptolemy.

Aisha looked at the pharaoh. Silence followed. She cleared her throat and glanced sideways at him.

"Of course. Join us, traveller," Ptolemy said with little enthusiasm.

Then he turned his back on Mac, spoke to Aisha in a hushed tone and swept out to the gardens with Pothinus in tow.

Aisha looked somewhat ruffled but brightened as she turned to Mac. "I look forward to enjoying your company then," she said. She turned to go then stopped. "Where are you staying?"

"On the edge of town," he answered, after a moment's hesitation. It wasn't entirely a lie.

"Aisha!" summoned Ptolemy from the garden.

"Coming, Your Royal Highness." Then to Mac: "Meet me here tomorrow, just before sunset," she whispered.

"Sure," he answered without thinking.

She hesitated. "You um… You have nice cheek pits."

She ran off, leaving him blushing.

And you smell like heaven, he'd wanted to call after her.

He frowned and raised a hand to his now invisible dimples. Cheek pits…

Mac watched her as she jogged down the path to catch up with the pharaoh. Ptolemy snatched her by the arm and yanked her close. Mac could tell from the pharaoh's expression that he spoke harshly to her. Ptolemy let her go and stalked off toward the palace with Pothinus. Aisha hung her head and fell in line behind them.

Mac's eyes narrowed. He'd already decided he did not like Pharaoh Ptolemy.

He looked around the room to find that most had lost interest in him for the time being. A few were still studying him and muttering to each other. He caught Elcor's eye, penetrating and enigmatic.

Elcor had witnessed the exchange and hadn't missed a thing. In fact, he'd been watching Mac and his granddaughter closely. The twinkle in Aisha's eyes when she spoke to the time traveller hadn't escaped his attention, nor had the boy's obvious fascination with his granddaughter.

That's right… thought Elcor. *Bind her to your heart. Protect her. Protect her with every grain of your existence, Deliverer.*

He disliked the pharaoh but tolerated Aisha's relationship with him. After all, he couldn't possibly offer his granddaughter the same start in life that marriage to the pharaoh could. It would mean wealth, social status, opportunity; it was the fairytale every Egyptian girl dreamed of. He should have been happy for her but he wasn't. Since they'd been seeing each other, he'd noticed Aisha had lost her sparkle. She just hadn't seemed herself for months.

Ptolemy had taken a shine to Aisha whilst visiting the Writing Room on a number of occasions. He had requested her as his personal scribe but, as Chief Administrator of the Library, Elcor had been able to use his sway to convince him that Aisha was not the correct choice. He had reasoned that Aisha was too inexperienced a scribe to be of personal use to the pharaoh and so she had remained in the Writing Room, much to Elcor's relief. He had no say, however, in whom Ptolemy chose to date, but he thought the less time she spent in his private company, the better. That kid was trouble. He didn't like the way Pothinus looked at her either. It made his skin crawl. He desperately hoped Rome would restore Cleopatra to power. The Ptolemies were a bad lot but at least Cleopatra had brains. With a bit of luck, Ptolemy and Pothinus would flee the country. He could only hope. Turbulent times were afoot and he worried for Aisha's safety, now more than ever – now that an ancient evil had resurfaced and now that he was about to knowingly expose her to it.

He massaged his jaw and stared into nowhere. How could he live with himself? He had to protect her.

Deliverer…

Elcor's focus returned to Mac. *Who are you, Time Traveller?*

He crossed the dining room to the boy and placed a hand on his bare shoulder. "Come, let's find some ointment for your sunburn."

Mac glanced at his pink forearms. He raised a hand to his face. It felt hot. He must have caught a bit of sun down by the harbour earlier, he thought. It didn't even occur to him that, back in the Now, his undiscovered body lay unconscious in the blazing midday sun, transmitting its physiology through time.

He followed Elcor down a corridor to his private chambers. Mac wondered how on earth he was going to warn him about the fire. He wasn't sure how to approach it. It would help if he knew when and how it was supposed to happen.

He was still deciding whether or not to tell him about yesterday's visit to the burning library, when they arrived at a decorative timber door. Elcor held the door open as the boy stepped past him into the office. Nefertiti, the naked cat, appeared out of nowhere to nuzzle Elcor's shins.

Mac looked around. The room seemed familiar. A sudden flashback lit up his memory. He knew this room. It was the burning room where he'd found Aisha. He spun to face Elcor, heart pounding. "I need to talk to you!"

"Sit down, boy," replied Elcor as he rifled through a collection of small bottles and jars on a shelf.

"It's important," Mac insisted.

The old man ignored him and mumbled to himself as he sniffed at a pot of greenish salve.

Mac plonked onto a small wooden stool that had legs fashioned into clawed lion's feet. He looked around the room and spotted the candelabrum in the corner. He glanced up at the ceiling. It was very high with huge timber support beams running its length. The room's only source of natural light was a small window with scrolled ironwork bars. He noticed a door on the opposite side and knew from experience that it led back through to the main library. Yesterday's incident was still raw in his mind.

He fidgeted with the bandages on his hands.

"Ah, here we are," announced Elcor, holding up a clay jar. He crossed to Mac, scooped out a glob of something that smelled faintly of lavender and smeared it across Mac's cheeks and nose. He replaced the stopper and turned back to the shelf.

Mac made a face and dabbed at the ointment.

Elcor sank into a chair behind his desk. He studied the boy for a moment. "Tell me of your When," he said. "From when do you come? And where?"

Mac took a deep breath. "I come from the year two thousand and twenty AD."

Elcor cocked his head. "Is 'AD' the name of the ruling dynasty?"

Mac realised he had no way of expressing the date in terms that had any reference for Elcor. The terms 'BC' and 'AD' were meaningless to him. The one man who split time wasn't even born yet and wouldn't be for about another fifty years. Mac stared at the ceiling for a moment. How could he avoid turning this into one *really* long story? "Okay, let's just say I come from a time about two thousand and sixty years in the future."

"Marvelous." The old man was enthralled. "Tell me," he said wriggling forward on his seat and leaning his elbows on the desk. "What is it like?" His eyes burned with the desire to know.

Mac struggled. He didn't even have the words in the Greek language to express cars, trains, planes, rockets and skyscrapers, let alone electricity, computers, the Internet, television, and smart phones...

"In some ways, it's very different. Everything's bigger. Well, not everything. Actually, some things are way smaller. But everything's faster. Almost instant communication with anywhere in the world," Mac attempted to explain.

"Ah, telepathy," Elcor nodded.

"Not quite. But in a lot of ways, the people are much the same as they are now."

Mac thought back to the bullies in the alley, the kids playing games on the steps, the tardy student, the gossiping girls, the pervy men, the arrogance of those in power and, right here in front of him, the quest of some to know all. It dawned on him that people were still people. Sure, their lifestyles had changed but, essentially, their lives hadn't.

In an instant of clarity, Mac saw that the human race didn't move through time – time moved through the human race. People stayed the same. Times changed. People didn't. Human beings the world over were still motivated by the same things. They were all still on a mission to find happiness.

His mother's words came rushing back to him.

Years ago, they'd been standing on a crowded platform in London's subway. They were being jostled and bumped by people pushing past. She had looked down at him with a smile and said:

"All these people are just like me;

They want to be happy and they want to be free."

He knew she'd just made up the little rhyme but it had stuck with him all these years.

Elcor interrupted his reverie. "*Where* is your When?"

"I come from..." He stopped. Australia hadn't even been discovered yet, according to the history books. He certainly didn't have a word for it in Greek. "It's a long way from here, to the south-east."

"Your land is south then? South of the black-skinned nations?"

"Sort of. It's way south and way east of here." Or was it west?

"Ah, the Far East. Their red-sailed ships are in the harbour as we speak."

"No, it's more south of that even. It's a big island. The biggest, actually."

Elcor's eyes widened. He gasped. "The Great South Land? I thought it naught more than a child's bedtime story – The Adventures of Lord Djes-eb, Son of Pharaoh Ra Djedef. Three thousand years ago, he sailed to the ends of the known world and never returned. Surely they are just fanciful stories. Who ever heard of giant jumping rats with pouches for their young?"

Mac was startled by the revelation himself. Could the ancients have known of Australia thousands of years ago?

"I've never heard of any Egyptian lord but we do have kangaroos." He used the English word. He scrunched his hands in front and jumped up and down on the spot like a kangaroo.

For a moment, Elcor was lost for words. He had read that the ancient Sumerians told of a lost Motherland in the Great Ocean. Could it actually be true? Was he conversing with an actual inhabitant of that mythical land?

"You must map it for me," insisted Elcor, reaching for an ink stylus.

"Maybe later, Elcor. I have to tell you something very important."

The old man became serious. He leaned back in his chair and repeated the prophecy. "The Deliverer cometh from afar."

Mac sat down, scraped his chair closer to the desk and leaned forward. He decided it was best to just be direct. "The Library of Alexandria is going to burn down unless we stop it."

Elcor sat expressionless.

"Do you hear what I'm saying? It burns down. All the scrolls are lost. Everything, gone."

His words failed to unfreeze Elcor.

Mac got to his feet. Everything tumbled out in a desperate torrent. "It burns! All of it! Poof! Up in smoke! You have to believe me. The history books will blame the Romans but it's not them. You *must* listen to me, Elcor. The Library of Alexandria burns to the ground." He banged his fist on the desk.

Ouch! His burns were still tender.

There was a noise at the door. Elcor swiftly opened it to see the retreating figure of Pothinus, robes billowing, as he swept down the corridor and turned the corner, out of sight.

Elcor wondered how long he'd been eavesdropping at the door. This was big news and he didn't want to start a panic.

It had to be contained. A strategy had to be set and action taken in a hurry. He didn't doubt the boy for a moment; the truth was in his eyes, yet it was still difficult to digest.

A shiver raised the hairs on his arms. The papyrus. He knew it was connected. He just didn't know how.

"How?" demanded Elcor, turning back to the boy. "When?"

Mac hesitated. "Well, that's the problem. I'm not a hundred percent sure." He dropped his eyes. "Actually, I have no idea. I just know that it does."

Elcor furrowed his brow. He paused for a while, thinking. "I'll have Candle Security on full alert and have extra barrels of water stationed around the perimeter."

"Candle Security?" asked Mac.

"Oh yes, yes." Elcor pointed to the candelabrum in the corner. "The threat of fire is a constant hazard. We have a division of security devoted entirely to keeping an eye on the candles and burning incense to make sure there are no incidents. The scholars and scribes are often working late by candlelight. Security ensures there are no candles still burning when everyone has gone home for the night or have fallen asleep at their desks.

"The scrolls, Elcor. We need to have them moved to a safe place."

"That's entirely impossible!" The man threw his hands in the air. "Look around you, boy. There are over half a million scrolls in this library. It's the largest collection in the world. I can't just pick it up and move it."

"Elcor." Mac was pleading now. "Elcor, you *must* listen to me. In the Now – in my When – not a trace of this great library remains. All the scrolls, all the knowledge… lost."

Elcor stared out the window.

The sun shone but he knew darkness lurked behind it. The papyrus document was safely locked in a chest in the Isolation Room. Its transcription hadn't even begun. Could he risk moving it now – hiding it and protecting it – until this real or imagined danger had passed? The sigh that escaped his lips stole a part of his conscience. Aisha. There was no other way. She was his fastest and most accurate scribe.

"At least we could try to move *some* of the scrolls to a safe place," Mac went on. "Perhaps just the really old ones or the ones that don't have copies stored elsewhere in the world."

Elcor was silent. He sat down and leaned back in his chair. He stared at the ceiling and stroked his silver beard. His gaze switched to Mac. It seemed incredulous, yet the stars didn't lie. 'A Deliverer', they had said.

Mac leaned across the desk. He held his bandaged left hand up to Elcor's face and waggled the finger with the ruby lion ring.

Elcor gasped and quickly checked his own left hand for the ring. It was still there. How had he not noticed it on the boy before? He had noticed the bandages but not the ring.

They stared at each other. Both rings started to pulse. They grew hotter.

"But, but… How did you get that?" spat Elcor. "My father had it specially made by a master craftsman. There is no other like it."

"I dug it up, here in Alexandria, over two thousand years in the future. That's what we do – me and my dad. We find things from ancient times to get a clearer picture of history."

"*Ancient* times?" Elcor could scarcely believe this modern-day city, with all its advancements and exceptional standard of living, could ever be relegated to the realm of the *ancient.*

"But, the ring… It belongs to *me*… That means…" His voice quavered. His bony hand shook as he stared at the ring and saw his own mortality staring back. The heavy chains of prophecy weighted his body. He sat like stone.

Mac continued. "You see, I travel through time by holding onto something from long ago and it just sort of… Takes me there." He shrugged.

Elcor took a while to speak. "I have heard of such a gift."

This surprised Mac but he went on. "Somehow I found myself in the library yesterday. It was on fire. Aisha –"

Elcor shot forward in his seat. "Aisha! What about her?"

"She was trapped in the flames but –"

"No!"

"It's alright. She's fine." Mac explained the events of yesterday's trip and how he'd saved Aisha's life. He left out the part about the kiss. He didn't think it was something her grandfather should hear. Besides, he didn't want to get on Elcor's bad side. Mac thought he might prove a force to be reckoned with when it came to protecting his granddaughter.

Elcor didn't speak for a while, seeming to wrestle with some internal torment that played across his face.

"The underground vaults. We could move the scrolls to the underground vaults. I will ask General Caesar's permission to rally a special detachment of his troops, along with ours, to move as many of the scrolls as possible. You see, there are catacombs that run under the Library and lead to secret storehouses. The tunnels also connect to the Palace."

Mac could see why Elcor had been appointed Chief

Administrator of the Library. He was cool and collected – a man who got things done.

Elcor scribbled quickly on a piece of papyrus, rolled it and sealed it with red wax, emblazoned with his official emblem. He whistled and a uniformed runner materialised at the door. Elcor spoke briefly to the runner and handed him the message. Off he went, his footsteps echoing down the hall.

The old man's thoughts turned to Pothinus. What was that snake up to?

CHAPTER NINE

THE SCENT OF the ocean laced with jasmine carried on the breeze as it stirred the potted palms on the balcony of the pharaoh's living quarters. The lounge area was lavishly decorated with expensive furniture, colourful cushions and rugs, and the finest of silk drapes that billowed with each breath of wind.

Ptolemy and Aisha sat cross-legged on the tiles of the balcony, playing a game that resembled chess, with figurines carved out of jade. The pharaoh was without his headdress and breastplate. His black wig was slicked into a ponytail at the nape of his neck and a trained parrot with exotic plumage perched comfortably on his shoulder. A blowfly buzzed around their heads. A musician reclined on a pile of cushions nearby, strumming away the afternoon. By the closed double doors stood a royal servant at dutiful attention.

"I still don't know why you had to invite the freak," snapped Ptolemy.

"Can we just leave it, *please*? Let's just enjoy the afternoon."

"I didn't like the way he looked at me," continued the pharaoh.

Aisha rolled her eyes. "It's your move."

Ptolemy's fingers lingered above one of the pieces while he considered his next move in the game.

Suddenly, the double doors burst open and a red-faced Pothinus barged in. "Out! All of you, out!" he yelled.

The musician and servant scurried off. Aisha and the pharaoh leapt up, knocking over the board and sending the pieces skidding across the tiles. The parrot squawked and fluttered to a safer perch on the balcony rail.

"That means you too, scribe girl!"

Aisha darted out of the room.

"See you tonight then," Ptolemy called after her. Then to Pothinus, "You might have considered knocking."

Pothinus stepped forward and slapped him hard across the face. The crack resounded off the tiled balcony. Tears of pain and indignation sprang to the boy's eyes as he raised a hand to his cheek.

"That's enough out of you," hissed Pothinus. "You've ruined everything, you and your loose lips. Who did you tell about the plan?"

"No one, I swear."

"Your girlfriend? Did you let her in on our secret?"

"Regent, I swear, I haven't told a soul." Ptolemy was backed against the stone balustrade.

Pothinus leaned over him. "Then tell me how, in the name of the Underworld, that glass-eyed little weirdo knows. I just overheard him warning the Chief Administrator about our plan to burn down the library," he growled.

Ptolemy gaped. He shook his head. He was speechless.

"He even said 'it's not the Romans' so he damned well *knows* we planned to pin it on Caesar!"

Pothinus whirled back toward the lounge. "Tell me, how

could he know that if you hadn't opened your mouth, you bumpy-faced little brat?" He was roaring now.

"Honestly, I don't know, Regent. I don't. I haven't said a word to anyone. Why would I? Framing Caesar for burning down the library is my one shot at turning public opinion against Rome and my bitch sister. It's my one shot at winning the respect of the masses."

"*Respect?*" Pothinus exploded. "You don't deserve their respect, you snivelling runt! You never have! The only reason you're still here is that, right now, the people like your two-faced sister even *less* than they like you and they resent her allegiance to Rome. Yet, despite that fact, it is my duty as your appointed regent to see you on the throne of Egypt, minus your trouble-making sister."

Ptolemy jutted out his jaw. His eyes glistened with hurt and rage. Eyeliner smudged at the corners of his lids. He knew Pothinus was just a cruel, self-serving snake. His regent just wanted the power for himself. With Cleopatra out of the way, there was nothing stopping him.

The boy pharaoh turned to look out across the city, to the harbour beyond. A storm was gathering far out to sea. He could see the red sails of the Easterners' ship among the ships of the Roman navy.

Why did it seem like everyone was against him?

His father had died just three years ago. He had barely known the man. Perhaps that was a blessing, given that his father had executed two of Ptolemy's older sisters – *the man's own daughters* – when they tried to seize power from him a few years back. Ptolemy had been terrified of his father, and with good reason. His mother, who also happened to be his father's sister, had been dead for years. He hardly remembered her.

Now Cleopatra had turned against him and who knew what she was plotting? She was fiercely intelligent and he was more than a little scared of her. And, to make matters worse, there were murmurings of an uprising from his other remaining sister, Arsinoe.

Then some stranger arrives in the city that his girlfriend won't stop talking about. He was sure the newcomer was trying to steal her. He desperately wished everyone would just leave him alone. He was the king! They should adore him. Why didn't they?

"We need a new plan," said Pothinus.

Ptolemy turned on him. "What, like your last big plan? Oh yes, 'cut off General Pompey's head, present it to Caesar and he will be your friend'. That's what you said. Well, that worked a treat, didn't it? Now he's really pissed off and it's all your fault!"

The pharaoh's cheeks were red, making his pimples stand out even more. His fists were clenched at his side and he was breathing hard.

Pothinus rushed at him and grabbed him by the throat. He squeezed hard.

"*How dare you?*" he hissed in the boy's face. "You're still alive because of me, you ungrateful piece of filth."

Ptolemy's face turned deep crimson and the veins at his temples stood out. He couldn't breathe. Tears streaked his make-up.

Pothinus flung the boy to the floor and stalked out of the room to leave him coughing and spluttering on the balcony.

Slowly, the pharaoh sat up and wiped his eyes. He felt very alone. How could he win back favour with his regent? He hated the man but he longed to please him.

A dragonfly buzzed past. In one swift movement, the boy caught it in his cupped hands. He held it by the tail and examined it. Its exquisite wings were shot with miniature rainbows. He watched them flitter up and down at lightning speed. Then he plucked them off, one by one.

CHAPTER TEN

WITHIN AN HOUR of dispatching the runner to the Commander, Elcor stood briefing a platoon of Egyptian troops in one of the lecture halls. He outlined the plan to move the scrolls to the safety of the underground vaults via the catacombs. He didn't elaborate on the details except to say that he had it on reliable sources that the threat of fire was imminent. The soldiers were to be divided into groups and assigned certain sections of the library to evacuate, starting with the oldest sections first.

In conclusion, Elcor held his hand up and blessed them so: "The Mighty Serapis, Sisterhood of the Muses and Enlightened Thoth be upon thy hearts and minds at this, the threshold of danger, and by the power of the Elder gods and the Eye of Horus, let the coming darkness be averted."

Minutes later, the troops reported for duty at the various sectors of the library. Already, tongues were wagging at the sight of troops marching into the library equipped with large woven baskets, one between two men. Elcor hoped that with the buzz of the coming festival, people would pass it off as part of the show's preparations or some such thing.

The storage compartments were emptied and the

cylinders containing the scrolls were neatly stacked in the baskets, which were then carefully labelled by library staff and dispatched to the vaults.

Mac shouldered a string bag stuffed with scrolls and followed Elcor down a narrow flight of stone steps which led from a concealed doorway in the library to the network of tunnels beneath. The temperature plummeted by several degrees as they descended and set off down the stone tunnel by flaming torchlight. The air was cool and dank. The smell reminded Mac of the underwater viewing gallery at Seaworld on the Gold Coast. His father had taken him and his cousins there when they'd visited last.

The floor of the tunnel had been worn smooth by three centuries' worth of footsteps. The ceiling was low. It was barely above Mac's head and, as he glanced over his shoulder at the column of soldiers behind them, he noticed many of the men were forced to stoop to avoid hitting their heads.

Elcor led the way, stopping to light torches mounted at intervals along the walls of the tunnel. There was only blackness ahead. Every so often, they passed iron gates that barred access to offshoot tunnels on either side. Here and there, water seeped through the walls and trickled in rivulets to the floor, forming shallow puddles.

The firelight cast eerie shadows on the rough stone walls as the troops marched on into the depths, carrying their baskets. Somehow the flickering play of shadows conjured memories of Mickey Mouse in The Sorcerer's Apprentice sequence in Disney's Fantasia cartoon. From what Mac could recall, things turned bad for Mickey.

A sudden chill pricked the flesh on his arms and he shuddered.

The floor sloped gently downward for a long while. Mac couldn't tell how long they'd been walking but, even in the cool of the catacombs, a thin sheen of perspiration covered his brow. He was beginning to realise the enormity of the task at hand. There were almost a hundred troops marshalled, carrying about twenty scrolls to a basket. Given that they still had well over a hundred trips back and forth to move the entire contents of the library, and that the distance to the underground vaults was significant, it seemed a mammoth undertaking. Mac wondered if it were possible to save the entire library before the fire. He desperately wished he knew when it was going to happen. They would have to just do the best they could.

Sensing the boy's misgivings, Elcor forged ahead with renewed urgency.

"Come on, men! Not far now. For the love of Isis, we must hurry," he called over his shoulder.

They hurried on. Mac took a deep breath and savoured the fact that he was able to be a part of it all. His chest swelled with self-indulgent pride that he was saving the vast storehouse of knowledge housed in the famous Library of Alexandria.

The Deliverer.

The thought quickened his pulse. He was reshaping history.

Before long, they arrived at what looked to be a dead end. Mac's heart sank as he stared at the solid stone wall in front of them. Elcor handed him the torch and swiftly pressed a series of barely noticeable indents in the wall. The stone rolled back with a rumble to reveal an enormous cavern. Elcor winked at him as he took the torch and went inside. The old man would be blown away by the modern-day notion of numbered keypads, fingerprint sensors, iris scanners and laser beam security, thought Mac.

Unlike the tunnel, the air in the cavern was dry and musty. Elcor lit the torches mounted on either side of the doorway.

The vault was huge. The walls were lined with large pottery jars, wooden furniture stacked high, bags of grain seed, statues and artwork. Shelving ran along one side cluttered with all manner of odds and ends such as animal bones, snake skins, feathers, more clay pots containing who-knew-what and geological rock samples.

Mac noticed a strangely shaped human skull on a shelf nearby. He set down his basket of scrolls to take a closer look.

The base of the skull was slightly elongated. Its jaw seemed oversized and the forehead bulged over heavy brows. Mac recognised it at once to be that of Neanderthal man. Beside it was another skull. This one was vastly different. The forehead sloped back into a high blunt cone. Enormous almond-shaped eye sockets stared blankly above diminutive teeth and jaws. It was like nothing Mac had seen in all his archaeological studies. The bone itself was strange. It was thin and almost translucent in places. It was not of this world; he was sure of it.

Then he spotted something else on the shelf above. What he could see beneath the dark fabric that partially cloaked it glimmered in the flickering torchlight. Curiosity snatched his will. He reached up to tug at the fabric. It slid off.

Mac gasped.

The gaping sockets of yet another skull stared out at nothing. But this skull was unlike the others entirely. This one was spectacularly carved out of clear crystal. It was breathtaking. It was perfect. He had to mentally pinch himself to remember that he wasn't caught up in some Indiana Jones movie. This was real. This was the Earth's living history. He could barely believe such an artefact existed – in this time frame at least. Of course, there were legends about the Mitchell-Hedges crystal skull found in Belize in the twenties but nothing had been verified and the stink of 'hoax' had clung to it for decades in the archaeological world. Could this be the very same one?

Mesmerised by the strange skull, he reached up a hand to touch it.

"Uh-uh," came Elcor's voice at his shoulder.

Mac's arm snapped back like a rubber band before he got a finger to it. He couldn't help looking guilty. For some reason, he felt he'd been about to desecrate something sacred just by his touch alone.

"I was just–"

"You were just going to help unload the scrolls," said Elcor in his usual sedate manner.

Mac glanced back up at the crystal skull then back at the old man.

Elcor leaned close and whispered, "Such things are for later discussion." He added a conspiratorial wink then turned away and started giving out orders.

Mac was more intrigued than ever. He wished he had more time to explore the whole vault. Who knew what treasures of antiquity were tucked away down there?

He dragged his attention off the strange skull and began unloading his basket. Men filed through the door, stacked their baskets at the far end of the cavern as instructed and marched out for the next load. Elcor stationed an officer at the door to oversee the project and returned to the library with Mac.

It was nightfall by the time they arrived back at Elcor's private chambers.

"As much as it pains me to do so, I must alert Pharaoh," said Elcor as he sat at his desk and scribbled on a sheet of papyrus. "No doubt the eavesdropping Pothinus has already been in his ear but it would be wise to follow proper channels all the same."

Within minutes a messenger had been dispatched to the palace.

Elcor squinted and leaned forward to study Mac's face. "Great whiskers of Cerberus, you did get a touch of the sun this morning," he remarked.

Mac raised a hand to his face. He was surprised to find the skin was still hot and tight, despite Elcor's supposed sunburn remedy. He really didn't think he'd been in the sun that long on his walk up from the harbour.

"I can offer you lodgings in the library grounds for the duration of your stay," said Elcor.

"Ah… no. Thanks all the same, Elcor, but I really should be getting back."

Mac was suddenly sick with dread. He had no idea how much time had passed in the Now. He cringed as he realised the cause of his sunburn. He must have been lying out in the desert for hours, days maybe. His father would be furious.

"I really have to go," he said, making for the door.

"But you'll stay in the city at least until the festival at Week's End?"

"I wouldn't miss it." Mac grinned. "Oh, and Elcor? You won't, you know, tell Aisha that –"

"No," he cut in. "I won't tell Aisha you fancy her."

"No, I mean…" Mac's face was instantly scarlet.

Elcor winked. "I won't tell her you're a time traveller either. That's your job."

CHAPTER ELEVEN

That's your job.

Elcor's words weighed heavily on Mac's conscience as he headed back towards his father's tent. The last rays of sun slanted across the desert as he plopped one lead foot in front of the other. Most of the workers had headed back to camp for the evening. He was drained. It seemed he'd been gone all day. At least he thought it was the same day but couldn't be sure. He exhaled and shook his head. His dad was going to go mental.

Mac hesitated outside the tent. It was quiet inside. He ducked through the flap. There was no sign of his father. Relief.

He sank down on his cot and pulled his boots off. That's when he saw the note. On the table beside the laptop, a tin mug weighted down a piece of paper with the words 'GONE TO TOWN. BACK BY DINNER. STUDY HARD. L.S.' scrawled across it in Leon's distinctive, capitalised handwriting. Mac thought it strange that his father initialled everything. He never just signed it 'Dad' and certainly never 'Love, Dad.' He knew his father loved him in some way. It just might have been nice to hear it once in a while – read it, at least.

Mac flung his dirty socks over his shoulder and lay down. He closed his eyes. By the sounds of it, his father had been gone since before lesson time. He allowed himself a sigh of relief. Gabriella would have assumed he'd spent the day with Ru and vice versa. That was one problem solved.

The next problem was how on earth he was going to get back to meet Aisha at sunset tomorrow *her time*. He wasn't even sure he could land in the same decade, let alone, the same week. It was amazing that he'd managed to get so close this morning. But what if his next attempt fell short by a few days and he had to find Aisha all over again? Or worse, what if he overshot the mark and she was already…? It didn't bear thinking about.

He slid his bandana off and ran his hands through his hair. He stared up at the khaki canvas that stretched overhead, his blinks long and slow.

By his calculations, time was running a little faster back in 'Old Alex', as he was now referring to it. It had been dark by the time they'd made it back to Elcor's chambers but he'd had no idea what the actual time was. He couldn't be sure how long they'd spent underground.

He sighed.

What difference did it make knowing the time? He couldn't tell what time it was from this end anyway. Even if he set his watch –

Dammit!

He whipped his left hand out from under his pillow. To his utter astonishment, his watch was still on his wrist.

He unclipped it to reveal a white band of skin that marred a very sunburned arm.

It seemed that he couldn't lose anything on a trip after all. If it went with him, it came back with him. He just couldn't bring anything from the Past back to the Now. He smiled as he realised he wouldn't have been in trouble for losing his watch after all. It was impossible to lose it.

He must have drifted off at some point. Voices outside the tent woke him. It was dark. He swung his legs off the cot and sat up. The smell of food wafted through the tent flap and his stomach rumbled.

"Hey, Sleeping Beauty," Leon said in his gruff monotone when Mac stuck his head outside.

"You're just in time, my good man," said Ru. "Your father was kind enough to pick up Chinese take-away in town."

"Cool, I'm starving."

Mac pulled up a camping stool while his father piled a plate high with sweet and sour pork, chicken chow mien and a dim sim on the side.

Mac's hand was halfway to his mouth with his second shovel of food when Gabriella's face came into view on the edge of the lamplight. His gut twisted.

"Evening, Gabby. Care to join us? There's plenty," said Leon.

"Thanks, Professor." Gabriella pulled up a seat as Leon searched for another clean plate.

"Glad to see you're putting the dig kid to good use at your end, my dear. Didn't lay eyes on him all day," said Ru.

Mac froze mid chew.

Gabriella's eyes narrowed as her sharp brain put the pieces together. "Sí, señor Ru," she said, levelling her gaze at Mac. "He was up to all sorts of things today. It no is a wonder he look so tired."

"And sunburnt," added Leon. "How many times do I have to tell you, boy? Sunscreen."

Mac lowered his eyes and swallowed his chow mien. He could feel his sunburnt ears turning a new shade of red. He was mightily relieved and grateful that Gabby hadn't spilled the beans about his all-day absence from the dig but now it meant he was obligated to let her in on his secret. He wondered how little he could get away with telling her. The worst part was that now she'd be keeping a close eye on him. It would be so much harder to sneak away. His stomach knotted as he thought about how and when he was going to keep his next meeting with Aisha.

Appetite gone, Mac merely pushed his food around his plate and pretended to listen to the dinnertime conversation. Try as he might, he simply could not drag his thoughts away from the Egyptian beauty for a second. He had to find a way back. He could not, *would not* disappoint her.

Mac tossed and turned on his cot. He couldn't get comfortable. He flipped his pillow over to the cool side. That usually worked. But not tonight.

He'd managed to dodge Gabby after dinner by excusing himself to study. He'd deal with her tomorrow when he'd had a chance to figure out what he was going to tell her. She knew all about his psychometry thing. She was one of the few on the team who did. That wasn't the problem exactly. It had more to do with the fact that she knew Leon didn't approve of Mac's psychometric time travel, and she was pretty loyal to the professor. Could she be trusted to keep his secret?

Mac puffed out a long breath. He didn't really have a choice. He'd just have to trust her and see what happened. His thoughts wandered back to Aisha. How the hell was he going to time his return trip so he didn't let her down? He just couldn't blow it.

His mind was still grappling with the problem as he finally slipped off to sleep.

Later that night, he dreamed of a lone heron standing on a rock in the middle of the ocean. Its eyes were closed and it stood perfectly still. The water was like glass and stretched to the horizon in all directions. The scene was washed in the dull greys of a cloudy pre-dawn. The bird's feathers were a dirty nothing colour and the sea was the colour of stone.

The clouds began to disperse as the sky lightened. Then the dream shifted. *He* was the bird standing on the rock, silent and still. As the sun pierced the overcast skies, he could feel the first rays of the day warming his webbed feet. A salty breeze ruffled the feathers around his face and neck. His world was orangey-red behind closed eyelids. He opened them.

Colour. Everywhere.

The sun breasted the Eastern horizon, flooding the sea and sky with its brilliance. Reds, golds and pinks bled into one another, pooling on the face of the water and sharply underscoring purple-grey clouds.

He was ready.

He stretched his long skinny neck skyward and opened his beak. The plumage on his breast shimmered as his lungs expanded. He reached down inside for the sound, drawing it up from his core, his very soul, from a deep sense of something beyond his already forgotten origins. He could feel the air rush over his vocal chords as a primeval cry rang out, shattering the silence and echoing to the very ends of the earth.

Time and space pivoted beneath him...

Then the dream became a frantic montage of imagery; cities rose and fell in a single instant; floods, famine and plague played out in unison; rulers and redeemers were born and died; countless deeds of good and evil obliterated each other in a never-ending struggle for equilibrium... And he saw all of it in the blink of an eye.

The horrific vision of some cataclysmic wave of blazing fire enveloping the earth evaporated as Mac woke. He sat up, unusually alert for such an early hour. He swung his legs over the edge of the cot and pressed his toes into the ground. Relief steadied his racing heart. It was one of those dreams he wanted to forget but remember at the same time. He worked his fingertips into his eye sockets, trying to erase the nightmare's final frame from behind his lids. It was no use though. He knew that dream would cling to him for a while.

He shook his head and reached for his bandana.

CHAPTER TWELVE

The smell of coconut sunscreen floated on the breeze. Gabriella hummed a tune as she worked nearby. Every now and then she glanced over at the dig kid, who was strangely quiet this morning. The number eleven between his brows was particularly deep today.

Mac avoided her gaze and kept brushing. He'd been surprised she hadn't asked him anything about yesterday. It seemed she was patiently waiting for him to bring the subject up. He didn't quite know how but, the more he thought about his 'travel' plans, it became clear he was going to need an ally at this end of the timeline.

Quite some time passed before he broached the subject. "Gabby, can I ask you something?"

"Sure."

Mac stopped brushing but didn't look up. "Do you believe in love at first sight?"

She laughed. It wasn't a derogatory laugh; it was almost a sympathetic laugh. "Of course." Gabriella noticed his reddening ears. "And so do you I theenk," she added through a smile.

Mac resumed brushing and said nothing.

"You gonna tell me about her or do I gotta beat it out of you?" she said, brandishing a trowel with mock aggression.

He snorted a laugh and put down his brush. Mac looked

at her. Tendrils of dark hair floated across her face, newly escaped from the thick twist of hair at the nape of her neck. She brushed at them with the back of her hand, leaving a smear of dirt on her cheek. There was a sort of raw unself-conscious beauty about her. Her warm eyes were patient and kind. Mac trusted her, he realised.

He pulled back the bandage on his left hand to reveal the ruby lion ring.

Gabriella gasped.

"I found it yesterday."

Mac went on to tell the whole story while Gabby sat in stunned silence.

When he'd finished, she merely shook her head. "MacKeenlee. What am I gonna do weetchu?"

"You're gonna promise not to tell Dad, that's what you're gonna do."

She crossed her heart. "Your secret is safe with me."

Mac nodded his appreciation. "So now how do I get back there on time? Any ideas?"

"For your beeg date, of course."

"It's not a date, Gabby!" His tone was defensive.

She giggled. "Alright, alright."

She was thoughtful for a moment. "My pappa used to say 'Intention is everything'. I believe heem, you know."

Mac drew his eyebrows together even further and studied her. "What? You're saying just concentrate on a particular time – hold a particular *intention* – and that's enough to direct the travel?"

She shrugged. "Be guided by your heart."

"Hmm," was all he said before turning back to his work. He pondered the idea of focused intention. He wondered…

The heavy textbook thumped shut as Mac leaned back in his chair. Studying was a waste of time when he was this preoccupied. He hadn't recalled a single thing from his lessons a day ago and had to backtrack a whole chapter. A quick glance at his watch told him his father would be back for lunch any minute. He took off his glasses and rubbed his eyes. A sense of urgency nagged at him.

"Be guided by your heart," Gabby had told him.

Well, it seemed his heart was getting anxious to be back in Old Alex. Mac decided to have lunch with his dad, then slip away to Gabby's tent, as they'd previously arranged. It had been her suggestion. No one would miss him for the afternoon and certainly no one would think to look for him there. Gabby had offered to cover for him so long as he was back by dinnertime. Mac had no idea how he was going to work that out. He would just have to cross his fingers and hope the whole directed intention thing worked.

He looked down at his dirty shirt and frowned. He took a tentative sniff of his armpits before pulling his shirt off over his head and heading for the barrel of water at the rear of the tent for a quick splash. He would put on a fresh shirt after lunch when Leon was back out on site.

Absently, he wrung out his wet bandana over the barrel. His heart was already off and running at the thought of seeing Aisha again and he noticed that strange stirring inside. Lunch with his father could not go quickly enough, he thought as he retied the bandana and rounded the tent in time to see Leon speeding towards him on the quad bike.

CHAPTER THIRTEEN

MAC OPENED HIS eyes to the green-gold glow of the Royal Gardens.

Right place.

It looked like afternoon at least but he couldn't be sure what day or decade he was in. Then he spotted her.

Right time.

Aisha was leaning against the trunk of a tree. She was side on to him, her lithe form backlit by the afternoon sun. She wore a cream robe of sheer fabric that came to just above her ankles and was caught at the waist by a braided gold band. The light streamed through from behind to outline her long slender legs. One knee was bent, the sole of her sandal resting against the tree. Her long hair fell loose and straight from a band of coloured stones at her hairline. She twirled a strand of it around her finger and bit her lip. Her eyes darted, searching. It was quite clear that she was waiting for someone.

Mac stared. She was beautiful. And all the more so because she didn't know she was being watched.

He adjusted his bandana and checked that the fly of his jeans was done up. The rolled-up sleeves of his white cotton shirt were too tight on his forearms so he wound them down a fold. It had been Gabby's suggestion to wear a long-sleeved shirt open over a grey singlet. Mac still wasn't sure about the whole ensemble but Gabby had said that he should look like he'd made an effort but not that he was trying too hard; whatever that meant.

He was surprised at how hard his heart was beating as he approached Aisha along the covered walkway. Butterflies harassed his belly.

Then she saw him.

Aisha straightened, smoothed her tunic and composed her expression but not before Mac noticed the split-second leap of her features the instant she laid eyes on him.

"I hope I'm not late," he said, walking towards her.

"You're early. I only just got here myself," she lied.

There was a moment of silent suspense while both searched for the next line.

Mac noticed Aisha had made extra effort with her make-up. Heavy lines of black khol ringed her eyes, making them look even bigger and greener than before. Her lips were a deeper shade and plumper, and he found himself wondering how she'd done it.

"So..." he started at the same time Aisha spoke.

"Have you been up to the lighthouse yet?" she said. "It affords an incredible view of the city. You know, it's one of Alexandria's finest architectural triumphs. It can be seen over thirty-five miles out to sea. You really should see it while you're here. I can show you, if you like." It came out in a rush, in one long unbroken stream that left her breathless.

Mac stifled a grin. It seemed he wasn't the only one who was nervous.

"Sure." He nodded.

Her breath rushed out over lips stretched into a smile.

The conversation didn't start up again until they were clear of the library grounds and strolling down toward the harbour.

"Grandfather tells me you're from the south."

"Ah, yes. That's right."

Aisha studied his strange leg garments. It seemed to be one piece of dark fabric that wrapped around the full length of each separate leg. "Your clothes. They're interesting. I like them."

In a city of togas and flowing fabric, Mac realised he must have looked a sight. He wished he'd pulled the sheets off his cot and worn them instead. At least he'd blend in.

Aisha went on. "That's what I love about this city. Fashion from all over. Food from everywhere."

She was right, thought Mac, noticing the different nationalities and costumes of the people in the street. He wasn't such a spectacle after all.

"So you sailed here then?" she asked.

"Um, not *all* the way."

"Are you travelling alone?"

He nodded.

"That must get rather lonely."

Mac shrugged. "Sometimes."

"I'd love to travel. I've never been out of Alexandria. My boyfriend –"

"Pharaoh," Mac cut in.

"Yes," she answered, blinking down hard on the word as she said it. "Pharaoh." She paused. "He keeps promising to take me on vacation somewhere nice but with talk of war on the horizon…" She trailed off.

Mac soured as he pictured Aisha with Ptolemy on some romantic tropical getaway. Although, he reasoned, they'd probably head somewhere cold for a nice change. He shuddered at the vision of the two of them curled up in front of some fireplace. The little muscle on his jaw line flexed as he clenched his teeth and kept walking.

"So, are you here on business? Trade?" she asked.

"Ah…"

Mac suddenly wished he'd invested some thought into what the hell he was going to tell her. He had no story. No story!

His mind raced.

"Ah… Research actually," he finally answered.

"Grandfather said he thought you might be a scholar."

Mac cringed as he recalled his cousins' singsong taunts. *"Schol-ar! Schol-ar!"* They'd busted him watching the history channel on cable in his room late one night.

"You look as though you spend some time outdoors though," said Aisha.

She bit her lip and stifled a smile. A strange little rush rippled through her as she revisited the image of him from yesterday's encounter, bare-chested and lean, bending over to pick up the toga crumpled at his feet. His flat, muscled stomach had creased neatly as he'd bent over, revealing a sliver of white skin at his hip, untouched by the sun.

"A bit," he said.

"Oh!" said Aisha, an idea popping into her mind.

She touched his arm. It felt warm through the thin cotton fabric of his shirt, the muscle hard and defined. Her fingertips thrilled to it.

"We should go horse riding one afternoon," she finished.

"Sure."

Somehow he'd managed to inject a whole lot more enthusiasm into his voice than he actually felt. What was he thinking? He couldn't even ride a skateboard, let alone a *horse*.

His cousins had laughed themselves stupid the first time he'd had a go on Luke's skateboard. He'd never ridden one before and it certainly didn't come naturally to him. His knees and elbows still bore the scars. However, undeterred, he'd begged his father to buy him a skateboard before they left Australia. Leon relented and the skateboard was, at that moment, gathering dust under Mac's cot in his tent back in the Now.

His panic finally subsided enough for him to pick up the thread of what she was saying.

"...and you can ride Ammit. You'll just love her."

Ammit, the Bone Eater... Mac pictured the crocodile-headed beast that featured prominently in Ancient Egyptian mythology for which the horse was named.

Mac let her gibber away beside him. He'd almost forgotten his terror at the thought of riding a horse. He was preoccupied with the sound of her voice, not so much what she was saying. It wasn't deep exactly but was without the manic high-pitched squeak that he found so annoying in most girls her age – the few he'd met at least. She sounded intelligent regardless of the words. He reckoned she could have been talking about lip-gloss and lollipops, and she still would have sounded like an authority on the subject.

She laughed at her own joke, whatever it had been. Mac

had missed it. There was a hint of huskiness to her laugh. He liked that.

He grinned at her.

Aisha watched the Roman numeral two between his brows evaporate when he smiled. The 'two' seemed to split and disappear, only to resurface an instant later as deep dimples in his cheeks. She was suddenly shy again under the force of that grin.

They continued on in silence for a time.

It was quite a walk from the library down to the harbour and by the time they reached the Heptastadion that led from the mainland to the lighthouse, a light sheen of perspiration covered Mac's forehead. He was grateful for the briny sea breeze that whipped his hair and tugged at his shirt.

Aisha's cheeks glowed under a swirling mass of tangled hair and she found herself wishing she'd opted for a different hairstyle. Glamorous long hair sounded good in theory but it wasn't at all practical in the onshore wind. She snatched a handful of hair from in front of her face and swept it to the side where she held it in her fist. She opened her mouth to speak but sucked in a cluster of stray hairs instead. Ink-stained fingers picked them out from between pursed lips.

They crossed to the lighthouse in silence.

Mac gazed up at the immense structure that towered above them. His skin prickled and he caught himself holding his breath. For some strange reason, he was captivated by it. There were bigger and better feats of modern-day architecture all over the world, many of which he'd seen first-hand, but somehow they paled before this one. The late afternoon light cast the white marble golden. It resembled some outlandish wedding cake. The lower storey was a huge square beneath an octagonal second tier set to the front of the square, with a circular tier on top. A statue of the mythological merman, Triton, Greek god of the sea, was mounted at each corner of the first square level. Mac was reminded again of the strong Greek influence in Alexandria.

"Are you coming in?" asked Aisha from inside the arched entrance.

Mac realised he'd been standing there gaping like an idiot. Blushing, he followed her inside.

"It's impressive when you see it for the first time. Most tourists have the same reaction," she said.

Mac nodded. But it was more than that. There was just something about the place; something he couldn't put his finger on.

He was surprised at the number of people inside. It was certainly quite a tourist attraction. A man stood at a makeshift booth inside the entrance collecting admission. Aisha smiled and waved as he nodded her through.

"I come here all the time," she said. "It's one of my favourite places."

The core of the structure was hollow with a wide, spiralling ramp that hugged the walls and rose upward on a series of trestled arches. A donkey hauled a cart of wood up the ramp with a laboured clip-clop. Its driver walked along behind, whip resting unused over his shoulder.

"That's how they get supplies up to the fire at the top," explained Aisha. "The donkey takes it to the top of this first level then the lift carries it from there to the very top. Tourists aren't allowed past the first level."

A variety of stalls selling souvenirs and food were

clustered together making the ground floor a noisy jostling marketplace.

Aisha led Mac through the crowd towards a pulley-operated lift in the centre where a group of tourists queued to be taken to an observation platform at the top of the first level. It looked dodgy to Mac. As he was herded into the tiny space with several other people, he glanced up at the ropes then back at the donkey on the ramp. The donkey looked like a much safer bet.

Not even the overpowering smell of Aisha's perfume so close to him could quite erase his apprehension. The lift jolted and swayed as it left the safety of the ground with a screech of some unseen pulley mechanism. Mac's palms sweated. His mouth was dry. He studied the sandals of the person in front of him as he tried to control his heart rate. The poor excuse for an elevator bounced and jigged within its rickety timber shaft as it reached the length of its pulley cycle before starting up again with another painful groan.

"Are you alright?" Aisha touched his arm as she whispered close to his ear. It brought the hairs on the back of his neck to life.

"I'm fine." He managed a lopsided grin.

The lift shuddered to a halt and swayed over the drop until an attendant steadied it and ushered them out onto a platform that opened through archways onto a wide, open-air observation deck that bordered the lighthouse on all sides. Tourists flocked to the edge of the balcony to take in the spectacular view of the city and its famous harbour. Mac found it strangely amusing that none of them had cameras. He desperately wished he'd brought his. The sun was setting over the city, blessing it with the rich colours of heaven, while the ocean made itself a worshipful tribute to the western sky. It would have made a magic photo.

"Come on. The best is yet to come," said Aisha.

She took him by the hand and led him to a small doorway in the wall. Mac found himself at the foot of a narrow staircase that was sandwiched between the outer layer and the inner layer of the lighthouse walls. It was only just wide enough for him to walk up it without scraping both shoulders. The lift was clearly the more sensible option for getting to the very top but he was glad they'd decided to take the stairs. It was somehow romantic.

Aisha took the lead as they wound their way up the steps, negotiating the sharp turns as the passage followed the octagonal shape of the second level. It was quiet and cool in the stairwell. Small windows were dotted here and there to let in light and afford a bird's eye view of the outside world. Every now and then, Mac stole a glance at the sprawling city below. That is, when he could manage to tear his gaze away from Aisha's shapely rump that bobbed at eye level as she climbed the steps ahead of him.

The cool air and romance of the passageway were soon forgotten as they neared the top of the second tier. Mac had worked up a sweat and both of them were puffing.

"Trust me," said Aisha, breathless. "It's worth it."

Eventually, they stepped out onto a small balcony and into the twilight magic of an Alexandrian evening. The spring air was fresh and cool. High above them, the first stars winked and twinkled.

"Whoa...."

"Told you it was worth it." Aisha grinned.

They walked partway around the balcony that ringed the base of the third cylindrical level of the lighthouse.

"This is incredible!"

"I bet you've never been this high up in your life," said Aisha.

Mac just shook his head. It didn't seem like such a lie if he didn't actually say it.

"I didn't think so," she said, looking pleased with herself.

Mac leaned his elbows on the stone railing to peer over the edge. The choppy sea broke in a cloud of spray on the jagged rocks below. He guessed he had to have been more than eighty metres above the water. The balustraded balcony rail seemed dangerously low, barely reaching to his hip. It would never have passed a modern-day safety inspection.

He twisted to gaze up at the tower above them. Its apex glowed brightly as the huge mirrors reflected the furnace out into the coming night. Mac tried to picture what it might look like from far out at sea.

"So, how long do you plan to stay in Alexandria?" asked Aisha.

Mac eased back around to look at her.

She was leaning on the railing beside him, so close that their elbows were almost touching. Suddenly and inexplicably, he took her by the arm and gently eased her back from the railing, away from the drop that seemed to suck gravity over the edge like an invisible waterfall.

Aisha didn't resist. She leaned into him an instant, before straightening up and stepping away with a nervous laugh. "Heights don't bother me. It's fine. But thank you."

Mac rushed to make amends. "No, it's just… That railing doesn't look very safe, you know. Low…" He was sure he sounded like some nerdy safety inspector. "I'm fine with heights too. Totally fine." He jammed his hands into the pockets of his jeans and pressed his lips together so nothing else stupid could tumble out of his mouth.

"You didn't answer my question," said Aisha.

The last hint of light from beyond the western horizon turned her green eyes golden. Her cheeks were flushed from the steep climb up the steps. They made a rosy bed for her little chocolate-moon birthmark. The dangly earrings she wore sparkled and clinked in the wind that blew her raven hair behind her. She looked as though she could have stepped right out of a twenty-first century music video.

Mac wasn't sure how much time had elapsed before he answered. "Um…However long it takes."

"However long what takes?"

The answer was simple – however long it took to make her fall in love with him. But he didn't say that.

"My research," he said.

"What is it you're researching exactly?"

"Er… history." He shrugged. "You know, ancient… things. Old stuff. I like old stuff. Pretty boring really."

Aisha smiled. "I don't think it's boring at all. I love history, especially ancient languages."

"Really?" The faint comment was simply his own addendum to the question: *Could a girl that perfect really exist? Really?*

She nodded and leaned closer.

"You know, I could get you access to the library's Isolation Room – the restricted area where all the really old secret stuff is kept," she whispered. The words were barely out of her mouth when a surge of guilty heat burned across her chest. What was she saying? It was a violation of the very code she lived by each day; worse, it was a violation of her grandfather's trust. What kind of dangerous power did this stranger have over her?

Mac raised an eyebrow. "Secret stuff?"

"Never mind," she said, shaking her head and wishing to the gods she hadn't opened her mouth.

He stifled a smile. It was so obvious she'd said more than she should have. He decided not to press her further but the thought of really old secret stuff excited him.

Aisha glanced across at the fascinating stranger and those irresistible cheek pits. What was it about him? It was so dumb, so unlike her. She considered herself a smart girl, so how in the name of the Underworld had she become so totally obsessed with the mysterious traveller? Obsessed? Yes, it was the right word, she guessed. After all, she'd thought of nothing else since meeting him yesterday. She'd changed her outfit four times that afternoon and spent ages doing her make-up. She didn't even do that for Pharaoh.

A flock of white gulls glided past at eye level.

She cleared her throat. "Grandfather says that one day man will fly like those birds. Crazy old thing."

"He's right." Then, catching himself, "I mean, he's right about a lot of things so he's probably right about that too."

"Perhaps."

"I mean, who knows?" said Mac. "Someday man might walk on the moon." He winked at her.

Aisha shoulder barged him playfully. "Grace of the Muses, you're full of it!" She rolled her eyes and laughed.

Mac grinned. But the grin began to fade inside as he realised she'd never see anything like that in her lifetime.

Flying like the birds, walking on the moon... It was all nonsense talk in her world. It was still a couple of thousand years away.

Suddenly, the gulf between their two worlds seemed enormous. Without realising it, he reached for her and pulled her close, as if he could somehow drag her back into his time.

Aisha was staring into his eyes, her lips slightly parted.

Mac's heart thundered. He could kiss her right now if he wanted to. He did want to. But... What was stopping him? He relaxed his grip on her arm and rubbed it. "Come on, you must be getting cold. You've got goosebumps."

Aisha's heart sank. She wasn't a bit cold. She was on fire! How could she explain that her goosebumps were merely the offspring of his touch? She bit down hard on her disappointment and swallowed it.

She nodded but said nothing.

Mac let go of her arm and they turned back toward the stairs.

"Miss Aisha," came a voice from the shadowy doorway.

They both jumped.

"Yes?"

"Pharaoh summons you."

"Of course." Her answer was brusque. "You may go."

"My lady, I'm to escort you personally. Pharaoh's orders."

The royal runner was a thin youth with big brown eyes and a nervous disposition. His eyes flicked back and forth between Aisha and Mac.

Aisha was furious – furious but scared. How long had Pharaoh's servant been standing there? How much had he seen, had he heard? Gods of the Underworld, she'd just invited a complete stranger to the Isolation Room, despite the lengthy lecture Elcor had given her about some new assignment she'd be starting the day after tomorrow. Was she out of her mind? She glanced at Mac, suddenly feeling very foolish that the novelty of him had so affected her better judgement.

"Very well," she said.

Abruptly business like, she turned to Mac. "So then, I trust you enjoyed the tour."

"Very much. Thank you."

"Goodbye, Mac."

Without another word, she disappeared down the steps, followed by Ptolemy's servant.

Mac wanted to call after her, to tell her to wait, to ask her when he could see her again, to beg her to say his name one more time. He stood there for a moment before turning back to the ocean view. The stars were bright and plentiful now, even against the dull remains of the day.

He reviewed the afternoon. Overall, it was good – better than good. It was more than he could have hoped for. He blew it at the end though. He should have just gone for it – just kissed her when he had the chance. Why hadn't he? Because, somewhere inside a little voice had said "Hold it!" and he'd actually listened. Who knew how long that skinny runner kid had been standing there spying on them? If he'd kissed her, it could have been death to both of them when Pharaoh found out.

His stomach rumbled. Figuring it was about dinnertime, he took a deep breath and prepared to go.

SWOOSH!

Black wings…

Mac ducked as huge dark wings swooped just inches above his head. The sudden rush of air ruffled his hair.

"What the – ?"

He swivelled to look up but saw nothing. It was gone. He dashed to the rail and leaned over. Nothing. Whatever it was, there was no sign of it.

Bats maybe? But the thing had been big.

He was breathing hard as he ran his hands through his hair. He was ready to go home. He closed his right hand over the ruby lion ring on his left and took a deep breath. *To the Now…*

CHAPTER FOURTEEN

The stone amulet began to take shape in Aisha's skilled hands. She sat cross-legged on the lawn. The twittering and giggles of jewellery-making class made a comforting contrast to the oppressive silence of the Isolation Room. She'd been sequestered in there all morning trying to finish off the document she'd been working on so that she could start translating some high-priority project for her grandfather the next day.

She shivered though the day was warm.

There had been an unsettling vibe in the Isolation Room that morning, something she did not like. She thought perhaps it had just been because the shelves had been emptied on Elcor's orders – something about a fire threat – and there hadn't been any other scribes working alongside her. The quiet emptiness of the place had made it seem eerie. Still, it had been a relief to bang the door shut and hurry off down the hall, like she'd slammed the black fingers of a demon in the door as she'd made her lucky escape. How ridiculous! She wondered if it was a full moon. How else could she explain her behaviour lately? And her grandfather's – he was going quite crazy, she was sure.

The laughter and gossip around her melted into the background as she let her thoughts drift. With expert strokes, she filed the jagged edges of the soft steatite into a smooth curve to form the head of the amulet. The stone yielded easily to her touch but was hard and durable once glazed. It was to be a special gift for Mac.

Mac…

The sound of his name in her head started her heart a-flutter all over again. It was silly. She couldn't explain why exactly. She'd only just met him and yet he seemed so familiar. It felt as though her mind was clutching at the remnants of an elusive dream. There was just something about him.

Aisha stopped filing and ran her fingertip along the smooth edge of the stone carving. She assessed her progress with a keen eye and continued sanding away at the stone, the midday breeze carrying away a fine shimmer of dust.

Before she'd even had time to monitor her thoughts, they were back on the newcomer. She replayed snatches of yesterday's conversation in her head. He was just so easy to talk to. A crystal-clear image of him smiling, his suntanned cheeks pitted with deep dimples, filled her mind.

Aisha knew it was stupid, yet she longed to talk to him again. She could barely wait to see him and found herself trying to think up excuses to visit her grandfather's chambers in the hope that Mac might be there. Yesterday's suggestion to go horse riding that afternoon hadn't exactly been set in stone so she wasn't sure if he'd even show.

Their date, if she could call it that, had been cut short just as she was getting to know him; just as he was about to – well, she was pretty sure what he was about to do. Resentment flared as she thought back to Ptolemy's rude interruption at lunch the day before. She wondered which one of his spies had tipped him off.

Sunshine bathed the garden in shades of green and gold. A cool breeze stirred the leaves of the canopy above. Aisha closed her eyes and stretched her neck, breathing deeply. She opened her eyes and inspected her craftsmanship critically.

"Hmm. Just a little off that edge," she said to herself as she held the amulet up to the light.

She resumed her work on the piece and, once again, visions of the intriguing stranger filled her head. She hadn't even had an opportunity to ask him much about where he was from. All she knew was that he was some sort of scholar doing historical research. She knew nothing of his family apart from the fact that his mother had died when he was a child. It was certainly a strange coincidence that they had both lost their mothers. She knew he hadn't lied about it either. She'd seen the pain in his eyes.

She glanced down at the amulet in her hands and smiled. She was sure he would find it special, once she explained its significance. Hopefully, he wouldn't think it too weird. After all, she had only just met him and here she was presenting him with a gift. She stopped work for a moment, suddenly troubled by that thought. Maybe it *was* too weird. Yes, it was too much. What was she thinking? She didn't even know the handsome stranger. She was being an idiot.

Aisha exhaled loudly and dumped the near-finished carving on a pile of rubble beside her. She let her shoulders slump.

The only feeling she could identify was anger but it seemed to be tangled up with other unnamed feelings as well. She wasn't entirely sure why she was angry either. It seemed a stupid unjustified emotion to be feeling. Following unspoken orders, her mind trawled for a culprit to pin it on…

"Besides," she muttered to herself, "he probably already has a girlfriend. Pig!"

No sooner had the thought escaped her lips, than she regretted it. She felt small for having even thought it. So what if he had a girlfriend? He hadn't been flirting with her. He'd been a perfect gentleman, shy even. In fact, she thought, he probably did have a girlfriend. Why wouldn't he? He was certainly a gift from the gods. And it certainly explained why he hadn't kissed her when she'd practically begged him to – in her mind at least.

Aisha glanced down at the discarded amulet and frowned. She picked it up and toyed with it. It was just a sign of friendship, right? Friends can give friends presents, she reasoned. It was just a souvenir of his time in the city and certainly much better than the tourist trash sold down in the marketplace. She sighed and picked up a pointy carving tool to begin adding detail to the stone.

It was time to exercise some thought control. Her heart just needed to stop running away with her head. It was all very foolish.

For a few minutes, Aisha tried to just focus her attention on her work but, before she realised it, she was fantasising about holding hands with Mac under the magical umbrella of the light show and then, just as things were getting good, the rational part of her brain stepped in.

"Ugh! Just let it go!" she hissed and thudded the ball of her hand against her forehead. What was wrong with her? Did she want to get the poor boy killed?

"Are you okay, sister?" came a sweet voice nearby.

Aisha glanced over to meet the quizzical stares of the other girls in the group, not sure which one had posed the question.

She blushed. "Of course. I'm fine." She forced a smile.

"Boy trouble?" asked a round-faced girl with thick eyebrows.

Aisha shrugged, uncomfortable with the line of questioning.

"What? Don't tell me your boyfriend's acting like royalty. Oh, wait… He *is* royalty!" another girl quipped sarcastically, her thin lips pursing into a nasty sneer.

The other girls laughed. Aisha half-smiled weakly at the lame attempt at humour. They all knew she was Pharaoh's chosen. Jealously flared among the other girls and Aisha was made to feel on the outer most of the time, despite her best efforts to just be one of the girls. She never flaunted the lavish gifts Ptolemy gave her. In fact, most of her jewellery was hidden under her mattress and the expensive silks still hung in her wardrobe, unworn. She chose to work, even though the pharaoh would have preferred she sit idly at his side all day for his sole amusement.

More than once, Aisha had regretfully declined party invitations because she knew Pharaoh was displeased with her mixing with the 'commoners'. Then the invitations simply stopped coming. Sure, she got to attend all the royal feasts and functions but they were tragically boring and she found the way in which Ptolemy wore her on his arm like she was some kind of fashion accessory sickening.

If only they knew how miserable she was with Ptolemy. Yes, 'miserable' was the word, she concluded, nodding to herself. Often, she felt like a prisoner. Sure, she was free to roam around albeit under the constant watch of the spies. Pharaoh told her what to wear, how he liked her hair styled, which of her friends she could and couldn't spend time with and pretty much dictated everything else in her day-to-day life.

Thank the Elder gods, she still had her scribe work, which she loved. Her career was hers alone, at least for the meantime. Already, Ptolemy was talking of marriage and heirs to the throne. She squirmed. She could barely stand to kiss him. More than once, she had narrowly managed to wriggle free of his more eager advances. She wondered how much longer she could hold him off. Even though a lot of her friends were already married at sixteen, Aisha simply couldn't get her head around it. It seemed like a death sentence. Marriage to Ptolemy probably was, quite literally! Even as Ptolemy's second wife, she would have a target on her head. She had met his sister and first wife, Cleopatra, only once. What a piece of work! She was one scary individual. Aisha had been terrified of her, as was Ptolemy.

Turning away from the other girls, Aisha put her head down and stared at the amulet in her hands.

Oh, Mac... Take me away from all this, she begged silently.

She brought the amulet to her lips and kissed it gently.

Then she concentrated on polishing the stone carving until it shone brightly in the glow of the gardens.

CHAPTER FIFTEEN

Mac fidgeted with the fresh bandages on his hands as he hurried south along the pathway that dissected the Royal Gardens. Yet again, his stomach was a knot of anticipation at the thought of spending the afternoon with Aisha, even if it was riding horses. He hoped it was still on. They hadn't had the chance to confirm anything at the lighthouse yesterday. So he just hoped.

Last night's return to the Now had gone smoothly. He'd been on time for dinner, much to Gabby's relief, and his father had suspected nothing.

Being Saturday back in the Now, it had been much easier to slip away to Old Alex for the day. As usual, Mac had risen early to have breakfast with his father. On cue, Gabby had arrived at their tent and asked if Mac would like to spend the day with her in town. He'd pretended to think about it for a minute while Leon encouraged him to go.

"Go on, son. It'll be good for you to get out, see the sights, spend the pocket money you still owe me," Leon had said, his flat tone lilting on the cheerful side. "You never know, you might even meet a pretty Alexandrian girl."

Mac had tried not to smile as big as he'd wanted to.

And so it was that the professor waved at the pair through a cloud of dust as the Jeep sped away toward the city.

Once out of sight, Gabby had stopped and let Mac out.

"Good luck, MacKeenlee," she had said with a smile. "Oh, and undo your top button. You look like a nerd."

Mac had heard her laughing as she'd driven off.

He'd managed to double back to her tent without being seen. The previous evening it had taken him a while to convince Gabby that he didn't need babysitting. She'd be better off shopping in town while he lay in her tent. His father and Ru had a museum function to attend in the city that night so Mac wouldn't be missed for dinner. Things had worked out perfectly.

As Mac neared the end of the path that crossed the Royal Gardens, a large group of giggling girls pushed past him carrying strings of beads and jars of pretty things. Aisha wasn't among them. Then he saw her.

She sat astride a zebra, laughing as one of the zookeepers led it by a rope through the gardens. A tiny foal trotted along behind its mother. It was like something out of a child's picture book, thought Mac. The sun was high overhead and light filtered through the canopy. A gentle breeze tickled the leaves on the trees and tugged at the wisps of hair floating about Aisha's face. Her smile was captivating as she leaned toward the foal and reached out a hand to pat its fuzzy mane.

Mac's heart was beating hard and he was aware of the strange stirring in his stomach again.

Aisha glanced up and noticed him. Her face lit up and she waved like a little girl. "Mac!"

He smiled and waved back.

She slid off the zebra with ease, kissed it on the nose and ran to meet him.

For a moment, Mac thought she was going to fling her arms around his neck and hug him but, instead, she stopped a few paces short and approached demurely, smoothing her hair and batting her long lashes.

She studied him for a moment. "You look…" she trailed off. How could she comment without gushing? She wanted to say 'handsome', 'adorable', 'amazing' but all those words seemed too over-the-top and inappropriate for just their third meeting. "You look…good," she finished. It felt like the most outrageous understatement, especially given his outlandish footwear. She'd never seen anything like it.

Mac blushed.

He looked down at himself. Seeing as they were going horse riding, he'd opted for denim jeans again and his usual white cotton shirt. He was wearing his Nikes. His father would have suspected something if he'd worn his work boots into town with Gabby.

"I have something for you," said Aisha, reaching into a fold in her robes. "I made it."

She held open her palm and presented him with an amulet carved out of reddish stone. It was shaped a bit like a person standing with arms by their side, the head an open loop. It was engraved with a knot design. A thin piece of leather was threaded through a small hole at the top so it could be worn around the neck.

"It's called a tyet," she explained as she leaned forward and placed it over Mac's head.

"The Knot of Isis," said Mac.

"Yes!" Aisha seemed pleased that he knew what it was. "It symbolises resurrection."

Aisha closed her eyes and bowed her head, so close their

noses were almost touching. She uttered a special blessing of protection taught by her grandfather. He could smell the sweetness of her breath. She pulled away. The close encounter was brief but left him feeling light as a feather.

Mac turned the amulet over in his fingers. She had inscribed his name on the back in neat Greek lettering. Beneath it, she'd etched a picture of a heron.

A heron!

The weird dream he'd had the other night flashed across his mind.

Mac was silent for a few seconds.

"Aisha," he said shaking his head.

"You do not like it?" she asked, biting her lip.

When Mac spoke, his voice was barely above a whisper. He was genuinely choked with emotion. "Aisha, I love it. It's the best gift I've ever been given. Ever."

The significance of the tyet symbol was not lost on him. It stood for the goddess Isis, Mother of the World, patron of nature and magic. It represented the idea of eternal life and resurrection. It symbolised welfare. He remembered that the tyet was mentioned in one of the spells in the ancient Book of the Dead. It stated that the tyet would drive off anyone who would perform a criminal act against the wearer.

Aisha smiled, clearly satisfied with Mac's heartfelt reaction.

"Isis stands for all mothers, in this world and the next," she said as she reached below the neckline of her robe and held up a fine chain. Sunlight glinted off gold as her own tyet amulet dangled in the space between them. "It was a gift from my mother. I've never taken it off."

Mac smiled back at her. He wanted to just grab her

and hold her but he didn't. He looked at the tyet again. "A thousand thankyous, Aisha." He closed his eyes and gave a little bow.

She clasped her hands behind her back, pushed her hips forward and twisted to and fro. Her eyes twinkled. She could barely conceal how pleased with herself she was.

Mac had to stop himself from laughing.

He turned the tyet over in his fingers. "This bird… It's a heron, right?"

"Yes, the Bennu bird."

"Bennu?"

"The god of Time, among other things. It's just tradition to put it on the reverse side of certain amulets, that's all."

The god of Time…

He wanted to ask more but Aisha seemed in a hurry to go. She kept glancing around as if they were being watched.

Taking Mac by the elbow, she led him into the shade of the covered walkway. "Come on, we need to hurry so that we can get a head start."

"A head start?"

"On Ptolemy's band of spying brats."

They hurried along the walkway to the south end of the gardens where a gate led through to the Royal Stables.

Despite his reservations about horse riding, Mac's spirit soared and somehow he managed to resist the temptation to hold her hand and skip.

Ptolemy was fuming. From his private balcony, high above the Royal Gardens, he watched the retreating figures stroll shoulder to shoulder across the gardens toward the covered walkway where he lost them in shadow. Aisha's back had been to him but he was certain he'd seen her present the stranger with a gift then lean in and kiss him. It was a long kiss. Ptolemy couldn't believe his eyes. His stomach knotted with rage and a burning sensation swept across his chest, up his neck and into his cheeks. He paced back and forth. He would make them both pay. How dare they insult Pharaoh!

A plan started to form. A sinister smile stretched his lips. Perhaps he had figured out a way to gain back favour with Pothinus whilst at the same time seeing to it that those traitors got what they deserved.

The original plan to burn down the library was sound. He wasn't sure that they could still frame Caesar for it. That part had been compromised somehow. But it seemed they had a new scapegoat in the form of a glass-eyed outsider. It was perfect. No one knew a thing about him. He suddenly appears out of nowhere in the very same week that the library burns to the ground and then disappears. Making him disappear would be easy. Evidence linking the stranger to the fire would be conveniently found at the scene of the crime and Pothinus' propaganda machine would go to work on the masses, claiming that the foreigner was an agent for Cleopatra's campaign against their beloved Egypt. Aisha would be named as an accomplice and publicly disgraced. Or maybe she would perish in the flames. He wasn't too concerned with the details.

Ptolemy nodded slowly. It was beautiful. Genius! All he had to do was find a minute alone with the stranger.

Just then the doorman announced the arrival of a messenger and ushered him into the lounge. The messenger knelt at the Pharaoh's feet and handed him the urgent report from the library's Chief Administrator. They were dismissed with a wave of his royal hand and Ptolemy walked back onto the balcony. He read the letter twice then started to laugh. It seemed the gods were smiling on him at last.

Pothinus arrived a short time later. Ptolemy told him about the plan and waited while he considered things.

Pothinus clapped him on the shoulder. "You're not quite as stupid as you look."

Ptolemy beamed.

"Come, there is much to do and the day is dying," said Pothinus and swept out of the room with the pharaoh in tow.

"The day will not be the only thing to die this evening," Ptolemy replied.

"Patience, young Pharaoh, patience. Timing is everything."

Pothinus laughed. It was a chilling humourless laugh that echoed through the halls of the palace.

CHAPTER SIXTEEN

On horseback, they cut a swathe through the waist-high field of yellow wildflowers. A flotilla of butterflies and bugs ushered them along toward a rocky outcrop in the distance. Its outline against the horizon reminded Mac of a sleeping giant in profile, with its flat broad forehead and big pointy nose that rose skyward.

The sun felt good on his skin now that there was some distance between him and the stables, between him and the overwhelming embarrassment at his comical attempts to get on the horse. Who'd have thought it could be so difficult? He had those stirrup things and everything but still couldn't manage. Aisha's giggles were still ringing in his ears. His cheeks had burned hot as he'd been forced to admit to her that he'd never been on a horse before. She was quite shocked but was certainly more patient and encouraging than he'd thought possible.

Aisha had told the stable hand that they were heading east along the foreshore. They'd set off in that direction but once out of sight, had switched back to head southwest, beyond the city limits.

Mac stole a glance at her.

She was wearing a loose, pleated shift in sea green, belted tightly under the bust. Her shoulders peeped through wide, slitted sleeves that fell to her elbows. She sat straight and elegant in the saddle with her hands folded on the horse's withers. A layer of her hair was swept away from her face and fastened behind her head with a white ribbon. A warm breeze played with the locks that fell loosely down her back. She sat astride the saddle and rode barefoot, her gold anklets tinkling as the horse plodded along.

Even over the smell of the horses, Aisha's signature scent of cucumber, watermelon and jasmine wafted over him. It transported him to some other place. There was a certain freshness, a purity, a loveliness that was hard to describe. What *was* that stuff? If he could bottle it and find some way to get it back to the Now, he reckoned he could make a million bucks.

"It's just over that rise," said Aisha, interrupting his thoughts.

"You still haven't told me where we're going."

She grinned and glanced sideways at him. "You're going to like this, I think."

"The last time you said that, I had to walk up a million steps and nearly had heart failure."

Aisha laughed that deep, husky laugh that Mac loved so much.

"No steps, I promise."

Mac toyed with the tyet amulet. Its weight felt strange around his neck but he liked it. He studied Aisha's perfect artwork on its reverse side. "Tell me more about this Bennu bird."

"The Bennu is the god of Time and its divisions.

Actually, there was a Temple of the Bennu at Heliopolis that was known for its amazing time-keeping devices."

Mac glanced at the white band of skin at his wrist where his watch should have been. After the near mugging in the alley on that first day, he'd decided it might be better not to wear it in Old Alex.

"It is believed that the Bennu is the Heart-Soul of God, the Ba of Ra."

"Ba of Ra?" Mac thought it sounded like a nursery rhyme.

"Ba. You know, your..." Aisha paused, searching for the word. "Your personality; the aspect of your soul that makes you uniquely you." She turned and looked at Mac.

Her gaze seemed to peel away his physical self like layers of an onion until it felt like she was staring at his bare-naked soul.

Mac looked down and fidgeted with the reins. He didn't relax again until he felt her look away.

"Ba is the part of you that continues on after death," she explained.

Mac glanced across at her. She met his eyes briefly.

"I believe that," she said. "I sometimes still feel my mother around and it's..." She trailed off.

"Like she never really left?" Mac finished.

Aisha nodded. She let a few minutes slide before continuing.

"Ba also represents creation and renewal; transformation and resurrection. That's the whole reason for the coming festival. It's the annual Festival of Transformation."

She flashed a smile at him. It transformed her face. Mac wanted to comment that her smile was like the Ba of her face but felt it would somehow just come out wrong so he merely nodded.

Then his familiar 'eleven' dropped his brow. "It's a funny name. Bennu."

Aisha cleared her throat before launching into an enthusiastic explanation.

Mac had to suppress a smile. She was a nerd. A gorgeous, brilliant nerd. And she was in her element.

"It comes from the old Egyptian word 'weben', meaning to rise or to shine forth." In her passion for the subject, her arms traced an imaginary fountain of energy exploding into the air. She lifted her face to the sun. Her lashes rallied against its rays while her smile flashed white. "Don't you think that's just beautiful?"

"Yes," was Mac's breathy reply. He couldn't take his eyes off her.

"It also means 'he who is created of himself'. The ancient Egyptian creation myth tells that the Bennu created itself; that it burst forth from the heart of Osiris as a living symbol of God. It tells of the first dawn and how the Bennu bird stood on a lone rock, surrounded by the primeval waters that covered the world. Its cry heralded the beginning of time, what is and what is not to be."

Mac had goosebumps. It was his dream exactly – the lone heron on a rock surrounded by water. He recalled the strange slideshow of world events that had streamed from the bird's cry; the slideshow with its nightmarish ending that still haunted him.

Aisha leaned closer. "It is also said that the Bennu bird offers unhindered passage through the Underworld. Legend has it that it appears every five hundred years but only to a select few. If you see it, it means you've been chosen to play a role in the destiny of the planet; the transformation of the world."

"When did it last appear?"

Aisha burst out laughing. "It's just a story, silly!"

Mac immediately felt stupid. "I know that."

His reddening ears hadn't escaped Aisha's attention and she hurriedly added: "But you never know, it could be true. The truth is stranger than folk stories, as they say."

"We have a similar saying," said Mac, brushing aside his embarrassment.

They fell silent.

The flowers and wild grasses petered out into sparse ground cover, which eventually gave way to hard rocky earth as they neared the outcrop.

Aisha eased her horse to a halt at the base of a massive red rock and dismounted gracefully, but not without sporting a fleeting view of her long shapely legs. An exotic-looking tattoo ringed her left thigh.

Mac's heart skipped a beat.

She patted her horse and turned to Mac. "It's just through there. See that gap in the rock?" She pointed to a thin vertical shadow that he would never have spotted as an opening.

Aisha held Mac's horse steady while he dismounted. It was a little better than his attempts to get on but still managed to elicit a giggle from Aisha when his shoe got caught in the stirrup and he had to hop on one foot as the horse skittered and shied.

Aisha cast a furtive glance back across the field behind them. Satisfied they hadn't been followed, she led Mac through the gap in the rock wall, horses in tow. Their hooves clattered on the stony ground as they entered the narrow cleft. The deep shade was cool and refreshing. They followed the path downwards. The cleft was a blind curve which meant that, apart from the sky above, rocky walls to each side, and the shiny rump of Aisha's horse in front, he couldn't see where they were heading until a few paces further on where the cleft gave way to open ground once more.

Mac caught his breath as he pulled his horse alongside Aisha's. "Almighty freakin' Isis..." he breathed.

Aisha grinned.

They were in a forgotten world. The high rock wall they were standing against rimmed a semicircular oasis that sloped away to fields in the west. Millennia ago, the site had been home to a huge stone temple. Weather-worn hieroglyphics wound their way around great hypostyle columns that bulged at the base and tapered at the top. The columns towered above them and cast eerie shadows in the afternoon sunlight. The roof was long gone and many of the columns lay in piles of rubble amid lush grass that sprouted up between the cracked flooring. A natural spring bubbled up from the earth and spilled into its own catchment of smooth stone. The original temple basin crafted around it had disintegrated entirely, leaving the water to its own designs. A stand of tall palms clustered around the spring. As the trees had grown, slabs of stone flooring had been thrust aside and lay crumbled against their trunks. A lonely wind whistled and weaved its way among the ruins.

Aisha dropped her horse's reins and let him saunter off to graze. Mac did the same.

"What is this place?" Mac whispered.

"No one knows for sure. These days it's just known as the Sleeping Giant's Temple but it's ancient. From the Reign of the Gods."

So, he wasn't the only one who thought the rocky outcrop looked like a sleeping giant. He knew his Ancient Egyptian timeline well enough to know that the period known as the Reign of the Gods pre-dated their recorded history which started at around three thousand years BC. That placed it somewhere more than five thousand years before Mac's time.

He let out a low whistle. "That is *old*!"

"You said you like old things," Aisha said with a flourish of hands. "Well, they don't get much older than this."

Mac shook his head in wonder.

"Rumour has it that this temple was somehow connected to Isis. It is said that the flowing spring here is her eternal river of tears for her beloved Osiris in the World of the Dead," said Aisha.

Mac's Egyptian mythology was a bit rusty but he was pretty sure Isis had been married to Osiris. He couldn't recall the details. He'd have to ask Ru when he got back.

Aisha crouched beside the spring. "It is said that this water has magical powers."

"Powers?"

"Yes. To drink from it gives you the ability to speak with your loved ones on the other side."

She held her hair back with one hand and scooped a handful of water into her mouth. "I don't know if that's true but the water tastes good."

Mac squatted beside her. He drank. It really did taste good.

"Who else knows about this place?" he asked.

"A few of the locals. It doesn't hold much interest for most people. It was plundered of anything valuable centuries ago."

They wandered in and out of the huge colonnades. There was a strangeness to the place – a subtle hum of ancient energy that still lingered there. Mac trailed his hands across the glyphs and stones, his fingers like organic antennae trying to pick up some signal from a long forgotten past. Whispers – voices only he could hear – hung on the air, desperate to tell their stories. Shimmers and flickers of light danced on the edge of his vision, ghostly traces of what once was.

Mac had visited countless temples and ruins but nothing matched this. He wasn't sure why. There were bigger and better temples all over Egypt but this one seemed to exist apart from them entirely. It was circular for a start. That was highly unusual. But there was something else.

He studied the curved rock wall that rose up behind the ruins. It was higher than the massive columns and slightly concave near the top. It looked as though the temple had been deliberately set against the protection of the rock face. He squinted, deep in thought. It was almost as if the temple had once been mostly underground but open on the western side. That in itself was unusual given that most important buildings in ancient Egypt faced east. He wondered why the westerly aspect was significant, if it was at all.

He glanced across at Aisha. She moved gracefully among the shadows, billowing green fabric and wild hair in her wake. Mac leaned against a pillar and watched.

She was haunting. She was beautiful. She was Pharaoh's…

He swallowed hard and turned away.

He looked up and tried to picture what the place would

have looked like in its day with a roof and perhaps even a mound of earth covering it from the rear. He caught his breath. "No way..."

His mind raced. He remembered snatches of a conversation he'd overheard between his father and Ru. They'd mentioned something about a 'holy mound' in connection with the famed Lost Tomb of Osiris.

For more than a century, archaeologists had argued over whether or not the mythic tomb of the god of the Underworld even existed. Many had devoted their entire careers to the fruitless search for it based on an obscure reference in an ancient text alluding to its existence. Some believed that the gods weren't gods at all but were, in fact, extraterrestrials – the original rulers or founders of Egypt long, long ago.

Mac wondered. If this turned out to be the 'holy mound', the Lost Tomb of Osiris, then it would be the biggest discovery since Howard Carter found Tutankhamun's tomb.

His hands were trembling slightly as he ran them over the carved hieroglyphics in search of clues.

He smelled her before he saw her.

"So what do you think?" asked Aisha, sidling up to him.

"It's incredible. I wish my father could see this."

It was then that he remembered the camera. He slipped his hand in his pocket and pulled it out. He grinned at the girl. "Now it's my turn to show you something."

He opened his palm to reveal the camera. Even though he knew most people these days used their smartphones as cameras, his dad still insisted on using compact digital cameras on the dig. He wasn't entirely sure why. Probably for security reasons but Mac didn't even own a smartphone so it didn't matter anyway.

Aisha stared at the shiny metal box with the string attached. "What is it?"

Mac didn't answer. Instead, he pressed the 'ON' button. With a little whirring sound, the lens cover slid back and the camera came to life.

Aisha gasped.

He held the camera up, framed Aisha within the viewfinder, and pressed the button. She squealed when the automatic flash went off.

"It's okay," said Mac, reaching for her arm. "Here. See this?"

Their cheeks were almost touching as he leaned in to show her the display screen on the back of the camera. Her perfume was overpowering. He blinked hard to concentrate. He slid the switch into Review mode and a crystal-clear image of a stunned girl with huge green eyes filled the screen.

Aisha squealed again, this time with delight. "Magic! I love magic!" She bounced up and down, clapping her hands.

"It's not magic. It's science."

Aisha laughed. "Of course it's magic. But, gods of the Underworld, how did you do it? Oh, wait. You can't tell me, can you? It's a secret but –"

"It's no secret and it's not magic. It's just science, you know… technology. It's called a camera." He used the English word.

She repeated it as best she could but somehow it just sounded funny coming out of her mouth.

"Almost everyone in my… my part of the world has one."

"But?" Aisha scrunched her nose up and shook her head. "But that's impossible." Her hands were raised, palms up, in a gesture of absolute incredulity. "How do you catch just a little piece of time and keep it in a small box? It has to be a magic trick."

Mac laughed. "No, Aisha. Anyone can do it. You try."

He handed her the camera. She took it in trembling hands as if she were holding something delicate but mildly disgusting – a frog perhaps. Mac positioned himself behind her left shoulder and reached his arms around either side of her to steady the camera in her hands. He held her gently by her wrists, careful not to press her bangles into her skin.

He could feel the warmth of her back against his chest. Her hair tickled his face as he leaned over her shoulder. He could see the little chocolate moon on her cheek out of the corner of his eye and fought the urge to press his lips to it.

"Look at that square. See? You can see whatever the camera sees through that square."

He moved her arms enough for her to notice the scene through the viewfinder change. They were facing west. Mac tilted the camera a fraction to frame up the spectacular sunset on the horizon. He lightly tapped her index finger with his. "Now press this button – see this little circle?"

She moved an ink-stained finger over the button. Nothing happened.

"Harder. Press it. That's it."

The camera clicked and buzzed. Aisha shrieked and almost dropped it.

Mac couldn't help laughing. "You did it! Here, let's have a look."

He flicked to Review and the screen showed a colourful but slightly blurry image of the sunset.

"Oh!" Aisha clapped her hands.

She was almost entirely encircled in Mac's arms. She

could feel his warm laughter on her neck. It raised goosebumps down her spine and made her shiver. There was nowhere in the world she would rather have been at that moment. She knew that if she turned to face him, they would be just inches apart. But she stood there, staring at the little magic box that held the sunset.

"How long does the time stay in there? Is it held forever or does it get out?"

Mac laughed again. "No, it's…" He trailed off.

It was actually a lot harder to explain than he'd thought. In a strange way, Aisha was right. A photograph was like a little piece of captured time; an instant snatched, stolen from its proper place and held forever.

"It's just a picture. You know, like a painting. It's just the exact image of a thing. The camera just sort of records it really fast somehow."

"Why is it blurry? Was time moving too fast to catch?"

"No, silly. *You* were moving too fast." He aimed a playful jab at Aisha's ribs.

"Ow!" She doubled over.

He caught her around the waist. They both laughed. Mac's heart dashed away in his chest and his insides flipped. Through her thin cotton shift, his fingertips pressed into the soft layer of skin at her waist. Underneath, he could feel lean muscle from many hours of horse riding.

"Here, try again," he said, straightening her up.

They repeated the process, although Mac was barely aware of the camera in Aisha's hands. He felt almost lightheaded. Cheek to cheek, they reviewed the perfect image of a palm tree silhouetted against an orange sunset.

"That's beautiful," said Aisha.

Mac slipped the camera from between her fingers and stepped around to face her. She was still smiling, her face and hair outlined brilliantly in amber. He zoomed in, snapped a photo then leaned in to show her.

"*That's* beautiful," he whispered into her hair.

Aisha blushed but said nothing.

She took the camera from him with a coy smile. Turning to face him, she stood with feet apart, took aim and slowly pressed the button. She was grinning as she lowered the camera.

"Okay, we're even," said Mac, snatching the camera off her with mock irritation.

"Let me see, let me see," she begged.

They both laughed at a smiling image of Mac with his eyes half-closed.

"You look like you've had too much good wine!"

"Wait, wait. Delete."

Plink! The image was gone.

"What happened?" asked Aisha, mystified.

"I got rid of it."

She rolled her eyes. "If only *you* were that easy to get rid of," she teased.

Mac wrapped an arm around her shoulders and pulled her close until they bumped heads. "Smile!"

He held the camera up in front of them with one hand and took a selfie. It was a winner. Their smiling faces glowed warm in the afternoon light. Aisha's eyes sparkled and her hair was wild. Even Mac had to admit he looked better than alright; the reflections on his glasses weren't too bad and the light had caught his dimples perfectly.

"Not so easy to get rid of now," he said and elbowed her.

Aisha was more serious as she continued to stare at the screen. Finally, she asked if she could keep it.

Mac considered it for a second. He could leave the camera with her and still have his camera on him when he arrived back in the Now but he wasn't sure if it would have any images on it. There was no point in Aisha keeping the camera. She couldn't charge it or download the images or anything. Besides, it would most likely attract the wrong sort of attention.

"I'll make you a copy of the picture," he said.

"You can get it out of the box?" Aisha sounded amazed.

Mac nodded. "It's like a drawing on paper. You'll see. I'll bring you one, I promise."

"Promise?"

Mac nodded again. "But it's our secret."

Aisha pressed her lips together and tied an invisible bow over them with her fingers.

Mac chuckled. "Lean up against that column. I want to get another picture of you."

Aisha did as she was told. She turned out to be quite the poser as Mac snapped away until the daylight faded so far that the flash was too bright and the background too dark.

"That was fun," said Aisha as the pair of them sank to a soft patch of grass between the rubble. Aisha sat with her dress pulled down over her knees and her arms wrapped around them. "I think I'd like where you come from."

Mac smiled in the near darkness. It was a rueful, sad smile. Every now and then the hopeless reality of the situation hit home. She would never see where he came from. He wasn't sure he could live with that.

Aisha watched his smile fade and the numeral two between his brows return.

"So, are you still keen to get into the library's Isolation Room tonight?" she said. She knew it was wrong, wrong, wrong… But she also knew it was the hook that might make him stay.

Mac's heart leapt. He'd forgotten all about it. "Sure!"

"Only if you're game, that is," she said.

"That sounds like a challenge."

She laughed. "It is."

"Oh, I'm game."

"Really?" She leaned against him playfully. "How game?"

Mac's heart thundered. "Game enough."

Slowly, he leaned toward her. Aisha's smile dissolved into an expectant half-pucker. Her eyes closed after a single slow-motion blink. Their lips were almost touching. Mac could smell the sweetness of her breath.

SWOOSH!

Rushing air… A black shadow…

Aisha screamed.

In an instant, Mac pushed her to the ground and rolled on top of her, shielding her from attack.

Massive wings beat the air above their heads and a loud cry echoed off the rock walls. The black horse whinnied and reared before bolting into the darkness.

Then the thing was gone.

They lay trembling in the grass.

"What *was* that?" Aisha sounded close to tears.

"I don't know," he said, rolling off her.

Whatever it was, Mac was sure it was the same bird-creature that had swooped him at the lighthouse yesterday and on the hill above the burning library the night of the fire. He decided not to mention it.

Mac took Aisha by the hand and pulled her to her feet.

"I hope I didn't hurt you," he said.

"No, no. Not at all."

She dusted off her robe as she blushed in the dark. If she hadn't been so utterly terrified, she probably would have thrilled to such a close encounter with the handsome foreigner.

"It's dark. We should get you home. Your grandfather will be getting worried."

"No, he'll be fine. He'll assume I'm with Ptolemy." A hot guilty rush swept over her. "But you're right. We should get going."

After whistling and calling for the black horse, they abandoned the search, mounted Aisha's horse and headed back across the fields toward the city.

"He'll make his way back to the stables when he's ready, no doubt," said Aisha.

She tried to sound light-hearted but the mood had changed. She was anxious to get home. The moon had risen, washing the ocean of rippling wildflowers in blue and silver.

The strange incident had interrupted a kiss that should never have been about to happen. Never mind how much she'd wanted it to. What was she thinking? It was insane! The interruption was a sign; she was sure of it. It was a sign that she was not to fall victim to her feelings for the newcomer. She resolved to get a hold of her head – her *heart* – and put a healthy distance between them. That is, just as soon as they got home and she could no longer feel his warmth at her back or his arms around her waist or smell the sunlight in his shirt and on his skin. She breathed deeply of the night air and nudged her horse into a canter.

Mac tightened his arms around her waist as the horse changed gait. Aisha's hair whipped him in the face, not that he minded in the least. Every so often her foot brushed against his shin. He wasn't even sure why that should be such a big deal but he found himself inching his legs forward in the hope they'd make contact again.

Way too soon, in Mac's opinion, they were back at the Royal Stables. Aisha seemed preoccupied with getting the horse fed and comfortable, having dismissed the stable hand on their arrival.

"So," started Mac. "What time do you want to meet later?"

Aisha stopped brushing the horse.

He lowered his voice. "Isolation Room?"

"Oh. Um… Look, do you mind if we maybe do that another time?"

"Sure," said Mac, swallowing a golf ball of disappointment. "I should probably get going anyway."

Aisha turned back to the horse and brushed harder, determined to fight off the threat of tears. "Okay," she replied without looking back.

Mac was suddenly awkward. He turned to go then turned back. "Aisha?"

She stopped brushing but didn't turn around.

"Thanks for today. It was… good." He'd wanted to tell her it had been the best day of his life.

Aisha bit her lip. "My pleasure," she managed to get out before a wave of silent tears choked her.

She listened to his footsteps recede then leant her

forehead against the rump of the horse. Tears rolled down her cheeks. What was she going to do?

It was already too late to not love him.

The white ribbon shone silver-blue in the moonlight. Mac stooped to pick it up. His fingertips traced the length of it. He spun back towards the stables to give it back to Aisha. As he reached the door, he could see her wiping her eyes with the ball of her hand. She looked like she was crying.

Mac shrank back to the shadows. His first instinct was to rush over and comfort her but somehow he figured he was the cause of it all. He wasn't sure what he'd said or done to upset her. She'd just suddenly changed. Maybe the whole bird thing had really rattled her. He sensed it was more than that though.

He watched as she set down the feed bucket and crossed to the torch mounted on the far wall. She took it and left via the rear door.

Mac was confused.

He held the ribbon in his hands, staring at it in the moonlight for a long while. He'd never used psychometry for snooping before, except maybe that one time with his cousin and the shark's tooth but that had been unintentional. Was it wrong to pry into Aisha's personal affairs? After all, he wasn't even sure if it were possible to make an object 'talk' against its will so he wasn't really doing anything wrong. Wondering if the ribbon would reveal any secrets, he eventually closed his hands over it and took a deep breath.

Fleeting images of Aisha flashed before his closed eyes like a living mosaic.

He saw a crowded stall in the marketplace, packed with pretty things. He could see her hands hover over a selection of different coloured ribbons that wavered in the breeze. He could *feel* her internal dilemma. *The gold one or the white one?*

Gone.

Skip to an image of Aisha's reflection in a mirror as she tied the ribbon in her hair that morning. He felt the texture of her soft shiny hair in her hands – *his* hands. He felt excited.

Gone.

Skip to the image of Mac's face – *his own face!* – just visible in the dusk, getting closer, lips slightly parted, his eyes locked with hers – *his*. He could feel the electric edge to her anticipation, her eagerness. It was *his* eagerness now. He could feel the power of her attraction to him as if it were his own. SWOOSH! Hot terror…

Gone.

Moonlight shining on flowers… The smell of the horse… The warmth at her back… Guilt, regret… Something underneath it.

And then he was sure.

Aisha loved him.

Mac opened his eyes. His heart pounded with elation. He had to find her. He wasn't even sure what he was going to do but there was no way he was heading home just yet.

CHAPTER SEVENTEEN

ELCOR GLANCED UP from his soup as Aisha opened the door to their modest quarters.

"Hello, Petal. I'm surprised to see you here. I thought you were attending that function at the palace tonight."

Aisha gasped and clapped her hand to her mouth. She'd forgotten all about it. Pharaoh was hosting a dinner party for visiting dignitaries and she was expected to be there. "What's the time?"

Without bothering to wait for an answer, she flew across the room and began rifling through a rack of robes. She knew she was late. Ptolemy would be fuming. Her stomach knotted.

"What am I going to wear? And, grace of the Muses, my hair!"

She dragged a hand through her unruly hair and pulled a blue and gold garment from the rack.

"Serapis damn it! There's a bead missing on this one."

She shoved it back on the rack and grabbed a yellow one, heavily beaded around the scooped neckline. "And this one's too itchy. I'm not wearing it again." She tossed it over her shoulder and kept hunting.

"The red one's always nice," said Elcor and slurped his soup.

Aisha made a face. It had been a gift from Ptolemy. It was a gorgeous dress worth a fortune, the colour only royalty could afford. She knew Ptolemy would be pleased to see her wear it, which made her want to wear it even less. She didn't have time to satisfy her rebellious streak so she snatched it off its hanger and slipped behind the curtain that served as a dressing room. She emerged a minute later and rushed to the mirror in the corner of the room. Trembling hands made certain her attempts at applying eye make-up were a disaster.

She swore.

"Calm down, girl. Sweet Isis, what's got into you?" asked Elcor.

He saw she was crying and came to stand behind her. Aisha hung her head while her shoulders heaved with each sob. Elcor picked up the brush from her dressing table and dragged it through her tangled hair with gentle strokes. He said nothing until her sobs became mere sniffles.

"Whatever is the matter, Petal?"

Aisha just shook her head.

Elcor braided her hair, as he'd done since she was a little girl. He handed her the hairpins. "Here, I'll let you work your magic."

Aisha piled the braids on top of her head in an elegant formal style and pinned them in place. Elcor handed her a handkerchief to wipe her nose and eyes. The second attempt with the eyeliner was much more successful.

She looked at her grandfather in the mirror as he fastened her necklace from behind.

"Thankyou, Grandfather," she whispered.

He placed his hands on her shoulders. "As always, you look more beautiful than a thousand sunsets. Pharaoh is well outshone."

She forced a smile.

Elcor became serious. "Is there something you'd like to talk about?"

Aisha shook her head. She simply turned and hugged him. "I'd better get going."

She slipped on her sparkly sandals and left.

Elcor remained in the doorway, uttering a prayer of protection after his granddaughter. He cursed that damned papyrus and he cursed himself for exposing her to it.

"Gods of the Underworld, what have I done?"

Mac sat perched in a tree, absently winding the white ribbon around his fingers as he watched the scene through the palace window.

Aisha sat beside Ptolemy at a long dining table. Mac could see the back of Pothinus' head opposite the pharaoh. The entire length of the table wasn't visible but there seemed to be quite a number of guests. Conversation buzzed and cutlery clinked. Servants scurried back and forth with that peculiar domestic invisibility which made them seem like part of the furniture.

Aisha was breathtaking. She wore a stunning scarlet robe and her hair was piled on top of her head, exposing her slender neck. Her bearing was regal. She indeed looked as though she belonged at Pharaoh's side, a true queen of Egypt.

Mac's heart sank. Who was he kidding? Why was he torturing himself like this? The girl was so far out of his league it was ridiculous, yet he couldn't have dragged himself away from that window if he'd tried. He brightened and shrugged in the darkness. Besides, he had the inside tip; he knew she loved him, however deranged her thinking may be.

He ran the ribbon between his fingers again. He'd put it in his pocket and set off from the stables in search of Aisha. As he'd rounded the corner of the library's living quarters, he'd glimpsed her running along the path toward the palace, skirts bunched high in one hand, hair kept in place with the other.

He'd hesitated not more than a second before deciding to follow her.

It had been surprisingly easy to slip past the guards stationed around the palace perimeter. He couldn't believe they were so lax, considering the Roman navy was at anchor in the harbour and there was talk of war. He'd ditched his white shirt for fear it would be too easily spotted in the moonlight and had stuck to the shadows until he'd found a suitable tree to climb.

Bare-chested, Mac shifted uncomfortably in his treetop vantage point. He wasn't sure how long he'd been there. He tried not to think about how much time had elapsed in the Now. So long as Gabby kept her end of the deal, he'd be fine. Still, he didn't want to push his luck. He wasn't ready to leave just yet though. And so he watched.

Aisha looked sad. She looked bored also, but mostly just sad. She made polite conversation with nearby guests and flashed that incredible smile of hers on cue but it didn't quite reach her eyes. She barely touched her food. Ptolemy ignored her entirely, almost pointedly so. His entire attention was focused on the plunging neckline of the curvy blonde sitting to his left. More than once Aisha had noticed the direction of his gaze, had rolled her eyes in disgust and reached for her wine glass.

Mac found his dislike for Ptolemy quickly turning to outright loathing. The guy was a creep.

The camera in Mac's pocket was digging into his hip. He wriggled it free and looped the string around his wrist. He turned it on and flicked through the images from the temple ruins.

He sighed as he zoomed in on the shot of the two of them, heads together, until Aisha's emerald eyes filled the screen. He *had* to be with her. There *had* to be a way. Surely life just wasn't this cruel…

Mac fumbled and almost dropped the camera. Thanks to the loop around his wrist, he recovered it but not before banging it against the trunk of the tree, setting the flash off.

He froze. There was no sound from the guards below. He turned his attention back to the feast. Everyone was engrossed in conversation… except Aisha. She was staring directly at him, eyes wide. There was no way she could see him but she must have seen the flash go off. She would know exactly what it was.

Mac held his breath.

He watched as Aisha politely excused herself and disappeared from view. Ducking and bobbing his head to try and get a better view between the branches, he spotted her on the balcony moments later. He shifted his weight and wrapped himself around a branch that very nearly reached the balcony railing.

Aisha glanced over her shoulder then leaned out over the railing, peering into the dark.

"Mac?" It was a hoarse whisper. "Is that you?"

"No. It's your friendly neighbourhood man-spider."

The Greek translation of the twentieth century comic hero hadn't come out quite right but Aisha shook her head and laughed all the same. She covered her mouth and looked back over her shoulder toward the party. No one had even missed her.

"Grace of the Muses, what are you *doing* here? Are you trying to get yourself killed?"

"I um.... You dropped your ribbon." He held it up.

Aisha was incredulous. "You risked your life for *that*?"

"Aisha... I just... I had to see you again." There, it was out. He exhaled with relief.

She shot a look back to the doorway. "Shhh! Someone's coming."

It was Ptolemy. Aisha spun to face him.

"What are you doing out here? Your absence is conspicuous." His tone was demanding.

"Just needed some fresh air. I'm surprised you even noticed I was gone, what with all the 'distraction'."

"Play nice, Aisha. Once you're my wife you'll have to learn to get along with all my *other* wives. Get used to it."

Mac watched Aisha's chest heave with fury.

She lowered her voice. "I'll *never* be your wife. Get used to *that*, Your Majesty."

Ptolemy snapped. He seized her around the throat with one hand and pushed her hard up against the railing so her back arched painfully. Aisha's tiny hands clawed at the grip around her throat. The pharaoh leaned over her so he was just inches from her face. She scrunched up her nose at the stench of alcohol on his breath.

He bared his gritted teeth in a snarl. "You will do what Pharaoh says. Let's just say it would be in your grandfather's best interests. Wouldn't want him to suddenly find himself out of favour with the gods now, would we?"

Mac launched himself over the railing and slammed the camera into Ptolemy's jaw. The pharaoh dropped like a rock. Mac stood over him, puffing.

"Are you okay?"

Aisha simply nodded, open-mouthed.

Mac stared at the unconscious pharaoh. He couldn't believe it had actually worked. He had his cousin to thank for that one. Corey was right into street fighting movies. Mac had endured hours of them when he'd spent a week with his cousins a few years back. Violence didn't come naturally to him and he'd found all the blood and the bone crunching a bit nauseating. Corey had explained in detail how a certain spot on the jaw line, if hit hard enough, would short-circuit the brain, knocking the person out. He'd then proceeded to demonstrate on Mac before Luke had come to the rescue.

Mac allowed himself a satisfied smile.

"Holy Serapis, what have you done?" breathed Aisha. "We have to get out of here." Her eyes were wide with fear.

Mac was suddenly aware of how much danger they were in. "Quick."

He led her to the railing and swung out onto the branch to face her. He steadied himself with one hand and reached the other out toward her. "Here, take my hand."

She hesitated. Voices neared the balcony doors. She hitched up her dress and stepped over the railing onto the branch. It sagged beneath their combined weight. She whimpered.

"It's okay. I've got you."

With one arm wrapped around the trunk, he held her by the hand and drew her against the safety of his bare chest. He could feel her heart hammering through the thin fabric of her gown as she clung to him.

From the safety of the shadows, they watched Pothinus and a couple of laughing guests barrel out the doors onto the balcony, wine goblets in hand.

A woman screamed.

"Gods of the Underworld!"

"Guards!" bellowed Pothinus. He nudged the unconscious boy with his toe.

Ptolemy groaned.

Pothinus squatted over the pharaoh and sniffed. He shook his head. "The boy never could hold his wine. Pathetic…"

They watched in silence as Ptolemy was carried back inside and the doors were closed.

Aisha breathed a sigh of relief. Still trembling, she let her body go limp against Mac's. She closed her eyes and dropped her chin while she soaked up the feeling of being wrapped in those arms; of being held securely against that hard chest that smelled like salty sunshine.

A shiver ran through her as she felt his lips brush against her forehead, soft as a butterfly. Her eyes opened but she didn't move. Moonlight filtered through the leaves to fall on the tyet necklace she'd given him. She put her finger on it. She noticed the rise and fall of his skin across the little hollow between his collarbones as he swallowed. Her heart beat harder.

She pulled back to look up into his eyes.

"I know I said this tyet symbolises resurrection from the dead but you needn't test its powers." Her smiled glowed blue-white in the moonlight. "You're going to need more than costume jewellery when Ptolemy's finished with you."

Mac chuckled in the dark. "He's got to catch me first. Come on. Let's get out of here before the guards grow a brain."

They scrambled down the tree and stood motionless against the trunk, listening. There was no sign of the guards. They ventured into the moonlight.

"HALT!" A voice boomed behind them. "Identify yourselves!"

They froze.

Mac palmed the camera still tethered to his wrist and spun to face the guard. He raised the camera and pressed the button. The flash was blinding.

"Aaargh!" The guard threw his hands up in front of his face.

"Run!" Mac grabbed Aisha by the hand and sprinted into the night.

"AFTER THEM!"

Angry shouts rose above the footsteps that pounded the earth behind them. They ran on. By the time they reached the closed gates to the Royal Gardens, their breath came in ragged gasps.

CLANG!

Mac rammed his shoulder into the gates. A bolt of pain shot down his arm. They were locked. He tried again. It was no use. The guards were gaining.

"This way! Hurry!" said Aisha.

She led him along the wall until they came to a small

wooden hatch at its base. She dropped to her knees, unlatched it and crawled through. Mac wriggled through after her.

Mac grunted with difficulty as he squeezed through the small opening.

"Shhh!"

They struggled to their feet amid dense undergrowth. Mac couldn't see a thing. Spindly branches slapped him in the face as he crashed through the foliage after Aisha until they stumbled onto open lawn.

She took his hand. "This way!"

They dashed across the courtyard and along the darkened walkways. Aisha knew the place like the back of her hand. She slipped through an unlocked door into what looked like some kind of lecture hall, an amphitheatre of sorts. Moonlight streamed through the windows on the far side, plunging the rest of the space into relative blackness. It was silent and spooky. Aisha hurried down one of the sloping aisles toward a central dais at the far end, which featured a large timber lectern for the guest speakers.

"They went in there!" The guards' voices echoed in the stillness as they barged through the door.

Mac and Aisha dropped to their knees and crawled between the pews.

"Go, go, go!" hissed Aisha, pummelling Mac's rear end in front of her. They crawled along on their hands and knees.

"Spread out, men!"

The fugitives scurried in and out of the pews, sticking to the shadows. A torch flared. They dropped to their bellies and wriggled forward. They had almost reached the dais. Aisha unhooked a chunky gold earring and hurled it toward the opposite side of the room as hard as she could. The torchlight followed the clinking sound, giving them a few precious seconds of darkness to slip into one of the aisles.

"Follow me," Aisha whispered.

She bolted onto the dais and disappeared behind the lectern. Mac was hot on her heels. He was startled to find himself alone when he ducked behind it too. He was certain that was where she'd gone but there was no one there. Mac whipped his head around in search of her. A hand reached out of the shadows and touched his arm. He jumped.

"In here."

Aisha hauled him into a tiny cupboard inside the lectern and pulled the door shut behind them. They were wedged together in the cramped space. Aisha was sitting on Mac's leg, her body curled against his chest. It was completely black. Over the pounding of his own heart in his ears, Mac could hear Aisha's breathing. He could taste it. Her signature scent was overpowering in the closeness. Neither of them dared move.

Several sets of footsteps drew near their hiding spot. They could see the flickering torchlight through the thin crack that outlined the door. Both of them held their breath. Mac closed his eyes and braced himself for the busting.

"What is the meaning of this?" came an authoritative voice from the far end of the hall. Aisha cringed as she recognised her grandfather's voice.

"Intruders on the palace grounds, Chief. Thought we chased them in here."

There was some confused mumbling between the guards.

"Must have given us the slip, Chief. A thousand pardons I beg."

Elcor muttered something they couldn't hear and the guards clomped away.

Mac's leg was losing feeling by the time they heard the wooden doors at the main entrance slam shut. A few seconds ticked by before either of them moved. The skin on Mac's chest tingled as Aisha let out a relieved rush of air across it. Neither spoke. There was no need. They both knew how close they'd come to very real danger.

Aisha pushed open the cupboard door and tumbled out into the gloom. The air was suddenly cold on their clammy skin after their cramped hiding place.

"Where to now?"

"This way," Aisha replied, leading Mac by the hand to a door in the corner.

The faint glow of the moon outside gave them enough light to tiptoe down a series of corridors until they reached what looked like a solid wall. Aisha let go of Mac's hand and fumbled with a concealed lock. A secret door slid back with a low rumble. She stepped inside.

Moonlight streamed through a set of high windows. Mac could make out several desks and a wall of pigeonholed shelving, recently emptied of scrolls.

"The Isolation Room?" asked Mac. He suddenly felt uneasy.

"That's right. It's where all the really secret stuff is transcribed."

"Secret stuff?"

"You know, documents of… " She hesitated. "Of a sensitive nature. Politically volatile information or military operations. Controversial historical finds. That sort of thing. Only a couple of scribes have security clearance to work in here."

"And, let me guess, you're one of them."

It was light enough to see Aisha's smile flicker. She rubbed the tops of her arms. Now that she was in there, she couldn't wait to get out.

"Sorry, most of the scrolls worth seeing have already been moved to the underground vaults. Grandfather's orders."

"Of course," said Mac.

Aisha took a step closer. "But that's not what I wanted to show you."

Taking him by the hand, she led him past the desks to the corner of the room. She groped for the familiar cord and yanked. A ladder unfolded from the ceiling. Aisha climbed the ladder and opened a trapdoor in the ceiling. Mac followed her through it to emerge on the rooftop.

The night air was cool against his skin. Exhilaration rushed through him as he took a deep breath and looked around. The roof of the Isolation Room was part of the east wing of the library complex but was considerably lower than the Musaeum and the main library building itself.

They crossed to a set of rungs bolted to a wall. Aisha went up first, the soft fabric of her gown billowing against Mac's face. He stepped over the rim after her to find himself standing on the very top of the library. The vast space was bathed in moonlight, broken only by the rectangular opening that looked down onto the indoor pond below.

"Well?" cried Aisha as she spun in a circle, arms wide. She grinned. Her scarlet dress was almost purple in the blue light of the moon and her skin was luminous. The night's adventures had played havoc with her elegant up-style, leaving her hair a mass of wild tresses blowing in the breeze.

Mac couldn't speak. A strange upsurging of some unnamed emotion took the words away.

He rushed to her, sweeping her off her feet and into his arms. Her laughter filled the night as they spun around and around.

Mac lowered her to the ground and they stumbled about, dizzy and near breathless with laughter. They held hands and ran the length of the roof to the front of the library. They stood there, chests heaving, overlooking the city and its magnificent harbour. The lighthouse stood against a dark sea and a starry sky beyond. Mac thought it strange to overlook a city in near darkness. There were no lights save for the odd glow of torchlight here and there. He realised Aisha would never see the spectacle of city lights in her lifetime. It made him sad.

He turned to look at her. In a moment of undeniable clarity, he admitted to himself the real motivation behind that first return-trip to Alexandria – *Aisha*. It had never been anything else.

He gently pulled her across to stand in front of him, wrapping her up from behind, his face buried in her hair. He breathed in the scent that was to haunt him for a lifetime.

Aisha shivered but not from the cold. Her hands curled over the arms that enfolded her. She closed her eyes and let her head fall back against him, a white flag of surrender. She wasn't sure if they were swaying slightly or the earth was tilting beneath them.

Neither spoke. Only the whip and rustle of the wind in silk broke the silence. And right there in that single instant was forged a love that dwarfed them, transcending time and space; a love that mocked the intellect, eclipsing all reason. In that moment, two thousand years no longer separated them. They were one heartbeat, one breath.

Only a secret stood between them now.

"Aisha," he whispered.

She spun in his arms to face him.

He looked into her green eyes and gently brushed a piece of hair off her face to reveal the little chocolate moon. She glanced down, self-consciously tucking a strand of hair behind her ear. Mac was still staring at her when she looked up again.

"There's something you need to know."

He felt her body go rigid. Courage deserted him. He couldn't tell her. He didn't know how. He exhaled.

"What is it?" she pressed, her anxiety tugging on some invisible string that puckered her brow at the centre.

"We can't – "

"Shush." She pressed a finger to his lips. Whatever he was about to say was going to ruin the moment, she was sure of it. Let it wait. Disappointment was for tomorrow. She raised a fingertip to touch his left dimple.

"Did I mention you have nice cheek pits?" she said softly.

Mac rolled his eyes and grinned, exaggerating his dimples further. She was good. She'd swerved the moment perfectly, he noticed. Maybe she was right. Maybe it wasn't the right time to bring it up. Maybe he'd do well to wait until he'd found a way for them to be together before he told her the truth. There had to be way. He would find it. Somehow.

"Mac, I didn't get a chance to thank you. Ptolemy can be… difficult."

Anger flared on Mac's face. "Aisha, I swear, if he so much as–"

"He won't."

"But–"

"Because now I have you."

"Aisha, we can't–"

"We'll figure something out. We can hide. We can run away. Take me with you, back to your homeland. We can–"

Now it was his turn to shush her with a finger to her lips. He wanted so desperately to make it all come true, to make the 'happily-ever-after' part real. He shook his head as he gently reached up and unlaced her hands from behind his neck and held them in front. He opened his mouth to speak.

"Then tell me you don't love me," she cut in before he had a chance to say anything.

She stared up at him. Mac could make out the unmistakable sparkle of brimming tears, threatening to spill over any second.

"You don't understand," he said.

Aisha's bottom lip quivered, as a single tear breached the rim and rolled down her cheek. With a gentle hand, he tilted her chin up toward him. He used his thumb to wipe away the renegade tear that marred her lovely face.

"*Tell* me," she said. It was no more than a whisper.

He didn't answer.

Gently, he cupped her perfect jaw with one trembling hand, his fingertips coming to rest behind her earlobe. He studied her in the moonlight.

Beautiful…

He leaned closer.

Aisha held her breath. The bandages on Mac's hands were rough against her soft skin. Her legs started to shake as he leaned in and drew her to him. She closed her eyes and waited.

Mac kissed her ever so softly. Her lips were cold but the

space just beyond them was warm and sweet. The faint rush of air from her nostrils tickled his face. An inferno blazed from his core, igniting his blood, radiating to every nerve and fibre.

Reality was suspended. All sense of time and space was lost as they surrendered to that single moment.

They didn't notice the dark shadow that passed low overhead and swept out to sea.

Time didn't matter that night. It simply slipped away as they sat together on the rooftop, Aisha tucked up between Mac's knees, his chest and arms wrapped over her like a blanket as they gazed out to sea. They talked. They laughed. They kissed some more. But for the most part, they just sat in silence, clinging to each precious second together. Who knew what tomorrow would bring? Things were so much more complicated than they'd started out that morning and Aisha didn't even know the half of it. Each was absorbed in their own thoughts, still intensely aware of the other yet careful not to tarnish the magic with serious discussion. There would be plenty of time for that… Mac hoped.

The eastern sky was beginning to lighten when they finally untangled themselves from each other. The pre-dawn chill had eventually become too much and they made their way back through the Isolation Room, through the maze of corridors, to the living quarters. They stood outside Aisha's door in the darkness of the covered walkway.

"There's a vacant room two up from ours. You're more than welcome to stay there."

"Thanks anyway, but I'd better head back."

Aisha looked disappointed. She was obviously excited at the thought of having Mac stay so close. "But it's too dangerous for you to head back across town, what with everything that's happened. Stay here. You're safer on library grounds where Grandfather has some authority."

"More authority than Pharaoh?"

She looked at the ground.

Mac nudged her chin back up with his knuckle. "Aisha, look at me."

She raised her eyes to meet his.

"We're in deep… camel dung." He offered a lopsided smile in the dark. "Ptolemy doesn't scare me but I need to lie low for a while, for *your* safety more than mine."

"*My* safety? But–"

"Listen to me. We'll figure this out but we have to be smart about it, okay?"

"But just for tonight? Say you'll stay."

How could he refuse her? "Alright."

She led him a couple of doors down, practically skipping with joy. "It's not much but it's comfortable," she said, pushing the door open and stepping inside.

There was just enough light through the window to make out a small bed with a blanket folded neatly at the end and a washstand in the corner.

Mac was uncomfortable. This made things complex. He really had to be getting back to the Now. He wasn't at all sure of the situation there which made it all the more difficult to ensure he was back in Old Alex by the time Aisha stuck her head through the door the next morning. It may prove tricky to slip away from the dig. Staying in his imaginary lodgings on the edge of town doing his imaginary research at least bought him some time the next day.

But it was too late. He'd already agreed to stay, albeit against his better judgement. He ran one hand through his hair, shoved the other in his pocket and bit his lip.

Aisha's smile was fading as she sensed his change in mood.

Mac stepped closer. The last thing he wanted to do was end such an incredible, crazy night on a bad note by upsetting her. He kissed her on the forehead. "Now, off to bed before your grandfather wakes up."

She hugged him and turned to go. "Paradise dreams. See you in the morning."

Mac swallowed hard and nodded. She paused in the doorway for a split second then disappeared. He closed the door behind her and plonked onto the bed with a huge sigh. "Paradise dreams…"

He took his glasses off, squeezed his eyes shut and worked his fingers into them before rubbing his palms across his forehead. He let his arm flop back onto the pillow. The low ceiling stared back at him. He was exhausted. It would be so easy to just drift off to sleep but he was anxious to get back home.

Focusing his mind on the Now, he succumbed to the quickening and slipped into the void.

CHAPTER EIGHTEEN

"MACKEENLEE! MACKEENLEE! WAKE up proper!"

Gabriella's panicked face came into focus.

"You are in beeg trouble. *I* am in beeg trouble."

Mac sat up. He held his head and squinted while he tried to orientate himself. It was daylight. He was in Gabby's tent sitting on her cot.

"What time is it?"

"Almost noon!"

Mac swore. "My dad– "

"He no is happy."

He stood up. His head throbbed and he sat back down.

Gabby steadied him with a hand on his shoulder. "You okay?"

He nodded. "What did you tell him?"

She looked sheepish. With her shoulders stuck in a shrug, she waved her hands about and worked her mouth but no sound came out.

"Gabby…"

"I deedn't know what else to tell him."

"*What* did you tell him?" Mac's stomach twisted.

"I tell him we had some wine and you got drunked and passed out."

"*What!*" Mac leapt to his feet. "Gabby! He's gonna kill me!"

"No, he keel me first."

Mac's outrage deflated as he realised Gabby had indeed taken the fall for him and in no small way. He put his hands on his hips and stared at the canvas ceiling, thinking. Leon would be furious. He was not a big drinker himself and was strict about under age drinking. Mac had not so much as had a sip of alcohol in his sixteen years – not that his father knew of anyway. He and his cousins had stolen a bottle of cooking sherry from the kitchen one time and had drunk it down at the river but they'd all vomited and had made a pact to keep it a secret. Mac had felt so bad after it that he had vowed never to drink again.

"Where is he now?"

"On the deeg with Ru."

Mac knew he'd have to face his father's wrath for something that never even happened; cop a punishment for something he didn't even do. He looked at Gabby. And, so would she, he thought.

"Gabby, I'm really sorry, honestly."

She shrugged. They stood in silence for a moment.

Gabby spoke first. "So did you kiss her or what?"

The 'eleven' between his brows vanished as Mac grinned wide but didn't answer. "I'd better go face the music."

He took a deep breath and smoothed his shirt which, he realised with mild surprise, he was still wearing.

"Do I look hungover?"

Gabby laughed. "You look like sheet."

CHAPTER NINETEEN

ALEXANDRIAN SUNSHINE STREAMED through the high windows of Ptolemy's royal quarters. The day was already hot. And so were tempers.

SMASH!

The red vase exploded off the wall.

"For the last time, I wasn't drunk! I was *attacked*!" cried Ptolemy.

Pothinus rolled his eyes and leaned forward on the couch to ease an overstuffed cushion out from behind him.

"So you keep saying, only there was no one there."

"Aisha was there! And the guards, they said they chased a couple of kids off the grounds. They must have been the ones who attacked me. It was probably that glass-eyed weasel and–"

"Oh, enough! There wasn't a mark on you. As for the scribe girl, I doubt you dragged your attention off that blonde long enough to notice when she left the party. And, really, do you think Glass Eyes has got it in him to best you? You saw the kid. He's soft. Easily outmatched. Besides, he couldn't have got past the guards and why on earth would he have any reason to 'attack' you?"

"Aisha! He's trying to steal her. I'm telling you, it was him."

Pothinus rolled his eyes again and got up. He paced the room. He was quickly losing patience. "So let him have her! She's nothing!"

"That's not the point. She's *mine*. She belongs to *me*."

"What do you care? Come tomorrow night, if all goes to plan, he'll be dead anyway. Problem solved. He'll take the fall for the fire, and little Miss Scribe Girl will be sorely disillusioned. Besides, just days ago you wanted the poor girl dead too."

"I'm going to marry her."

Pothinus was exasperated. "I don't have time for this." He turned to leave.

"What if he really *is* an agent of Cleopatra's?" asked Ptolemy.

Pothinus stopped. "He's *not*. We'll just make it *look* that way after the fire."

"How do you know for sure? What do we really know about him? Maybe *we're* the ones being played. After all, the spies can find nothing on him. He's a ghost. No one knows anything about him. They can't even find where he's staying. I've had him followed for days and every time he just disappears. We don't even know what country he comes from. How can we be sure who we're dealing with?"

Pothinus rubbed his eyes. It had been a late night and the young pharaoh was sorely testing his patience this morning. "So what would you like to know about him before we kill him?"

Pharaoh folded his arms and pouted. He looked out the window and shrugged.

Pothinus shook his head. "Fine." Then, turning to the servant waiting at the door, "Summon the Crone!"

A short time later, the wizened husk of a woman knelt before the pharaoh's throne, a bagful of bones scattered on the tiles at his feet. Ptolemy held a silk handkerchief over his nose. The smell was dreadful. He wasn't sure if it was the woman or the unusual runes, or both. Pothinus' sweaty bulk sat on his right. Heavy drapes blocked the windows. Candles and incense burned. Ptolemy felt claustrophobic.

"Hurry *up*!"

The hag waved her hands over the bones and muttered. She fixed Ptolemy with an unnerving, one-eyed stare. The white eye made him shudder. He broke eye contact and stared at the runes on the floor.

Minutes passed before she spoke. Ptolemy squirmed. His make-up felt heavy on his skin and his scalp was itchy under the headdress.

"The one you seek is no longer among us, Your Majesty." Her voice sounded like her throat was rotten.

"Where is he?" asked Ptolemy.

Pothinus leaned forward. They couldn't afford to have him vanish just yet. The plan hinged on him.

"Another world."

"Dead?" asked Pothinus.

The crone shook her head. "But beyond your reach."

"No one is beyond my reach. I am Pharaoh!"

A thin smile split her ugly face. "He will be your undoing."

Her words hung in the silence.

"Who is he?" asked Pothinus.

She studied the lay of the bones. "He is death and deliverance."

Pothinus and the pharaoh exchanged confused looks but said nothing.

She went on. "Death for the pharaoh, deliverance for the Future."

"Speak not rot, woman!" Spittle flew from the corner of Pothinus' mouth.

The hag was unperturbed. She looked mildly amused.

"And what of Aisha?" asked Ptolemy.

"She is naught to you so why do you ask, Your Majesty?"

Pothinus leapt to his feet. "Such insolence! Out!"

The guards stepped forward but Ptolemy halted them with a raised hand.

"Answer my question, hag."

The woman hissed out a fetid breath and let her head drop back. Her eyes rolled in their sockets.

"The scribe is the junction of history and destiny. The traveller is the catalyst, unwitting yet wise; a necessary but dire complication to the forces that be. The agents for good and for evil cast lots on events unplayed. The laws of probability cease to apply and Earth's future teeters in the balance."

She fell silent, eyes closed.

Suddenly her head snapped forward, eyes wide. She held the thigh bone high and shook it. "This is bigger than all of us, I tell you!"

The pharaoh and Pothinus shrank back in horror. They were mystified, afraid. Neither could make enough sense of her words to even form the next question. Pothinus tossed her a piece of silver and dismissed her with a wave of his hands. She snatched up the coin, scooped her bone runes into a bag and turned to go. She looked over her shoulder to fix Ptolemy with a wicked smile. Her eyes were mere slits glinting in the candlelight.

"And she loves him."

She shuffled away with an inhuman sound that could have been laughter.

CHAPTER TWENTY

Mac sat in front of the computer. His eyelids were heavy. A fly buzzed around in the tent, a hypnotic accompaniment to the rhythmic whip-crack of canvas flapping in the noonday breeze.

His father hadn't given him the serve he'd expected. Instead, Leon had been distant and disappointed. That was worse. Mac would rather have been yelled at. His father had simply shaken his head, his mouth a thin line, and turned away. Ru had said nothing but wore a sympathetic expression. Mac had apologised as best he could but he may as well have been talking to a brick wall. The Cardiff boys, Rhys and Gavyn, had ribbed him and shared their tried and tested hangover cures but Mac was quite sure sauerkraut and tomato juice wouldn't fix the kind of 'hangover' he was suffering.

He'd hung his head and retreated to the tent.

He knew he'd be expected to catch up on lessons and was quite sure the tent was being watched closely. There was no sneaking away today.

The computer pinged sweetly as Mac plugged in the camera to download the photos. He wasn't at all sure if there would be any images there. Seconds later, the computer informed him there were thirty-seven new images to download. He clicked the mouse with a sigh of relief and waited for the thumbnails to appear.

As exhausted as he was, the thought of seeing Aisha's face lifted his spirits. His pulse quickened as a string of colourful squares appeared on the screen. He clicked on the first and laughed out loud as Aisha's startled features filled the screen. He moved on to the next, and the next. He paused on the shot of the two of them, heads together, smiling.

He was breathing hard and his heart pounded with the tide of emotion that swamped him. Static frizzed as he placed his hands on the screen in front of him. Why couldn't she be *there*; right *there* with him, right in that Now moment?

He scrunched his eyes shut, willing her into his reality. Nothing had changed when he opened them and stared at the photo again. He studied every inch of her face; those big green eyes, her chocolate moon, that smile that made you forget your own name…

Could life really be that cruel? Could it dangle heaven in your face, taunting you from the other side of a two-thousand-year gap? Could it tease you to the point of insanity? Mac chewed on his bottom lip. He reckoned it could.

He took a deep breath. He was being melodramatic. It was probably just the lack of sleep.

His attention flicked to the tyet amulet that hung around his neck in the photo. He instinctively reached a hand to his throat but, of course, it wasn't there.

Damn!

He continued through the array of photos. One in particular held his attention. It was an image of Aisha and the ruins in hues of sunset amber. She must have moved just as the photo had been taken, resulting in a phantom effect of blurred streaks trailing after her. She was a ghost, a shiny spectre of loveliness in a forgotten world. The angle of the sinking sun had sharply highlighted the carved hieroglyphs on the columns.

Mac zoomed in. "What the...?"

He had never seen hieroglyphs like them. There was what looked like the distinct image of a helicopter. He leaned toward the screen until his face was just inches from it. It was a perfect rendering of a modern-day helicopter, no doubt about it. He scrolled the mouse to view the glyphs around it. To his astonishment, there was a picture of a spaceship, a submarine and what may have been a tank.

"No way..."

Meshing his fingers behind his head, he leaned back in his chair and stared at the screen, eyebrows knotted together in thought. He chewed the inside of his cheek. What could it mean? Was he seeing things? A trick of the light perhaps? Maybe he really did need sleep.

He grabbed a pencil and began to sketch the glyphs exactly as they appeared. The same column appeared in other photos from different angles. Always the pictures looked the same – a helicopter, a spaceship and a submarine. He copied down the carvings from some of the surrounding columns.

Mac had a superior knowledge of hieroglyphics for his age but these were not like anything he'd previously seen. He couldn't decipher them. It would take an expert. He was debating whether or not to show them to Ru, when he had an idea.

He selected an enlarged area of the photo and hit

PRINT. With an efficient buzz, the printer spat out a colour image on glossy paper. Mac retrieved it from the tray and waved the photo for a second to let the ink dry. He studied it closely. The carvings looked as though they were related to hieroglyphics somehow, perhaps a pre-cursor to them, he thought.

He peered around the computer screen to check he was alone. Holding the printout in one hand, he used the other to wipe his brow with his bandana. He scrunched it in his hand and hooked his index finger through his mother's wedding band on the string around his neck. He took a deep breath, closed his eyes and placed the photo against his forehead.

At first, there was nothing but the sound of howling wind. Then the nothing became grains of sand, swirling and blowing in gusts across the blackness of his mind. Some of the sand began to clump together. The clumps grew. They became stones. Gusts of sand blasted across the stone in channels, carving out mysterious symbols. The wind roared, eroding the symbols back to nothingness on the surface of the stone. Then, strangely, the stone itself was blasted away by the savage sand-wind, leaving only the symbols in stunning relief against the dark. The wind died down and the symbols became brighter. There was an undercurrent of sound, a primeval hum that fluctuated. The symbols began to move and flicker; they came alive in a bizarre sort of pantomime. It had meaning, Mac was sure, but to try and touch it with his mind would send it dashing away again. Instead, he relaxed and let the meaning come to him like a trusted friend.

Mac opened his eyes. He pulled the photo from his

forehead and frowned at the small ink smudge caused by his sweaty skin. At least the carvings were still readable. They were readable!

He read in hushed tones, barely moving his lips. "... for in his veins runs the true blood of the most ancient of ancients from across the water, descended in purity from the Lord of the Horizon, Ruler of the Western Domain, Cleaver of the Earth. This blood shall forever carry the memory of the great catastrophe that darkened the sun and disturbed the gods, lest we forget the Tuat..."

Tuat?

Mac gazed outside for a moment, tapping his finger on the printout and trying to remember where he'd heard that word. Tuat...

"Of course!" He remembered that it referred to the place where people's souls went after death – The World of the Dead. Nudging his glasses further up his nose with his finger, he continued reading.

"...and he shall rule the heavens as he ruled the earth..."

Who? Who were they talking about? Mac scanned the image for more clues. Some of the text was difficult to make out, as the carvings were lost in shadow at the edge of the column.

"...the last of the god-men..."

God-men?

"...who gave us the New Ways. His light will shine on learnings not forgotten."

It wasn't making any sense to him but he was intrigued. He glanced at a different area of the photo and studied the symbol that appeared to be a helicopter. An indistinct word hovered at the edge of his understanding but the translation was something like 'spin flyer'. He moved on to the spaceship symbol. This time the translation was less clear but was along the lines of 'transporter'.

His eyes widened.

The submarine carving yielded 'seeker in the seas'.

He was sitting on the edge of his chair with his face just inches from the printout, when Ru stuck his head through the tent flap.

"What is so fascinating, my good man? Do share," he asked, noting the deeper than usual 'eleven' carved between Mac's brows.

Mac jumped and tried to shove the photo under a pile of books but instead, sent them crashing to the floor. In his hasty dive to recover them, the photo slipped out of his grip and floated to a stop at Ru's feet.

Ru drew his bushy eyebrows together and groaned as he bent to pick up the photo. He tilted his chin up and peered along his nose, scrutinising the glossy image in his hand.

His expression changed. Mac watched it morph, reading the play of emotions across the man's chubby face until he finally blurted:

"What in the w– ? Where did you – ? What *is* this?"

Mac was so glad he'd cropped Aisha out of the photo. He wasn't ready to reveal her to the world just yet. Without even glancing at the computer, he minimised the images on the screen with a deft click. He stared at Ru for a long moment while he tried to figure out what to say.

"I, ah, came across it."

"Where? What's it from? I don't even recognise the glyphs."

"Ah no. See, that's the thing…"

Ru stared at him, as if trying to extract the information by the very power of eye contact. "*Well*?"

Mac weighed his options: lie and say he stumbled across it on the net, which meant Ru would have dismissed it immediately (he thought Google was overrated and despised the misinformation bandied about on the internet), or tell him the truth and deal with the consequences?

He was too tired to be inspired enough to lie successfully. "Okay, but you can't tell Dad."

Ru held a hand up. "MacKinley, I make no such promises and –"

"Alright, alright." He would just have to take his chances. "I wasn't drinking with Gabriella last night. I went on a… on an excursion. You know." He made spirit fingers in the air and do-do-do-doed the Twighlight Zone theme.

"I thought as much," said Ru, lowering himself to perch on the edge of Leon's cot. He had a feeling this was going to be a long story. He glanced at the photo in his hand and back to the dig kid. He nodded for him to continue.

Mac took a deep breath.

He fumbled with his bandages, prised the ruby lion ring off his finger with a grunt and passed it to Ru who studied it closely.

"I found this the day before yesterday. I think." Time travel was messing with his head. He couldn't be sure of the days. All he was certain of was that he'd known Aisha for three Alexandrian days since rescuing her from the fire. Just three days. Had he really only loved her for just three days? It felt like eons, lifetimes.

Mac explained the strange pull the ring exerted and how he'd let himself be drawn back to ancient Alexandria. He described the lighthouse and the library in detail. He told of his meeting with Elcor and his granddaughter, careful to play down Aisha's part in the story for fear of revealing his true feelings for her, and went on to outline the events of that first day.

Ru was riveted. "Ptolemy X111 *himself*?" ... "Underground tunnels?" ... "How many scrolls to a basket did you say?" ... A moment's silent calculation.

Mac left out the following afternoon's 'date' with Aisha at the lighthouse and skipped straight to their visit to the mysterious ruins.

"Luckily, I remembered to take the camera."

Ru concentrated on the glossy print in his hands as Mac described the odd semicircular layout of the ancient temple that faced due west and how he thought it looked as though it had once been buried beneath a mound of earth.

Ru's head snapped up. "A *mound*, you say?"

His eyes bounced around with the rush of thoughts through his mind. "Could it be?"

"The Lost Mound of Osiris? I wondered the same thing," said Mac.

Ru spoke rapidly. "Legend has it that the dismembered body of Osiris is buried under a mound. According to the stories, and there are many variations mind you, Osiris was killed by his jealous brother, Set. He was sealed alive in a box and thrown into the Nile. His wife, Isis, eventually found him and brought him back to life using her father's ancient spells. The evil Set found out and had Osiris killed again, this time dividing his body into fourteen pieces and scattering them to the ends of the earth. Isis gathered them up and bound them together. It is said that she buried them in a secret place."

"The Lost Mound," said Mac.

Ru nodded. "And this secret place supposedly marks the portal between this world and the next."

"A *portal*?"

"Or so the legend goes."

"But wasn't Osiris a god? How can he have a dismembered body if he wasn't human?"

"Well now here's the thing," continued Ru. "Some versions of the myth say Osiris was a king – a regular human king – before he became a god. Some even suggest he was an extraterrestrial, believe it or not. Other accounts relate that he was the very first king, the father of civilization in Egypt. The history of this country is so ancient it's been lost to the mists of time. But you… You, my boy," he said, waggling a fat finger at Mac, "can see through the mist!"

"The last of the god-men…" said Mac in a faraway voice.

Ru didn't seem to hear. He was even redder than usual as he studied the photo again. "Show me the others."

Mac hesitated. The colour rose in his ears and cheeks.

"Oh for heaven's sake, boy. It's not half obvious you fancy the girl. Now show me the blasted photos before I burst!"

He did look as though he might burst. His round face was flushed with excitement and Leon's cot sounded as though it was about to snap under Ru's bouncing bulk.

Mac turned to the computer and restored the window to full size, wondering how Ru had seen through his carefully constructed façade.

The Englishman was at his side in an instant, squinting at the screen. "Zoom out."

Mac did as he was told.

"Hmm. Interesting," said Ru as he hit the arrow key to advance the next frame.

An image of Aisha leaning against a column with her hands behind her back, one knee bent and her head tilted to one side filled the screen.

Ru whistled out a breath and elbowed Mac in the arm. "My word, she *is* something else!"

The colour in Mac's cheeks deepened but he said nothing.

Ru scrolled through the remaining images, making comment here and there. Thankfully, thought Mac, he'd taken quite a few images of the ruins that didn't feature Aisha. The temperature in his ears returned to normal.

"If only we knew what the devil it said," muttered Ru. "How I do miss your mother at these times."

"I know what it says."

Ru stared at him, astonished.

"I can read it… With Mum's help, of course."

Ru glanced at Emily's wedding ring hanging around Mac's neck and nodded slowly.

Mac translated some of the strange glyphs that appeared in the photos.

"God-men?" breathed Ru, his eyes just slits sandwiched between bushy eyebrows and big cheeks. "Lord of the Horizon… That's the god, Thoth or Tehuti, as he's often known. Keep going."

Mac read aloud between Ru's outbursts of illumination.

"Cleaver of the Earth is from the Papyrus of Ani. It refers to Thoth also. Keep going."

Mac continued.

"Uh-huh. Yes, the Book of the Dead refers to Thoth

as 'Ruler of the Western Domain'. It seems they're talking about a descendent of Thoth."

Mac stared at Ru. The man was an encyclopaedia on legs.

"Still no mention of whom they're talking about," said Ru, shaking his head. "We need a name."

Mac was less interested in old kings and more interested in the mysterious pictograms. "But see, here's where I get stuck," he said, pointing to the helicopter symbol on the screen. "I can get the word for it but I can't fit it into any context. Is it a prediction of future times? Our time? Or are they talking about current events back *then*?"

Ru shook his head, his eyes never leaving the screen. "We need more information. You have to go back."

"But Dad –"

"Shh!"

With a glance toward the tent opening, Ru leaned closer. "Look, I know your father doesn't see the positive side of your gift but if it got us closer to discovering the Lost Mound of Osiris, I know he would understand – be *grateful*, even."

"I dunno…" Mac feigned hesitation but already his heart was beating hard at the thought of going back to Old Alex, back to Aisha. "If Dad finds out he'll – "

"He won't. I mean… I'll talk to him. It'll be fine."

"Well…" Mac drew the word out, as if considering his options. "Seeing as it's for the furthering of knowledge. History and all that, you know. I suppose I could go back just one more time."

Ru could feel the boy's eagerness through the charade and had to stifle a smile. "Only if it's not too much trouble of course. I wouldn't want to overburden you, MacKinley."

"It's no trouble," said Mac, a little too quickly.

Ru nodded. "But perhaps we should keep this to ourselves for the meantime."

"Yeah, you're probably right. I'll need that back though," said Mac nodding toward the ruby lion ring that Ru still held in his hand.

"Not so fast." Ru closed his fist over the ring. "There are some conditions."

Mac frowned.

Ru was very serious. "MacKinley, your safety is paramount. If you get even the slightest whiff of danger, you're to high-tail it out of there. Clear?"

Mac nodded.

"And there's to be no interaction with events. You cannot mess with history, Mac. Is that understood? You are merely an observer. You've already meddled way too much even by rescuing the scrolls from the library."

"Yeah, yeah. 'Look but don't touch' and all that."

"And don't go falling in love or anything stupid like that, okay?" Ru winked and clipped him lightly on the back of the head.

Mac blushed scarlet and scowled.

Ru handed him the ring and turned to leave. "Now get some sleep. You look exhausted, boy," he said and ducked out of the tent.

Suddenly, Mac realised just how tired he was. He merely nodded after Ru and half waved.

He turned back to the screen and flicked through the last couple of images; an out of focus tree branch and the headless torso of a palace guard at full sprint, flashlit against a black background. Mac snuffed a laugh. So far, that camera had proved itself quite a weapon.

A few clicks of the mouse later, and his drooping eyelids closed over the image of a smiling Egyptian girl, just moments before his forehead dropped onto the keyboard.

CHAPTER TWENTY-ONE

AISHA WIPED THE tears that ran down her face. She sat on the bed that had clearly not been slept in and stared through blurry eyes at the tyet she'd found abandoned on the pillow. She nodded slowly.

So, it's like that then, is it? she thought bitterly.

She was gutted. She'd really believed he was different.

She sniffled.

Maybe he *was* different and she'd just scared him off. All that talk about running back to his homeland with him… It would make any man run a mile. Why did she always have to be so intense? Why couldn't she just keep her feelings to herself and shut up?

Aisha stood up. She looked down at the tyet then shoved it in her pocket and left.

She made her way along the covered walkway toward the Isolation Room, still blinking back tears. A busy day of scribe work awaited her and she was glad for that. She needed a distraction, something to focus on other than her shattered heart. Besides, she wasn't sure if Mac was coming back or not but she wanted to avoid seeing him if he did.

What had gone so horribly wrong? When she'd left him

last night, it had sounded like they were planning some sort of future. Had she misread what he'd been saying? Maybe his sudden disappearance was part of the 'lying low' bit. But then why had he purposely left his tyet behind? It seemed like a message that said, for whatever reason, "thank you but goodbye". How could she possibly take it any other way?

Her pace quickened as she fought back a fresh wave of tears.

Aisha knew she was late for work so she was relieved to find The Isolation Room deserted when she unlocked the door and slipped inside. There were usually several other scribes working in there on various projects, all with the proper security clearance.

She slid the heavy door shut, locked it as usual, and leaned back against it. A few deep breaths stilled her quivering chin while she tried to gather focus for the day ahead.

Her grandfather had assigned her a special project. He'd been very serious at breakfast as he'd explained the importance of keeping it a secret – more secret than any other document she'd ever transcribed. At the time, she'd simply nodded distractedly, her train of thought barrelling along tracks that led only to Mac. She'd wondered whether he was awake. She'd been dying to see him.

Serapis damn you, Mac! More tears brimmed.

Elcor's words had barely registered. After all, a secret was a secret. How much *more* secret could something be? She hadn't paid much attention to the rest of what he'd said as she'd bolted down breakfast in a rush to get to Mac's quarters. She'd wondered what his hair looked like first thing in the morning. It would be bed-wild for sure.

"Are you *listening* to me, Petal?" her grandfather had

asked. The unusual sense of urgency and frustration in his tone had briefly magnetised her back to the breakfast conversation but she'd missed most of what he'd been saying.

Now, standing alone in the Isolation Room, she wished she'd paid more attention. She couldn't explain her uneasiness. It was something apart from her aching heart and lack of sleep. Daylight poured through the tall windows to fill the room yet somehow it still seemed too dark.

She crossed to her desk and lit a candle. The room's cold light diluted the flame. It was a dim flicker that barely illuminated the charcoal rubbing that was pinned to the easel mounted on her desk. Her grandfather must have set it up for her earlier.

Aisha hesitated before sitting. She rubbed the tops of her arms. The invisible dark chilled her. It wasn't until she reached across to light a stick of incense that she noticed the array of amulets and stones, strategically placed on the desk to form a magic shield of protection. Goosebumps swept across her skin. Her grandfather knew the craft and Aisha recognised his work immediately. She quickly withdrew her hand to stare at the spread of talismans. What had her grandfather told her this morning? She wished she'd been listening.

Aisha studied the strange papyrus in front of her. The glyphs were ancient. She wasn't even sure she could translate all of it. It was complex, obscure. Detailed formulas were interspersed between vertical panels of text.

She turned to face the life-size statue of the ibis-headed god, Thoth, patron of scribes, which stood by the door. She uttered a quick prayer for clarity and accuracy before turning back to the papyrus.

What was this thing? Where had it come from? She leaned closer.

Her sudden proximity to the ancient text allowed its dark power to make her its victim. Symbols, stark against the black rub, appeared to morph and move, to coalesce into one another then re-emerge a whisper in her mind. Their dark tentacles reached for her; their energy slithered around her throat, drawing her closer. Snatches of meaning proclaimed the fierce and terrible knowledge of the thing. She knew it to be true. Just as she knew it was her destiny to salvage and preserve that knowledge.

Trance-like, she picked up an ink stylus and began to write, her world forgotten and the hurtful foreigner along with it.

"With all due respect, Your Majesty, this is highly irregular," came Elcor's voice from outside the Isolation Room.

Aisha's head snapped up. She squinted and blinked, trying to get her bearings. The slant of light through the windows told her several hours had passed. She felt as though she'd just woken from some dark dream.

The door rumbled open as Ptolemy pushed past Elcor and into the room.

The ink stylus dropped from Aisha's hand and clattered to the floor. She leapt from her seat, heart in her mouth. "Pharaoh! What a… What a surprise."

A blaze of guilt swept across her chest and up her neck. Every ounce of moisture evaporated from her mouth instantly. Why was *he* here?

Oh, Sweet Isis, he knows about last night. Suddenly she felt sick. Where was Mac? What had Ptolemy done to him?

"Is everything alright, my lovely lotus?"

Aisha tried to swallow but couldn't. She thought she nodded but wasn't sure.

He offered her the crook of his arm. "Come. Walk with me."

"But um, I have work to –" She shot a look at her grandfather.

Elcor nodded once, instructing her to do as she was told. He could tell Pharaoh Ptolemy was in one of his moods today. Aisha would do well not to provoke him.

She was trembling slightly as she took his arm.

Ptolemy just happened to glance past her to the charcoal rubbing. It seized him. He stared at it, transfixed. Then he took a step toward it.

Elcor saw his eyes, saw them 'listening' to Evil as it called a brother's name.

No... thought Elcor. *He will not be your puppet. I will not let it happen.*

"What is this you're working on, my dear, clever Aisha?" drawled Ptolemy without shifting his gaze from the papyrus.

Aisha was mute.

Elcor rushed to the easel and whipped the papyrus off it. He rolled it rapidly and spun to face the pharaoh. "It is nothing that cannot wait until Aisha's return, Your Majesty." He forced a smile as he tightened his fist around the scroll to silence the black whispers.

Aisha dragged her eyes off the scroll in Elcor's hand to look at the sunlight in the trees outside. True, the document was darkness, but there was light in it as well. There was balance if one knew how to identify the light, how to use it. She must finish it – find the key to controlling it.

"You wished to speak with me, Your Grace?" She feigned innocence with her big green eyes while her stomach made an oily tumble.

What could he want?

Aisha glanced over her shoulder at her grandfather as they made their exit. There was no mistaking the concern on his face.

In silence, Ptolemy walked her to a secluded corner of the garden. He spun to face her with a whirl of his cape.

"Lovely day, isn't it?" His voice was sickly sweet.

Aisha hadn't noticed the weather but nodded anyway.

"A trifle steamy though," he went on. "Possible storms tonight, they say."

Aisha shifted uncomfortably but said nothing.

Ptolemy folded his arms across his bare chest and rocked back on his heels. He peered up at the canopy above. "My associates tell me you've been spending quite a bit of time with the traveller. Moc? Muc?"

"Mac." She could barely squeeze his name out through lips that started quivering again.

"Ah, yes. Mac." Ptolemy said the name with an especially hard 'C' that was enough to make Aisha flinch. "Tell me, what do you actually know about him?"

Aisha gulped. She shrugged and tried to seem casual. "He's from somewhere south and is in the city doing historic research of some sort."

Suddenly, she was very aware just how little she actually knew about the handsome stranger. All she was sure of was that he'd stolen her heart right out of her chest. And then broken it…

"So it comes as no shock to you then to learn that this Mac is an agent of Cleopatra's?"

Aisha gasped.

Ptolemy pulled one side of his mouth into a mean smile. He reached for her and drew her close. He gripped her tightly by her arms and leaned over her. The smell of stale alcohol from last night's dinner party still hung on his breath.

She cringed.

"He is not what he seems, my sweet one. He had us all fooled. We've uncovered his plan to set fire to the library."

Aisha brought her hands to her lips. She was speechless. She was confused. Her knees felt weak. Part of her simply refused to believe it. She felt the weight of the discarded tyet in her pocket. Then the other part of her stepped in. Maybe Ptolemy was right. But it didn't make sense. If the plan to burn down the library had been Mac's, why would he beg Elcor to move the scrolls to safety? Her grandfather had believed him and he was not an easy man to fool.

"Where is he now?" she finally asked, her question laced with dread.

"My men are scouring the city for him as we speak but, according to my sources, he was last spotted in the intimate company of that blonde from last night's party."

Aisha felt like acid had been poured on her already wounded heart. She couldn't breathe.

"He may try and contact you, Aisha. Manipulate you into helping him. You mustn't speak to him." Ptolemy squeezed her arm harder. "So help me Serapis, if he so much as utters a word to you, I'll have his tongue cut out," he hissed.

Aisha looked horrified. Even through her hurt and confusion, she couldn't bear the thought of Mac being harmed.

"But what if you're wrong? What if –"

The pharaoh shook her. He spoke through clenched teeth, spittle clumping at the corners of his mouth. "You are forbidden to speak to him, do you understand?" His eyes were crazed.

Aisha was truly scared of him.

"DO YOU UNDERSTAND?!" he roared.

She jumped. "Yes, yes… I understand." The sting of tears pricked her eyes.

Ptolemy released her and smoothed his wig. "Good. Now you'd best not keep your grandfather waiting. You've got a lot of work to finish off before we announce our engagement at the festival tonight."

Aisha gaped. She was sure her heart had stopped beating.

"Wear the blue dress I gave you. Oh, and do that thing with your hair that I like."

Pothinus cleared his throat loudly as he approached Pharaoh from behind.

"One moment, Regent," said Ptolemy over his shoulder. He leaned over and whispered in Aisha's ear. "And if you even think of sending him a warning, you shall share his punishment." He kissed her on the cheek and strode away.

Too shocked to even wipe his vile kiss from her face, Aisha simply stood there staring after him.

"Is everything alright, Petal?" asked Elcor as his granddaughter ran past him in the hall. She looked like she'd been crying.

"Fine," she called back.

He watched as she turned into the Isolation Room and slid the heavy door shut behind her with a bang. Elcor gnashed his teeth as his loathing of Ptolemy swelled. He wondered what the pharaoh had said to upset her this time. He made to follow her then changed his mind. She probably needed to be alone.

CHAPTER TWENTY-TWO

Mac jolted awake.

He wasn't sure what had woken him. There was no one else in the tent. The computer screen was black. He scrunched his eyes shut, stretched his stiff neck and groaned. His mouth was dry and his left cheek was deeply indented with a grid of neat squares from the keyboard. Faint snatches of a dream haunted him but he couldn't quite get it back. He knew it had something to do with Aisha – *searching* for Aisha, he thought.

He looked out the window. The sun had crossed the sky and was heading toward the horizon. Without checking his watch, he guessed it to be about mid afternoon. Mac wondered what time it was in Old Alex. He was anxious.

A rumbling in his stomach reminded him he hadn't eaten in… in… He couldn't remember how long. The passage of time was all mixed up.

As he yanked open the door of the gas fridge, he realised he was starving. He grabbed a couple of mint slice biscuits and shoved them in his mouth. Still munching, he followed it with a milk chaser, straight from the carton. His father hated the way he did that but it didn't seem to stop him.

He paused mid gulp. Actually, now he thought about it, he did a lot his father didn't approve of. And yet Leon loved him unswervingly. He was sure of that. His father wasn't an openly affectionate man; sometimes he almost seemed like a stranger but Mac never doubted that he was loved. Not liked perhaps. Certainly not understood. But loved all the same.

He lowered the milk carton. Guiltily, he wiped the biscuit crumbs off the lip of the carton and put it back in the fridge. He didn't notice the change in pitch of the fridge motor as he stared blankly at the contents inside.

Slowly, his unspoken unrecognised plan to be with Aisha was being dragged up from the depths of his subconscious to sit uncomfortably at the forefront of his mind. He hadn't even realised he'd been toying with the idea of staying permanently in Old Alex to be with her.

What had he been thinking? How could he even entertain the thought when it would mean abandoning his father? He was horrified at himself. Leon would be devastated. He knew that. Unless there was some way of bringing Aisha back to the Now, how were they going to end up together? And even if he could figure that out, she would never leave her grandfather. He would never ask her to.

And yet, Mac simply could not bear the notion of a future without her.

He decided it was time – *almost* time – to be honest with his father. He'd tell him everything. He'd make him understand somehow; understand that he could not be apart from Aisha. Besides, he was sixteen, almost seventeen. In less than two years he'd be eighteen, a legal adult, and he could do whatever he wanted. Technically, it could mean that he might leave his father anyway to study abroad or something.

It was a possibility that Leon would have to face sooner or later. Why not just fast-forward it by two tiny years?

Nodding at the open fridge, Mac resolved to have a long talk with his dad just as soon as he got back from Old Alex tonight. Hopefully, by then he'd have gathered more compelling evidence of The Lost Mound of Osiris, if that's what it was, and Leon would be a little more pliable.

After scoffing down leftover savoury mince without even bothering to heat it up and a handful of pizza shapes, Mac decided it was time to get going. Quickly, he organised a few things.

He remembered that the festival was on tonight in Old Alex so he picked out his very best shirt – a grey, collared one with a faint pinstripe. Gabby had helped him choose it months ago when they were on a shopping break in Greece. She'd said it made him look handsome. It had only been worn once. He went to put it on and stopped, caught in a dilemma.

He'd planned to trip from the comfort of his own cot so that his father would presume he was sound asleep. He was sure Ru would cover for him. But he couldn't exactly fake a nap wearing his best shirt and shoes. Instead he tied it around his waist. He'd simply pull the blanket over himself so it looked like he was sleeping bare-chested as normal and change into the shirt once back in Old Alex. Using the shoelaces of his Nikes, he tied each one around his legs so his bare feet would be sticking over the end of the bed. The jeans he still wore were the only ones he owned so they would have to do.

There was just one more thing.

Mac crossed to the laptop, selected a photo and printed

it out on glossy paper. He smiled as he took it from the printer tray and waved it to dry. It was the shot of him and Aisha.

He went to slip it in the top pocket of the shirt hanging from his waist but hesitated. He stared at it. An inspired smile spread across his face. He reached for a pen and tapped it on the table, thinking. After a few moments, he wrote something on the back of the photo in his neatest handwriting. It was something his mother used to say. Careful not to crease the photo, he tucked it in his shirt pocket. Mac was still grinning as he stuffed the camera in the front pocket of his jeans.

Suddenly, he remembered Ru. He'd have to make a quick trip back to the ruins before finding Aisha. Keeping Ru satisfied with information was his free pass back and forth between the Now and the Past without bringing his dad into all this, at least for the time being. He grabbed a compass from a box of stuff in the corner of the tent. He thought it might come in handy. If he could get his bearings from the ruins, he might have more chance of finding what was left of them, if anything, in the Now. Ru would be stoked if he knew where to start looking at least.

Moments later, in a tent on the outskirts of the modern city of Alexandria, a boy with bandaged hands appeared to be sleeping deeply.

Mac opened his eyes to a sea of wildflowers.

He could see the red rocky outcrop in the distance ahead.

He'd tried to focus his mind on the ruins in order to direct his travel there. It had worked the last couple of times. He'd ended up pretty much where he'd wanted to be. This time however, his thoughts had slipped just a little at the last minute. A clear picture of Aisha riding beside him through the field of wildflowers, hair flowing in the breeze, had flooded his mind, making his heart leap. And so, that is where he ended up.

The sun was high in the sky. He guessed it was roughly the same time here as it was back in the Now. He hoped it was the same Alexandrian day he'd left that morning.

Mac slipped on his shirt without bothering to button it up and rolled up the sleeves. It was a little tighter across the shoulders than he remembered. He put his shoes on and set off toward the ruins.

He covered the distance fairly quickly and, before long, stood at the entrance to the ruins. The temperature dropped as he made his way along the passage to emerge in the columned oasis. It was eerily still and silent, except for the bubble of water from the spring. He felt a chill, despite being hot from his walk across the field. The place was kind of creepy now that he was totally alone there. He couldn't shake the feeling he was being watched. He glanced around slowly, peering into the shadows. There didn't seem to be anyone else there.

He knelt by the spring, soaked his bandana then wiped his brow and the back of his neck. The water was cold but strangely enticing. He scooped up a double handful of it and drank. It tasted so pure. He scooped another, this time tipping it over his head. He closed his eyes and ran his hands through his wet hair.

A presence… He spun, eyes wide. Nothing.

His heart pounded as he scanned the ruins. There didn't

seem to be anyone or anything behind him. Yet something had startled him. He was sure he hadn't heard anything. But he'd *felt* something. He took a deep breath.

"Get a grip," he told himself.

Mac retied his bandana and took the camera from his pocket. He was keen to get the job done and get out of there. Yesterday, the place had been mystical and magical with Aisha by his side. Today, all alone, it was... disturbing, haunted.

The light was better than the day before and the glyphs on the columns stood out in brilliant relief. Mac snapped away, trying to capture every angle. Even in his eagerness to get out of there and go to Aisha, his sound archaeological training prevailed and he diligently recorded as much of the place as possible. He tried to keep his brain busy to shut out the incessant whispers.

After pacing out the length and breadth of the ruins to gauge the area, he tried to get a compass reading. He stood at the centre of the old temple and examined the face of the compass. The needle spun wildly.

He tapped the face of the compass casing with his finger. The needle swung clockwise through all the cardinal points then suddenly reversed direction. He'd never seen a compass behave like that. It made the hairs on his arms stand on end. He shoved it back in his pocket.

There was a faint vibration on the soles of his feet and in the pit of his stomach, an almost mechanical hum but smoother. He stared at the ancient stone slabs underfoot. Squatting, he placed his right hand on the stone floor. The vibration intensified. Mac closed his eyes...

A brilliant flash of light... A circle... So bright... Moving, liquid light...

A noise.

Mac's eyes flew open in time to catch the passing of a shadow from overhead. He looked up to see nothing but columns against the sky. He was breathing hard. Every hair stood on end.

He glanced over his shoulder. Much sooner than he'd realised, the sun had dipped toward the west. The thought of being there on nightfall made him shudder as he hurried back toward the entrance. He glanced up at the rim of the rock wall that rose above the eastern end of the ruins. If he could get a shot from above, looking down onto the layout of the place, it would certainly help Ru.

The rocky outcrop was already in shade when Mac scrambled up it. It was a tougher climb than he'd expected and he was puffing by the time he hauled himself over the lip to look down on the ruins below. The circular layout of the place was more evident from this vantage point and the concentric rings of columns, minus quite a few that lay in piles of rubble, were precise and evenly spaced. He wriggled the camera free of his pocket and took a few photos. Something astonishing caught his attention as he reviewed the images on the LCD screen.

The ground surrounding the spring was depressed, as if the space beneath it was hollow and the floor had started to sink. The really weird thing was the fact that the depression was an absolutely perfect circle with the spring pouring forth from its centre. Mac hadn't been aware of it at ground level, probably because the stone flooring was so cracked and uneven, and strewn with rubble. He wondered if there was some kind of circular underground chamber or cave beneath the spring.

He caught his breath. For an instant, he could have sworn he saw light shining up from beneath the waters of the spring. He stared at it but saw only the twinkle of the sunset glinting off the water. It must have been the play of light, he reasoned.

He looked back over his shoulder. In the distance, the city of Alexandria gleamed golden in the setting sun. If he hurried, he might just make it across the fields before dark. He didn't want to be late for the festival. Moments later, he was pulling up handfuls of blue and yellow wildflowers as he jogged across the field, open shirt billowing behind.

A sick feeling of dread squirmed in his gut. He wondered how Aisha would be feeling toward him. She would have discovered him gone that morning without a word of goodbye and hadn't seen hide nor hair of him all day. What must she be thinking? He was determined to make it up to her at the festival tonight. He patted his top pocket and felt the photo still there. He hoped they would get a moment alone. He planned to tell her everything. She needed to know. If she truly loved him, she would accept it. Then they just had to figure out how to be together. The pharaoh wouldn't take the break up lightly. It would be better if they just slipped away in the dead of night and went to… hmm… Rome perhaps. At least her father would be there. Maybe they could convince Elcor to go with them but he doubted it.

Then another thought struck him. He wondered if Ptolemy suspected who his attacker had been last night. He wondered if the palace guards got a good enough look at him to be able to identify him. Would Pharaoh's men be on the lookout? Mac decided he would have to be careful. He wondered how he and Aisha might slip away from the crowd tonight without being noticed. He also wondered if Aisha was okay. Was she in trouble with Ptolemy? Mac was really starting to worry – about everything. He ran faster.

CHAPTER TWENTY-THREE

Cucumber and watermelon laced with jasmine; soft overtones of freshly cut grass on a summer's afternoon… He smelt her even before he opened his eyes. And there she was, sitting at her writing desk with her back to him. She was so focused on her work, she wasn't even aware of his presence.

Mac was only a little surprised to find himself standing in the Isolation Room.

Out of breath and sweating, he'd arrived outside the library grounds just a short time ago, wondering where on earth he should start looking for Aisha. Deciding that it was too dangerous to wander around searching for her, he'd opted for a quick psychometric hunt instead. Mac had made his way to her quarters without being noticed. He'd been pretty sure it would be deserted and he'd been right.

The dressing table in the corner of the room had been covered in pots of make-up, hair accessories and jewellery. Mac had simply laid the bunch of wildflowers aside, closed his eyes and put his hands on her things.

He'd been shown a clear picture of the Isolation Room, empty except for Aisha working alone at her desk. Even though he knew where to find her, he had no way of getting to her without being seen. He'd wondered how far he could push the boundaries of time travel. Was it possible to travel to a specific *location* in time-space? If it were, he'd reasoned, since it was technically the same *time*, he shouldn't need to leave a duplicate of his body behind. It was worth a shot.

One dizzying instant later, he was standing in the Isolation Room, minus the bunch of wildflowers he'd picked for her. Of course, they would still be sitting on the dressing table in her room.

Dust motes floated lazily along a shaft of late afternoon sunlight that still found its way through the western window to fall on Aisha's head and shoulders.

Mac caught his breath.

She looked angelic. She was hunched over her writing desk, pen in hand, her head turned to the side. Her left ear was so close to the desk, it must have been almost touching. Mac could make out the velvety finish of her cheek glistening in the dying sun. He wanted to reach out and stroke it but he didn't. Her hair was splayed out across her left shoulder, exposing the right side of her face and neck. Mac could see the soft whorls and wisps of fine hair that swept up the nape of her exposed neck. The patch of skin behind her ear was lighter, almost caramel. He fought the overwhelming urge to kiss it.

Instead, he just stood in silence and let the scene wash over his senses. How he wished he could stop time, arrest the beauty in that single instant.

Then he remembered the camera. He quietly slipped it from his pocket and switched it on. It made a soft ping. Aisha stopped writing and listened but didn't turn around. Mac framed her up and pressed the button.

Aisha dropped her pen and spun. "Mac!"

Her chair crashed to the floor as she leapt up.

Her eyes were huge. Mac watched the lightning parade of different emotions flash through them. It began with surprise, closely followed by a bolt of joy, only to be quashed by anger and hurt, with an encore of surprise as she glanced at the locked door across the room.

"What are you–? How did–?" She was breathing hard. "You can't just…" Aisha trailed off as she watched his dimples dissolve and the cheeky smile fade. She stared into his tawny eyes. He looked unsure. Strange, but her first instinct was to rush to him. Then she remembered the empty bed, the abandoned tyet, the 'no goodbye', the hurtful revelations and dire warnings from Ptolemy, and the feeling suddenly evaporated.

She folded her arms across her chest and clamped her jaw. He was clearly uncomfortable now. A tiny part of her enjoyed that. The manufactured image of him with the blonde from last night's party bolstered her. She lifted her chin slightly but didn't speak.

"Aisha, we need to talk."

"No actually, we don't. I have important work to do and it was wrong of grandfather to let you in here."

"He didn't," Mac interrupted.

"Oh, I suppose you just walk through walls, do you?"

She turned back to face her desk.

Mac crossed the small space between them and grabbed her by the arm, spinning her back to face him. "Aisha, listen to me. This is important."

Aisha glanced at his bandaged hand on her arm. "Get your hands off me," she said in a low voice.

Mac let go of her arm immediately. He held his palms up, facing her. "Please listen to me."

"Here. You forgot this in your hurry to leave." Aisha tossed him the tyet from her pocket.

He caught it easily and stared at her a moment longer before looking down at the amulet in his hand. How had everything gone so horribly wrong in such a short space of time?

"Will you at least let me explain?"

Aisha folded her arms again and glanced out the window. The sun had disappeared. She chewed the corner of her lip. "Fine," she said, still staring out the window.

Mac bent and picked up the chair on the floor. He motioned for her to sit.

Aisha hesitated a moment before sitting down and crossing her legs.

His stomach flipped. He could feel the colour drain from his face as he glanced nervously at the floor then back at Aisha. How could he not make it sound completely ridiculous – completely *insane*? Surely it would have helped his case if Elcor had been there to endorse his story, to lend it some credibility. Where was the old man when he needed him?

He drew in another deep breath and exhaled with a rush. His palms were sweating under his bandages. He tried to remember how he'd launched into the story with Elcor. The problem was that he hadn't really been too worried about what Elcor thought of him, so long as he got the message across. This was different. He really, really cared what Aisha thought of him, message or no message. His whole future depended on it.

She was everything.

Aisha listened intently as Mac explained the situation. He kept nothing from her, despite his instincts screaming at him to shut up. When he'd finished, Aisha sat in silence, an odd look on her face. He gave her a moment to absorb things. It was a lot to take in.

"A time traveller?" She arched one eyebrow as she said the words.

Her tone was not reassuring. Her eyes narrowed as she stared at Mac.

He noticed she'd made no mention of the fire, which was the whole point of the story. Not a good sign at all. He couldn't tell what was running through her head but he was quite sure it wasn't good. He had no idea that, in her mind, his words were suddenly crystallizing all of Ptolemy's accusations.

Aisha leaned back in her chair, pursed her lips and gave a short sharp snort through her nose. She blinked slowly, condescendingly. With a slight tilt to her head, she stared at him in silence for a moment.

Mac swallowed hard. He felt tiny beads of sweat break out on his top lip.

"And I thought you were different from the rest," she said, barely above a whisper, yet shouting contempt.

Mac was speechless. Why was she suddenly so hostile? He'd expected laughter, confusion, ridicule even, but not this.

Aisha folded her arms across her chest, lips still pursed. "I'm used to boys trying to get my attention in all manner of ways but *this*... This is the most *outrageous* nonsense I've ever heard." Her voice was still low and angry.

Mac's mouth dropped open.

She went on. "You really must be desperate if you feel the need to concoct such a fanciful story to impress me. Do you think I'm some kind of idiot? Just a dumb girl?"

"No!" Mac cut in.

She got louder. "Do you honestly think I'm gullible enough to buy any of that rubbish? A time traveller, indeed!"

"Hey, wait just a minute –"

"No, *you* wait just a minute! You wait until I tell my boyfriend – until I tell *Pharaoh* – that you tried to lure my affections with your crazy stories about danger and time travel." She pretended to cringe and waggled her fingers dramatically. "Unbelievable!" she snapped, re-folding her arms across her chest.

Mac gaped for a second. "You honestly think you're so desirable that guys make up stories to impress you – sorry – *lure* you, I believe was the word? *You're* the one that's unbelievable!"

Aisha gasped indignantly. She'd never been spoken to that way by anyone but Ptolemy. Secretly though, she knew she deserved it this time. She winced inwardly but carried on despite herself. She jabbed a finger at him as she stood up and stepped closer.

"And don't think you're fooling my grandfather either. He can spot a lie a mile away. If he's pretending to humour you, it's only because he knows I can take care of myself and take care of big fat liars like you!"

Mac's confusion was quickly turning sour.

"You little *princess*!"

"Almost," she quipped. "Pharaoh and I plan to marry."

Her stomach heaved with the words. Then her heart imploded at the look on Mac's face.

"What happened to 'I'll never marry you'?"

Aisha flashed back to the scene on the palace balcony the night before. Her protests still echoed in her head. She swallowed guiltily. "Things change."

They stood just inches apart. Mac was easily head and shoulders taller than Aisha. He couldn't help but look down at those full, pouting lips. They had seemed so lovely just a short time ago. Now they seemed almost cruel. Mac looked into her eyes. They blazed with anger.

But, what was that?

The tiniest shadow of something passed behind her eyes. Was it doubt? Regret? Fear? Yes, he thought perhaps it was fear. He couldn't be sure but it seemed as though it was almost easier for her to snap than to allow herself to believe him, to love him.

Mac sank down into a chair. When he spoke, his voice was calm and resigned.

"If Elcor thought I was lying, why would he have ordered that the scrolls be moved underground?"

"Because... Because..." She hesitated, blinking rapidly. "Because he knows you're an agent of Cleopatra's and you plan to burn down the library yourself!"

"*What?!*" His voice bounced off the empty shelves that lined the walls as he leapt to his feet.

He was gob-smacked. Surely Elcor didn't believe that. Wait... This had Ptolemy's stink all over it.

Mac was suddenly seething.

Aisha sensed the change and, for the first time, became afraid. She backed against the desk.

"*Ptolemy,*" hissed Mac.

He turned away from her and ran his hands forward, over his hair and across his face. He stared at the ceiling, hands on hips.

Almost a full minute passed before Aisha spoke. "I've decided I won't mention this visit to Pharaoh, for you own safety."

"That's big of you," Mac replied sarcastically over his shoulder.

She stepped closer. "He's looking for you, you know."

Mac didn't reply. He merely shrugged.

Aisha's eyes narrowed. She studied the back of his head. Any other boy would have been – *should* have been – terrified at the very mention of Pharaoh's name. They should have been begging her not to tell. Mac had seemed unfazed by the threat. He *was* different.

Mac turned to face her, hurt and outrage on his face. He was shocked at her reaction; shocked that she would behave like such a prima donna. It seemed he'd sorely misjudged her. He felt stupid that he'd fallen for her in the first place; stupid that he'd somehow elevated last night's escapade into the romance of the century. His throat tightened.

For a moment, they glared at each other in silence.

Aisha relaxed the set of her jaw slightly. She desperately regretted her snotty little performance but she couldn't take it back now. Besides, she still didn't believe the story. Who would? It was ridiculous but she realised now, looking into his eyes, that *he* believed it. Oh, why did she have to be such a cow? She was kicking herself. Of course he wasn't in league with Cleopatra and of course he didn't run away with that blonde from last night's party. She knew Ptolemy was full of camel dung.

Wrinkles in her forehead were as close as she could get to an apology.

For some bizarre reason, despite his anger, Mac was still fighting the urge to lean down and kiss her. It would be so easy. She was just inches away and, even though she was a total pain, she was maddeningly beautiful. At this close range, she smelt divine. As he gazed at her, he found it difficult to breathe.

He squeezed his eyes shut for a second. The anger seeped away. His shoulders sagged. Of course she wouldn't understand. Had he honestly expected her to? It was too much to hope for.

When he opened his eyes, Aisha was staring at the floor.

Neither spoke in the dim room. The situation didn't seem salvageable.

"I'm, ah… I'm gonna go," he said.

Aisha simply nodded.

Without another word, Mac turned and melted into the shadows across the room.

Aisha's vision was too blurred with tears to even make out his silent exit. She let her knees buckle beneath her and sank to the floor as the quiet sobs wracked her.

The room was almost completely dark before she stilled herself enough to carry on. The festival would be starting shortly. She needed to get ready. Ptolemy would be waiting. Another burst of tears flowed as she stood up and smoothed her tunic.

"Get a hold of yourself, girl! You can't change a thing so deal with it," she ordered.

She wiped a hand across her face and sniffled as she headed for the door. The sound of paper underfoot stopped her. She bent and swept a hand across the floor where her fingers found a small piece of paper. Curious, she lit a candle on the nearest desk.

Aisha gasped. She covered her mouth with her hand and blinked back more tears as the candlelight flickered across the crumpled photograph of her and Mac, heads together and smiling in the afternoon light. The paper was so thin and smooth, the image so real, so lifelike. It was like a shiny sliver of time pressed onto the whitest paper she'd ever seen. She rubbed her thumb across Mac's face and closed her eyes. The memory of that moment came flooding back. She could hear their laughter. It was only yesterday. Gods of the Underworld, what had happened in the short time since?

She flipped the paper over. Her heart quickened as she read.

Aisha,

Love was not born of this world so is not bound by it.

Yours Forever,

Mac.

There were two dots and a curve scrawled after his signature. It reminded her of a smiling face but obviously, the symbols must have meant something in his language that she couldn't understand – his family name or emblem perhaps.

A thousand thoughts collided in a split second. Aisha stuffed the photo in her pocket, blew out the candle and ran for the door.

"Sweet Isis, please don't let it be too late."

CHAPTER TWENTY-FOUR

Mac sat on the library steps, turning the tyet over in his fingers, trying to make sense of what had just happened. The evening cool did nothing to dull the hotness in his cheeks. The 'eleven' between his brows was even deeper than usual and his jaw worked furiously. He was angry – mostly with Ptolemy, a lot with himself and a little with Aisha.

Ptolemy… Mac swore under his breath.

Man, he'd love to smash that guy into the middle of next week. He winced in pain as he balled his fists, the burnt skin under his bandages stretching tight. Clearly, the pharaoh had some hold over her. She was scared of him. That much was obvious. Mac knew she didn't love Ptolemy. Hell, just last night she'd suggested running away to a foreign country together; a country she knew nothing about with a guy she barely knew.

Mac shook his head.

Maybe he shouldn't have told her the truth after all. Maybe it was all too soon. But things had happened so quickly. Circumstance had practically forced him to be honest with her, for their own safety. Maybe it would have been better coming from Elcor. She loved and trusted her grandfather.

Well, it was too late now anyway. It was all too late.

Mac's thoughts returned to Elcor. He'd made up his mind to go home right then and there but felt weird about just disappearing without a word of goodbye to the old man. He suddenly realised he hadn't even said goodbye to Aisha. He pounded his forehead with the butt of his hand. "Idiot!"

Things had ended awkwardly. It was too late to say anything further to Aisha but he felt he should at least see Elcor before he left.

He stood up and took a deep breath. Elcor would most probably be in his office, he thought.

Mac knocked on the door. Seconds later, Elcor answered it.

"Mac! All ready for the festival?"

"Ah, actually I won't be staying for the festival. I came to say goodbye."

"Oh, Aisha will be disappointed, you know," said Elcor.

Mac shrugged.

Elcor's silver eyebrows meshed in the middle. So, that's what had happened, he thought. Mac had told the whole truth and his granddaughter hadn't believed it. He felt there was a little more to it than just that.

"Hmm..." was all he said. He scratched his beard.

He thought it would have been a good idea for Mac to tell Aisha the whole story before they got too involved. Perhaps it was too late for that. He thought Aisha would have been enthralled and amazed by the traveller's story. Sadly, it seemed, he didn't know his granddaughter anymore. Once upon a time, he was sure, a tale like Mac's would have lit up her mind and set her heart on fire. She would have been hurling a thousand questions at the boy, her eyes sparkling with wonder all the while.

Elcor shook his head imperceptibly. She had changed so much under Ptolemy's influence.

The old man smiled weakly – guiltily almost – at Mac. Admittedly, he felt a little sorry him. He had noticed the newly acquired tyet around the boy's neck and recognised Aisha's handiwork. He'd known it would be unwise to allow them to get too close. After all, it could only end in sadness. Perhaps it already had, by the look of things. Mac had to return to his When eventually. Still, he found himself drawn to the boy. He trusted him. Mac was the Deliverer after all. Could it hurt to let them find happiness, however fleeting? He thought that if Aisha found she had feelings for another boy, perhaps she would start to distance herself from Ptolemy.

He sighed.

That in itself could prove dangerous. The boy pharaoh was controlling and possessive. He didn't think Ptolemy was the sort of boyfriend that would take a break-up well, to say the least. Although he knew his granddaughter was a strong and independent young lady, he was also pretty sure she was scared of Ptolemy. It would take a strange and unexpected turn of events to set things straight.

Elcor studied Mac for a moment before speaking. "I take it your story was not well-received then?"

Mac snorted. "That's an understatement."

"Hmm."

"I really think she hates me."

"Hates you?" asked the old man, staring up at the ceiling. "Hates you or likes you too much to admit it even to herself?"

He levelled his gaze at the boy.

Mac shrugged.

The thing was, now he'd had time to think about it, he didn't believe she really felt that way at all. He was convinced the whole episode had been motivated by fear. Maybe it was the fear of believing something that might not be true; maybe it was the fear of Mac's freakish ability to travel through time; the fear of Ptolemy; maybe she was just in denial and couldn't face the thought of her beloved library and all her hard work going up in smoke; or maybe, just maybe, if he dared to allow himself to think it, Elcor was right and it was the fear that she might actually be falling in love with him; falling in love with an impossible future.

He told Elcor of his doomed attempt at convincing Aisha of the imminent danger she was in, leaving out the hurtful outburst that had taken him entirely by surprise.

"And now Ptolemy has her convinced that I'm an agent of Cleopatra's and that– "

He was cut off by Elcor's laughter. "Indeed! Have you ever heard of anything so ridiculous?"

The sound of footsteps neared the door.

Mac turned to see Aisha. Somehow, in the short time since he'd left her, she'd managed to reinvent herself. She was wearing an azure blue robe and matching veil. She had put on an array of stunning jewellery: gold bangles, dangly earrings, a dazzling necklace set with colourful gems and a gold arm band in the shape of a ruby-eyed snake. Her hair hung in a thick plait at the back and she'd woven the tiny blue and yellow wildfowers all through it. She was a goddess incarnate. And her perfume…

Why did he find it so hard to breathe around her?

"Oh," was all she said as she paused in the doorway but her expression finished the sentence for her… *"Thank the Elder gods you're still here,"* it said.

Mac thought she looked relieved to see him, yet she still seemed troubled. Her incredible eyes were superbly outlined with black khol but he could tell she'd been crying. He knew he should say something but he was struggling.

"You look… nice," he finally managed to utter. The truth was she looked a billion times better than 'nice'.

His cheeks glowed hot and he could feel his ears turning red. His heart thumped.

"Thank you," she replied without looking at him.

Awkward silence followed.

"Ah, Petal." Elcor stepped forward and hugged his granddaughter, momentarily diffusing the tension.

"Did I miss something funny, Grandfather?" she asked as they pulled apart.

She'd overheard the last few words of the conversation as she'd neared the office and assumed she'd caught her grandfather's reaction to Mac's time-travel story. Her tummy twisted.

In the hurry to get dressed and find her grandfather, she'd managed to convince herself that Mac had been telling the truth. How else could he have the technology to trap time in a box if he wasn't from the future? Now it seemed Elcor was having the same reaction to the story that she'd first had. It was crazy, right? Of course it was.

Her hand closed over the rumpled picture of time in her pocket. But? She was torn.

"An agent of Cleopatra's?" Elcor's voice bounced with laughter and he put his hands on his chest. "Absurd!"

Aisha looked at the floor and blushed. "I owe you an apology," she said without looking up.

Mac shrugged and stared out the window. "Forget it." His curt reply came out more harshly than he'd intended. He blinked hard and bit his lip. He'd just blown his chance to put things right. Out of the corner of his eye he could see Aisha straighten up and look away. He groaned inwardly at his own stupidity.

Elcor cleared his throat and crossed to his desk. "Well, Mac, I am glad to hear that you're able to stay for the festival after all," said the old man, shuffling some sheets of papyrus on his desk.

"Ah…" Mac just nodded dumbly.

Elcor stifled a smile but the twinkle in his eye betrayed him.

Mac looked down and blushed. He'd just been railroaded by Cupid with a beard.

Mac and Aisha glanced nervously at each other. Secretly, each could think of no better way to spend an evening – in the other's presence – yet the extreme awkwardness of their earlier exchange had altered things between them. Both desperately wished they could start over, each wondering if it were possible to get things back on track.

Quite suddenly, Elcor turned serious. An icy sense of foreboding uncoiled itself in his stomach.

"I want you both to stay close to me at the festival tonight," Elcor told them.

Neither protested.

Mac knew the only way he'd be safe from Ptolemy and

his men was to stay in Elcor's company. He doubted the pharaoh would cause a fuss in front of the Chief Administrator. Pothinus wouldn't allow him to do anything rash in public. But it was Aisha he worried about.

He looked at her. She was staring blankly and chewing her bottom lip.

Aisha's stomach knotted with dread. She simply couldn't see how she was going to avoid Ptolemy all night. She knew she'd be safe in her grandfather's company but she worried for Mac's safety.

She looked at him. He was looking back at her with equal concern.

"We'll watch the skyfire from the lighthouse. It will afford a magnificent view," said Elcor as cheerily as he could.

Skyfire... Skyfire...

Slowly, the word tumbled over in Mac's mind like it was coated in treacle. He knew Elcor was talking about fireworks but...

"Fire! That's it!" cried Mac. "The skyfire!"

The others jumped.

"Holy..." Mac didn't finish the sentence.

His mind raced. Could the fireworks start the library fire? It seemed plausible – quite possible even. Actually, he thought it highly probable. The history books suggested the Roman navy was at anchor in the harbour at the time of the fire.

"They're in the harbour right now," he muttered to himself, eyes darting. "It all fits. The history books have it wrong. It wasn't Caesar, it was the fireworks."

The Roman general's love of books and learning was well known. There was no way he'd burn down the library for political gain. It *had* to be the fireworks.

Mac looked at Aisha. Goosebumps swept over him. The night of the fire she'd been wearing the same blue dress, the same jewellery; that snake armband with the ruby eyes. Even her hair was plaited the same way, minus the wildflowers. Everything fit.

"Mac? Are you alright?" asked Aisha, eyes huge.

He grabbed her hand and made for the door. "We have to get out of here. Now."

Elcor was alarmed. "What's going on?"

"Elcor, it's the *skyfire*! The skyfire starts the blaze! We have to stop it. It's not too late."

The old man processed it in a split second. Instantly, he was a whirl of robes, a man in action. Elcor held the door open for them. "Go! Go! I'll send a runner to the ship. Meet you at the lighthouse later."

They almost ran smack into Pharaoh Ptolemy in the doorway.

"Hail Pharaoh," said Elcor, recovering quickly.

"Greetings," replied Ptolemy. His voice was poison in wine.

The pharaoh looked at Mac. If Ptolemy was surprised to see him, he didn't show it. Neither was he openly hostile.

Mac's skin prickled. He wasn't sure why. Ptolemy was smiling pleasantly enough but there was something disturbing lurking in his dark eyes.

Elcor shifted nervously. His extrasensory perception was also picking up an unspoken darkness in the room. "You are alone, Your Majesty?" he asked.

It was unusual for the boy pharaoh to be seen without Pothinus at his heels.

"My regent has been dismissed for the evening to enjoy the festival."

"I see." Elcor did not like the sound of this. Evil was afoot.

"I've come to escort my pretty lotus – " He leaned forward and planted a kiss on Aisha's cheek. " – and our esteemed visitor to the show."

Mac's cheeks burned hot.

Ptolemy smirked at him before turning back to Aisha. "You look ravishing, as always, my sweet thing," he said a little too smoothly.

The pharaoh continued. "But first, I feel it is my duty and responsibility as Pharaoh to personally lend my support to the troops doing such a fine job of caching the scrolls underground. Positively marvellous."

Now Elcor was sure something was amiss. Pharaoh Ptolemy had never shown much sense of duty or responsibility before, certainly not right before a big event and certainly not out of the public eye. Elcor sensed he was up to no good. "Very well then, Your Royal Highness, I shall escort you to the vaults."

"No need, Chief Administrator. I know the way," replied Ptolemy. From early childhood, Ptolemy had been made to study maps of the labyrinth of tunnels that connected the palace to the library and ran under part of the city to the harbour. He needed to be familiar with them in the event that he should be forced to flee for his life via the underground network.

"Come along," he said to the others.

They dared not argue.

Mac glanced back at Elcor as they were swept out of the

room. The old man looked worried. Mac's stomach knotted. He didn't like this at all.

They went down the steps and into the tunnel, Pharaoh leading the way. The last few Egyptian soldiers to leave the tunnel knelt before him and hurried up the steps when he'd passed.

Elcor had ordered all the soldiers out of the catacombs at sunset and the library was to be evacuated and locked during the festival. Even though Mac had said he had no idea when the incident was likely to occur, Elcor was taking no chances. He knew potential disaster was close at hand. Its cold fingers had been tickling the edge of his mind all day. The old man hadn't had a second to himself to meditate on things so he wasn't able to get a clear vision of future events but he trusted his instincts all the same. He couldn't risk anyone being left in the library that could pose a threat – Egyptian, Roman or royalty.

The echoes of the soldiers' footsteps faded and they were alone in the tunnel. The torches along the walls had been snuffed out as the troops vacated. Ptolemy held a single torch to light the way. They walked in uncomfortable silence for a short time before Aisha spoke in a nervous voice. "Grandfather tells me they moved more than a hundred thousand scrolls. That's no small feat in a just a few days."

"Absolutely," agreed Mac.

"Our army is second to none," said the pharaoh. "Hurry, there's something I want to show you. It's a surprise." He smiled wickedly.

"Oh… I love surprises," said Aisha unconvincingly.

She exchanged a nervous glance with Mac who was

struggling to speak under the heaviness of an increasing sense of dread.

They continued on in silence but for the sound of their footsteps and the jingling of jewellery.

As they neared the end of the tunnel, Ptolemy stopped suddenly and turned to a gate on his right. He produced a set of keys and unlocked it. He turned and smiled at them. "Not long now. It's just through here." He winked at Aisha.

Mac shivered. The pharaoh looked evil in the flickering torchlight. His teeth glinted as he smiled and, with all the dark make-up, his eyes looked demonic. He was wearing the more traditional style headdress that wasn't as high at the top and had long flaps that hung down past his shoulders on each side, similar to that of the Sphinx in Cairo.

Ptolemy pushed the gate open and Aisha stepped through.

Mac hesitated. He glanced back to the darkness from which they'd come. His every nerve tingled. He knew that Ptolemy was up to no good but he had no choice but to follow and protect Aisha. He stepped past the pharaoh into the side tunnel. The gate slammed shut behind them.

"Come along," said Ptolemy and pushed past them to lead the way once more.

They seemed to be going deeper. The temperature dropped sharply. They passed several more gates along the winding tunnel before Ptolemy stopped again to unlock one and stepped through into yet another tunnel. Mac was struggling to keep his bearings. The place was like a maze. With a sick feeling, he realised they would never find their way out without the pharaoh to guide them. He had no choice but to cooperate.

"How much further?" whined Aisha. Her beaded sandals were wet from the puddles on the floor and the hem of her robe was filthy. She shivered with cold.

"Not much further, my flower," Ptolemy answered.

"By the stinking breath of Cerberus, this had better be good," she muttered.

"We really should be getting back, Your Highness," said Mac.

Ptolemy ignored him and opened yet another gate for them. It was clear to Mac that they were being led deep into the catacombs. He dared not imagine why. His palms began to sweat. He felt sick. He touched the carved tyet hanging around his neck and looked back over his shoulder. There was no one to come to their rescue, no one to hear their cries for help. They were all alone.

Or were they?

Mac couldn't shake the creepy sensation that they were being watched.

They came to another gate, which Ptolemy opened for Aisha to walk through. Before Mac could follow her, the pharaoh stepped in front, barring his way.

"And this, my honoured guest, is where your underground tour ends," he said to Mac, swinging the gate shut behind his back, cutting them both off from Aisha.

"NO! What are you *doing*?" she cried, gripping the bars of the locked gate and shaking it furiously. It clanged against its hinges, echoing throughout the labyrinth.

Ice-cold terror turned to white-hot rage in a millisecond. Mac roared and pushed Ptolemy hard up against the gate with all the strength he could muster, sending the torch flying. The dig kid was no match for the pharaoh who had been trained in the art of fighting since he was a child. Ptolemy overpowered Mac easily and slammed him against the wall of the tunnel so hard that the wind was knocked out of him. He wheezed as the pharaoh pinned him to the wall by the neck and whipped the ivory-handled dagger from his belt. Ptolemy held the point at Mac's throat.

"Stop it! Please, stop it!" screamed Aisha, face pressed to the bars.

"Think you can impress my girlfriend with that pathetic display?" he spat viciously at Mac's face. "Hah! You make me laugh, that's what you do."

Ptolemy's face was twisted into a psychotic mask. He was panting through gritted teeth and spittle clung to the corners of his mouth.

Mac gurgled. He was struggling to breathe. His face was swollen and red. His temples throbbed and the veins in his neck felt like they were going to pop. The pharaoh relaxed his grip just enough for him to suck in some air. Mac coughed and struggled for another breath.

"Oh wait, did I just say 'girlfriend'? I meant *fiancée*," said Ptolemy.

"For the love of Isis, what on *earth* is all this about?" Aisha demanded.

Ptolemy may have had a vague sense of what transpired on the balcony the night before but Aisha was sure he had no proof that his attacker had been Mac. And she was quite sure he had no idea what had happened on the rooftop of the library afterwards.

"Oh, you didn't think I saw that kiss in the gardens yesterday, did you? Pharaoh sees all."

"*What?*" Aisha was confused. Then she remembered

presenting Mac with the tyet and leaning close to bless him. From the palace, it probably would have looked like a kiss. She cursed silently.

"And don't think I'm not aware of the attempt on my life last night."

"You're insane!"

"On the contrary, my sweet. I'm saner than I've ever been. And do you know why?" He didn't wait for an answer. "Because I've come up with a brilliant solution to turn public opinion against my sister and Rome's intervention. I don't want to give away too much and spoil the surprise but let's just say, long live Prometheus." His deranged laughter bounced off the walls of the tunnel.

Mac's eyes bulged. Prometheus was the Greek god of fire.

"It's *you*!" Mac hissed. "*You* set fire to the library!"

"NO!" Aisha screamed.

"I don't know how you know that but, yes, that's the plan," stated Ptolemy. He smiled. "And you, my friend, will take the fall. Pharaoh thanks you."

Mac whipped his left fist up and punched Ptolemy in the side of the head. The headdress took most of the blow and the pharaoh managed to stay on his feet. He strengthened his grip on Mac's throat. The blade of the dagger pressed hard against the skin under his chin, sending a trickle of warm blood down his neck. Mac held still. He could just see the handle of the dagger out of the corner of his eye. Ptolemy's fingers clutched the carved ivory so tightly, his knuckles turned white. One of the coloured gemstones was missing. Mac could see the empty divot that marked its absence. It bugged him in the same way that a crookedly hung frame on a wall bugged him. It's funny what you notice in a crisis, some detached part of his brain was thinking.

Ptolemy's face glowered.

"Enough." His tone was chilling.

He tore Mac's red bandana off his head. "Oh look, a handkerchief for Pothinus' snotty old nose. And I'm sure you don't need these," he said as he plucked Mac's glasses off his face. "After all, Aisha tells me you're a seer." He snickered. "Well, tell me, did you see *this* coming?"

Mac was silent. The panic rose in him like a tidal wave and threatened to choke him, even if Ptolemy didn't. He had promised to protect Aisha.

His brain ticked over furiously. He could try and pull out of the 'trip' and flash back to the Now, then try coming back later to rescue Aisha and stop the fire. The only problem was that he couldn't guarantee where and when the ring would deposit him next time, even with his newfound technique of directed intention. It may be too late. It was risky. He decided it was not an option.

He shot a glance in Aisha's direction. She was on her knees, face pressed against the bars of the gate. Tears streaked her face. She clasped her golden tyet necklace and chanted low and fervently to the goddess Isis.

Mac's bandaged hands were clamped around the pharaoh's wrist as he tried to ease the pressure of the vice-like grip on his throat. The torch burned steadily on the floor. The ruby lion ring on Mac's left hand reflected the flames brilliantly. It seized Ptolemy's attention.

Mac noticed the pharaoh's gaze shift to the ring. "No!" he croaked and tried to shake his head.

He didn't know what would happen if he lost the ring.

Would he be stranded there with no way back to the Now? Or would the connection be broken instantly? Neither scenario was appealing given the current situation.

Ptolemy increased the pressure on the knife, meanwhile using his free hand to wrench Mac's left arm down and flat against the wall. Then the pharaoh pinned that wrist with his knee and prised the lion ring off Mac's finger. Mac thought his third finger was going to just pop off at the knuckle. The fact that it was so cold in the catacombs was probably the only reason the ring came off at all.

Mac braced himself for the time vortex that was sure to follow. He was breathing hard. Nothing happened. He was still face to face with the pharaoh. If he was still there, that meant…

No…

By Mac's reckoning, the fact that he was still there and not instantly transported back to the Now meant he was stuck in Alexandria. He had to get that ring back!

Ptolemy held the ring up and examined it.

"That's my grandfather's ring! Give it back, you swine!" yelled Aisha, at the same time wondering how, in the name of Serapis, Mac came to be wearing it.

"Your grandfather couldn't afford anything like this," scoffed Ptolemy. Obviously, he had never noticed Elcor wearing it, but then, he probably didn't notice the shiny baubles of the middle class, thought Mac bitterly.

The ring distracted the pharaoh just long enough for Mac to wriggle out of his grip and duck under his arm. He darted to the side and faced Ptolemy square on, tunnel to his back. The pharaoh still stood between him and Aisha.

He could feel the blood flowing freely down the front of

his throat and down his chest. It was only a nick but it bled like mad. Instinctively, he reached for his mother's wedding band but instead clasped the tyet Aisha had made for him.

An idea struck him. The Egyptians were superstitious. Mac guessed that Ptolemy, being of rather weak character, would be particularly suggestible.

The pharaoh roared and advanced toward him. Mac clutched the tyet and held it up in front of his face. Ptolemy stopped dead. Mac assumed a powerful stance and began to intone 'prayers' to invoke the goddess. He spoke in English to further mystify Ptolemy. "Mary had a little lamb. Its fleece was white as snow," he boomed.

Ptolemy looked uneasy. So did Aisha. The pharaoh stared at the tyet and slowly backed away. He was familiar with the 156th spell in the Book of the Dead and knew the Knot of Isis was a powerful talisman. He didn't dare reckon with the gods.

"…and everywhere that Mary went… the lamb was sure to go."

He couldn't believe it was working. He started to laugh, despite his best efforts not to.

Ptolemy looked scared and confused.

Just then a massive wave of vertigo swept over Mac. He stopped laughing and swayed on his feet. At first, he thought it was just because he wasn't wearing his glasses and his vision was a bit off. Then his heartbeat became erratic and a pulse boomed in his ears. His chest tightened. The quickening. He was breathing hard. What was happening? He was being drawn back. But *how*?

The horrified faces of Aisha and the pharaoh blurred into nothingness. He was falling, falling… falling…

CHAPTER TWENTY-FIVE

"Here he comes. He's waking up."

Mac could hear his father's voice. He opened his eyes. He was lying on his cot in the tent. Fuzzy outlines slowly took shape as his vision sharpened. He was relieved to realise he was still wearing his glasses. The concerned faces of his father, Ru and Gabriella hovered above him. It was dark outside. A gas lamp burned in the corner. He could smell Betadine. Mac tried to sit up. He was weak and dizzy.

"Aisha… I have to get back," he mumbled.

Leon placed a firm hand on his son's chest and eased him back down. "You're not going anywhere, son." His voice was gruff but tinged with concern. "You've had one hell of a trip by the looks of it."

"Here, MacKeenlee, dreenk," said Gabriella, handing him a tin mug of water.

Mac was thirsty. He guzzled it and asked for another. He noticed that the makeshift bedside table was littered with blood-soaked swabs. He touched the cut under his chin. It was still bleeding a little. He reached for the tyet necklace but, of course, it wasn't there. He knew he couldn't bring anything back with him.

Mac rolled onto his side and propped himself up on one elbow. He took a deep breath and groaned.

Leon was perched on the edge of the cot holding the ruby lion ring. "What the hell happened, MacKinley?" he asked.

"Dad, please, I'll explain everything but you gotta let me go back. It's a matter of life and death," he pleaded desperately.

"Not a chance."

"Dad, pleeeease – "

"NO!" yelled Leon, getting to his feet. "No more of your foolish adventures! We were worried sick. We've been trying to wake you for hours and then you just start bleeding from a cut that suddenly appears on your throat. What the hell am I supposed to think? Are you being murdered somewhere? What?"

He was waving his arms about as he yelled. Leon Sanderson was furious. Mac couldn't recall ever having seen him this angry.

"We damned near had to snap your finger to get that ring off and bring you back."

So, *that's* what happened, thought Mac.

"You're grounded until… forever!" yelled Leon. "And all Internet privileges are out the window. Do you understand?"

"But Dad – "

Ru laid a chubby paw on the professor's shoulder. "I think we could all do with some rest. We can discuss this in the morning."

"But you don't understand –" Mac protested.

Ru cautioned him with a glare.

Mac shut his mouth and looked down.

Leon handed Gabriella the lion ring. "Put this in a safe place, Gabby. Now go get some sleep."

She slipped the ring in her pocket. "Hope you're feelink better," she said to Mac and ducked out through the tent flap to return to her quarters.

Mac flopped back on his pillow. He had a cracker of a headache but sleep was a long way off.

"Goodnight, my good man. I shall see you in the morning. We have much to discuss," said Ru with a wink and left.

Leon stood by the cot with his arms folded for a few minutes. He exhaled with a rush and ran his hands through his thinning hair. He softened.

"Son, you really had us worried, you know."

"Sorry, Dad. I really am."

Leon squatted beside the cot. He studied Mac's face. "I just don't know what I'd do if I lost you too." His voice trailed off. "Get some rest, son."

He stood up and turned off the gas lamp then retired to his cot. It wasn't long before his snores reverberated through the tent.

Mac sat up and slipped off his bloodied shirt. He scrunched it into a ball and threw it across the tent in frustration. It was a humid night. It made him all the more irritable. He reached for his watch on the bedside table and strapped it to his wrist. The illuminated hands told him it was thirteen minutes past midnight. He lay back down on his cot with a heavy sigh and rolled over. His stomach churned with worry. He agonised over Aisha's safety. Was she okay? What would she be thinking? He had literally vanished in front of her eyes!

He pictured Elcor dispatching a runner to the Chinese ship with warnings to stop the skyfire. He wanted to scream across the millennia, "It's not the skyfire, it's Ptolemy! Your king is your enemy!"

He rolled over again.

"Ouch!"

The camera in his pocket dug into his hip. He eased it out of his jeans, along with the compass, and put them on the bedside table. His hand lingered a moment on the camera before picking it up again and switching it on. The last photo he'd taken was of Aisha working in the Isolation Room. She looked beautiful, as always. He zoomed in on the image. The detail was brilliant. He could even make out the document she was transcribing. It was a large roll of dirty papyrus clipped to an easel, which was mounted on the desk. Upon closer inspection, the document looked more like the charcoal rubbing of a carved stone. He was sure of it. He'd made a number of them over the years. Many times, he'd placed a piece of paper on top of stone carvings, rubbed the broad side of a charcoal stick over it and watched with fascination as the inscriptions in the stone appeared in relief on the paper.

Mac zoomed in further. He was astonished that he could read it. It was the same ancient language as the one written on the columns in the ruins. The document in the photo contained complex diagrams and mathematical formulas. He wondered what it was all about. Using the toggles on the back of the camera, he slowly scrolled over the image.

... but be ye warned,
Mysteries of the Cosmos be they dangerous to those mortal minds
not learned of the key,
Minds starved of wisdom and righteousness,
Bloated by the emptiness of undiluted intellect...

He raised his eyebrows. "Deep."

Leon grunted and rolled over.

Mac decided to wait until his father was snoring again before attempting to sneak away. He turned back to the LCD screen.

He scrolled further down the image of the document when something snagged his attention.

...shall in some distant day
raise armies from the dead,
Summoned through the portal to exact vengeance
upon a sleeping planet
And hell will reign.

A shiver passed down his spine. He wondered who was seeking vengeance. He also wondered if the ominous prediction had already happened in the long-forgotten past or whether it was yet to happen in some distant future. Perhaps it was neither – just nonsense. Still, the words clung grimly to his mind.

Aisha's head blocked the bottom of the document so he couldn't read further. But now he was intrigued. He scanned from the top of the document.

Few are they who secure safe passage
To the Light that shines beyond
For his minions, strange and terrible,
Lie hungry for the Soul that attempts the crossing
but to dwell in the body once more.
Heed ye well this warning:
Keep to the curves of space where his minions
cannot follow.
Only in angles do they move
and in angles will hunt thee relentlessly.

Curved is the pathway to Truth, The Circle, Protection.
Abandon all grievances
For such dangerous treasure shall slow you before his minions' pursuit
And the sharp edges of guilt and unforgiveness
fit not the curves of Light and Truth.

Mac was clueless as to what it all meant, yet he couldn't help feeling it should mean something to him. It all seemed so cryptic though. His head was still fuzzy and it hurt to think too much. He switched the camera off and put it on the floor under his cot.

He wondered how much time had elapsed in Aisha's When. The passage of time between the two dimensions was so unreliable. He figured he'd been gone for about eight hours but not even three hours had elapsed in Old Alex. Time was flowing faster in the Present. However, he knew from past experience that it wasn't always so. On more than one occasion, he'd spent hours in another time, only to return to find just minutes had passed in the Now. He wished he had some control over it. For all he knew, the Library at Alexandria could already have burnt to the ground and Aisha may be dead. He *had* to do something.

Careful not to wake his father, he got up and went outside. He breathed deeply. He hadn't bothered putting on another shirt so the fresh night air was welcome relief against his clammy skin. His headache receded a little and he felt steadier on his feet. He gazed across the dig. It was bathed in bluish moonlight. He looked up at the crescent moon. It reminded him of Aisha – Aisha and her chocolate moon beauty spot.

He considered climbing down into the remains of the library and lying on the tiles, as he had previously, but dismissed the idea. It was too general. The ring was still a safer bet. It emitted more energy. He had felt the difference as soon as he'd put it on. The signal was stronger. There was more chance of landing somewhere near Aisha and Elcor. He needed the ring.

He set an alarm on his watch to go off just before dawn. He was hoping the watch still functioned properly in Old Alex and kept accurate time for the Present. That way, he could try to gauge the passage of time between the two Whens and, hopefully, make it back before his father woke up and discovered him gone. Mac figured he really would be grounded forever if his dad found out he'd been deliberately disobeyed. It was a risk he was willing to take. Aisha was worth a lifetime of being grounded.

He noticed a gas barbecue lighter beside the camping stove and decided it may prove useful. With a click of the button, a bright flame sprang from the stainless-steel nozzle. He slipped it in his back pocket and set off toward Gabriella's tent. He didn't have a plan exactly but he knew he had to get the ring back and she had it. It was his best shot at rescuing Aisha.

Mac crouched outside Gabriella's tent. He smiled as he listened to her loud snoring and wondered how such an attractive woman was capable of such horrendous noise.

Without making a sound, he slipped inside. A portable camp light beside the cot cast a dim yellow glow. Gabriella lay on her side with one long slender leg hanging just over the edge of the cot. She wore a white t-shirt that didn't quite cover her belly and pink lacy underpants. Her wild hair was splayed out across her pillow. Apart from the string of dribble at the corner of her mouth and the quivering nostrils, she was quite beautiful. Mac wondered how many of the guys on the dig team wished they could trade places with him at that moment.

He tiptoed closer to the sleeping Gabriella.

The ring!

The ruby glistened. It was on the third finger of her left hand, which rested on the pages of an open book written in Spanish. He crouched beside the cot, just inches from her face. He wasn't sure what to do. He thought about just yanking it off her finger and running like mad but thought better of it. Gabby was a loyal friend but she was equally loyal to the professor. She'd go running to Leon purely out of concern.

Maybe he could somehow just ease it off without waking her. Spying a bottle of coconut tanning oil on a trunk nearby, he reached for it and drizzled a little on her fingers. She grunted. Mac froze. He watched her slip back into a regular snore pattern again and slowly reached for the ring. No sooner had he touched it, than she groaned and rolled over to face the wall, tucking both hands under her cheek.

Damn!

Mac sat back on the floor of the tent and considered his next move. The tiles in the library dig were the only option now. He would just have to try and direct the travel as best he could and see what happened. He had to at least try.

As he got up to leave, he knocked over a crate of artefacts at his feet. He held his breath and waited. Gabriella didn't stir. One by one he carefully picked up the scattered odds and ends and placed them back in the crate. He recognised the shards of pottery with the blue square-shaped design that he'd found just days ago.

Suddenly, his heart leapt. Goosebumps cloaked his body. He reached out a shaking hand to retrieve a carefully labelled object carved out of red stone. Hot tears stung his eyes as he stared at it. Fate squeezed his chest.

The tyet!

Slowly, he turned it over and ran his thumb across the eroded Greek letters that spelt his name. The Bennu bird had been disfigured by time but he could still make it out. The leather string had long since perished and the reddish stone had been polished smooth by millennia in the sand. He couldn't believe his luck. Was it luck, he wondered, or were divine forces at work? Either way, he had his ticket back to Old Alex, back to Aisha.

Seconds later, the tyet hung around his neck, alongside his mother's wedding ring. He wrapped a hand around them and held them tight before setting off into the moonlit night toward the library ruins.

CHAPTER TWENTY-SIX

THE DARKNESS WAS suffocating. Mac strained to see anything apart from the vaporous squiggles and sprinkles of pretend light that always seemed to occupy total blackness. Judging by the cold stone under him and the faint 'plink, plink' of dripping water, he guessed he was back in the catacombs.

He sat up slowly. The energetic force of the tyet and the lapis-lazuli tiles on the floor of the library ruins had combined to pull Mac into the most intense time vortex he'd ever experienced. His head was still spinning. He felt nauseated and claustrophobic.

Breathing hard, he reached into his back pocket for the gas lighter. He clicked the button and it burst to life. He scrunched his eyes up against the bright, but welcome, light. Instantly, his nerves settled. He could make out the rough tunnel walls on either side. But where in the labyrinth was he? With rising panic, he realised he had absolutely no chance of navigating his way out of the catacombs. The imagined weight of tonnes of earth above him set his heart racing once again. He pictured himself doomed to wander the network of tunnels until he died of thirst and starvation.

No one would be looking for him. After all, Aisha had witnessed him vanish into thin air.

He took a deep breath. Thinking rationally again, he realised that scenario was never going to happen. If worse came to worse, he could always just pull out of it and return home.

Mac stood up and moved along the wall in search of one of the mounted torches. He found one almost straight away and lit it. The torch blazed. Lifting it from its bracket, he looked around. A gate stood ajar in front of him. He hoped it was the same gate through which Ptolemy had escaped with Aisha. Could he be that lucky? He wondered. He glanced back over his shoulder and spotted a small object on the ground.

The tyet!

It was the one he'd left behind when he'd been sucked back to the Now.

"Hah! You little beauty!" He retrieved it and slipped it over his head to hang with its present-day twin.

With renewed purpose, he went through the open gateway and ran off down the adjoining tunnel, torch held high.

He wondered how much time had elapsed while he was gone. He ran faster. It seemed amazing that he'd somehow managed to return to the exact same spot. Perhaps it was the double whammy of the tyet and the tiles that strengthened the signal. He wondered just how much heightened emotional charge or focused intention had to do with it. The field of time was vast indeed but not beyond his influence. Even so, he knew there was still much he had to learn about time travel.

After a short while, another gate appeared on his left.

He slowed. Aisha and Ptolemy could have gone through any number of gates. How was he ever going to know which way they went? The gate was still locked. The fact that Ptolemy hadn't bothered to stop and lock the previous gate behind him was probably a safe bet that he was in a hurry and hadn't locked any of the remaining gates, thought Mac. He kept going.

Further down the tunnel, a shallow puddle shimmered in the torchlight as he skipped over it. A trail of splashed water in front of him caught his attention. He stopped. The splashes on the stone floor weren't exactly in the shape of footprints but it was clear that someone had run through the puddle recently. He took it as a good sign that the others weren't far ahead. He ran on.

Then, above the sound of his footfalls and laboured breathing, a loud clang echoed down the tunnels to reach him. Mac stopped. He knew it was the sound of a gate banging shut somewhere up ahead.

"AISHA!" he yelled.

He took off down the tunnel at a sprint. "Aisha! I'm coming!"

There was no reply. He kept running.

Suddenly, he tripped and went sprawling face first onto the floor of the tunnel. The torch flew through the air and rolled to a stop in a puddle up ahead. The flame guttered and died with a hiss.

"NO!"

Total darkness once again. Mac lay on his belly, breathing heavily. He reached a hand to his face. His glasses were missing. The floor of the tunnel in that area was not nearly as smooth as the area near the vaults. Blood oozed from scrapes on his elbows. He eased himself up into a crouch and groped for his glasses. It was hopeless in the dark. Mac reached for the gas lighter in the back pocket of his jeans. It was gone.

Chills seized him. He held his breath and listened. There was a presence. He was not alone; he was sure of it. Something was in the tunnel behind him. Another desperate scrabble for his glasses turned up nothing.

A sound.

Mac froze.

Every hair on his body stood to attention. Adrenalin prickled at his fingertips and toes. Without a sound, he moved to the edge of the tunnel and crouched with his back against the wall, knees drawn close. His eyes were wide with terror. They darted to and fro in the inkiness of the tunnel. A trickle of sweat ran down his temple. His heartbeat thudded in his ears.

Whatever was in the tunnel with him was getting closer. He couldn't hear a sound but sensed it moving toward him. He clasped the tyet and considered flashing back home but he knew Aisha wasn't too far ahead. He couldn't just bail out now. Maybe whatever it was wouldn't even know he was there and just keep going.

He pressed himself up against the wall as hard as he could. It was right in front of him now; he could feel it. He dared not breathe. His hand closed over the tyet. Time to go.

There was a metallic clink as his foot changed position and nudged something on the floor beside him.

The gas lighter!

Mac grabbed it and clicked it on. He swung it in an arc.

"Holy mother of..." Mac trailed off, panting. He held the lighter out in front of him. The hideous creature had been just inches from him but leapt back before the flame. Without his glasses, he couldn't make out what it was exactly but it was about the size of a cat with huge eyes and bat-like ears. Its wrinkled white skin was covered with blotches and… Wait…

"Nefertiti?"

The cat merely stared at him a moment before she sat and began licking her paws.

Mac puffed out a sigh of relief. Nefertiti was a bit creepy, no doubt, but right now he was glad to see her. Elcor must have sent her to keep an eye on them. He stood up slowly and held the lighter with shaky hands. He shook his head in amazement. "You are one freaky cat but, man, am I glad to see you."

The cat stopped licking and glanced at him indignantly. The expression on her face told him it certainly wasn't her choice to be there; she had better things to do so be grateful, kiddo. She was weirdly humanesque, especially with her hairless skin. He made a move to stroke her but she dodged him easily, leaving him feeling foolish, as only a cat can do. She made a high-pitched trill in the back of her throat and started down the tunnel. She turned and looked back at him as if to say, "Are you coming or what?" then continued into the darkness.

Mac followed.

A few paces along, he spotted his glasses glinting in the dim light. To his relief, they were undamaged. He put them on and continued down the tunnel until he found a torch on the wall and lit it. The torch flared and he was back on his way to finding Aisha.

Mac guessed, by that time, they had a fair head start

on him. He wondered what Ptolemy had planned to do with him. Surely he hadn't intended to let him live. Then again, maybe he'd planned to just abandon him in the tunnels between locked gates to starve to death slowly, leaving a pile of bones to be discovered in some distant future. He shivered. It didn't bear thinking about. All that mattered was that Ptolemy's sinister plan hadn't worked. He wouldn't be expecting Mac to pop up again anytime soon. Although, thinking back on his disappearing act earlier, perhaps the pharaoh wouldn't be entirely surprised when Mac resurfaced but he would certainly be pretty unsure of himself when next they met.

He smiled and followed the cat.

Mac was deep in thought when they came across an open gate on their right that led to yet another tunnel. This was the first gate he'd come across that was unlocked. He stopped. That must be the way they had gone, he figured, but the cat hadn't so much as glanced in that direction.

Nefertiti meowed impatiently from further up the tunnel and kept going straight ahead.

Mac stared after her. Should he trust a cat over his own powers of reason? He guessed she probably knew the way out but did she realise he was looking for Aisha first? He had to find her and make sure she was safe.

As if in answer, Nefertiti gave a short sharp mew and kept going.

Mac followed her.

Further ahead, the tunnel split. The cat didn't hesitate but trotted purposefully down the right fork. Mac followed, somewhat reluctantly trusting the cat's instincts. They continued on for a short time before Nefertiti suddenly stopped.

She stood rigid, head cocked. She sniffed the air then darted to her right and disappeared.

Mac froze. The torchlight flickered across solid stone. The cat had walked right through the wall!

"Nerfertiti?" he whispered.

He took another step then saw a narrow crevice in the wall – a concealed opening that switched back on itself so it couldn't be seen by anyone coming down the tunnel from his direction. He'd never have noticed it had it not been for the cat.

Mac squeezed through the narrow entry to find himself in a small hallway at the base of a set of rough stone steps that spiralled upward. Nefertiti brushed up against his leg then dashed ahead. Mac had trouble keeping up with the nimble shadow several steps ahead of him. He was puffing by the time he reached the top to find himself in yet another tunnel, identical to all the rest. There was the faint sound of running water from up ahead. They kept going straight until they came to a gate directly in front of them. It was locked. Mac took a step back and rammed his shoulder into the bars as hard as he could. The gate clanged. He groaned.

"Now what?" Mac's voice bounced off the walls.

Nefertiti spun and hissed at him to be quiet. He obeyed. He sensed by now that this was no ordinary cat. She crouched low and slipped easily under the bars of the gate.

"Alright for you, cat. What am I supposed to do?" he whispered.

He untied his bandana and wiped his face. According to his feline guide, this was the way out, or the way to Aisha at least. There had to be some way to get through. Nefertiti sat patiently on the other side of the bars wearing a rather condescending expression, Mac thought.

Then he had an idea. He slipped the tyet over his head and stared at it. Reaching through the bars, he draped the tyet over Nefertiti's head. It hung almost to the floor. The cat stared at it for a moment then lay down on top of it. She closed her eyes and started purring. Mac let a few minutes slip by before reaching through the gate to retrieve the amulet. He put it on again. He could feel the warmth of the stone against his chest, along with faint vibrations of another energy. He wrapped a hand around it, closed his eyes and breathed deeply.

In his mind, he formed a crystal-clear image of the cat sitting on the other side of the bars. He'd barely completed the thought when he found himself standing beside her on the other side of the locked gate.

"Awesome!"

He couldn't believe it had worked. Nefertiti's energetic signature had been strong enough – or fresh enough – to pull him through. The torch still burned on the floor on the opposite side of the gate. The tyet lay nearby. It seemed he couldn't even transport objects a short distance through time-space.

He crouched and reached through the bars to retrieve the amulet but wasn't able to reach the torch. He stood up and pulled the gas lighter from his pocket.

Mac took a second to steady himself then hurried down the tunnel after Nefertiti.

The ceiling of the tunnel got lower and, in just a short while, he was forced to bend almost double to prevent hitting his head. The sound of running water came from up ahead. As they rounded a bend, the tunnel opened into a small cavern with an underground pool.

Colourful Egyptian scenes and hieroglyphics decorated every inch of the walls and roof. They were exquisitely painted in the traditional old style of the ancients. The ceiling was only a little higher than it was in the tunnel so Mac was still hunched over as they came to a stop at the water's edge.

To his horror, he could see only solid rock walls bordering the pond. A stream of water bubbled from an invisible cleft in the rock to his left and tinkled into the pool. He guessed it was a natural spring. But still, there didn't seem to be any way out. They were at a dead end. He put his hands on his hips.

"That's what you get for listening to a stupid cat," he muttered to himself.

As if she understood, Nefertiti glared at him over her shoulder and twitched her whiskers. She started toward the pool's edge and dipped a tentative paw in the water. Quickly, she withdrew it and shook the water off. She sat for a moment longer and stared at the pool before slowly walking into the water until just her head remained above the surface. Silently, she glided across to the wall on the far side of the pool and then disappeared.

Mac was in shock. He stared at the ripples radiating across the pond toward him. He wasn't sure if Nefertiti had just drowned or had simply vanished, or perhaps had dived into a secret passageway or something. Or had some unseen creature snapped her up?

He was breathing hard. He shook his head. It was like something out of Alice in Wonderland. He held the lighter above his head and started forward. He stopped at the edge of the dark water and ran a hand through his hair. Was she coming back? Was he expected to follow?

"Here, Puss, Puss," he called softly.

He bit his lip and frowned. If she was leading him out of there somehow, he was letting her get away. He took off his glasses and put them in the front pocket of his jeans. He was glad he'd left the camera at home this time. He stared at the flame of the gas lighter. The thought of having to extinguish it was horrifying. Then he thought of Aisha.

Mac took a deep breath, clicked off the lighter and shoved it in his back pocket. He waded into the pond, shoes and all. The water was icy. He gasped but kept going. It deepened quickly and was up to his chest by the time his outstretched hands felt the far wall. He ran his hands over the stone in front of him, hoping to find a secret panel or something. He couldn't figure out where the cat had gone. He ducked under the water and felt along the wall a bit lower down. To his relief, the wall gave way to the smooth edge of another opening. He ran his hands around the perimeter. It wasn't big but he figured he could squeeze through it.

He rose to the surface and took a deep breath. This time he dived with more force and quickly located the edge of the opening. He gripped the stone edges and hauled himself into the space. It was only just wide enough to get his shoulders through. His hands were pinned by his side so he had to use his legs to propel himself forward. Despite his eyes being wide open, he couldn't see a thing. He could feel the whisper-soft touch of disturbed algae and grunge from the tunnel floor on his cheeks as he squeezed his way through. His jeans snagged on something. He kicked harder and freed himself but the panic had surged through his blood stream; he was desperate for air. Heavy shoes made it harder to kick and his legs felt like lead. His lungs burned.

With a wave of near hysteria, he realised he couldn't even reach the tyet at his throat to try and get home. He kicked furiously and finally wriggled out the other end of the underwater tunnel into shallow open waters. He was face down. Through a swirling cloud of muck, he could just make out the bottom of a tiled pool, just inches below him. He rolled to look up. Above him, he could see a bluish light at the surface. He pushed off the bottom and burst through the water, gasping for air. He was on his knees, the water level only reaching to his chest. He was in some kind of man-made pond. He leaned over the edge and sucked in air until he got his breath back. It was dark but there was blue light coming from above.

Mac groped in his pocket for his glasses and put them on. At once, he recognised The Musaeum. He was in one of the long pools that ran down each side of the building. Moonlight streamed through the open ceiling of the observatory. The place was deserted. The torches were unlit and even the candles at each of the shrines had been extinguished on Elcor's orders. The place was in relative darkness but for the blue cast of the moon, which illuminated only the centre of the immense space. It was eerie. The sculptures atop their plinths looked ghostly in the cold light and deep shadows. The only thing that broke the stillness was the trickling of the waterfalls.

Nefertiti sat on the tiles nearby, her long neck craning to lick the water off her back. She sensed Mac's attention and paused. Her big blue eyes fixed him with a contemptible look. She shook herself from head to tail and stalked off into the shadows. It was clear that her 'duty of care' was over. Mac stared after her. He sat on the edge of the pool, contemplating his next move. In the distance, he could hear the boom of the first fireworks and a pink glow briefly illuminated The Musaeum. The skyfire had begun. He had to find Aisha.

CHAPTER TWENTY-SEVEN

Outside the heavy wooden doors of The Musaeum, Mac could hear voices approaching. He hauled himself out of the pool and squelched his way into the shadows near the shrine of Melpomene, The Muse of Tragedy. Keys jingled in the lock. He shrank further into the gloom as the cedar doors swung open.

Immediately, he recognised the distinctive figures of Pothinus and the pharaoh. There was no sign of Aisha.

Pothinus crossed the room in a swirl of purple robes. A large set of keys hung from a length of plaited gold cord that looped around his waist. Mac noticed he also had a sword sheathed on his hip. He was carrying a wooden bucket in each hand. He reached the pool nearest Mac and poured the contents of the first bucket into the water. Mac wondered where on earth the guards were. Elcor said he had them stationed around the perimeter.

"What are you waiting for? Hurry up, you fool!" Pothinus snapped over his shoulder at Ptolemy. The boy tipped his bucket of fluid into the other pool.

"And don't forget to plant the evidence!"

The pharaoh reached into his tunic and pulled out the

glasses and red bandana he had taken from Mac earlier. He considered his options for a moment before tossing the bandana in a corner. Then he carefully placed the glasses at the foot of a towering statue of Thoth, the god of science and learning, patron of scribes. Having emptied his buckets, Pothinus, walked to the other end of the hall and returned with a flaming torch.

"May I do the honours, Regent?" asked Ptolemy politely.

Pothinus ignored him and touched the torch to the surface of the water.

WHOOMP!

The entire pond burst into flames. The Musaeum was aglow as they set fire to the second pond. They must have used some kind of fire accelerant, Mac guessed. He hid behind a statue and watched in horror as they set fire to anything that would burn. Ptolemy's eyes were huge with the sheer rush of destructive force he was unleashing on everything combustible. He grinned like a maniac.

Pothinus was coolly evil. He hoisted his robes and held the torch high as he climbed the spiral staircase to the observatory. At the top, he mounted the torch in a bracket. From the belt around his waist, he unlooped a small bow and arrow, lit the end of the arrow with the torch, and shot the flaming arrow into the timber rafters of the ceiling. The first arrow didn't hold and fell to the floor. The second one held fast and slowly the huge beam began to smoulder and burn. The timber was already more than three hundred years old in that section of the building and the flames became voracious.

Mac quivered with rage. He didn't have a plan but he knew he couldn't just sit back and watch one of the greatest tragedies of history unfold before his eyes. He looked back at the pharaoh. Ptolemy was at the far end of the building facing the other way.

The roar of the flames muffled Mac's footsteps as he darted across the open space toward the staircase. He bounded up the steps, two at a time. He reached the observatory and hurled himself at Pothinus' back, slamming him into the railings. The bow and arrow went flying. Mac clung to the regent's back, trying to get his arms around the man's neck.

"YOU!" roared Pothinus as he lurched backwards in an attempt to throw Mac off.

They went crashing into a table covered in astronomical instruments and charts. Mac was winded and let go of Pothinus. Before he had time to recover, the regent had whipped his sword from its scabbard and let fly with a blow that would have cut Mac's head clean off had he not rolled away in the nick of time. The sword quivered as it bit deep into the timber tabletop. Pothinus struggled to free his weapon. Mac used the advantage to slip behind him and grab the flaming torch from its bracket. He rounded on the regent as he swung it in a wide arc.

WOOSH!

Pothinus reeled. Mac took a step forward and swung his arm back for another flaming swipe at the man. As he opened up, Pothinus ducked the flames and jabbed forward with his sword. The blade just caught Mac on the left hip. It was deep but not mortal. He backed off.

Pothinus smiled cruelly. His rotten teeth were long and squished together, and he showed way too much gum. The tip of his nose almost touched his top lip when he smiled.

Mac held the torch in front. It lit the regent's features

from below, the flames reflected in his black eyes. It was the face of a thousand nightmares.

He gulped and took another step backwards. He knew at that moment that Pothinus hadn't the slightest intention of letting him live. He would have to fight for his life. He could hear Ptolemy yelling from down below. In a moment, it would be two against one.

Their eyes remained locked as the man inched forward and the boy inched back. Mac could feel the shudders as Ptolemy pounded up the staircase. The railing was at Mac's back. He had nowhere to go.

Just as the pharaoh reached the top step, Mac hurled the flaming torch at his head. Ptolemy screamed and tumbled backwards. Pothinus was only momentarily distracted but it was enough for Mac to aim a kick at his sword hand. It connected. The weapon flew through the air and clattered down the steps. Pothinus bellowed in fury and ran at Mac. He hit the boy with such force that the timber railings gave way with a crack. Before Mac knew what was happening, he was airborne.

As if in super slow motion, Mac could feel the railing fall away in pieces and the void below sucking at his back; gravity's next victim. Above him, he could see Pothinus' gaping mouth and terrified bulging eyes. Mac's world tilted. His glasses went flying. Then, with a sudden jolt, he was suspended in mid air by his right ankle. Somehow his foot had become tangled in the cord that hung around Pothinus' waist. The man had managed to grab onto the stump of a snapped balustrade and hung at arm's stretch over the drop, with Mac dangling upside down below him. Mac gasped for breath as he twisted to and fro above the inferno.

Pothinus screamed for Ptolemy. He managed to get his other hand up and onto the stumps of the railings so he hung by both arms.

Mustering all his strength, Mac managed to curl up and grab hold of the cord above his ankle.

"STOP! Stop it, you stupid boy! You'll kill us both!" yelled Pothinus as they swung dangerously over the drop. "PTOLEMY!"

Mac gripped the hem of the man's robes with both hands and somehow managed to wriggle his foot free of the cord. He hung on for dear life, coughing and gasping in the thick smoke.

"Let go of me!"

Mac looked around, frantic. He squinted to try and see without his glasses. The smoke didn't help. By his reckoning they weren't far from the staircase. It was his only hope. He kicked his legs and swung in an arc.

"NOOOOO!" Pothinus screamed. "What are you *doing*? Are you out of your *mind*? PTOLEMYYY!"

Back and forth they swung, the staircase rails inching closer to Mac's fingertips with each swing. Suddenly, Pothinus lost his grip as one arm was wrenched off its anchor with the momentum of Mac's trapeze act. The slip was enough to give Mac the few extra inches he needed to make the leap.

In one split-second movement, he let go of the robes and latched onto the railings of the staircase with both hands, legs flailing madly. The staircase shuddered. Mac pulled himself up and over the rails until he stood on the steps.

Pothinus almost lost his handhold just as Ptolemy came to the rescue. The pharaoh grabbed his regent and began hauling him up.

Mac glanced back at them for a moment then bolted down the stairs. The bunch of keys that Pothinus had worn on his belt glinted on the tiled floor, along with the shattered remains of Mac's glasses. He scooped up the keys and ran. The intense heat singed the hairs on his arms as he rushed through the blaze toward the door. He almost crashed into the statue of Thoth on the way.

"My glasses!" It was the pair Ptolemy had planted as evidence. He snatched them up and ran on. He had to get to Aisha.

CHAPTER TWENTY-EIGHT

In a cloud of smoke, Mac stumbled out the door. He coughed furiously. The building was well alight. Greedy flames raced along the timber support network of the ceiling to reach the adjoining library and lecture halls. Smoke billowed from the windows and doors but the flames, as yet, weren't high enough to have alerted the masses down by the harbour; their attention was on the spectacular fireworks.

Over the roar of the flames, Mac could hear the angry shouts of Pothinus. "He's getting away, you imbecile! After him!"

Mac knew they'd be hot on his heels. He had to keep going. He took a few hurried steps along the walkway and tripped over something large. He managed to avoid hitting the ground and regained his balance as he tried to make out what he'd stumbled over. With alarm, he realised it was the body of one of the Egyptian guards that had been stationed at the door. An empty goat-skin canteen lay in a puddle on the path nearby. Mac squatted beside the guard and checked for a pulse. The man was still alive but unconscious. Pothinus must have slipped a sleeping potion in his water. Mac turned and ran on. A short way along the path, he came across another unconscious guard lying beside a discarded water skin. The barrel from which they filled their canteens must have been spiked. He leapt over the body and kept on going.

Without even thinking, he turned into the hall that led to Elcor's private chambers. His footsteps echoed down the corridor. Instinctively, he knew where to find Aisha. Of course, she would be in Elcor's office. It made sense considering that was where he had found her on that very first visit to Alexandria. He wondered why he hadn't thought of that before. It was so obvious.

By the time he arrived at Elcor's office, the smell of smoke was thick in the air. The room was already on fire. Mac tried the handle. It was locked. He pounded on the door with his fist.

"Aisha! Aisha, are you in there?" he yelled.

"Mac!" came the near-hysterical reply. "Mac! We're in here! We're trapped!"

He fumbled with the bunch of keys until he found the one that fit the lock. He burst into the burning room. Aisha and Elcor were sitting back to back, tied to chairs with thick rope. It seemed Ptolemy and his regent couldn't afford to leave any loose ends.

"Mac!" cried Aisha with relief. "I knew you'd come back. I'm sorry. I'm so sorry. I believe you. I honestly do."

He ran to her. He cupped her tear-streaked face in his hands. "Of course I was coming back for you." He held up the desert-worn tyet around his neck. "You made sure of that." He grinned.

Aisha's eyes flew wide as she stared at, not one, but two tyets. Her mouth formed the start of a question.

Mac cut her off. "I'll explain later."

Aisha gasped. "You're bleeding!"

He glanced at the trail of blood running down his side and soaking into his jeans. "It's nothing. Just a scratch. It doesn't even hurt."

The last part was true. It didn't hurt. He knew Pothinus' sword work was more than just a scratch though and probably needed a stitch or two but he couldn't afford to think of that.

"Hurry up and free us, my boy," said Elcor impatiently. "There isn't much time."

The beams above them were on fire and it was spreading to the timber shelves of scrolls that spanned one wall. The room was quickly filling with smoke. Mac grabbed an ornamental dagger from its mount on one of the shelves and hacked away at the ropes. He had just freed them when the door slammed shut with a loud bang. They heard the metallic snap of the key as it was deliberately broken off in the lock.

"NO!" they screamed in unison.

Mac leapt up and raced to the door. It wouldn't budge. Stupidly, he'd left the keys in the lock. They were trapped. Pothinus' evil laughter carried clearly over the flames as he retreated down the hall.

"Curse you, Pothinus!" cried Elcor, his voice hoarse. "Curse you and five hundred of your kin!"

The room was silent but for the crackle and pop of the flames and the distant boom of fireworks.

Mac rushed to the small window and gripped the ironwork bars. He stared out at the Royal Gardens, washed orange in the glow of the burning building. In the sky, he could just make out the intermittent shimmer of colour from the fireworks against the clouds.

"There must be another way out," he thought aloud.

"Both doors are locked from the outside and the window is barred. I fear we will die of smoke inhalation long before the doors are charred enough to break through with force," countered Elcor, his face grave.

Mac was silent a moment, thinking. He knew he couldn't take things back through time with him but he'd never tried taking back people. Perhaps it could work. After all, the nuances of time travel had surprised him more than once already that day. Maybe time travel would surprise him again.

He turned away from the window. Elcor had his arm around Aisha as she stood rubbing her wrists. Mac crossed to them and took Aisha by the hand. He spoke rapidly. "Listen to me carefully. I've never done this before so I don't know if it's going to work."

He went on to explain his idea of transporting them back to his When. They both stared at him for a moment. Elcor and Aisha looked at each other. Aisha nodded. Elcor closed his eyes and prayed.

"Sacred Bennu Bird, god of Time and its divisions, Heart-soul of Ra, your grace, protection and guidance be upon us now and evermore." He opened his eyes. "Let us do this."

They sat cross-legged on the floor and joined hands. The smoke swirled overhead. The heat was intense. They closed their eyes. On Mac's instruction, they tried to block out their surroundings and focus all their mental attention on the tyet, their link back to the Now.

"Just breathe. Slowly now. In… and out…" Mac guided. "Empty your minds. Slip into the vast ocean of quiet. So quiet…"

They breathed in unison, despite the gathering smoke. Mac concentrated on the tyet and within seconds, the quickening was upon him. Everything was spinning. He was aware of Aisha and Elcor. They were there but he was losing them. Their energies were flickering. Mac was teetering on the edge of 'the fall'. He used all his will to resist the pull.

Stay with me! You can do it!

Their energies surged and he felt them come unstuck from the grip of the Now.

That's it! Keep going! I'm right here.

Mac felt an energetic drag from his core. He was literally hauling them over the edge into the void. Just as he slipped over, he felt their energies scatter and disintegrate, like fine sand through his fingers. He'd lost them. He was sucked into the rush, unable to prevent it.

Nooooooo!

As the spinning slowed, he had a split-second flicker of awareness of cold lapis lazuli tiles, before ricocheting back into the vortex. The next thing he was aware of was immense heat and sweaty hands holding his. He opened his eyes to see the out of focus faces of Aisha and Elcor set against the backdrop of the burning room. He disengaged their grip and rolled onto his side, heaving with nausea. His head screamed.

"Mac!" Aisha leaned over him and laid a hand on his forehead.

"I'm okay," he groaned.

"It almost... It almost worked," coughed Elcor. "Did you feel it?"

"I did, Grandfather!" said Aisha, rubbing her eyes.

The smoke was thicker now and the flames were eating

their way through the shelves. They struggled to their feet and moved to the window trying to suck in fresh air.

Mac was weak. He felt sick. He gripped the bars and rested his forehead against them with a gentle thud. As he did so, the ironwork vibrated. He studied the windowsill. The scrolled bars had been cast as a single piece to be inserted snugly into the window casement. He couldn't see any fastenings. It was simply a really tight fit, probably sledge-hammered into position. The beginnings of an idea swirled around in his head. Mac pushed and pulled on the bars as hard as he could. The single cast iron grill shuddered in the casement, sending up little puffs of dust.

He turned to Elcor. "Help me push."

Aisha stood aside while Mac and Elcor put their combined strength behind nudging out the bars. The ironwork gave a little but the prisoners soon fatigued and collapsed on the floor panting and coughing.

Suddenly Mac jumped to his feet. "Elcor, whistle for Suru!"

Elcor hobbled to the window. He leaned on the windowsill and cupped his hands around his mouth. He tried to whistle but nothing came out. He licked his lips, swallowed hard and tried again. A high-pitched whistle pierced the night. Seconds later, the pure white bulk of the baby elephant emerged out of the shadows like some holy apparition.

"Good boy!" croaked Elcor and patted Suru's snuffling trunk through the bars.

Elcor reached into his pocket and pulled out a handful of sticky melted treats for the baby elephant. He held them just out of reach of the probing trunk but close enough for the sweet smell to be maddening.

Suru trumpeted and pushed his trunk further through the bars. The smoke irritated the elephant and he sneezed, sending a blast of warm gooey elephant snot all over them. Still, Suru seemed undeterred and made another grab for the treats in Elcor's elusive hand. He trumpeted again and stomped his feet.

"Come on, my baby," coaxed Elcor. "Mmmm… They're yours if you want them." He waved the treats just under the elephant's nostrils.

Suru flapped his ears and waggled his head in agitation.

"Come on, Suru. You can do it," urged Aisha.

The elephant wrapped his white trunk around the bars and heaved. The ironwork screeched in its casement.

"Yes, yes! That's it, boy!" Elcor offered encouragement.

"Good Suru," Aisha crooned.

Mac bit his lip. "Come on, one more. Just one more big one."

Suru spread his front feet, lowered his head and yanked as hard as he could on the bars. With no more than an instant's resistance, the square of ironwork shuddered out of the casement in a flurry of dust.

"Deliverer," Elcor rasped.

Aisha threw her arms around Mac. "You're a genius!"

She drew back and stared at him. Her eyes danced in the firelight. She was so close. His stomach twisted and flipped. For a split second he was sure she was going to reach up and kiss him. Instead, she darted away to her grandfather's side.

Elcor insisted Aisha go first but she wouldn't hear of it. The old man was pale and shaking. He could hardly breathe. Mac and Aisha helped him onto the windowsill and eased him down on the other side.

No sooner was he safely outside, than an ear-splitting crack signalled the collapse of a ceiling beam. Mac flung himself on top of Aisha and they hit the floor as one. The beam split on impact sending a searing blast of heat and sparks across Mac's naked back. He rolled away, hugging Aisha to his bare chest with both arms. The heat was unbearable. The smoke was too thick to see anything. Aisha coughed violently. Her body spasmed with each painful hunt for air. Mac knew they couldn't stay there. They were out of time.

The burning beam cut them off from the open window and the main door was locked. Mac peered through the smoke toward the other door; the door he'd escaped through last time. He knew it was locked too but he couldn't help thinking that it was the way out, just like last time. Things were different yet strangely the same.

He whipped off his bandana. It was only just damp but it was better than nothing. He clamped it over Aisha's mouth.

"Breathe through this," he yelled over the roar of the flames.

She didn't argue.

Mac scooped her into his arms then hoisted her up and over his shoulder like a sack of flour. He crossed the room with powerful strides and dropped his shoulder to barge the door. Before he could, it swung open like magic! He lurched through it in a billow of smoke, almost losing his balance with the momentum of the charge. He failed to notice the old man on his knees to the left of the doorway, keys still in hand.

Mac ran. He was spurred on by the sound of beams crashing to the floor behind him. The smoke was so thick he could barely see in front of him. He looked down at the tiles

– those familiar lapis lazuli and obsidian tiles – and guessed from the pattern in the floor that he was nearing the centre of the library. He slowed to avoid crashing into the pond like last time. Too late! They tumbled over the lip of the pool and into the shallow water. Mac was arrested by an eerie sense of déjà vu. It was just like last time… only different…

Mac struggled to his feet and hauled Aisha to hers. "Come on!"

They splashed through the pool and out the other side. This time Mac knew which direction to go in. He led Aisha off to the right at a sprint. Moments later, they burst into the fresh air.

They lay sprawled on the steps, gasping and coughing. The cool air was almost painful to breathe. Mac took off his glasses to rub his stinging eyes. He was surprised to realise he was still wearing them, unlike last time when he'd lost them in the pond and the beautiful stranger had retrieved them.

Mac turned to Aisha. She looked almost as she did the night he met her, only she was even more beautiful this time. Her plait had come undone and her damp hair hung long and loose down her chest. He reached for her. "You okay?"

She nodded through a coughing fit.

He held her against his chest and stroked her hair. She shivered and coughed and sobbed.

Mac looked across the gathering crowd to the harbour. The lighthouse shone brightly. The moon had disappeared. Lightning streaked across a sky that was heavily pregnant with storm clouds. The thunder that followed was barely noticeable above the commotion around the library. The onshore wind carried the scent of rain.

A bright burst of colour suddenly lit up the sky. Mac had

almost forgotten about the festival. It looked horribly wrong somehow, like fireworks on the sinking Titanic.

"Ugh!" Something slammed Mac in the shoulder.

A group of soldiers carrying a barrel of water yelled obscenities and ran on. He watched them disappear into the burning building.

Dreamlike, his attention turned to the strange little Oriental man in the orange robes praying nearby. It was a weird sensation – like watching a movie he'd seen before, only this was the director's cut. The same but different…

Wait! This *was* different.

Elcor!

He wasn't on the steps where he should have been. Mac scanned the crowd for any sign of him. Nothing. He eased Aisha to her feet and stood on tiptoes to see above the people. He couldn't see Elcor anywhere. He'd last seen the old man climbing out the window. Surely he'd have had the good sense not to go back into the burning building. But then again…

Mac flashed back to the magically opened door. His heart bolted.

No!

"Grandfather?" Aisha had noticed his absence at the same moment. "Where's Grandfather?" She was panic-stricken.

"Aisha, listen to me," said Mac. His eyes drilled into hers. "Go to the lighthouse and wait for me. You'll be safe there. I'll find your grandfather."

"No, I'm coming with you!" Her voice cracked.

Mac shook her. "Listen. Go to the lighthouse. Go now."

Tears streamed down her face.

"*Please,* Aisha."

Her bottom lip quivered as she nodded and blinked away the tears.

He pulled her close and whispered into her hair. "I love you."

Mac kissed her on the side of the head then pushed her away. "Go. Hurry!"

She stumbled a few paces then turned and looked back over her shoulder.

"Go!"

She pushed her way through the crowd. Mac watched her get swallowed up by the mob then ran up the steps into the blaze.

CHAPTER TWENTY-NINE

It was hopeless. Mac was beaten back by the searing heat almost immediately. The smoke was choking. He'd never find Elcor in it. He tried calling out but his voice was no more than a hoarse yelp. He retreated back down the steps coughing.

He thought perhaps Elcor had escaped via the main entrance. Mac pushed his way through the crowd in a frantic rush for the front steps of the library. As he rounded the corner of the building, he could barely move through the press of bodies, through the sea of spectators frozen in collective horror.

He had almost elbowed his way to the base of the steps when the first big raindrops of the approaching storm plopped on his head. The drops were icy and a chill wind blew off the harbour. Lightning flashed overhead. A mighty boom of thunder broke the spell, scattering the crowd. Suddenly, a bolt of lightning struck the burning library with a deafening crash. The ground shook. People screamed and ran. From where Mac stood it looked to have hit the observatory. Seconds later, another zigzag of lightning bolted right through the library's atrium, sending an explosion of tiles, smoke and hissing steam out through the pillars. Mac dropped.

Soldiers streamed out of the library, buckets abandoned. It was like something out of an Armageddon movie; hundreds of people screaming and running, mothers clutching children, rain driving through blinding smoke, ear-splitting thunder and vicious lightning.

Mac abandoned all thought of searching for Elcor. He had to get out of the storm and get to Aisha. He took one last look at the burning library.

Something on the steps caught his attention – a small silhouette against the flames, a perfect statue, unaffected by the nightmare. Mac rubbed the ash off his glasses with the back of his bandaged hand.

"Nefertiti!"

Mac dashed up the steps and fell to his knees.

The cat was silent, her expression grave. Her ears were charred and disfigured. Her whiskers were gone and the skin on her naked body was badly burned. She was hideous yet strangely dignified. Mac couldn't bring himself to touch her. She just looked too proud. He started to cry.

Eyes narrowed against the rain, Nefertiti slowly turned her head to the side and croaked a meow.

Mac followed her gaze.

"No…" The word drew out as a devastated sigh.

Elcor lay face down in the pouring rain, a river of blood cascading down the steps beneath him.

Mac scrambled to the man's side and rolled him over. "Elcor!"

The stench of burnt hair was sickening. He reached to check for a neck pulse. Lightning flashed. Mac recoiled.

Frozen by the momentary flash of cold blue light was a gaping throat slash, black with blood.

Elcor lay murdered.

Mac's temples throbbed; rage surged through his veins. Neither wind nor rain could dull the fury that swelled in him.

He stood up and screamed into the night. "PTOLEMYYYY!!"

The rain beat down. Mac stood there, breathing hard. Reason was seized by rage. He couldn't think.

Lightning. Thunder.

Aisha!

Mac ran.

CHAPTER THIRTY

By the time he reached the third level of the lighthouse, the rain had eased. He was gasping for breath and his lungs burned as hot as the library far below. He stumbled out onto the balcony. It appeared deserted. Then he saw her.

Aisha spun from the railing to face him. She looked exquisitely tragic. The wind lashed her wet hair wildly against the backdrop of burnt orange storm clouds and smoke that hovered low in the sky. She was a vision of untamed loveliness.

Mac stared. For once, time seemed to stand still. He had never seen anything so… so… He couldn't quite finish the thought. There were no words. There was only a feeling; a powerful feeling that started in his chest and spread to every cell in his body like liquid fire.

He rushed to her.

They held each other fiercely. Aisha sobbed. Mac was silent. He knew she knew. Elcor was gone. There was nothing more to say.

Mac pressed her head to his bare chest and let her cry. Her breath was warm against his skin, her tears hot. He plucked a lone yellow wildflower from her hair and twirled it in his fingertips before letting it drift away on the wind. He wound his fingers loosely through her wet hair until he gripped a handful of it in his fist. It seemed he couldn't hold her tight enough. He closed his eyes and kissed her lightly on the head again and again.

She was his. He would never let her go. Never. He would find a way to make a life together. Their destinies had collided for a reason.

Sensing his resolve, Aisha lifted her eyes to his. Rain dripped off her chin and ran down her throat, following the trail of tears.

Lightning flashed.

Mac cupped her face with both hands and kissed her, slowly at first, then more desperately with each second, as they were swept away in a torrent of emotional release. Surely every horrible thing could be erased by that single kiss, washed clean by the pouring rain.

They got lost in each other while the world disappeared for one precious moment that sidestepped time.

Gently, he eased her away but still held her face. "Aisha, we can't stay here. It's not safe. Ptolemy will be looking for us. His men will be everywhere. We have to leave the city tonight."

"And go where?"

"We'll hide in the old temple ruins until I can figure something out. We need to get to Rome, to your father. Just for a while. We'll be safe there."

"But –"

Mac slid his hands down to her shoulders and shook her lightly. "Listen to me, Aisha. Egypt is on the brink of war. Even now, Pothinus has got General Achillas amassing an army of twenty thousand to march on Caesar if he makes a move."

"*What?* How can you know this?"

"Because in my When it's already happened, long ago. Caesar wins. Cleopatra's restored to power. Pothinus gets his head chopped off and, in December next year, Pharaoh Ptolemy Theos Philopator winds up dead in the Nile." Mac shrugged. "And no one knows how."

"That's quite a tale, Traveller," came Ptolemy's chilling voice from behind.

They jumped apart.

Mac whirled. A surge of adrenalin coursed through him. For a single nauseating second, the life force drained from his legs and he was rooted to the spot.

Sheet lightning flickered. The pharaoh's headdress was gone, along with his plaited wig. His skull was shaved smooth. He was spattered with arterial blood. Black eye make-up streaked down his face, zigzagging from one pimple to the next. There were superficial burns on his forehead and neck. Blood seeped from a cut on his bottom lip. Apparently, the old man hadn't gone down without a fight.

Mac recovered in an instant, stepping in front of Aisha.

Ptolemy eyed him warily. He was still disturbed by the traveller's vanishing act in the tunnels. The pharaoh moved his right hand to the bloodied dagger on his belt.

"And what manner of trickery can we expect this time?" he said.

Mac didn't respond. He backed Aisha toward the railing behind them.

Ptolemy continued. "Come now, Aisha. We've a wedding to plan."

He advanced a step.

"Get back!" hissed Mac. "You touch her and I swear I'll kill you." His voice was low and gritty. He was charged. He was ready; ready to die fighting for the one he loved. His weight shifted almost imperceptibly to the balls of his feet.

Ptolemy spotted it immediately and smirked. This fight would be easy.

There was a blur of movement.

Aisha screamed.

Lightning glinted off the knife just in time for Mac to dodge a fatal wound, the blade slashing his shoulder instead. He clamped a hand over it. Warm blood oozed through his fingers. His eyes didn't leave Ptolemy. The pharaoh was grinning but had backed off to reset.

Slowly, Mac began to circle to his right, putting distance between himself and Aisha. He thought if he could draw Ptolemy away from the door, she'd have a chance to slip past him and escape. Mac waited for Ptolemy to make the next move.

A noise.

Ptolemy was momentarily distracted by the groan of the elevator as the next load of timber – fuel for the lighthouse beacon – arrived in the shaft behind him.

Mac took the advantage. He rushed Ptolemy. His good shoulder caught the pharaoh under the ribs and lifted him off the ground. The knife flew from his grasp as Mac slammed him against the wall.

Ptolemy rammed the point of his elbow into the top of Mac's skull. He dropped, stunned. The pharaoh twisted away and lunged back through the doorway. He seized a length of wood from the stack in the elevator and came out swinging. Mac retreated before the lethal timber assault. Ptolemy advanced, forcing him back toward the railing until he stood an arm's length from Aisha.

The pharaoh sneered at him. "Aren't you going to sprout wings and fly, Magic Boy? Now would be a good time."

His face twisted as he put all his force behind another deadly swing.

Mac ducked. The timber sailed in a powerful arc above him. It smashed into Aisha's jaw with a sickening crack. The force of the blow hurled her over the edge.

Mac lurched for the rail but he was too late.

"NOOOO!"

The cry exploded from deep inside, escaping his soul, echoing into the void. It ripped through every dimension of time and space; agony given wings.

Mac leaned over the rail and searched the black ocean below. The storm had whipped it into a frenzy. Monster waves crashed over the lighthouse foundations, sending an explosion of spray skyward. He couldn't see anything. An inhuman whimper was coming from somewhere nearby. He didn't realise it was coming out of his mouth.

Neither was he aware of the winged shadow that swooped low overhead and the mournful birdcall that pierced the night.

MacKinley Sanderson didn't even see the blow coming. It struck him on the back of the head and sent him tumbling over the edge into space. He was unconscious long before he hit the water.

Blessed blackness.

CHAPTER THIRTY-ONE

AWARENESS FILTERED INTO his mind.

It was dark… Almost.

Yes, there was definitely light coming from somewhere.

Somehow he seemed to have wound up back in the tunnels. He was in some kind of circular chamber – a junction or hub from which multiple tunnels led off in different directions.

Mac was confused, disoriented.

Then a single memory assaulted him like a blow to the head.

Aisha.

He wanted the dark to just swallow him up forever. And yet he was aware of a strange insistence, a pull, a silent calling. He didn't have the strength to resist. It seemed to be tugging him toward the tunnel directly in front of him. The light coming from the mouth of that tunnel seemed brighter than the others. It must have been daylight outside, he thought. He could also hear faint voices up ahead.

He moved toward the sound.

The tunnel seemed long but he was surprised to reach

the end of it in no time. The brightness was dizzying at first. Shapes began to emerge from the light.

Aisha?

"Aisha!"

She looked like an angel, bathed in light and loveliness. She was smiling.

Mac thought he was dreaming until he found himself wrapped up in her familiar heavenly scent. He rushed to her but stopped short, overwhelmed by the sight of her. She looked radiant; perfect – not so much as a scratch. But *how*? He'd seen her fall.

Suddenly, it didn't matter…

"Thank God. I thought you were –"

Aisha cut him off with a silencing finger to her lips. She was still smiling, emerald eyes sparkling in the bright white that seemed to be coming from everywhere.

Mac was powerless to tear his gaze from her. Part of him wanted to look around and figure out where they were but the dominant part was occupied solely with soaking up the beauty right in front of him. Recent events seemed to recede in his mind as if they weren't important anymore. Somehow, all the tragedy and turmoil just drifted away.

"Aisha…" He trailed off. He was finding it difficult to form a coherent thought. He tried to concentrate. "Aisha, we need to get to…" Where? Wasn't there somewhere they needed to get to? Something about… something. Everything was hazy now.

Aisha moved closer. Mac could feel the warmth of her energy mingle with his own, sending a powerful ripple across time.

"Mac." The sound of her voice pulled all his senses

taught. "Mac, listen to me. You can't stay here. You have to go back," she said gently, patiently, as if she were speaking to a child.

"I know, Dad will be awake soon but then I promise I'll –"

Aisha blinked slowly as a sad smile tweaked her mouth for a moment. She shook her head. "You have to go, Mac."

"But..."

"We will be together. Destiny wills it. But you must go now."

It was like a blow to the chest.

Suddenly, Aisha seemed to be further away but she was still speaking.

"I will be with you always. Always." She smiled, sending the little chocolate moon on her cheek higher. "Love was not born of this world so is not bound by it."

They'd been his mother's words. Now, they came from the only other woman he'd loved.

Another powerful blow to the chest pushed Mac further back down the tunnel. He stared back at Aisha, stunned. She was waving. He heard another voice calling her name.

"Coming, Grandfather," she called back over her shoulder.

Elcor?

Mac could just make out the bearded old man standing behind her.

"Wait!" yelled Mac as something whacked him hard in the chest yet again.

The brightness seemed distant now.

"No..."

Whack! That hurt. What was happening?

Tears were lost in the falling rain as they streamed down Gabriella's face. She threw her weight down into another straight-armed pump to Mac's chest.

"Unos... dos... tres..." she sobbed in Spanish as she counted in time with the pounding on the dead boy's chest. "Please, MacKeenlee," she cried, exhausted.

Again, she pinched his nose shut, placed her mouth over his and breathed out.

Mac lay motionless.

"Mack-een-lee," Gabriella sobbed hysterically. "Please! Come back to me!"

Out of sheer desperation, she abandoned the conventional CPR routine and just hammered his chest as hard as she could with a double-fisted thump.

His body jolted with the force. He coughed.

"Sí, sí, MacKeenlee! That's it! Breathe!"

Mac coughed again, harder this time. He sucked in one ragged breath, followed by another. Of course, there was no water to cough up. He couldn't bring it back from the Past, even in his lungs.

Gabriella scooped his shoulders onto her lap and cradled his head against her chest, which heaved and shuddered as she cried and cried.

CHAPTER THIRTY-TWO

DRIZZLING RAIN SPRINKLED Mac's face. His eyes fluttered open to a dull, pre-dawn sky above. He shivered. It was cold. Yet he was aware of another energy encircling him. He tilted his head back to look up into Gabriella's face. It was framed by dripping tendrils of dark hair and was rumpled with concern. Her big brown eyes were puffy and teary. She offered a lopsided smile.

"Gabby." It came out as a croak.

"MacKeenlee, you horrible, horrible boy." Her smile broadened as she wiped the back of her hand across her nose and sniffled.

Mac struggled into a sitting position. He felt like hell. His head screamed. He realised he was sitting on the floor of the dig. Miniature waterfalls trickled over the edge of the excavation. He turned to face Gabby. She wore the same white t-shirt she'd been sleeping in and a pair of grey sweat-pants. She was soaked to the bone and cold.

"What happened?" he asked.

"You tell me!" said Gabby, throwing her hands up in exasperation. "I hear you leaving my tent so I follow you. I no could stop you but someone's gotta keep an eye on you, right? Besides, who am I to stand in the way of true love?" She shrugged, eyes wide in the gloom. "So I watch you for a while then your hip is bleeding, then your shoulder is bleeding, and then you just stop breathing. No heartbeat, nothing. I freak!" Her face broke, making way for a fresh wave of tears. "I thought I'd lost you!"

Gabby reached across and hugged him tight. "You stupeed, stupeed, MacKeenlee," she mumbled into his wet hair.

Mac could feel her body shaking. He was still too shocked himself to register just how much he'd scared her. He hugged her and closed his eyes. He let his own tears fall as he and Gabby rocked back and forth on the floor of the dig.

They jolted apart at the sound of a high-pitched electronic beeping. Mac swore as he fumbled to switch off the alarm on his watch.

"You okay?" asked Gabby.

Mac nodded. But he wasn't okay.

There was silence. A light rain fell.

Finally, Mac found his voice. "Gabby, thanks. Thanks for…" He couldn't bring himself to say "bringing me back from the dead." If he was totally honest, he wasn't entirely sure he was grateful anyway. He wanted to stay with Aisha. His heart ached; his soul was in pain. He didn't care if he lived. It could only ever be a half-life now without her. If only there was some way to bring her back, some way to be with her in her world.

Mac stiffened as Ru's words flashed back to him. *"And this secret place supposedly marks the portal between this world and the next."* He'd been speaking of the Lost Mound of Osiris. Mac hadn't paid much attention at the time but now Ru's words took on a new significance.

A portal between this world and the next...

The thought churned in his mind. Was such a thing even possible? He recalled the cryptic document from the Isolation Room photo. Hadn't it mentioned something about a portal and raising armies from the dead and returning to the body or something? He thought back to that magical afternoon with Aisha in the Sleeping Giant's Temple. She'd said the spring was connected to Isis – her eternal river of tears for Osiris in the World of the Dead. According to her story, the spring gave you the power to communicate with dead loved ones. It sounded insane but, at that moment, it was pretty much how he felt anyway – insane.

He had to get to the ruins, to the spring. He had to try.

"Gabby." His voice was croaky. "Gabby, you gotta let me go back. Right now. I *have* to go back."

"No!" Water dripped off her wet hair as she shook her head. "No way."

"Please, Gabby. You don't understand– "

"I understand you almost died. You *did* die! Look at you. You're a mess. You're not going anywhere."

"Please." Mac forced the word through unmoving lips. Veins in his neck stood out with the strain of keeping his emotions in check.

Gabby noticed the glint of tears building behind the rim of his eyes and the determined set of his jaw. He was serious. She let her head drop back and exhaled skyward. The moment drew out. Her head flopped forward to meet the ball of her hand as it ran over her forehead and snagged in her wet hair. Anguish twisted her face and she swore in Spanish. She knew she was powerless to stop him. All she could do was watch over him like some blind and deaf guardian angel. She glanced at the sky. Leon was an early riser but she figured he'd probably sleep late in the overcast weather. It would buy them some time.

"One hour, MacKeenlee. You have one hour."

Mac blinked a tearful thanks and lay back on the wet tiles. He placed his palms flat on the floor, eyes closed. He felt Gabby's warm kiss on his forehead as he slipped over the edge, into the void.

The familiar smell of the Alexandrian seaside mingled with the smell of smoke. Mac opened his eyes to find himself standing on the beach not far from the lighthouse. It was barely daylight in Old Alex. The city was shrouded in an eerie haze. Apart from the desolate caw of a lone gull, it was silent. The absolute stillness was unnerving.

A wave of fatigue buckled his legs and he dropped to his knees in the sand.

Dust.

He felt like dust.

He was disintegrating from the inside out and was sure the very next breath of wind would scatter him in all directions. Mac knelt at the water's edge and let the waves lap at his knees before crumpling onto his side, cheek pressed to the wet sand. Maybe the wetness would bind the dust, turning him into some sort of mud boy at least. Surely that would be better than dust. Yes, he could feel the guilt lodged, thick and gluggy, in his mud body. Somehow 'guilt' seemed an altogether inadequate word for the deep remorse that choked him now.

He had killed her. He had let her die. It was the same thing, wasn't it?

Words from a half-forgotten Longfellow poem seeped through the mud.

Let the dead past bury its dead…

But the Past was very much alive. The dead though… They were still dead, weren't they. It was not a question. Perhaps it should have been. But who could have answered it anyway?

"She lives," came a beastly voice nearby.

Mac jerked his head up in surprise. A ghostly figure wrapped in a dirty blanket emerged through the haze a little way down the beach. He pushed himself up into a sitting position and squinted to focus.

"But not in this world," the voice rasped.

Mac recognised the voice. It was one he'd never forget. It belonged to the hag from the alley.

She turned a milky eye on him. Her face wore the same amused expression he remembered. Somehow it made her all the more chilling in the grey dawn. She moved toward him through swirls of haze.

Mac struggled to his feet and steeled himself to face her. He fought to find his voice. "She's dead."

The old crone shook her head. "There's no such thing. Not really."

Frayed nerves made his temper flare. "What the hell would you know about reality?" To Mac, the old hag seemed about as far removed from it as you could get.

Laughter gurgled in the back of her throat. "I'm well acquainted with both hell *and* reality."

Mac was silent.

"Death is a place of sorts," she continued. "So is hell." She stepped closer. "But you don't have to be dead to exist in hell, as I think you well know." She was smiling broadly now, her cracked lips peeled back over toothless gums. She seemed to derive some perverse pleasure from the obvious pain that was etched into Mac's face and imprinted on his frame.

He choked back his anger and composed himself to speak. "If death is a place then tell me how to get there, how to find her."

The hag gave an amused snort.

"Tell me!" he barked. His throat hurt.

The hag was suddenly serious. Mac took a step back.

"That is knowledge you have not earned, boy."

"Oh, I've earned it."

"Hmm." The start of a smile curled one corner of her mouth. It wasn't a humorous smile. "Heed me, boy, death's threshold is a dangerous place to play. Osiris' minions guard the Borderland well. 'Tis no place for a novice."

He shuddered.

Suddenly, it dawned on him. He could simply travel back in time before the fire, before Aisha's death. He could change things, protect her, do things differently. It was so simple that he wondered why he hadn't thought of it earlier.

The hag seemed to read his mind. "The fire, her death – it was written. It is destiny – unchangeable, immutable," she explained. "You could do things a thousand times over but all outcomes, all timelines, would still coalesce at the same point."

"Nothing is unchangeable."

"Some things are, boy. You'd do well to accept that and move on. Destiny's no fool." She hawked up a glob of phlegm in her throat and spat it on the sand between them. "But it seems *you* are."

"Fine then. We're back where we started. Now tell me how to find her."

The hag briefly glanced southwest then back to the dig kid. "Even if I did, you cannot bring her back. The price is too high."

"Price?"

"Would you wager the future of the world on some girl?"

"She *is* the future of the world – *my* world!" His voice cracked. "And she's not just *some* girl. She's *my* girl!" Mac was shaking.

The hag threw back her head and cackled. "Stupid boy. Selfish boy." Then she was suddenly serious again. "You are the Deliverer."

Deliverer? Mac was confused. Elcor had said the same thing but it didn't make sense, especially considering he hadn't managed to stop the fire or save Aisha. He hadn't delivered anyone from anything.

The hag went on. "Bennu chose you…way back in the beginning, when your destiny was written in the stars."

"Bennu… that bird – the heron." Mac touched the tyet at his throat. He stared at the sand and tried to recall what Aisha had told him about the Bennu bird. *"If you see it, it means you've been chosen to play a role in the destiny of the planet; the transformation of the world."*

Mac shivered. "But –" He looked up to speak.

She was gone. The hag had simply vanished.

"Damn you!" He kicked up a spray of sand.

He looked back toward the library, hands on hips. A tall column of smoke drifted into the bleak sky. A heaviness hung over the city. The entire place seemed to be in silent mourning.

Mac's chest ached. All of him ached. Still, he found himself plodding along the waterfront toward the lighthouse. He wasn't even sure why. Maybe some part of him needed to stand on that second-floor balcony and make sure that somehow Aisha wasn't still standing up there waiting for him; that somehow it all hadn't just been a horrible nightmare, now dissolved in the cold light of day. Part of him was terrified that he'd look over the edge to see Aisha's mangled body dashed against the rocks below. He pushed the thought aside and walked on.

The hag hadn't answered him when he'd asked how to find Aisha but he noticed she'd glanced to the southwest, in the direction of the temple ruins. It was enough confirmation for Mac to make the decision; he would direct his efforts there. He desperately hoped that the legends had some foundation in truth. He had to at least try. If death was a place – a location – then it had to exist in time, he reasoned. And the fact that he was blessed with the gift of time travel surely meant there was at least the possibility that he could travel to death and back. Hadn't he already done it?

The trouble was that he needed a psychometric trigger. Anyway, whether or not he could bring Aisha back with him was another thing. He wasn't totally averse to the idea of staying there himself if he couldn't bring her back, although the notion of 'suicide' appalled him. He couldn't look at it that way. It was more like going on an overseas trip and deciding to stay permanently.

Mac shook his head. He just couldn't do that to his father… to Ru, to Gabby. It would crush them. There had to be another way.

Somehow, through the haze of the morning and his

mind, he found himself standing on the lighthouse balcony. He was alone. He felt every bit of it too.

He went to the edge. Trembling hands gripped the railing. Without opening his eyes, he leaned over the drop. A deep breath of sea air filled his lungs as the sick dread of what lay below filled his gut.

He opened his eyes.

Nothing.

The nothing-coloured sea washed over the nothing-coloured rocks on a nothing-coloured day in history.

He puffed out a sigh of relief and leaned his forehead against his crossed arms on the railing. He stared blankly at the floor, not even registering the fat tears that plopped onto the tiles at his feet.

Who knew how much time had passed before he roused himself from his stupor?

As he went to straighten up, something glinted on the floor. It looked like jewellery, a chain of some sort. Curious, he picked it up.

A blast of electricity surged through him. White light flashed.

He staggered. Breathing hard, he examined the necklace he held. Shining back at him was the golden tyet Aisha had worn around her neck. Tears flowed freely down Mac's face as he gripped the necklace tightly and held it to his lips.

"Thank you, thank you, thank you," he whispered.

Now he had his link, his psychometric link to Aisha. He had hope at least. The signal was strong – stronger than anything he'd ever felt. Aisha had probably worn the chain for most of her life. It rested near her heart and it seemed to embody her very essence. He could even smell her perfume.

He wanted to set off to the ruins right then and there but he knew he wouldn't make it that far. He was physically and mentally on the brink of collapse. He could feel it. If the hag's warnings were anything to go by, it sounded like he'd need his strength for the journey. Common sense and total exhaustion prevailed. That trip would have to wait. First, he needed to stash Aisha's tyet somewhere safe so he'd find it on his return. How he wished he could just take stuff back to the Now with him!

Then he had a brilliant idea.

He looked down on the smouldering ruins of the library. It was a disaster. The roof had partially collapsed, along with a number of columns. The living quarters at the rear looked to be almost totally destroyed and, from what he could see, the Royal Gardens had suffered too. He thought of the baby elephant, Suru, and wondered if the zoo animals had survived. It was still early and aside from a few people who picked their way through the smoke and rubble, the library was deserted.

Mac forced himself into a trot and headed back down the lighthouse steps.

By the time he reached the library, heavy skies had rolled in and the plume of smoke that had risen skyward a short time ago now tumbled low, shrouding the place in an eerie fog. The smell of smoke and wet ash stuck in Mac's throat as he slowly approached the front steps. Through the rolling smoke, his eyes were fixed on the spot where he'd last seen Elcor's body. A swirl of smoke lifted briefly and Mac could see the steps, washed clean of any blood by last night's storm. Elcor's body was gone. A fresh flood of anger bolstered him, as he strode up the steps and into the smoke, his mouth a thin line of determination.

Ptolemy would pay, he decided. He would pay with his life.

Unnoticed, Mac made his way through the devastation to the pond. It was black and filthy and full of rubble. He looked up. The ceiling was still intact on one side, plunging the far corner of the pond into deep shadow. He wouldn't be seen there.

Crouching at the dark edge of the pond, Mac studied the lapis lazuli and obsidian tiles artistically arranged along its rim. He knew for a fact that they survived the test of time to remain unchanged in the Now. He took a deep, smoky breath and coughed. It was his only shot.

By some miracle, the gas lighter was still lodged in the pocket of his jeans. He pulled it out and began running the pointy end back and forth along the groove between two tiles. The grout was already three hundred years old so, in no time, Mac had managed to gouge a deep crevice and prise loose the triangular piece of blue lapis lazuli that marked the very corner of the pool. With a quick glance around to make sure he was still alone, he carefully lifted the tile and began hollowing out a small depression in the cement underneath.

Sweat trickled down his temples by the time he pulled Aisha's golden tyet from his pocket. He kissed the amulet and offered a silent prayer that it would still be there, undiscovered, in the Now. He put the necklace in the hole and replaced the tile. After making a sorry attempt at re-grouting it in place by scraping the powder back into the groove and splashing some pond water on it, he rested one hand on the tile and cradled his head with the other. Exhaustion, grief and debilitating guilt overwhelmed him.

Movement in the shadows pricked his senses. He stood up slowly. Smoke curled lazily in the stillness. There was no sign of anyone. But something lingered close. It was creepy.

Unnerved, Mac headed for the steps. As he did, the ceiling above where he'd been standing just seconds before began to creak and groan. With a thundering crash, it collapsed in a violent explosion of stone and dust. The floor shook underfoot. Mac was horrified. He'd missed being crushed by a matter of seconds. The shock drained the last of his energy. He felt weak and fragile. It was time to go.

A heartbeat later, he was homeward bound.

CHAPTER THIRTY-THREE

VOICES. HE COULD hear hushed voices nearby. They stopped as his eyelids fluttered open. Ru and Gabby peered down at him. He was still on the floor of the dig. Rain fell from a dark sky.

"Ru," he croaked and struggled to sit up.

"Easy now, my good man," said Ru. He was wearing a yellow, hooded raincoat over blue and white striped pyjamas. All Mac could think of was that kids' show, 'Bananas in Pyjamas'.

"Ru, what are you doing here?"

"I could well ask you the same question, my boy," he said, arching his bushy eyebrows. "I came to check how the dig was holding up in all this rain. Imagine my surprise to find you and Miss Gabby down here."

"What's the time?"

"Time to get you out of here before the professor wakes up," said Gabby.

He noticed the anxious edge to her voice.

"Oh, you know he sleeps like a mummy in its tomb," said Ru light-heartedly but it didn't mask the concern in his eyes.

Mac mustered a tired half-smile. "Depends on what movies you've seen lately."

Ru grinned, relieved the boy seemed okay, albeit totally exhausted. Mac was deathly pale, he noticed, and his blood-shot eyes were heavily underscored with black. Nasty purple bruising decorated his jaw and blood trickled from a deep wound to his shoulder and another on his left flank.

Mac groaned as he touched a sore spot on the back of his skull. He figured it must have been where Ptolemy whacked him but he couldn't quite remember it.

"You're shivering," said Gabby wrapping an arm around him.

"So are you."

Gabby shrugged.

Ru slung an arm under Mac's shoulder and hoisted him to his feet. "Come on. Let's get you dry and fed."

"Food…" Mac couldn't remember when he last ate. His stomach rumbled at the realisation it was so empty.

Ru and Gabby supported him as he took a few painful steps toward the ladder.

"Wait!" Mac whirled and stumbled back toward the pond.

Gabriella and Ru exchanged puzzled looks as they watched Mac fumble with a particular triangle of lapis lazuli on the floor of the dig.

A few seconds later, Mac lifted the tile free and let out a triumphant yell. Aisha's tyet glinted bright, even in the gloom. The thin gold chain was broken in several places but the tarnished amulet had remained intact over the millennia. Instantly, he could feel it pulsing in his hand, eager to communicate. He shoved it in his pocket just as he thought he smelled the faint whiff of jasmine.

First things first – he needed to get his energy back.

Ru and Gabby looked suspicious but said nothing. The three of them set off through the rain for Ru's tent and a hot cup of tea.

Once inside, Ru hung up his raincoat, handed Mac and Gabby towels and blankets, and put the kettle on. No one spoke. The rain drummed on the roof of the tent. With a whistle of the kettle and the clinking of cups, tea was ready. Mac wrapped his cold hands around the mug.

"Let me have a look at that shoulder," said Ru.

Mac flinched away from his touch. "It's nothing. Really." He knew it needed stitches but he was cold and stiff, and he just couldn't face the thought. It had stopped bleeding at least.

Ru shrugged and returned to his tea.

"You won't tell Dad will you, Ru?" asked Mac after a while. "After all, it *was* kind of your idea."

Ru frowned. He laid a hand on Mac's knee. "Make no mistake, MacKinley. I am your father's oldest and dearest friend. I don't appreciate being put in a position where my loyalty is compromised. Do we have an understanding?" His gaze was penetrating.

Mac nodded. "I really am sorry. But I thought you said – "

"Uh!" Ru cut him off with an air-chop of his hand. "No excuses. Promise me you will not put me in that position again. No more sneaking around behind your father's back. No more midnight escapades."

Mac nodded and studied a floating tealeaf in his cup.

Ru sighed and patted the dig kid's good shoulder. "It was wrong of me to suggest we keep things from your father."

Mac nodded again and chanced a look at Gabby who turned away guiltily. He decided then and there that he would not involve either Gabby or Ru in any more of his plans. It wasn't fair to either of them. He was on his own from here on in.

It was Ru who broke the awkward silence. "Well, come on, my boy. Don't keep an old man in suspense."

Mac shrugged hopelessly. "Not much to tell really. I failed. Simple as that. The library burned, and Aisha… she…" He couldn't finish the sentence. It felt like a fat man was sitting on his chest. It was a struggle to breathe, to swallow.

Ru and Gabby averted their gaze as tears welled in his eyes. He pretended to sip his tea as he grappled with his emotions.

Gabby felt his pain as though it were her own. She didn't let on. She simply got up to make more tea when her own tears started to flow. Ru's subsequent attempts at light-hearted conversation fell flat. The boy was shut down and withdrawn. The mood in the tent was grim.

Mac finished a cup of tea and a piece of toast with strawberry jam without even tasting it before glancing at the slate sky outside. It was still heavily overcast but well after daybreak.

"I'd better get back," he said. "Dad will be wondering where I am."

Ru tossed him an old Cardiff University sweatshirt that one of the volunteer workers had left on site. "Your father will have a heart attack if he sees those wounds."

"Thanks." Mac winced in pain as he pulled it on over his wet hair.

"You also might want to remove that amulet from around your neck too," said Ru. "You know the old buzzard doesn't miss a trick."

Mac nodded his thanks. He chewed on another slice of toast as he left and headed back toward his tent. He tried not to limp as the wound on his side stiffened up. It had stopped bleeding but was still tender. His shoulder was okay so long as he didn't try to lift his arm. He unwound the filthy and bloodied bandages on his hands as he walked on legs made of lead.

Leon was frantically pulling on his boots as Mac ducked through the front flap.

"Mac! I thought – "

"Just having breakfast with Ru, Dad," explained Mac as he stuffed the last bit of toast in his mouth.

The tyet was safely in his pocket with Aisha's gold one. The ruby ring was still on Gabriella's finger, as far as he knew. The borrowed sweatshirt concealed his wounds. There was nothing to alert his father as to his overnight escapade.

Leon scanned his son from head to toe. "You look tired, son," he said, gruff but concerned.

That was an understatement, thought Mac. He could see his father examining the bruises on his jaw but Leon chose not to comment.

The professor finished lacing up his boots and said, "I'll make some tea."

Mac nodded and smiled weakly.

All he wanted to do was curl up and die.

CHAPTER THIRTY-FOUR

It was well after midday when Leon roused Mac from a deep, dreamless sleep.

"Hey, you ready for lunch? I picked up some local spicy soup in town."

Mac squinted through groggy eyes. He was totally disoriented. What day was it? It was still overcast outside. It had been raining last he remembered. Perhaps it was still the same day but it felt like he'd been to the moon and back.

Mac nodded. He was hungry.

He put his glasses on and sat up. "Ow!" His shoulder ached. So did his side and his jaw, and the back of his head. And so did his heart. It ached like it would never mend. A crushing wave of grief smothered him. He took a ragged breath and exhaled. Gradually, he felt his energy return with each breath. The fuzziness in his brain began to clear and he felt somewhat capable again. He forced himself up to pull on a pair of shorts and a fresh shirt.

He retrieved Aisha's golden tyet and the stone one she'd given him from the pocket of his wet jeans and threaded them together around his neck. Aisha's familiar perfume lingered magically in the air – or was it in his mind? Her perfume, her energy, her love… it lingered still; intangible, maddening but it was all he had now. It was all he had…

And so, he clung to it like a castaway to a raft.

Strangely enough, along with his grief came a newfound respect for his father. He'd lost the love of his life when she'd died from a mysterious illness when Mac was just a kid. Yet he'd managed to carry on. Mac couldn't remember seeing him shed a tear, couldn't remember seeing him struggle to make it through the day. And yet he must have struggled. He must have been hurting just as much as his son was now. Leon wasn't exactly the smiley type but he seemed content enough these days, which meant it was possible to get over grief, given enough time, thought Mac.

"Just get the hell over it," he said to himself as he tightened his bandana a little too much.

Light drizzle fell with a muted pitter-patter against the tarpaulin lean-to overhead as Mac joined his father and Ru for lunch. Unseeing eyes gazed out across the deserted dig. It was too wet to work so most of the team had either retreated to their tents or had gone into town for the day. His gaze strayed to the flat grey sky. It was an altogether depressing day.

Leon handed him a steaming bowl of soup.

Mac mumbled his thanks and stared at the assortment of colourful vegetables and tender chunks of meat bobbing in his bowl. He knew it should smell wonderful but his senses didn't seem to register anything. He just felt weirdly anaesthetised. Luckily for Mac, the soup had cooled to a nice eating temperature on the drive back from town so it didn't scald him as he ladled it into his unfeeling, untasting mouth. He was vaguely aware of conversation around him.

Whether or not it was supposed to include him, he wasn't sure, nor did he care.

With a slow osmosis of awareness, he realised he'd been staring blankly at a mysterious brown package on the foldout table. He found himself wondering what it was but his curiosity wasn't sufficiently piqued to give him enough energy to bother taking a closer look. He just continued to stare, his trademark eleven burrowing deeper into his brow.

Leon noticed the direction of his son's gaze. "I almost forgot. This is for you." He reached across and handed Mac the package. "Early birthday present."

"Thanks, Dad," said Mac, intrigued. It was weighty. The bowl of soup was carefully laid aside as he tugged at the knot of string that bound the package.

"I picked it up at the bazaar in town for next to nothing," said Leon. "I almost feel bad. The poor old lady obviously didn't have a clue what it's worth. A small fortune, I'll bet. She only had one good eye, poor old dear."

Mac flicked his eyes up to his father's as a little shiver ran down his spine.

Leon kept talking as Mac unwrapped the package. "Lucky it didn't find its way into the hands of an antiquities dealer. That would have been a whole different kettle of fish. I thought perhaps blah, blah, blah…"

His father's voice was tuned out the instant Mac recognised the object in the brown paper.

Total shock stole his breath.

His world seemed to hover in suspended animation as he stared at the ivory-handled dagger in his hands.

"Hey, if you don't like it, I'll keep it myself. I rather fancied the piece."

Mac struggled to find his voice for a second. "Dad… It's absolutely… It's perfect!" He looked up at his father. "You have no idea how much this means to me."

His father cracked a rare smile. Mac stood up and hugged him. Leon patted his son awkwardly. "Eat up. Your soup's getting cold." Then he ducked inside the tent.

The soup was forgotten as Mac sat down and examined the ancient dagger. Its distinctive craftsmanship was unmistakable. Surely there was no other like it. A scaly serpent was intricately carved into the yellowed ivory scabbard and wound its way along the hilt, its writhing body weaving through a maze of coloured gemstones. Age upon age of dirt had lodged in the grooves of the carving, which highlighted the remarkable detail. Slowly, he turned the dagger in his hands. He knew what he was looking for. And there it was – the little divot where the missing stone should be. Goosebumps!

A hot wave of hatred flushed through him.

Ptolemy…

He gripped the hilt in his right hand. His fingers nestled comfortably between the contours of the twisting ivory serpent. Without even trying, he could feel the dagger's psychometric signature seeping into him like a toxic oil spill. The energy was heavy and dark; it was evil.

Mac unsheathed the dagger. The tarnished bronze blade was dull, and dusted blue-green with the passage of time. He was surprised that it was bronze but he guessed the weapon was probably already very old when it was handed to Ptolemy, most likely a family heirloom from the Bronze Age.

"That looks like Apep, the Evil Lizard," said Ru, nodding at the dagger in Mac's hand. "He was the snake-demon, Enemy of Ra. See, he's trying to swallow the sun."

Mac tilted the handle. The weighted pommel at the base of the hilt was set with a large yellow stone. The snake was carved in such a way that it did indeed look as though it were trying to swallow the sun.

He nodded but didn't speak. He was transfixed, held in the grip of some dark power. Thoughts of violent revenge filled his head as he ran his finger along the double-edged blade. Polished and sharpened, it would be as good as new, he thought; ready for action.

An eye for an eye, Ptolemy…

No sooner had he thought it than Ru leaned close to him and whispered, "Karma is a double-edged sword too. Remember that."

Ru was deadly serious.

Mac stared back at him.

"It means that karma is both fulfilled and created at the same time," Ru explained.

"I didn't think you believed in all that hippy crap," said Mac.

Ru shrugged. "I'm not sure I do but I do know this – what goes around, comes around. And I know trouble when I see it." He glanced at the knife in Mac's hands then back to his eyes. "Whatever you're thinking, MacKinley, don't do it." He got up and went inside to join the professor.

Mac swept Ru's comments from his mind and smiled a cruel thin smile. Ptolemy's time was up. Newly flared hatred burned away the cold residue of grief. Vengeance fuelled him.

"Yaaah!" He sprang to his feet and sliced the dagger through the air. Whoosh-whoosh! It felt good. He laughed. Then stepped back on his bowl of soup, flipping it up and all over his leg.

He stopped laughing.

The last rays of sun glinted blood red off the shiny bronze blade in Mac's hand. In the distance, he could just make out the turret of the Lighthouse of Alexandria above the horizon. A chill December wind blew off the desert. He didn't feel it. He was hot with hatred. Besides, he'd prepared for the cold. Before he'd left the Now, he'd pulled on a black hoodie of lightweight stretch knit that clung to his lean frame. He wore the same dark jeans he'd had on the last time he confronted Ptolemy. They still bore the bloodstains. Knowing he was headed for combat, he'd swapped his glasses for contact lenses.

He stood motionless, waiting; a dark figure against the lonely desert.

Mac had commanded the ivory dagger to lead him to Ptolemy. A heartbeat later, he'd found himself facing another Egyptian sunset in the desert east of Old Alex with the Nile River just metres to his back. Only this time, the sunset held no romance.

The ground beneath his feet trembled as an orange cloud of dust billowed from beyond the nearest rise. Seconds later, a black stallion and rider breasted it at full gallop, straight toward him. Ptolemy was twisted in the saddle, looking back over his shoulder through the dust, desperate to put more distance between himself and the other, bigger cloud of dust that churned on his trail.

The stallion spotted Mac just in time and skidded to an abrupt halt, throwing the boy pharaoh from the saddle. It bolted away as a stunned Ptolemy swore and struggled to his feet. He whirled to face the mysterious figure in black.

Mac pushed back the hood.

"YOU!" roared Ptolemy. His eyes were like saucers. "But you're dead. I watched you die. I watched you… fall…" His voice trailed off as he realised he hadn't actually witnessed Mac's death. He'd seen him fall over the lighthouse balcony but that's all. The rapid flicking of his eyeballs said that he guessed the boy could have survived the fall although he found it shockingly difficult to believe. Yet there he was, standing right in front of him.

The pharaoh's mouth hung open. He cradled his injured right wrist and stared at Mac.

Despite having thought of nothing but this moment since getting the dagger, Mac was strangely lost for words. He just stood there. He hadn't a clue just how sinister his silence was to Ptolemy.

The pharaoh's attention flicked to the dagger in Mac's hand. Instinctively, his hand moved to his belt and curled around the familiar carved ivory hilt. A strange breathy wheeze of shock came out of his mouth but it didn't quite form any particular word. Suddenly, his hanging jaw clamped shut and his eyes narrowed. He slid his dagger from its sheath. Wha-ching! The bronze blade scraped the scabbard.

Ptolemy crouched low and began circling to his left with cat-like grace.

"Do your worst, Sorcerer," he said with a lopsided grin. "I don't have time for this nonsense."

"No," said Mac, surprised at the steadiness of his own voice. "By the looks of it, you don't," he added with a nod at the advancing dust cloud. He could faintly hear the thunder of hooves. His heart beat with fresh urgency. Mac did not want to be robbed of vengeance by Ptolemy's pursuers, whoever they were. He had to act fast.

He mirrored the pharaoh's sumo crouch and began to circle to his left.

Ptolemy made the first move. He dashed forward like lightning and slashed the air under his opponent's chin.

Mac jerked his head back with a nanosecond to spare.

Confidence tugged at the corner of the pharaoh's mouth. This would be over in no time, he thought. Then he'd make a dash for the river and try to evade his pursuers. He desperately wished his horse hadn't bolted. He changed stance, ready for the next thrust.

Mac dodged it easily this time and managed a back-handed clout to the side of Ptolemy's head.

The blow upset the pharaoh's wig but was largely ineffective. Ptolemy tore his wig off and threw it on the ground. The sun had gone and he looked truly terrifying in the cold light of its aftermath. He shrugged his shoulders forward and danced on the spot the way a boxer does before a big fight.

Mac rushed at him with a roar.

Ptolemy sidestepped and Mac careened headlong down the short sloping bank and into the shallow waters of the Nile.

The pharaoh was on him in a flash. The blade flew from Mac's grip as Ptolemy landed on top of him and pushed his face under the water. Mac squirmed onto his back in time to deflect the stab with his forearm. He felt the blade scrape the bone and cried out in pain.

Ptolemy retracted for another blow but he wasn't quick enough. Mac grabbed the pharaoh's injured right wrist and twisted it as hard as he could. Ptolemy screamed and dropped the knife. He staggered backwards and lost his footing in the mud. They fell in a tangled writhing heap.

Without weapons, they were evenly matched in strength. The upper hand shifted from one to the other as they struggled and splashed amid the reeds at the water's edge. Mac managed to get in a few of his best punches but so did Ptolemy. Blood gushed from Mac's nose. He was sure it was broken. Somehow it incensed him further and he fought on with blind rage.

Ptolemy was pinned face down but he reached back to grab a handful of Mac's hair and pulled for all he was worth. The dig kid gnashed his teeth. He was sure his scalp was going to peel off his skull. With one hand, he whipped his red bandana off his head and had it wrapped around Ptolemy's throat in the blink of an eye. It took all his strength to pull it tight against Pharaoh's clawing hands.

Ptolemy made a horrible gagging sound and thrashed his legs and arms. Mac held on, possessed by vengeance. "This is for Aisha, you bastard," he said between gritted teeth.

The pharaoh's searching hands pulled a rock loose from the riverbank above him. He threw his arm back over his head and smashed it into Mac's face. Mac saw it coming but he wasn't quick enough to dodge it entirely. The skin was ripped from his right cheek as the pain bolted through his skull. He let go of the bandana and staggered backwards with a splash.

Ptolemy coughed and rolled onto his back. He clutched his throat. His heels found purchase in the mud as he pushed himself up the riverbank on his back, trying to buy time to recover before making his next move.

Mac plunged through the knee-deep water after him.

Rocks and stones fell away beneath Ptolemy's fingers as he groped for a suitable weapon.

Mac looked on in horror as a big yellow scorpion scuttled out from under the disturbed rock and ran up the pharaoh's arm. Ptolemy shrieked and flung it off but not before it stung him twice. It was the deathstalker scorpion. Mac had read about them and knew that its sting caused death within minutes.

Ptolemy screamed as the searing pain travelled up his arm and into his shoulder. Within seconds, his hand was completely numb. He managed to stand but stumbled as he tried to climb the bank. Struggling to his feet, he turned and lunged back toward the water. His hands pawed at his throat as the deadly venom in his bloodstream made his throat swell. Frothy saliva clung to his lips. In sheer desperation, he latched onto Mac. They fell to their knees in the water. Ptolemy splashed and writhed as his face turned purple from lack of air. It was hideous to watch. Terrified eyes bulged in his swollen face and the veins in his neck stood out like rope. Ragged gasps turned to silent gaping as his airway closed over. He clung to Mac, his eyes begging for help before they flickered and rolled back in his head. Limp hands released Mac's shirt then the pharaoh's lifeless body lay still in the shallows.

Mac was breathing hard. His whole body trembled. He wasn't sure he could stand but the blood dripping off his forearm into the muddied water sent alarm bells ringing somewhere in the back of his mind. Nile crocodiles were deadly. He glanced nervously along the reed bed at the water's edge before slugging his way out of the water and up the bank. He nursed his arm as he looked back at the river to see Ptolemy's body bobbing gently amongst the reeds. Then he noticed something half-buried beneath the mud – the ivory-handled dagger. He shuffled back down the bank and dug it out. It was caked in mud so he couldn't tell if it was Ptolemy's or his (which he guessed was still really Ptolemy's anyway).

As he squatted to rinse the mud off the blade, there was a sudden eruption of water and reeds nearby. He jumped in fright the instant a water bird took flight with a mighty beat of its massive wings. It looked like a heron but he couldn't be sure. He was overcome by a nauseating wave of relief. His brain's split-second panic had screamed "Crocodile!"

Every ounce of energy drained out through his toes. He shivered with cold and shock. His swollen and bloody right cheek throbbed. The deep stab wound to his forearm was caked with mud and blood, and would most likely need stitches. He imagined infection working its way into his bloodstream.

It was time to go home.

But before he could, the earth beneath him shook and the thunder of hooves at his back sent him darting into the reed bed.

He could hear voices, along with the squeak and jingle of saddlery. They were so close he could smell the horses. Mac eased up to peer over the reeds. There were perhaps twenty Roman soldiers on horseback. Several had dismounted and were huddled around the pharaoh's discarded black wig lying in the dirt. He ducked as their gaze drifted toward the river. Ptolemy's body floated close by. The footprints, spattered blood and churned up mud at the water's edge made it obvious there had been a struggle. Even though the Romans would probably thank him for making their life easier, Mac thought it best to make a hasty exit.

Heavy footsteps approached as he closed his eyes, gripped the dagger and flashed home.

Leon's snores rumbled away, unbroken. It was still dark outside. Mac was glad he'd decided to go after Ptolemy from the comfort of his own bed. Every bit of him hurt. His arm was still bleeding. He groped on the floor for a towel and wrapped it around the stab wound.

He lay there wondering how he could possibly explain his fresh injuries to his father. He felt like a train wreck…

A quad bike wreck!

Details of his plan to stage a crash slotted into place one by one as the stars trekked across the sky. Timing was the tricky part. He'd have to be up and about before his father woke.

The watch on his bedside table read 4:17 when Mac slid off his cot and checked the sheets for blood. Luckily he'd made the trip with his arms folded across his chest so he'd mostly bled into his clothes. There were a few spots on the sheets, which could be explained by his previous injuries. There was quite a bit of blood from his nose on the pillow. He flipped it to the clean side. He'd deal with that later.

He stood in front of the mirror. Even in the near dark of the tent, he was shocked at just how bad he looked. The bridge of his nose had spread out under both eyes, which were quickly turning black underneath. Dried blood caked his top lip and chin. His right cheek was twice its normal size under a nasty graze, and the bruise on his jaw hadn't faded any. At least it was a relief to take the irritating contact lenses out and put his glasses back on, although they sat painfully on his swollen nose and cheek.

He left the tent, taking the blood-soaked towel with him.

The quad bike, a red Suzuki Kingquad 700, was parked quite a distance from the rear of the tent. His father was a sound sleeper so it was unlikely he'd wake when the bike was started. Mac straddled the quad and started the ignition. He eased on the throttle and sped off into the desert.

He knew the site. He'd planned it all from his cot. There was a rocky shelf not far from camp. It wasn't very high and many a time he'd had fun doing jumps off it in the quad. Of course, his father knew nothing about that.

The sky was getting lighter as Mac pulled the quad to a stop at the edge of the drop off. The spot he'd chosen for the crash was more of a steep slope than a vertical cliff. He wasn't actually crazy enough to crash it for real. He just needed it to look that way. Hopefully, he could keep the damage to a minimum. He knew he'd be expected the pay for any repairs out of his own pocket. Luckily, quads were usually pretty indestructible.

He sighed. It seemed ridiculous to go to all this trouble. Then he remembered what his reflection had looked like in the mirror. It had been pretty horrific. His father would never let him time travel again if he knew the truth.

It was a struggle to push the quad bike over the edge but eventually it bounced and jolted down the steep slope before slamming into a pile of rocks at the bottom. Minutes later, Mac was inspecting the damage. It wasn't much but just enough to make his story plausible. It was certainly still rideable. After rolling around in the dirt and tearing a bigger hole in his sleeve around the stab wound, he mounted the bike and tore back to camp.

Leon Sanderson dropped the tin mug of hot tea when he saw his son pull up on the quad beside the lean-to. "Mac!"

"It's just a few scratches. Nothing serious," said Mac as he got off the bike and sauntered over to his father, doing his best to look pain-free.

"*Nothing serious?* Look at you!" Leon nudged his son's chin up to study his face. He touched a thumb to the boy's bludgeoned cheek.

Mac flinched and sucked in a breath between clenched teeth.

"You're going to need a doctor, son."

"No, Dad. I'm fine. Just some disinfectant and some ice."

"I think your nose is broken."

Mac tried to smile. It really hurt. "Yeah, but my glasses aren't. How 'bout that?"

CHAPTER THIRTY-FIVE

Nightmares plagued him. If it wasn't Ptolemy's puffy corpse floating in the Nile, it was Aisha's horror fall from the balcony. Other times, he was hopelessly lost in the catacombs, chasing her calls for help but never finding her. He'd wake from the dreams shaking and sweating, overcome with guilt and dread.

Every night before sleep, he'd remind himself that he hadn't actually killed Ptolemy; the scorpion had. He was innocent, right? But deep down he knew he'd have killed the pharaoh given the chance. Hell, he'd practically choked the last breath out of the guy. If Ptolemy hadn't walloped him with that rock, he would have been guilty of murder in the first degree. Gabby once told him "Intention is everything." Well, if that was the case, he was certainly guilty; his intention had been murder, although he hated to use the word. 'Vengeance' sounded less violent, certainly more romantic and heroic.

And Aisha… His guilt over her death would haunt him forever.

Three nights of turbulent sleep had left him exhausted. In the few days since Ptolemy's death, Mac's swollen nose and face had gone down, and the bruising was beginning to yellow. It turned out his nose wasn't broken after all. He'd been diligent with the dressing on his arm so there was no sign of infection. It seemed his body was on the mend. His mind though... That was a different story.

He stared blankly at the computer screen, an open textbook in his lap. It was pointless trying to concentrate on his lessons. His thoughts kept drifting to the Lost Mound of Osiris and its rumoured portal to the next world. He fidgeted with Aisha's golden tyet around his neck while he pondered the possibility for the umpteenth time.

The intermittent sunshine of the past few days had finally given way to heavily overcast skies. The computer screen glowed bright in the gloom of the tent, as Mac clicked on the file of photos from the temple ruins. He hadn't looked at them since that day he'd had the argument with Aisha; since that day the library burned down; that day Elcor and Aisha were killed... That one, long, horrible day.

The cursor hovered over an image thumbnail. Mac took a deep breath and clicked.

The smile that burst to life on the screen almost strangled him with grief. He didn't even bother fighting back the tears as he clicked through the images of that magical afternoon. It seemed like a lifetime ago – a different life, even. And he'd been a different person then.

He took off his glasses and wiped his eyes on his shirtsleeve. He shook himself and sat up straighter in his chair. He needed to concentrate on the glyphs. Surely they held a clue to the portal, if there was one. He quickly downloaded the fresh images of the ruins from his camera. They were much clearer than the first lot. Zooming in on a photo of the ancient columns, he let the whispered translations come. He could read everything.

Hours dissolved.

Messy notes littered the keyboard and desk. Then he found it. The reference to the portal was etched into a column in the corner of a photo. He enlarged it further. His lips moved slightly as he read and he was leaning so close to the screen, his breath fogged it. The translation was almost identical to the text from the Isolation Room photo. He scrolled to that very last picture on his camera. His jaw clenched against the pain of seeing Aisha's image, haloed by the late afternoon light. She was lost in her work, unaware that *that* sunset would be her last.

He dragged his eyes off her and studied the document she'd been working on. It was almost word for word the inscription on the columns. He was onto something here. The chair creaked as Mac leaned back and threaded his fingers behind his head, deep in thought.

"Today is the day," he told himself. "I go today."

The decision was made.

As he went to get up, Gabby ducked into the tent carrying two mugs of hot chocolate.

"Hey," said Mac.

"Thought you could do with a treat," she said, setting the mug down beside the laptop. "Careful, it's hot."

"Muchas gracias," Mac said in Spanish.

Gabby smiled that incredible smile of hers and sat cross-legged on Mac's cot. "The professor no is here?" she asked.

"No, he and Ru went into town to get new tyres fitted on the truck." His eyes narrowed. "And don't act dumb, Gabby. I know he asked you to keep an eye on me."

She scratched the back of her neck under her ponytail and looked away.

Mac tried to sip his drink but it was still too hot so he set it back down on the desk. Small talk floated back and forth for a few minutes. When she asked how he was, he just shrugged and turned back to the computer.

Gabby sighed and stood up. "I thought you might need this."

Mac turned. The ruby lion ring glistened in her palm.

He stared at the ring then met her big brown eyes. "Come here."

They hugged.

Gabby ruffled his hair as he slipped the ring on the third finger of his left hand and felt the familiar hum of energy from it.

They faced each other in silence.

Gabriella folded her arms and rocked back on her heels. "I'll watch over you, you know."

Mac shook his head. "You don't have to do that, Gabby."

"I do. Someone's gotta." She smiled, making her eyes crinkle slightly at the edges. She was beautiful, no doubt about it, thought Mac.

"Tell you what," he said. "Why don't you come for a drive with me?"

"Okay, but I'm driving."

"No, no, *I* am doing the driving." Mac said with more levity than he felt. He jingled the Jeep keys in the air.

Gabby feigned a frown. She knew Mac didn't have a driver's licence but he'd been driving since he was twelve years old and she knew he was actually very good at it.

"So where are we off to?" she asked, adjusting her thick ponytail.

"I'm not entirely sure yet. Hey, do you still have that topographical map in your tent?" asked Mac.

"Sure. I'll go grab it."

No sooner had she left than Mac snatched the compass from the bedside table and darted out of the tent to the Jeep parked nearby. The top was down so he vaulted over the driver's door and landed easily behind the wheel.

Seconds later, he was speeding southwest across the desert. A dark sky hung low overhead. Wind and misty rain buffeted his face. It was exhilarating! The cool air was charged and he felt invigorated as the Jeep bumped and jolted over the rugged terrain, kicking up a spray of wet dirt in its wake.

He felt terribly guilty about ditching Gabby like that but he just had to do this on his own. He couldn't afford to involve her any further. Of course, she only had his best interests at heart but she would never understand what he intended to do or how important it was to him. Even if she did, she'd probably still try to stop him. Hopefully, she'd forgive him. He'd find a way to make it up to her when he got back. *If* he got back…

Mac shook off the fear and concentrated on the horizon.

He was looking for the distinctive rocky profile of a sleeping giant. He had to remind himself that over two thousand years had passed and the outline of the landmark would have changed a lot. He desperately hoped the ruins would still be there. The back of the Jeep was loaded with shovels and digging tools but he knew the chances of the ruins being easily accessible after so long was remote. Still, it was his only shot. He had to try.

It couldn't be far. He remembered it hadn't taken all that long to get there on horseback with Aisha. But then, time had always seemed to fly when he'd been with her. He couldn't be entirely sure how long it had taken but it was surely no more than a couple of hours. The Sanderson Team was already camped on the outskirts of the city, so he reckoned it wouldn't take long to get there by car. He'd better keep his eyes peeled, he thought.

Sure enough, just a short time later, the Jeep slowed as a mound of red rock came into view up ahead. As he neared the outcrop, Mac squinted to try and relate its outline to the sleeping giant's profile he remembered. He thought it could be the same place, however, the centuries had taken their toll. Now the giant's flattened forehead and chin receded toward the ground, and his nose was short and blunt.

Mac pulled up at the base of the outcrop. He sat for a second, reliving the memory of Aisha dismounting from her horse with a flash of both her brilliant smile and her long legs. His heart started pounding.

He retrieved a shovel from the back of the Jeep and headed for the invisible cleft that was the entrance.

He hesitated at the head of the pathway. It was much as he remembered, even two thousand years on. The curved path between the high rock walls sloped downward. It was gloomy and still. He glanced at the slit of sky high above. The rain had stopped but it looked like the black heavens were about to dump the motherlode any second.

Mac made his way along the path until it opened onto what was once the temple ruins. Not a trace of the stone columns had survived to the present. They'd probably served as cheap building materials for other projects somewhere through the ages. Now, there was just a tranquil oasis around a spring that still bubbled up from somewhere deep within the earth.

Isis' eternal river of tears...

There was still a cluster of palms surrounding the spring but Mac was sure they weren't the same trees. These were probably several generations of plants later. A lush patch of wild grasses and flowers radiated from the spring before dissolving into the surrounding desert. Minus the columns, the place resembled more of a natural stone grotto in the middle of nowhere than the site of an ancient temple. The energy of the place, however, felt anything but natural.

Mac shivered. Two thousand years hadn't dulled its spookiness any.

Pulling the compass from his pocket, he took a deep breath and knelt beside the spring. The compass needle did its crazy dance once again, raising the hairs on his arms. It was definitely the same spot. He had no idea what he was supposed to do now. He hadn't really thought that far.

A portal between this world and the next...

There was nothing that he could see that remotely resembled any kind of portal or doorway. Unless...

Mac stared at the bubbling pool. Could it be underwater? But the spring was so small; just a gurgle of water that barely filled the shallow pool before trickling off on its own course. Then he remembered the view of the ruins looking down from the lip of the semicircular rock wall. The water sprang from the centre of a circular depression. He recalled thinking that there looked to be some sort of underground chamber beneath it.

As he stared at the eruption of crystal clear spring water,

he could have sworn he saw a flash of light below the surface. He took his glasses off and rubbed them clean with his bandana. He looked back at the water. This time the light burned bright and steady from deep below. His pulse raced.

He grabbed the shovel and struck at the rock around the mouth of the spring. The clang rang out in the silence and echoed off the walls. He didn't stop. The dig kid went to work and within a few minutes, the spring had become a fountain gushing up from a hole the width of his shoulders.

He mopped the sweat from his brow and retied the bandana. He stood with hands on hips and stared at the fountain. It seemed like the only way in but it was dangerous. What if the spring didn't open into an underground cavern? Or at least, what if he didn't make it there before he ran out of breath? What if he got stuck, wedged in the narrow hole? Fear threatened to smother him.

He put his hands on his head and looked at the sky. He roared through gritted teeth. The sound bounced off the rock walls. "Come on!" he yelled. His own voice echoed back at him. Somehow the loudness seemed to chase away the bad spirits he imagined and reality kicked in.

He puffed out a breath and sat down to take off his boots and socks before he could chicken out. He pulled his shirt off over his head without bothering to unbutton it. It was a habit his father hated as it meant he had to turn the shirt the right way out then unbutton it before it went in the wash each week. Mac had been mindful of it lately but right now he didn't give it a thought.

Gingerly, he stepped into the knee-deep water. He gasped. The water was icy. Out of nowhere a chill wind funnelled through the grotto. Mac shivered. He looked around. It felt like a hundred pairs of eyes watched him.

He squeezed his shut. "You can do this."

Mac sat in the water and slipped one foot into the newly made fountain. The gush of bubbles tickled his skin. He cringed a moment, waiting for some ancient monster below to chomp his foot off. With an effort, he pushed the fear from his mind and slid the other foot into the hole.

He shook his head and wondered at what point he'd stepped off the edge of reality into insanity.

Suddenly, there was a rush of air above his head. He ducked as a huge bird swooped low. He blinked in utter astonishment as a large heron landed on the edge of the pool with a graceful flap of its wings. The bird was big – way bigger than a regular heron. It stood just inches away, towering over him. At first glance, its plumage was the same dark grey as the sky above but when it moved, its breast feathers were shot with purple and crimson. Even in his shock, it reminded Mac of the iridescent fleck in the paintwork of his Uncle Terry's Porsche; that certain shimmer that made the heart beat faster.

Mac stared at the bird.

The heron dipped its long neck and angled its head to the side so that it was eye to eye with the boy. The golden eye that fixed him with its intense gaze seemed to draw him in, to pull him into some ancient past. He was completely transfixed.

"Bennu," he whispered.

He felt his focus scatter. His surroundings melted into nothingness as he let himself be drawn into the world upon golden world that lay deep in the bird's ancient eye.

Aisha's words echoed in his mind: *"Bennu offers unhindered passage through the Underworld."* Is that where he was really headed? He wasn't sure he even believed such a place existed.

A shrill wind howled through the oasis. It raised goosebumps along Mac's spine and ruffled the bird's feathers. There came a dark presence. The heron sensed it immediately. It broke focus, raised its beak and cried out. Mac could tell it was angry.

CRACK!

Lightning bolted to the earth just metres away. The ground shook; the air sizzled. The heron took flight with a single flap of its giant wings.

Terror surged through Mac. In one quick movement, he propelled himself feet first into the fountain, without a thought of what lay beyond.

CHAPTER THIRTY-SIX

THE UPSURGE OF water was powerful. It tore his glasses off his face. Torrents of bubbles rushed over Mac's skin as he gripped the rocky walls on either side with his fingers and pulled himself deeper into the hole. He knew it was suicidally crazy. Still, he kept going.

He felt the hole widen and the current ease. Air released in a stream of bubbles soothed the pressure in his lungs as he sank deeper. He started to panic when he lost touch with the rocky sides. He was submerged in icy blackness with no way of knowing where he was or what lay ahead, or when and where his next breath was coming from. The whole thing was a bad idea.

He extended his legs to set himself for a powerful return kick toward the surface when he felt his feet break through the water into cold rushing air.

Total confusion…

Light shone beneath him.

Immediately, he thought he must have somehow become disoriented in the water and spun upside down without even realising. How else could his feet be poking through the surface? Perhaps the spring surfaced somewhere else and he'd mistakenly presumed he'd been descending when he'd really been carried along some subterranean channel to pop out further along from the oasis.

He tumbled over until his head broke the surface.

Air! A chill wind blew in his face as he sucked in a welcome gulp of it. He squinted against the brightness. Something wasn't right. He felt as though he was upside down, like his feet were somehow *above* him in the water. And with that realisation, he started to *fall* through the surface of the water toward a perfect circle of wavering light.

Mysterious symbols were carved around its entire circumference, which looked to be made of some sort of shiny metal. The light emanated from the centre of the circle but possessed a strange quality; it looked and moved like liquid. It was beautiful. Mac had always been a fan of the television series, Stargate SG1, and owned the entire first season on DVD. To him, this was the closest thing to a stargate he could possibly imagine.

Even through his panic, he wondered if this was the actual portal between the two worlds. He held his breath as he hurtled towards it.

A mixture of fear and excitement coursed through him as he plunged into the rippling circle of light. A dazzling flash of white swallowed him, leaving blue shimmers of electricity spiderwebbing across the circle. The surface wasn't solid exactly but was strangely resistant as though he were swimming through jelly, only the texture was different; it felt tingly and sort of electric. It wasn't an unpleasant sensation. Everything was brilliant white inside the circle. He felt expansive, as though he'd dematerialised somehow.

An instant later, he emerged out the other side.

He was falling through black space.

Terror!

"AAAAARGH!" He was sure he was screaming but no sound came out.

Stop, stop, stop!

And suddenly he did.

He just stopped dead, suspended in mid air. His mind was paralysed with shock. He couldn't feel anything under him and it didn't feel like he was hooked on anything from above. He'd just stopped the instant he willed it. Above him, he could just make out the wobbly blue shimmer of liquid light. Cold air whistled all around him.

Maybe he was still underwater and hallucinating from lack of oxygen; maybe he drowned without realising it; maybe he was already dead…

He did an automatic mental body check, the way you do when you've just come out the other side of any horrific experience. He moved his hands to his face but they touched nothing.

Huh?

He tried to touch one hand to the other but missed. Through rising panic, he tried to bang his knees together; you can't miss your knees, right?

Nothing. Air.

The realisation came slowly. *I don't have a body…*

Mac wasn't sure just how he felt about that. In the complete darkness, he tried to look at where he thought his hands should be but saw nothing.

No, not nothing.

Something very faint glowed in the darkness. He tried to concentrate. Yes, there it was – the faintest outline of a hand. In fact, it wasn't really an outline but more of a blueprint; it was a biological map of thin glowing lines, energetic pathways.

Mentally, he flexed his fingers and watched in amazement as the glowing blueprint mirrored his silent command.

Did that mean he was dead? He didn't feel dead. He felt perfectly alert, albeit utterly confused. But it did seem that he'd somehow shrugged off the physical density of his flesh-and-blood body.

He wished there was light so he could see where he was. No sooner had he wished it than a weak light began to emanate from his core. His belly had turned into a beacon! It felt warm and soothing. The light was comforting even though it didn't penetrate the darkness enough to show him where he was.

The comfort was short lived as his imagination got the better of him. What if something lurked in the dark waiting to snatch him?

Stop it! Just keep going. He brought his thoughts under control and moved forward.

Mac stopped, surprised that he'd been able to move forward in the first place. After all, he didn't have a body and he wasn't even on solid ground. As far as he was aware, he was still suspended in mid air.

Forward!

His ethereal body moved forward again. The air rushed through him. He stopped.

Left!

The wind changed as he moved left, then right at will.

He smiled in his mind; the mind that seemed to be his own mental joystick.

Mac continued forward, careful not to move too fast in case he smacked into a wall or something. Mind you, he thought, he could probably go right through them!

He wondered where on earth – or *not* earth – he was. Perhaps this was the void he flashed through so quickly when he time travelled. He didn't think so though. It felt different. There was a certain vibration in the air that buzzed through him. It reminded him of the feeling you get when you press your lips together and hum, only the feeling wasn't just confined to the lips, it zinged through his whole being.

When Aisha... Well, the last time he saw Aisha anyway (he still couldn't bring himself to say 'she died'), he had woken in some sort of tunnel arrangement. He wondered if that's where he was now. He wished he could see the way.

Gradually, his mental eyes adjusted to the dark.

He was travelling parallel with a wide, curving ribbon of pearly blue light that swept gently upward and away like the twisting double-helix of a strand of DNA. He hadn't realised he'd been moving up as he'd moved forward but now that he could see relative to the glowing curvature, he sensed the upward motion. He reached out to 'touch' the curve that ran alongside him. His fingertips raked long shimmers of electric blue light along the curve as they meshed with the strange substance. It was some sort of force, he was sure. It wasn't solid but had definite presence and parameters, and his fingers could interfere with it energetically, sending tingles all through him. He felt as though he were slightly magnetised to it; as though there was a magnet moving behind the curve and he was a paperclip being dragged along the surface of a piece of paper, just like the game kids play when they're bored in science class.

Mac peered into the gloom beyond the blue curve. The double-helix pathway seemed to be bordered by a vast matrix of shafts and hallways that intersected at shadowy alcoves and angles.

The Borderland…

He thought he saw light coming from the end of one of the tunnels. He stopped for a better look. He couldn't be sure. The subtle shadings of blacks and greys shifted and changed before his eyes but he was certain he'd seen something. He looked way up the central shaft of the spiral he was on. He thought he saw a pinprick of light in the far distance but, again, couldn't be sure. The light he thought he'd seen in the space behind the curve had seemed much closer, easier to get to.

With a bright shimmer of blue and mauve, he pushed himself through the light-curve to emerge on the other side in a square-shaped tunnel.

There it was again. For a split second he thought he saw light.

He glanced back at the glowing spiral path and was surprised at how far away it suddenly appeared to be. He could just make out the blue residual glow from the spot he'd passed through.

He turned back to face the dim tunnel and caught the peripheral play of light somewhere up ahead. He started forward, boldly at first, then slowed as he began to question the direction he was heading in. Could it be that he was heading downward again? He glanced left and realised that the tunnel also morphed left at that very point. He turned and followed it.

Fleeting reflections of light gave him momentary hope

that he was heading in the right direction again. He continued straight for a time then realised he hadn't passed by any offshoot tunnels as he'd expected, based on how the matrix had looked from the curved path. Almost instantaneously, a tunnel appeared on his right. He hesitated. Only a moment ago, he was quite sure, that tunnel hadn't been there. As he looked ahead again, he could make out a dull grey dead end.

With a mental shrug, he headed down the right-hand tunnel. As he moved he raked his fingers along the walls, expecting the blue shimmer. Instead, he saw nothing. His fingers dragged through a sluggish energy that felt almost solid, yet wasn't. It was still some sort of force but was certainly very different from the curve.

The first twinges of indecision nipped at his mind.

He turned around and started back toward the curve, careful to reverse the way he'd come.

Okay, it was a left followed by a right, wasn't it?

That should have brought him out on the edge of the matrix where he could still see the curve. But it didn't. Instead, he found himself in yet another square tunnel. Confusion quickly turned to panic. He spun around to retrace his steps, only to find a dead end at his back.

That's impossible! I just came that way… didn't I?

A tunnel stretched away to his right. He took it. In his panic, he moved quickly, following the sharply angled twists and turns of the hellish labyrinth, every now and then catching fleeting glimpses of the elusive witch-light that taunted him. Finally, his fear turned to outright rage.

He roared silently and punched the wall as hard as he could. The wall just swallowed the blow with its sickening viscosity. Mac withdrew his hand and hovered there, trying to calm down.

This is all Ptolemy's fault! He's the reason I'm in this mess. He got everything that was coming to him.

Then he turned the anger on himself.

No, it's your fault, idiot! You *messed with time,* you *fell in love,* you *let her die. Your fault!*

Okay, so I deserve to die. But so did Ptolemy!

Suddenly, he wondered where Ptolemy was. If this was indeed the Underworld then it stood to reason that the evil pharaoh could be lurking around anywhere, just waiting for his chance to exact vengeance.

A segment of the strange papyrus rubbing flashed across his mind.

...shall in some distant day
raise armies from the dead,
Summoned through the portal to exact vengeance
upon a sleeping planet
And hell will reign.

Anger seeped away as fear rolled back in triumphantly.

Was it referring to Ptolemy? Was *he* the one to raise armies from the dead to exact vengeance on a sleeping planet? Mac couldn't imagine anything more terrifying than Ptolemy leading an army of the dead. And all because of *him*... Mac couldn't live with that and he sure wasn't about to die with that.

"It's *me* you want!" His silent scream stayed trapped in his mind.

Mac tried to think, tried to cling to sanity. Why hadn't Ptolemy made his move yet? Wasn't this all about some stupid vengeance? For an instant, it all seemed so petty, so insignificant. Even the memory of Ptolemy seemed small now. Then another memory

… but be ye warned,
Mysteries of the Cosmos be they dangerous to those mortal minds
not learned of the key,
Minds starved of wisdom and righteousness,
Bloated by the emptiness of undiluted intellect…

He couldn't just teleport out of there like he did on his psychometric trips seeing as he hadn't got in that way. He needed to find his way back to the curve for a start. It was a mistake to have left it for the angled matrix he'd thought was the easier route. Then, with a hideous surge of horror, snatches of the ancient document he'd inadvertently photographed came flooding back.

Keep to the curves of space where his minions cannot follow.
Only in angles do they move
and in angles will hunt thee relentlessly.

The instant he had the thought, he was aware of something in the tunnel nearby; more than one 'something' … Osiris' minions!

Darkness seemed to pour forth from either side of the tunnel and his energetic beacon of light dipped and dimmed. He *felt* the darkness growl rather than *heard* it.

Mac didn't wait to see what materialised. He flew. He flew fast.

Grey-black corridors zoomed by as he took corner after corner, deeper into the nightmare. He felt more of the 'somethings' join the hunt as though his terror drew them like moths to a flame. He wondered if they – whatever 'they' were – were picking up the scent of his fear. They seemed to come out of nowhere. He couldn't see them but he felt each new presence add to the hunger. Their collective energy was dark, primal, yet intelligent.

Then he felt them switch strategies. So far, he'd managed to outrun them. Now, he felt the pack behind him disperse, only to spring up in clusters ahead of him, blocking his path.

He propped.

UP!

He zoomed up through the heavy drag of the tunnel ceiling and broke free on the other side to emerge into yet another shadowed purgatory. Instead of a clearly delineated tunnel, he found himself in a weirdly angled cell with no way out except through the strange walls that jutted out and switched back on themselves to create even more… angles…

WOOSH!

Mac felt their black formless forms flash to him from every crevice. He screamed in silence as one of the things ripped at his being. Little sparks and shimmers exploded as it tore hungrily into his energy. He flung himself across the space and into the far wall.

The thing was sucked off him as he hauled himself through the barrier and wound up in another angled chamber identical to the last. He got the impression he was in a sort of dark honeycomb, with chamber after chamber fused together.

They were on him almost instantly – ripping, tearing, gnawing at his being. The pain! It felt as though the shapeless monsters were savaging his very soul. The dig kid mustered every ounce of strength to fight them off.

Aisha! He called to her in his mind.

His beacon swelled bright from his core. The things recoiled briefly but were on him again as they watched his light fade.

AISHA!

This time the call was stronger. His light blazed. The evil shadows shrank back. His core settled into a bright pulsing. His attackers withdrew to the dark angles but he could feel them watching, waiting.

He held a picture of Aisha in the forefront of his mind like a torch while he decided what to do. He thought of Aisha's golden tyet.

No!

Mac's heart sank as he realised he couldn't possibly still be wearing it. His hand moved to his throat anyway. To his surprise, he felt its energetic imprint and noticed a faint residual glow, despite the fact that the physical object wasn't there.

His ethereal fingers soaked up the tyet's glowing residue. Fascinated, he watched its energy spread through the circuits of his hand like the veins in a butterfly's wing. His mind reached out for Aisha, searching. He felt a light go on somewhere in the recesses of his mind.

Where are you, Aisha?

He could feel her ever so faintly on the fringes of his awareness. The heaviness of the labyrinth seemed to be blocking the signal. He needed to get back to the curve.

The space vibrated slightly. Mac's light faltered as the dark ones circled.

How do I get back there?

In answer, his mind recalled another excerpt from the mysterious document in the photo.

Abandon all grievances
For such dangerous treasure shall slow ye before his minions' pursuit,
And the sharp edges of guilt and unforgiveness
fit not the curves of Light and Truth.

He fought to maintain distance between himself and the encroaching others while he grappled with the meaning of it.

Grievances... Dangerous treasure...

Mac wondered how a grievance could be referred to as treasure unless it was something you valued. A tiny spark of understanding brightened his mind somewhere. He felt the menacing things around him recoil an instant. He was onto something.

Guilt and unforgiveness... Dangerous treasure...

According to the ancient document, all grievances must be abandoned. That sounded simple enough – simple perhaps, but not easy.

Okay, let's see... Number one grievance – Pharaoh Ptolemy Theos Philopator. He killed my girlfriend and murdered an innocent man.

Fury and vengeance hunger surged through him. His light dimmed. The hunters moved in.

Aisha, Aisha, Aisha...

His light burned once more, holding his pursuers at bay.

Mac wasn't dumb. If the ancient text was right (and from what he'd observed so far, it quite possibly was), it was clear he needed to let go of his hatred of Ptolemy. He needed to forgive him to get back to the curve, to rid himself of the dark hunters on his heels at least. But the simple truth was that he just didn't want to get over his hatred. It irked him to have to let go of it. He wasn't ready to forgive Ptolemy. He felt he shouldn't have to. It wasn't fair. With horror, he realised he'd rather cling to his grievance – protect it fiercely, even – than abandon it. He just wasn't willing. It was his treasure… His dangerous treasure…

The space reverberated with his silent scream of frustration. He could feel dark laughter all around him. His light started to fade.

God… Osiris, Isis… Aisha… Whoever the hell can hear me, tell me what to do! Help me!

The angled cell shook and the air around him thrummed as a thin sliver of white light pierced the ceiling through a narrow crack. His attackers darted for cover. Mac flew to the light. He tried to slip through the crack but couldn't. His energy wouldn't fit.

And the sharp edges of guilt and unforgiveness
fit not the curves of Light and Truth.

The relentless hunters snapped at him from below. He could feel the pack spread out and sensed their dark presence in the high angles either side of him. They were going to try and cut off his escape.

No!

In an instant Mac weighed up the choices. What did he want more – the safety of the light or the 'wealth' of his petty grievances?

He chose the light.

In the moment of that single decision, he felt his entire energy lighten. He felt freedom like he'd never known. He *became* the light and streamed through the narrow crack to find himself back on the curve.

Yes!

He was ecstatic! Had he had physical eyes to cry, he would have bawled them right out of his head then and there. He was back on the path. He was safe.

A distant light shone, high above him. He moved toward it with renewed strength.

Take me to Aisha, he commanded the glob of pulsing energy at his throat that was once the golden tyet.

He moved faster. Up and up, he went, pulled by some unseen force through bands of wonderful colour toward the brightness. The light streamed through him and he was aware of music that wasn't really music; it was melodic vibration but he couldn't actually be sure if it was sound exactly. He felt like he was a single string in some cosmic violin.

Aisha was close. He could sense her. He felt his violin string vibrate faster.

From the brightness, there came another light, this one more intense with an oscillating rainbow of colours at its shimmering tips.

"Aisha? Is that you?" His voice was a thought pattern that flitted like static across the space between them.

"No," came the calm reply. "But she is near." The vibration was as soothing as a lullaby.

"Can I see her?"

There was a pause, a fluctuation in the light. "Not yet."

Mac noticed the strange ripple he put forth as he fought his frustration. "But I've come all this way."

"You needn't have, my friend. The veil is thin. She is

always near. Always." The light seemed to shift as it 'spoke' so that it encircled him.

The calm returned almost instantly. He couldn't think of what to say next. There was an overwhelming desire to just sit, to stay; he wanted to just soak up the peace, the beauty, and forget everything he ever knew.

The voice went on. "There was the agreement… In the beginning, remember? You must finish what you set out to do."

Agreement?

The ticklings of a memory so distant it barely existed brushed his mind… Yes, there *was* something, he thought. A mission…

If light could be said to 'smile', it did. "Do not force it, child. There is a part of you that remembers. The Plan was well laid out and as time burst forth into existence, so too The Plan rushed forward to meet it head on. Always has it danced and adapted to time's unfoldment. You, MacKinley Sanderson, are part of that Plan."

Mac's beacon flickered and faltered. "But I don't want to be anymore. Bennu chose me. I didn't ask for any of this."

"Oh, but you did. Bennu chose you from many volunteers, much to your great honour and delight. And the heavens did rejoice along with you, Deliverer."

"I don't understand any of this."

"You do not need to. Go back and live your life. To know too much now would alter everything."

Mac wondered if he hadn't already altered everything.

"Worry not, dear mortal. Every age has its Deliverer and with every Deliverer, there goes forth at least one Balancer. It is the way. What will be, will be but forget not this Plan is foolproof in the end. It will not fail. Only the smoothness of its execution is subject to circumstance, not its effectiveness."

Mac's mind felt stretched to breaking point.

He felt the light withdraw.

"Wait," he said. "How will I know what to do? I've already wrecked everything. I should have protected Aisha and her grandfather. I should have stopped the fire. I probably shouldn't have gone after Ptolemy and I never should have fallen in love in the first place. I just should have–"

The light strobed with gentle laughter. "There are no 'shoulds' and 'shouldn'ts' in life. Just live it and forgive it."

Mac was still.

The light pulled back further.

Then there came another light – another presence. This light had a different quality. It was not as bright yet it was strangely compelling. The light floated and flowed into form.

"Aisha!"

Mac recognised her instantly. The space between them responded to the fresh vibration with a subtle shift and shimmer. Somehow she still looked like Aisha but she was a portrait painted in living light. Had it been possible to translate her perfume into colour, this is just what it would have looked like, he thought. Subtle shades of green tinged with indigo blue and a hint of pink radiated from a white-gold core. Her new beauty stunned the senses; her Ba, he thought – her beautiful Ba.

She smiled. Her light flashed.

They rushed *into* each other. Their energies meshed in a great surge of brilliance. It was an embrace like no other. It was a total melding of spirit – a soul kiss. Each was lost in the other as they became one.

Unity.

Aisha was the first to extract. She twinkled bright and fast before him.

"You must go now, my love."

Waves of energy stroked his being. "No, I'm staying."

"Time needs you."

"And I need *you*."

Her light tickled as she moved closer. "Remember, I am with you always."

She pulled back.

"Wait! I love you, Aisha!"

"And I love you." Her thought-voice was further away.

Another light joined hers.

Elcor.

And then another…

Mum? MUM!

He felt his mother's love rush in…

An instant later everything flashed brilliant white.

CHAPTER THIRTY-SEVEN

GREY SHEETS OF rain overlapped as the wind swirled around the ancient grotto. The palms overhead lashed wildly but Gabriella ignored the storm. Fearful of snags, she'd stripped her button-up shirt and cargos down to just a white singlet top and flowery boy-leg underpants. She squatted in the shallows of the spring and prayed. As she stared at the spring's widened mouth and the discarded shovel nearby, she cursed MacKinley Sanderson for the thousandth time since she'd heard the Jeep roar off into the desert without her.

Gabby hadn't wasted a second. She'd headed straight for the quad bike only to find it was low on fuel. Precious minutes were lost filling it from the drum so by the time she was following Mac's tyre tracks across the desert, he'd had a pretty solid head start.

"Bastardo pequeño estúpido!" she hissed under her breath. She was furious – *worried* and furious – and more than a little scared of diving in after him.

She squinted through the driving rain at the boy's boots and shirt lying on the ground and eased into the cold water with a gasp as it gushed up over her navel. The rope around her waist chaffed her skin. She adjusted it and glanced over her shoulder at the end tethered around a palm trunk. There was no way she was going down any hole without a guide rope. She'd dived sinkholes in the Amazon jungle and knew how dangerously easy it was to become disoriented or stuck and drown. A yellow all-weather torch was in her hand. Thankfully, it had been in the back of the Jeep, along with the rope. She switched it on. Slanted raindrops sparkled in its beam. The torchlight glinted off Mac's glasses lying in the shallows. Worry galvanised her into action. She tossed them on his discarded shirt then, with one big breath, Gabby pushed herself into the hole.

A white-hot flash of pain!

"Aargh!" Mac's cry was just a muffled explosion of bubbles.

His elbow banged hard against the side of the hole as he was dragged up through the water toward the surface. Yellow torchlight bounced erratically somewhere above him. He knew where he was but couldn't remember a thing after jumping into the spring. He figured he couldn't have been down there more than a few seconds, as he still had air in his lungs. And now someone or something was hauling him to the surface.

He burst through the spring into the pouring rain. Someone's feet were planted on the rocks either side of his head. He spun to meet a wall of wet dark hair.

Gabby sat behind him, her grip still locked under his armpits. The hair that washed down over her face parted around the torch between her teeth. She was breathing hard. Her knees were bleeding from having scraped them all the way up the walls of the hole. She'd had to tuck them up and reach down between them to grab Mac under the arms and drag him to the surface, using her toes to push off the sides.

She spat out the torch, let go of the boy, and wiped the hair off her face. The loop of rope around her waist slipped off after a moment of fumbling with the knot. Mac hadn't registered she was in her underwear until she stood up and stalked off through the rain.

"Gabby, wait!"

He got out of the spring and stumbled after her. He caught her arm as she stooped to pick up her sodden clothes. "Gabby…"

She yanked her arm away. "What the hell is wrong with you, MacKeenlee?" Her eyes blazed. Rain streamed off her chin. She was fuming.

Mac put his hands on his hips and looked at the ground. He pinched the end of his nose. He couldn't think of a single thing to say. He simply looked on as she struggled into her soaked button-up shirt. She didn't bother pulling on her wet cargos before heading back toward the entrance. Mac stared after her through the driving rain.

What the hell *was* wrong with him? He wondered.

Vague snatches of events flashed across his mind. A circle of light… Fleeing through the darkness… More light… A conversation with… with someone. Aisha! Yes, she'd been there. Though none of it made enough sense to string together in any way.

He heard the Jeep start up. It idled, waiting. Quickly, he gathered up his things and ran for the entrance, scooping up Gabby's forgotten shoes on the way.

Gabriella sat behind the wheel, chewing her bottom lip.

Mac tossed the stuff in the back of the Jeep and went to her door. "Gabby, please," he started.

"See you back at camp," she said without looking at him. She jammed the Jeep into gear and sped off, tyres slewing in the wet.

Mac watched her go. He walked slowly back to the quad bike. He shivered as he realised he'd dumped his shirt and boots in the back of the car. It was going to be a cold ride home.

By the time Mac heard his father's old truck rumble to a stop outside the tent, he'd bathed in hot water, changed into dry clothes and found a spare pair of glasses in his trunk. He lay on his cot with a copy of Space Journal lying open on his chest, not that he'd so much as glanced at the page. It wasn't quite nightfall outside but a gas lamp burned steadily in the corner of the tent. The afternoon had all but drifted away while Mac lay lost in thought.

He couldn't say for sure if he'd found the portal or not. Something had happened; he knew that much. He'd had some kind of experience but it was like having had a dream that you can't quite get back once the alarm has gone off. One thing he was sure of was that he'd found Aisha. He couldn't remember it precisely but the feeling lingered like the warmth in your belly after a long kiss.

Strangely, he felt calm inside. Sure, he was confused and felt bad about Gabby – *really* bad – yet the fog of grief had started to lift somewhat. It felt like he'd found some sort of closure. A future glimmered on the horizon at least.

Mac jumped at the loud clash of pots and pans that rang out from the cooking area in the lean-to.

"Hey!" yelled Leon from outside. "Get out of there, bird! Shoo!"

An instant later, a large grey heron darted into the tent. Mac jumped off the cot. The bird squawked in fright and flapped its big wings in the small space. Loose papers went flying off the desk into the air.

SMASH! The gas lantern toppled to the ground.

The heron hopped and flapped and screeched.

FIZT! Sparks flashed from the laptop computer.

"NO!" yelled Mac. "You stupid bird!"

He hadn't been quick enough to stop the heron from knocking over the mug of stone-cold hot chocolate he'd left sitting beside the laptop earlier that day. The brown liquid had raced across the keyboard and seeped into every crevice. A thin coil of smoke accompanied a dreadful electrical burning smell.

"Now look what you've done!"

The bird stopped flapping, folded its wings neatly and rose to its full height. It fixed the boy with a golden stare. Mac could have sworn it smiled. It seemed to wear a satisfied expression at least; one that said "My work here is done." And with that, the bird turned and bobbed out of the tent.

Leon stuck his head through the tent flap. "Did you see that?"

Mac rolled his eyes at the stupid question. "Yeah, I saw it." He ran his hands through his hair and shook his head in disbelief.

"Looks like we're up for a new computer," said Leon.

All Mac could think of was how lucky he was to still

have the photos of Aisha on the camera. The hot chocolate spill had missed it completely. He picked it up and flicked it on. There she was. His heart leapt.

My Aisha. My everything… Always.

He tucked it safely in his back pocket. He would make sure it stayed there until they got another computer.

CHAPTER THIRTY-EIGHT

MAC SAT ON a concrete block, soaking up the morning sunshine in the modern-day city of Alexandria. His skateboard lay across his lap. Blood and clear goo oozed from a nasty graze on his left knee. The palms of his hands hadn't fared much better. Aside from the ever-present red bandana, he wore a pair of knee-length cargos and a red t-shirt atop his Nikes, which had made it out of the trunk yet again.

After checking that the camera in his pocket had survived his clash with the pavement, he gazed out across the gentle sweep of the Eastern harbour. Gone was the magnificent tower of white marble that was the ancient lighthouse, toppled into the sea by an earthquake centuries ago. In its place stood Fort Qaitbey, built in 1480. Mac thought it looked more like a storybook castle than a fort.

Behind him rose the grey granite wall of the new Bibliotheca Alexandrina – an impressive new library of international proportions built, supposedly, close to the sight of the original Library of Alexandria. True to the Egyptian standard, it was an amazing piece of architecture and engineering. It was a modern building, built in the shape of a low broad cone that had been sliced through on an angle to leave an elegant slanted disc. Apparently, so Mac had read, its shape symbolised the rising sun, an important concept of the Egyptian people since ancient times. Its unique sloping roof was its crowning glory. It looked almost space-aged in design. It had eleven storeys but several of them were underground so it didn't loom massively above ground level. In fact, it was an interesting yet quite modest building from the outside. It wasn't until the visitor entered the building that its immense scale became apparent.

Mac had been inside the library on several occasions when his father had business in the city. Physically, the only resemblance to the original building, in his opinion, were the lofty columns that rose high into the air to meet a ceiling through which natural light streamed in. Otherwise, they were vastly different structures. However, the thing that struck Mac was that both buildings were imbued with the same atmosphere. There was a strong tone of peace, harmony, knowledge and a passion for learning. There was an almost magical air of reverence that had indeed been recaptured from ancient times.

Mac plonked the skateboard on the ground and rolled it back and forth with his foot while he waited for his father to return from the post office.

Four long weeks had dragged by since he'd lost Aisha. He had dreamt about her almost every night. The nightmares were now mostly good dreams. Sometimes he couldn't see her face clearly or her features seemed to morph and change but always he knew it was Aisha. He would know her unmistakable aura – her Ba – anywhere. Somehow she had become a part of him, fused to his very existence.

He longed to see her again and had been tempted more

than once to pop back to a time before the fire just to see her. So far, he'd managed to resist the temptation. It wasn't the sensible thing to do, as he well knew. It would only stir up feelings he'd only just managed to get a hold on. She was gone. That was a simple fact. Still, some weird program in his brain couldn't help scanning the crowd for a glimpse of her everywhere they went, as if she'd just magically pop up in the Here and Now. Mac thought he had spotted her more than once out of the corner of his eye but, of course, he knew it was just his mind playing tricks.

He toyed with the pair of tyets around his neck – the red one and Aisha's tiny gold one – and, eventually, his thoughts turned to other matters.

He was one hundred percent certain they'd discovered the original library just kilometres away, even though government officials and so-called experts refused to believe them. There was absolutely no mistaking the distinctive lapis lazuli and obsidian tiles. But that wasn't really something he could present to the authorities. Despite vigorous campaigning by his father to convince them to grant permission to launch further exploration into the original library and the catacombs that led to the secret vaults, they had flatly refused and his plea was denied. It was heartbreaking for Mac. He was pretty sure that if he could locate the original entrance to the tunnels, he could navigate his way to the vaults. He remembered it being a single tunnel with no turns.

For weeks, Mac, along with his father and Ru, had been obsessed with the thought of what may or may not still exist in the lost vaults. Mac had shared his glimpse of the enigmatic crystal skull with them, which had sparked ongoing debate between Ru and Gabby. He desperately wished he'd had the opportunity to ask Elcor about it. He had so many questions and wondered just how many of the answers might lie entombed amid those lost scrolls.

The team had spent countless hours pouring over maps and satellite intelligence trying to gauge where the vaults might lie. From all that they could gather, it was most likely that, if the vaults and tunnels still existed (there had been a few devastating earthquakes over the millennia), they would most likely lie directly beneath the man-made canals of the prime waterfront real estate in the city. There was little chance they hadn't been totally flooded by the developers. Ru had become quite teary at the prospect of those ancient scrolls having once been saved from the flames only to perish under several metres of water.

"It's the Aswan Dam all over again," he had lamented.

The construction of the Aswan Dam further up the Nile Valley had forever put beyond archaeologists' reach countless valuable sites and antiquities, buried under billions of cubic litres of water.

"We don't even know for sure if anything of value remained in the vaults," Leon reasoned. "It could have been moved or destroyed eons ago."

He had a point. Perhaps they were chasing vapours. It was difficult to let go of though. In the end, Mac figured that if the contents of the vaults had been meant for the betterment of mankind, they would have been revealed somehow, some way, at some point in time over the course of history. Who knew? Perhaps they already had. Maybe things were unfolding exactly as they should be after all. He couldn't help feeling that underneath the surface and behind the scenes, there was some grand plan at work.

A bunch of gossiping girls walked past. They shot admiring

looks in his direction and giggled. He smiled. He assumed they were students studying at the university, which was part of the new library complex. A scruffy youth wearing ripped jeans and a stained t-shirt sprinted past carrying an armload of books. Mac guessed he was late for lectures. He couldn't help drawing comparisons between the Past and the Now. Sure, the buildings had changed but, essentially, the people were still the same. Their lifestyle may have changed but life hadn't.

Suddenly, Mac had the creepy sensation that he was being watched. He turned to his right and was startled to see a hairless cat sitting nearby, studying him intently.

His heart thumped. Could it be? Surely not.

He glanced around then leaned toward the naked cat. "Nefertiti?" he asked in a hoarse whisper.

The cat seemed to offer him a knowing half-smile. He could have sworn it actually winked at him then darted off in the direction of the markets. Mac was speechless.

"You look like you've just seen a ghost," came Ru's voice.

Mac jumped. In a funny sort of way, he *had* just seen a ghost… or something like one.

"Care for a cinnamon doughnut?" asked Ru as he eased his portly frame onto the concrete block beside Mac and opened the box.

"Huh? Ah… I'm good," the boy answered, still staring after the cat. "You know, I'll meet you back here in five. Gotta go check something out." Mac leaned the skateboard against the block at Ru's feet and left.

The Englishman chuckled through a mouthful of doughnut as he watched Mac disappear into the crowd after a group of girls. He didn't see the fleet-footed cat that darted through the marketplace ahead of them.

Mac was puffing by the time he rounded the corner into a dark alley. He slowed to catch his breath and let his eyes adjust.

"Puss, puss! Where'd you go, girl?"

The cat had led him on a crazy chase through a maze of stalls. The crowded marketplace was layered with too many sights and too many smells. Mac was dizzy with exertion and sensory overload.

He heard the cat meow from further up the alley. Swept along on a wave of déjà vu, Mac followed the sound. He caught a glimpse of the cat disappearing into a doorway on his left.

He paused in the spill of yellow light and peered inside. The small dwelling was sparsely furnished. A dirty old armchair took up the corner beneath an orange tasselled lamp that glowed weakly. The chair's faded green fabric was tatty and worn but it matched the equally worn Persian rug on which the cat sat staring at him. A crude kitchenette ran along the other wall to meet an old bookcase stuffed to overflowing. Strange odds and ends were squeezed onto the shelves along with the books – religious figurines, feathers, animal bones, polished stones, melted candles…

There was a vile smell to the place that was only just masked by the cigarette smoke that hung in the air.

"Salutations, traveller."

Mac jumped.

The milky white eye stared at him from above a grinning toothless mouth. The old woman stood to one side of the door with a cigarette dangling from between her lips. Her one good eye was squinted against the smoke curling from its glowing tip.

She plucked it from her mouth between yellowed fingers and shuffled across the room to sink into the armchair. She gestured for Mac to take a seat on a rickety kitchen chair nearby.

Despite his urge to run, he sat.

"I've been expecting you," she said after another puff of her cigarette. She spoke in heavily accented English.

"But *how*?" Mac was incredulous. It just seemed entirely impossible that she even still existed, let alone was *expecting* him. He was utterly mystified.

The hag dismissed his question with a waft of her cigarette. It was a somewhat insulting gesture that assumed he wouldn't understand even if she answered. "But you want other answers, no?"

Mac shrugged. He guessed he did but he hadn't yet formed the questions in his own mind. The past weeks had been such a whirl of emotion and confusion that he'd barely begun to process it.

The first question he could think of tumbled out of his mouth. "So how does the whole time thing work?"

She gargled a hairy ball of laughter. "Time is a complex thing, if indeed you could call it a thing. For it is no thing really."

That wasn't an answer. Mac shook his head to clear it. It was too big a question to start with. He asked the next thing that popped into his head.

"How did you know about Osiris' minions – about the Borderland?"

"It was written."

Mac thought back to the document in the Isolation Room. It was supposedly top secret. Mind you, he'd discovered it on the columns in the ruins so it couldn't have been too secret. It was ancient and forgotten perhaps but not exactly secret.

The hag went on. "And now, thank the gods, no trace of the writings remains. The future of the world is safe. For now."

"What do you mean?" asked Mac as he moved his hand to the camera in his back pocket. Not every trace was lost, he thought. He still had the photos.

The old woman stubbed out her cigarette on the arm of the chair and leaned forward. Her breath was rank. "The knowledge they contained held the power to destroy the world. It was knowledge from the Dawn Times, buried, hidden, until its untimely discovery threatened the planet yet again. Interpreted correctly and in the wrong hands, it could give one man power to annihilate his enemies and every living thing along with it."

Mac recalled reading something about raising armies from the dead to exact vengeance on a sleeping planet.

"And hell will reign," she quoted in her raspy voice.

The dig kid shuddered. Yet there had been light in those ancient writings; there had been truth in them.

She went on. "And so the forces that be went head to head. The force for good pushed to eradicate every trace of such dangerous knowledge and they won. This round, at least."

Mac's mind raced. "So you're saying that's why the Library burned down?"

She nodded. "Either by arson or an act of the gods, it was destined to happen exactly when it did."

He remembered the violent electrical storm on the night

of the fire. "So for me to have prevented the fire, I'd have been getting in the way of the 'good guys'?" He drew the parentheses in the air with curled fingertips.

The hag nodded again.

"And you're one of those supposed 'good guys'?"

She shrugged. "I am merely a Balancer. An instrument."

Balancer... Mac knew he'd heard the term but couldn't place it.

The hag went on. "So you see the girl had to die, taking that knowledge with her."

Mac swallowed hard. "She didn't have to die."

"Oh, but she did. It was part of the Plan."

"Screw the stupid *Plan*!" he said, leaping to his feet and knocking over his chair. The cat bolted out the door. "If it wasn't for me, she'd have lived."

"Yes, Deliverer, but only until we all perished in the dark events that were to follow. Do you dare imagine the awful power Pharaoh Ptolemy would have wielded with such information at his disposal?"

Mac was still.

Deliverer...

He felt sick. Huge chunks of the puzzle slammed into place. His mind reached out to touch the delicately balanced web of events. As it turned out, he hadn't messed with time; it had been his destiny all along... His tragic, heartbreaking destiny. His lip quivered.

The old crone held out her hand, palm up.

Mac stared at it.

"Nothing comes for free, kid."

He realised he was expected to pay. "Oh..." He fought the rising resentment as he fumbled in his pockets for some coins. "This is all I've got," he said, dropping them into her palm.

The hag let the coins slip through her fingers to bounce and roll away on the floor.

Instinctively, Mac turned and picked up the money. When he turned back, she was standing right behind him. It was creepy. "Here," he said.

Her toothless pit of a mouth grinned wide as she took the coins.

Mac left without another word.

Amazingly, he managed to find his way back through the markets to where Ru was waiting outside the library with an empty doughnut box beside him.

"What the devil did you get up to, my good man? You've been gone for ages. She must have been a looker," he said with a wink.

Mac cringed. "She wasn't my type."

"Your father's chatting to an old colleague up the street. Something about another project in the pipeline. Sounds intriguing. Some rather interesting leads have turned up regarding the fabled lost Hall of Records in Peru.

"Hall of Records?" Goosebumps raced up Mac's spine.

He couldn't help wondering if, buried somewhere in an ancient Hall of Records, if such a thing even existed, there might be an answer as to how he can be with Aisha in that other world. He wondered if an ancient copy of that now destroyed document from the Dawn Times might still exist. For some reason, he couldn't help thinking there was light – there were *answers* – to be found in it. It had led him to her once. Maybe it would again.

"Mmm. It might be worth a look," said Ru and mopped

his sweaty brow with a handkerchief. He stuffed it back in his pocket before going off on a conversational tangent that Mac simply didn't have the energy to follow.

Ru sensed the boy was preoccupied and left him to his thoughts. "I'll go see what's taking the professor so long." He waddled off.

Mac's thoughts drifted over the bizarre series of events… the oh-so-convenient 'finding' of the ivory-handled dagger, meeting Nefertiti's equally ugly twin, his encounter with the hag that seemingly lived forever…

It was all so very strange. His mind flashed back to her words, *"Time is a complex thing, if indeed you could call it a thing. For it is no thing really."*

His mind grappled with the concept. *No thing… It is no thing…* If it were 'no thing', that would make it nothing. Is that what the old bag was saying? That time is nothing? An illusion perhaps?

Well if that was the case – if time *was* an illusion – then he seriously hoped he would eventually find a way to punch a hole in it and be with Aisha again in the next life.

He sighed. It was all too much. His face tilted up to meet the sunshine and he closed his eyes.

He longed to see her, to feel her.

Send me a sign. Anything… Something…

Then he smelt her – soft jasmine interwoven with the freshness of cucumber and juicy watermelon on a bed of freshly cut summer grass.

"Mmmm…"

"You like?" asked Gabby.

Mac's eyes flew open.

Gabby held her wrist under his nostrils. "I buy this

scented oil in the markets. I theenk I got reeped off but I like it." She pulled her wrist back to smell it.

Mac's heart was hammering. The scent was like a drug to him. It took him to good places. He shook himself.

At least things with Gabby were slowly getting back to normal. They'd had a long talk and she'd forgiven him. It was good to see her smiling again. The awkward tension of those few days after the 'spring thing', as they now referred to the incident, wasn't gone completely though. Mac wondered if their relationship would ever go back to the way it was before. He was sick of Gabby telling him to snap out of it. It just wasn't as simple as that. He was changed. Transformed.

"And check this out," Gabby went on. She leaned forward and swept her hair off her face. "Cute, eh?"

Mac gasped.

A stick-on crescent moon high on her left cheek sparkled in the sunlight. He was too stunned to mask the total shock on his face.

Gabby shrugged. "I know. It's just a silly girl thing. Just a bit of fun. Here," she posed dramatically, "Take a photo of me before I peel it off."

"Don't peel it off," he said in a faraway voice as he reached for the camera in his back pocket. To his horror, it was gone. He flashed back to the dropped coins in the old hag's hut. She must have pick-pocketed the camera when he bent to pick up the money. "That bitch!"

He jumped up and headed for the markets.

"Hey, where you goink?" Gabby called after him.

"Someone stole my camera!"

She laughed without humour. "Forget it, MacKeenlee. You no are gonna get it back now."

He stopped. She was right. It was totally futile. He'd never get it back. His shoulders slumped in resignation.

So, the forces for good had prevailed; no trace of the ancient writings remained. It seemed beyond belief that the disgusting hag – that vile thing – had been one of the good guys. It was too much to get his head around.

He took a deep breath and gazed out to sea. The sun sparkled on crystal waters. Mac fidgeted with the ruby lion ring on the middle finger of his left hand. He had begged his father to let him keep it and, as his birthday was coming up, Leon had relented and let him have it. The heart of the ruby blazed in the sunlight.

Gabriella curled an arm around his shoulders. "Come on. I buy you a new one for your birthday and then you will love me forever," she said, tossing her head back. Her laughter floated up into the cloudless blue sky as they strolled along the waterfront.

Mac sighed.

For an instant – just an instant – he wished things could go back to the way they were; that he could go back to who he used to be when life was simple and uncomplicated, and love was just something in song lyrics.

But then, why would he want that?

ACKNOWLEDGEMENTS

Well here we are again, folks. Three long years after the successful release of my debut thriller, *Powder*, I find myself at the end of the first instalment of what is promising to be an epic saga, spanning at least four books. Did I really just sign myself up for this?

I penned the very first words of *The Lingering* way back in 2008. Since then, the story has been loved and hated, shredded and dissected, abandoned and rebirthed more times than I can count. Even the title changed several times – it was originally *The Fire And The Ring*. The final adventure turned out vastly different from its original inception, metamorphisising over the years, as I did.

Writing and releasing this book has proven far more challenging than my previous novel, where I could hide behind the blockbuster action and blistering pace. My heart and soul have been poured into *The Lingering* so I needed to get it just right. It exposes my little-known softer side (most people don't know I'm a giant marshmallow on the inside), leaving me feeling quite vulnerable as I share it with the world.

I am blessed to have a handful of friends who keep me

sane, be that with coffee or a well-timed meme or random text message. You know who you are. Thanks, guys. There are also a number of people who have helped me overcome my fears and limitations and perpetual self-doubt, as well as those who have contributed to the overall storyline with constructive feedback and encouragement. The following acknowledgements are in no particular order for everyone involved has offered me invaluable support and I truly appreciate each and every one of you.

I'm grateful for the incredible love and and support of my immediate and extended family, whose laughter lights my days and whose weirdness is my salvation. Massive thanks must go to my parents, both avid readers, who instilled a love of books in me at an early age. Thanks, Mum, for being my very own on-demand sounding board and personal editor, always willing to drop everything just to read the next little snippet I send you and for offering your honest opinion and insight.

Dad, from the time I could read, you ignited in me a passion for general knowledge and gathering information that allows me to write this type of thing. I remember reading about the fire that destroyed the Great Library of Alexandria in one of the World Book Encyclopaedias you bought us that cost you a small fortune back in those days and I'm truly grateful.

And to my beta readers of the final version, Jen Millar, Kathreen Cruz, and Mary Pearce, you'll simply never know how much your positive feedback and enthusiasm lifted me up and inspired me. Jen, I still remember the day I told you I wasn't sure if I wanted to publish it and you put your hands on your heart and said very dramatically, "Dan, that book *consumed* me!" Haha! I was stunned but humbled to my core. Thank you for your friendship and for believing in me.

Kim Vercoe, you were the first person to read one of the early versions of the manuscript and you very kindly ran it past your friend's son, Daniel, who was only 13 at the time (he'd be all grown up now!) because you felt it was important to test it on my target market. I know you're both blissfully unaware that your glowing feedback at the time created a pivotal moment in my life that allowed me to glimpse possibilities. Kim, I still remember the voicemail you left me telling me, "He LOVED it!" I never deleted that message and only lost it when I changed phones somewhere along the way.

A big thank you must also go to Maggie Kerr for her sage advice and counselling in helping me bring my inner child out to play and reassuring me I won't disintegrate if people discover I'm secretly a hopeless romantic at heart!

And to Matt, my husband and soulmate, you are my world, my everything, my sunshine. You're the reason I'm even capable of writing a love story in the first place. I'm grateful for you and to you, every moment of every day.

And to YOU, the reader, who took a chance on this story, I hope you enjoyed it. Thank you from the bottom of my heart!

Love is all there is.
Dani Mathewson 2021

ABOUT THE AUTHOR

After twenty-one years as a professional photographer, Dani Mathewson sold her studio to pursue her indie publishing career.

With a passion for reading and creating exciting young adult fiction, her subject matter and target age range vary across a number of titles, some of which are still in the pipeline, but the one reliable constant is her commitment to action, pace and authentic characters.

Described by her friends as a loveable weirdo, Dani calls inner city Brisbane, Australia, home. Her healthy appreciation for the unknown extends to controversial theories of human history, ancient civilizations, metaphysics and cryptozoology, not all of which are reflected in her work (yet…). When not fused to her laptop, her spare time is an imperfect balance of hiking in nature and Netflix on the couch.

The 2018 launch of her first eBook, *Powder*, a murder-mystery thriller set in an abandoned ski lodge, debuted in the iTunes Charts Top 100 Books across all genres and remained there for eight months. It is available for download from leading eBook retailers. *Snapshot*, a paranormal mystery, is also slated for release in late 2021/early 2022.

The Lingering is the first instalment in a proposed series of four books. Stay tuned for more of Mac Sanderson's captivating time travel adventures and mind-bending discoveries in his quest to find answers and to master his runaway heart.

"Be curious, not judgemental."

WALT WHITMAN

Thanks for sticking with me. Did you enjoy the book? Share the enjoyment with others by recommending to friends and leaving a review at your favourite eBook retailer.

Discover other books by Dani Mathewson:

POWDER

A young adult murder-mystery thriller
set in an abandoned ski lodge
Available for the price of a coffee at Smashwords
and other leading eBook retailers

SNAPSHOT

A young adult paranormal mystery
This one is still in the pipeline but will be
available at Smashwords and other leading
eBook retailers in late 2021/early 2022.

Connect with Dani Mathewson

Website:
https://danimathewson.com/
Instagram:
https://www.instagram.com/danimathewsonbooks/
Facebook:
https://www.facebook.com/dani.mathewson
Smashwords author page:
https://www.smashwords.com/profile/view/danimathewson

Printed in Great Britain
by Amazon

22423121R00218